98

DOUBLE BLIND

DOUBLE BLIND

◆

KEN GODDARD

A TOM DOHERTY ASSOCIATES BOOK
NEW YORK

This is a work of fiction. All of the characters and events portrayed in this novel are either fictitious or are used fictitiously.

DOUBLE BLIND

A Forge Book
Published by Tom Doherty Associates, Inc.
175 Fifth Avenue
New York, NY 10010

Forge® is a registered trademark of Tom Doherty Associates, Inc.

Library of Congress Cataloging-in-Publication Data

Goddard, Kenneth W. (Kenneth William)
    Double blind / Ken Goddard.
        p.   cm.
    "A Tom Doherty Associates book."
    ISBN 0-312-85796-9
    I. Title.
  PS3557.0285D6   1997
  813'.54—dc21
                                    97-13269
                                    CIP

First edition: November 1997

Printed in the United States of America

0 9 8 7 6 5 4 3 2 1

This book is dedicated to the sad passing of two treasured friends,
Harold Mays and Dave Siddon . . . and to the joyful arrival of
a like soul: Brittany!

ACKNOWLEDGMENTS

My sincere thanks to Dr. Myrna Milani, who took time out from the exploits of her own fictional StC character to offer a fascinating definition of "cat-ness"; to Special Agent (Lt. Colonel) Commodore Mann, who provided some chilling insights into the capabilities of an Army Ranger hunter-killer team; and to Elliott, Bucky, and Bob, fellow USFWS employees whose editorial comments are probably best thanked by allowing them to remain cheerfully anonymous.

Double Blind: a quality control and quality assurance procedure in which none of the people directly involved in the process — the participants *or* the observers — know the true nature of the system or object being tested.

> "But who would rush at a benighted man,
> And give him two black eyes for being blind?"

> —THOMAS HOOD (1799–1845), ENGLISH POET
> ODE TO RAE WILSON

Excerpts from the Field Notebook of USFWS Special Agent Henry Lightstone

DEPARTMENT OF THE INTERIOR

U.S. Fish and Wildlife Service

Division of Law Enforcement, Special Operations Branch:

David Halahan	Chief, Special Operations Branch
Freddy Moore	Deputy Chief, Special Operations Branch
Larry Paxton	Supervisory Special Agent, Bravo Team Leader
Henry Lightstone	Special Agent, Bravo Team
Dwight Stoner	Special Agent, Bravo Team
Mike Takahara	Technical Agent, Bravo Team
Thomas Woeshack	Special Agent/Pilot, Bravo Team
Samuel Riley	Supervisory Special Agent, Charlie Team Leader
Natasha Marashenko	Special Agent, Charlie Team
Frank Wu	Special Agent, Charlie Team
Antone Green	Special Agent, Charlie Team
Mark LiBrandi	Technical Agent, Charlie Team
Augustine Donato	Special Agent/Pilot, Charlie Team

Division of Law Enforcement—Region One:

Wilbur Boggs	Resident Agent

National Fish and Wildlife Forensics Lab:

Margaret Kuo	Wildlife Forensic Scientist
Ed Rhodes	Wildlife Forensic Scientist

<u>Office of Personnel Management—Washington, DC</u>

"Robert"   Administrative Specialist

DEPARTMENT OF DEFENSE

U.S. Army Reserve Forces

<u>Third Battalion, 54th Army Ranger Reserves:</u>

John Rustman   Lieutenant Colonel, Reserve
                              Battalion Commander
Aran Wintersole   First Sergeant—H/K team
                              leader ("One-One")
"Bill"   Corporal—weapons specialist
                              ("One-Two")
"Azaria"   Specialist Four—
                              communications ("One-Three")
"David"   Private First Class—combat
                              rifleman ("One-Four")
"John"   Private First Class—combat
                              rifleman ("One-Five")
"Tim"   Private First Class—combat
                              rifleman ("One-Six")
"Rick"   Private First Class—combat
                              rifleman ("One-Seven")

UNITED STATES CONGRESS

House of Representatives

<u>15th Oregon Congressional District:</u>

Regis J. Smallsreed   Congressman, 15th District
Simon Whatley   Congressional District Office
                              Manager
Keith Bennington   Congressional aide
Marla Cordovian   Congressional intern

FRIENDS OF HENRY LIGHTSTONE

Bobby LaGrange   Retired San Diego Police
                              homicide detective
Susan LaGrange   Wife of Bobby LaGrange

THE ICER COMMITTEE

Aldridge Hammond	Chairman, ICER Committee
Sam Tisbury	CEO, ICER Committee
	Chairman/CEO Cyanosphere VIII

DEPARTMENT OF JUSTICE

Federal Bureau of Investigation

Medford, Oregon, Resident Agent Office:

George Kawana	Senior Resident Agent

Special Investigations Team:

Al Grynard	Assistant Special Agent in Charge/Team Leader

MISCELLANEOUS PLAYERS

Lou Eliot	Foreman for Rustman Family Hunting Preserve
"Jim"	The soothsayer (AKA "Sage")
"Karla"	The witch
"Sasha"	The cat
"Danny"	The Dogsfire Inn cook
René Bocal	Call girl

Prologue

He was mad, or so they said . . . but others thought only "disturbed."

A loner, and a wanderer.

And in so many other ways, far distant from his present world.

So it was perfectly understandable, and perhaps even predictable, that a thoroughly paranoid, moderately self-sufficient, and quasi-militant group like the Chosen Brigade of the Seventh Seal would accept this ragged outcast into their remote and isolated private community . . . in their continued search for defendable truth and purpose within the boundaries of their determinedly secluded lives.

They liked to talk at length and quote scripture frequently; he listened well. They liked to shoot guns, hunt and guide illegally in the surrounding forests, eat freshly killed game, reload ammo, drink home brew, and talk about putting the government on trial well into the late-evening hours; he abhorred meat, guns, alcohol, and violence of any kind. They talked proudly of owning the donated land upon which their community had been built, and being independent from the big brotherhood of government, but never failed to collect their monthly allotment of food stamps or cash their disability, welfare, and social security checks; he professed no connections to any government data bank. They engaged in carnal activities as often as possible, to maintain their "genetic flow" in peak condition so that they could repopulate the earth following the nuclear holocaust; he embraced celibacy.

The Sage did, however, serve as a willing audience and a welcome diversion. And best of all, he made few demands upon their carefully hoarded resources. They were deeply superstitious by nature, but they sensed that somehow, in some yet undetermined manner, he might serve them well in the coming days.

So they let him stay.

By consensus, of course, and for a predictably self-serving reason: if they were sufficiently patient and minimally generous, this scrawny, scraggly-bearded, hollow-eyed mystic might, someday, give them a glimpse of the inner truth that he so adamantly claimed to see.

So they had hoped for several weeks now.

Which, in retrospect, probably explained why — toward the end of a late-evening council meeting, when all of the adult males gathered in small clusters around a dwindling fire—the men felt startled, but not necessarily surprised, when their resident Sage suddenly began to mumble about the woman.

At first, his soft, slurred, mostly unintelligible words, separated by intermittent periods of silence, attracted little attention. The men had long since grown accustomed to his random efforts at social intercourse, and their conversation flowed easily around his occasional mutterings.

The council meeting continued.

But the Sage persisted, as if driven by a chorus of inner demons to connect—and somehow, to communicate—with his fellow cave-and-cabin-dwelling misfits . . . and suddenly the words began to pour forth as if released from a rapidly breached dam.

In a matter of moments, he held their complete attention.

Much of it consisted of pure rambling, and very little of what *was* intelligible made any sense. He called himself Tiresius, and claimed he'd been both a rogue and a scoundrel before Hera, the wife of the supreme Greek god Zeus, blinded him and thrust him out into the world to be a messenger—a soothsayer—for those seeking the truth.

That explained his abstinence, and the dark glasses, and the faded white walking stick that never left his side, the council members whispered among themselves. But not the ancient motorbike that provided wobbly, noisy, and smoke-belching transportation for the demented old man.

The irrational, disjointed nonsense poured out of him, yet no one got up and wandered away, as many of the old-timers often did at these usually unfocused and unproductive gatherings. Even when the coals in the fire pit barely glowed, no one dared risk aborting the breathtaking flow of words by doing something so mundane—but possibly distracting—as fetching more wood.

It was as if God Himself had suddenly appeared before the men of the Chosen Brigade of the Seventh Seal to offer His insight into the importance and meaning of their self-imposed isolation.

But there was more.

Much more.

"The Beast will return," the Sage announced with certainty, referring not to the Soviet Beast, which had given them an excuse to abandon their lives and take to the hills those many years ago, but rather to Bigfoot himself, the creature that virtually everyone in the group *except* the Sage claimed to have seen at least once . . . but not recently.

"The government is still the enemy," he reminded them again and again. "But not in the same way. It can change before your eyes. Nothing is ever as it seems."

The Sage repeated that phrase often during his rambling discourse. *Nothing is ever as it seems.*

"And the woman will come," he insisted time and time again.

Soon.

Any day now.

"And she will draw the two terrible warriors who lead the forces of darkness and light," he bellowed fiercely, his wild eyes glowing hotter than the dying embers of the fire.

"And when those forces meet, right *here*" — he pounded the rock-hard soil with a scrawny fist — "the battle you've prayed for all these years will finally begin."

Several of the older men shifted uncomfortably. A lack of exercise and excess of home brew had left most of them overweight and blurry-eyed. Their limited cash flow and dwindling ammunition stocks had long ago reduced their live-fire practice to a few ragged volleys more or less aimed at a handful of tin cans down near the garbage pit every week or so. Their training forays into the surrounding old-growth forest represented nothing more than an excuse to escape the continual harping of the women. And truthfully they hadn't hoped to meet any adversary, much less one driven by the forces of darkness, for years.

They definitely wanted more details about these two terrible warriors, but the Sage returned to the woman again.

"She is the key," he emphasized. "Everything depends upon her arrival."

His sunken eyes bored into those of every man seated around the fire.

"And if she doesn't come, the battle between light and darkness won't occur until the next millennium, and," he added in a deep, foreboding voice, "you must disband and rejoin the outer world."

Then the Sage fell silent, apparently exhausted by his unaccustomed, emotional outpouring. As he fumbled for the canteen at his belt, the elders of the group sat in silence, numbed by the mere thought of going back to the mundane and inglorious existence of their past lives; back to low-paying jobs, unsympathetic bosses, suffocating mortgage payments, nosy neighbors, jackbooted cops, and — worst of all — the women in control again.

Thus it was left to a younger "man" of barely fifteen years to ask the obvious question:

"What will she be like, this woman?"

The Sage blinked in momentary confusion, then paused for a long moment, as if gathering the necessary strength to summon the demons one more time. Finally he spoke again in that hoarse and foreboding tone:

"Slender and stealthy, sleek and sensual, warm and alluring, cold and calculating, highly intelligent, a priestess and a whore, and" — he paused

long enough to sip from the canteen he brought to his parched lips—
"very *very* dangerous."

The young man considered this for a long moment, then volunteered
timidly, "Gee, that sounds just like my cat."

"Of course it does." The Sage nodded his grizzled head slowly up
and down as if it were all so perfectly obvious. "Because that's exactly
what she is. A cat . . . and a witch as well," he added with a mischievous
smile.

A palpable wave of relief swept over those seated around the now
dead campfire.

Laughing and clapping each other on the back, the men stumbled to
their feet, suddenly aware that they were stiff and cold, and thirsty for a
good warming shot of home brew. They were also, to a man, secretly
relieved that their resident Sage had turned out to be truly crazy after all.

It was a good story, about the forces of light and darkness being drawn
to this sensuous cat-woman/priestess/whore/witch, who would pit these
terrible warriors against each other and evoke the Apocalypse. Even better
when told by a demented old blind man who could see. Yes, a good story
indeed.

But nothing worth taking too seriously.

Feeling in a celebratory mood, they tapped a new keg, poured everyone a generous shot, and a second . . . and went home to bed, comforted
by the knowledge that life as they had known it for the past twenty years,
a life of dreary, poverty-stricken, and invariably paranoid delusions, would
go on as always.

And it did—until the next day, when they awoke and discovered that
the woman had appeared.

Chapter One

At precisely 5:45 in the morning, the first flight came in low on the
horizon.

Eight glistening figures, flying in a near perfect V-formation and sil-
houetted against the brightening sky. An increasingly rare sight in the
southern marshlands of Jasper County, Oregon.

Congressman Regis J. Smallsreed smiled in anticipation.

"Look, over there!" Marla Cordovian whispered excitedly.

The eighteen-year-old intern — just completing one of the more miserable hours of her life, crouched down and shivering in the far corner of the concealed duck blind with a heavy shotgun cradled awkwardly in her arms — started to come up from the low wooden bench as she pointed in the direction of the oncoming V, but a cold glare from the imposing white-haired figure seated in the padded center shooting chair warned her back down.

"You stay put, young lady, and keep that shotgun out of sight," Smallsreed ordered as he slowly brought his own intricately engraved and tightly choked auto-loading shotgun up to a ready position. "I can see them just fine."

"My God, Regis, I think they're all cans," Simon Whatley, the congressman's longtime district office manager whispered hoarsely as he lowered his binoculars. "Every damned one of them."

Cans.

Canvasbacks.

The elusive Holy Grail of the southern Oregon duck hunter.

For a brief moment, every pair of male eyes in the concealed blind — both human and canine — watched in lustful awe as the unbalanced formation of migratory birds announced their approach with intermittent quacks, long necks craning forward as their powerful wings sliced through the chilled morning air in precise, synchronized strokes.

From his crouched position in Lt. Colonel John Rustman's spacious VIP blind, Congressman Regis J. Smallsreed convinced himself that he could actually hear the cold air hissing through the microscopic gaps in the primary feathers of the glistening wings that stroked the air with choreographed precision.

Seconds passed, the soft anticipatory whine of the pair of chocolate Labrador retrievers underscoring the reverential silence that enveloped the occupants of the expensively constructed, below-water-level blind as they each absorbed, in their own way, the richness of the moment.

It was one of those precious intervals of time that any true waterfowler would later describe in hushed and respectful tones, in the quiet corner of a darkened bar or the luxurious solitude of a pristine boardroom, as being as close to absolute perfection as mankind could ever experience.

But like all such moments, it ended too soon.

The concussive roar of the 12-gauge auto-loading shotgun instantly shattered the treasured memory into illusionary fragments as the lead canvasback erupted in an explosion of feathers, tissue, and blood.

The shock wave had barely registered on the gun-wary instincts of the remaining birds when four more blasts erupted from the blind, sending four more tight patterns of lead pellets streaking upward in intersecting paths with the entire left side of the rapidly separating formation. Four more bloody explosions sent four more lifeless canvasbacks plummeting into the water.

In the brief interval it took for the remaining three canvasbacks to veer off in three separate zigzagging paths in a desperate effort to escape the deadly barrage, Regis J. Smallsreed quickly set the still-smoking empty shotgun against the insulated wall of the blind. Then he reached down and took an identical, fully loaded shotgun out of the ice-cold hands of the stunned young intern, all the while keeping his eyes locked on the nearest surviving canvasback.

In one smooth, swift motion, he brought the stock of the handcrafted weapon against his right cheek, calculated the lead in his head, and squeezed the trigger.

Nothing.

Cursing furiously, the congressman glared down at the offending weapon, quickly spotted the problem, and thumbed the safety to the OFF position. Looking back up, he whipped the shotgun to the left, *sensed* rather than saw his target, and instinctively fired . . . then grunted in satisfaction when the close-range shot caused a shower of canvasback blood, tissue, and feathers to rain on the occupants of the concealed blind.

A spectacular shot by any measure . . . and one well worth a momentary pause to savor the appreciative nods and comments of his hunting companions. But at that particular moment, one of the country's most powerful and influential politicians didn't care about applause. Smallsreed could get all the ego-massaging he needed simply by stepping outside the door of his congressional office on any morning of the congressional work week.

What he wanted on this particular morning, or more to the point, what he craved far more than any of his usual pleasures—expensive liquor, illicit sex, exquisite food, or completely untraceable campaign cash—was the thrill and taste of blood.

Congressman Regis J. Smallsreed was greedy.

He wanted to kill them all.

Completely focused on the frantic escape efforts of the remaining birds, Smallsreed swung the smoking shotgun barrel directly over the rapidly ducking heads of his companions and fired two more times, the expended hulls ejecting over his shoulder in wide parabolic arcs.

The seventh canvasback died instantly as three of the tightly patterned number-two shot pellets tore through its neck and fragile skull.

But the delay created by the mistakenly armed safety on the congressman's backup shotgun allowed the eighth to come within an extra fifteen feet from the blind before the white-haired legislator triggered his last two shots—just far enough to reduce both the number and the velocity of the number-two lead pellets striking the bird.

Smallsreed saw a small cloud of feathers burst away from the rear of the bird, and started to smile. But his pleasure gave way to anguished disbelief when the injured bird remained airborne—desperately quacking and flapping its wings as it tried to reach the reed-choked sanctuary of the far-distant western shoreline.

John Rustman, fourth-generation owner and manager of this private hunting preserve, and a retired lieutenant colonel in the U.S. Army Ranger Reserves, took one look at the directional vector of the duck's erratic but determined course, cursed silently, activated a small radio transmitter on his belt, and made a minor adjustment of the headset microphone almost completely hidden by his black knit cap and the high collar of his windbreaker.

"Wintersole," he whispered tersely into the mike. "Take it out."

Congressman Regis J. Smallsreed was still standing there, clutching his empty smoking shotgun and staring at the rapidly escaping canvasback—*his* canvasback—a good eighty yards away and gaining distance with each frantic wing stroke, when a dark-hooded figure suddenly stood in one of the smaller adjoining blinds.

A moment later, a single sharp, explosive crack echoed across the water.

Ninety yards away, the injured bird suddenly tumbled in midair, its bloody feathers momentarily fluttering protectively over the splash point where the dead canvasback struck the water.

So that's Wintersole, Lou Eliot, Rustman's foreman, thought. *Damn.*

For reasons that he didn't care to think about right then, Eliot suddenly felt very grateful that Rustman had unexpectedly taken him off perimeter duty and ordered him to assist in the VIP blind that morning.

"Holy shit!" As Simon Whatley's astonished exclamation rang out across the water, Regis J. Smallsreed wheeled and stared openmouthed at the dark-hooded figure casually replacing the .223 Ruger Mini-14 semiautomatic rifle in the blind's gun rack.

Before Smallsreed could say anything, however, the hooded figure locked eyes with the stunned congressman for a brief instant, then shrugged with visible indifference before sinking out of view into the blind.

"Who . . . the *hell* is that?" Smallsreed gasped, his voice—when he finally found it again—tottering on the brink of uncontrolled rage.

"That's Win—uh, one of John's new employees," Simon Whatley quickly corrected himself when he noticed the deadly look the military officer shot in his direction.

"I don't give a good goddamn how new the son of a bitch is," the furious politician spit at his district office manager. "I want to know who gave him permission to shoot at one of my cans . . . and with a rifle—a goddamned rifle—to boot. That's . . . that's *outrageous!*"

Although Whatley cringed, Smallsreed's anger failed to ruffle the re-tired military officer long accustomed to the temper tantrums of his su-periors.

"Guilty as charged, Congressman," Rustman admitted calmly. "My people have standing orders to pick off any cripples that fly out of shotgun range."

"But . . ." the congressman started to protest, but Rustman continued.

"Thing is, it's a real pain in the ass trying to find the damned things when they get out too far. And I don't like leaving a bunch of birds lying around where people can find them and maybe get curious, especially when we're running one of our, uh, lead-shot experiments," he added, a casual but deliberate reference to the fact that the only hunter shooting in this particular instance was already six canvasbacks over his limit—not counting the one blown apart with a single .22 rifle round—and had killed them all illegally with unplugged shotguns and lead shot.

"Makes a lot of sense to me," Simon Whatley automatically pitched in.

But the sixteen-term congressman was in no mood to be mollified that easily.

"Well, as far as I'm concerned, there aren't going to be any more cripples flying out of shotgun range when I'm the one driving the god-damned lead around here."

Smallsreed looked at the expensive shotgun in his hand, then at the pretty young intern who stared wide-eyed and openmouthed at the car-nage floating around the sunken duck blind.

"Damn it to hell, young lady!" he roared, hurling the shotgun into the corner of the blind with such force, the startled young woman nearly wet her pants. "When I put that safety in the OFF position, I expected it to stay that way!"

Simon Whatley quickly stepped in to protect the terrified underling.

"That was my fault, Regis. My fault all the way," he whispered sooth-ingly behind Smallsreed's left ear. "I should've checked the safety myself. I forgot that this was Marla's first time out duck hunting. You know how easy it is to get caught up in the excitement of seeing that first V coming in low over the water, and taking in that first lungful of burnt powder. Bet you probably remember *your* first time like it was yesterday."

"The first time" was one of Congressman Regis J. Smallsreed's most reliable response buttons, and Simon Whatley knew exactly when and how to press it to get the desired effect.

The first time.

Oh yes.

Regis J. Smallsreed nodded his head slowly. "It's been a whole bunch of yesterdays since my first duck hunt. Hate to think how many. But I certainly do remember every minute of that gloriously beautiful morning." The congressman's anger visibly subsided as he reminisced, one beefy hand rubbing his chin thoughtfully.

"Glorious as that day was, though, I bet you didn't even come close to the kind of shooting you did today," Whatley added, automatically massaging the congressman's shoulder while Rustman signaled Lou Eliot to release the two increasingly anxious retrievers. "That was a damned fine recovery shot. Best I've ever seen."

"It *was* a hell of a shot, Congressman." Rustman smiled agreeably as his two highly trained dogs hit the water and joyfully churned toward the closest of the floating carcasses.

Incapable of letting it rest there, Smallsreed's chief local sycophant and deal-maker turned to the lieutenant colonel's longtime foreman. "You've seen a few drops in your day, Lou. What do you think? Forget that the man happens to be one of the most powerful congressmen in the entire country—hell, one of the most powerful men in the whole damned world. Tell him what you think."

Lou Eliot smiled, savoring the underlying ironies for a long moment while he absorbed the breathtaking beauty of the marshland that comprised the huge northern shore of Loggerhead Lake.

His lake.

His marshland.

His preserve.

He never thought of it in any other way.

Lou Eliot had long since lost what little awe or respect he once felt for the select representatives of wealth, power, and influence who frequented the Rustman family preserve to savor the end of a sport doomed to disappear for the simple reason that the flyways were rapidly running out of ducks. Few of those privileged men and women possessed the vigor or hunting skills of a dedicated waterfowler like Regis J. Smallsreed. Fewer still would forsake the comforts of a warm bed—and an even warmer companion—in one of the three VIP cabins to camp out in a cold, damp duck blind on the far northern shore of Loggerhead Lake, awaiting daybreak when the pleasures of waterfowl hunting peaked.

As Eliot learned, a late-morning shoot at a few dozen pen-raised and covertly released mallards easily satisfied the sporting urges of most of his employer's VIP guests. And the avian survivors—the sixty-some percent of the birds which somehow managed to evade a virtual blizzard of shot pellets, often fired at distances of less than twenty-five yards—earned the right to make that same suicidal run over the next visiting "hunter."

All of which explained why Simon Whatley's comment so amused Lou Eliot.

Forget that the man happens to be one of the most powerful congressmen in the entire county—hell, one of the most powerful men in the whole damned world. Tell him what you think.

Yeah, right.

Okay, Congressman, I think you're a greedy, self-serving son of a bitch, who'd rather drink smooth whiskey, shoot wild ducks, screw willing and not-so-willing women and backstab people over money than anything else in the world, Eliot thought to himself. *Just like me.*

Powerful words, those.

Just like me.

For a brief moment, he wondered what it would feel like when he destroyed Smallsreed. Destroyed one of the most powerful men in Congress. Hell, in the whole damned world.

Probably just like wringing the neck of one of them goddamned grain-sucking Canada geese that spent their entire whole lives screwing, honking, and shitting all over the place and driving decent, hardworking people crazy.

The irresistible imagery caused Eliot to smile, and momentarily to forget the chilling presence of the hooded figure in the nearby blind.

But in spite of his treacherous thoughts, and most recent treacherous actions, Lou Eliot never allowed himself to forget the most critical element of his job: the need to be ready and willing—if not necessarily eager—to soothe and stroke and bolster a wide range of terribly fragile egos. Even a skilled waterfowler like Smallsreed, who certainly knew better than to trust the ready status of his weapons to a young and inexperienced aide, required an occasional, albeit exaggerated, reaffirmation of status.

Fortunately for the veteran foreman's self-respect, however, he didn't need to exaggerate his praise this time. Simon Whatley, the shameless ass-kisser, and U.S. Army Ranger Reserve Battalion Commander Lt. Colonel John Rustman—who, as Eliot knew all too well, much preferred to kick ass than kiss it—had called it exactly right.

It *was* a hell of a shot.

"First-rate shooting, Congressman. Can't think of more than a half dozen times I've ever seen anyone match it, far back as I can remember." The deeply tanned marsh foreman flashed Smallsreed a thumbs-up sign of approval before accepting the two canvasback carcasses from his employer's prize retrievers.

The genuine praise from a respected waterfowl expert like Eliot placated the testy legislator.

"God as my judge, it felt right all the way." Smallsreed squinted up at the empty sky smugly. "Been lucky that way all my life. Blessed with good genetic stock. Steady hands, sharp eyes, clear lungs. And a nose for the kill," he added, tapping his prominently veined and pockmarked beak with a mischievous wink.

"Looks like the dogs approve, too." Simon Whatley chuckled as the two exuberant chocolate Labs shook and sprayed the blind's occupants after enthusiastically retrieving another pair of the dead canvasbacks.

"If the rest of my constituents were that cheerful, loyal, and obedient, I'd never need to attend another fund-raiser for the rest of my career," the congressman cracked to his solicitous audience as he wiped the water from his face.

"Uh-oh, looks like another flight coming in from the north." His host nodded toward some distant flecks of black in the sky as he expertly reloaded the first shotgun and handed it to Smallsreed. "Better hold the dogs, Lou," he added, pointing at the grinning Labs eager to retrieve the floating remains of the last duck.

Eliot quickly wiped his bloody hands on his jeans and grabbed the dogs' collars.

"Another batch of cans?" The gleam of unsatiated greed made Smallsreed's deep-set eyes appear much larger than they actually were.

Rustman nodded his head thoughtfully. "Wouldn't surprise me one bit. Maybe even a redhead or two, if our luck holds. Been having some real nice shooting out here the past couple days."

The military officer didn't bother to mention that the congressman owed most of his luck to Lou Eliot's considerable skill in capturing young wild canvasbacks from Canadian nesting sites, smuggling them across the border, and concealing them in pens in a remote area of the Rustman family preserve. There, fed sparingly and protected from natural and human predators, the ducks awaited the opportune moment—such as a visit from a dependably generous and influential congressman—when another well-trained employee released them, a few at a time. Like plump golden magnets, they flew right back into the migratory flyway, and directly over the Rustman Preserve's VIP blinds.

Not exactly like shooting ducks in a barrel, the lieutenant colonel thought. But close. Damned close.

He smiled, pleased by the idea that even an experienced waterfowler like Smallsreed could be fooled if enough money were put into the effort.

"Redheads?" The politician's porcine eyes blinked greedily. Redheads were even rarer than canvasbacks.

Rustman nodded. "Keep your eyes peeled. We . . ."

But before the wealthy landowner could expand on his meticulously orchestrated optimistic prediction, a pair of barely audible beeps caused him to reach for the small transmitter/receiver on his belt again.

"Rustman," he acknowledged the summons softly into the collar mike, his wary eyes systematically sweeping the surrounding weeds, waterways, and sky while everyone else in the blind fell silent. Other than a single small plane flying high above the distant clouds to the west and the approaching flight of birds, he saw no other signs of life in the area.

"Looks like we got ourselves a bogey on your four o'clock position, Colonel."

The voice Rustman heard through the small receiver in his right ear sounded flat and monotone, a result of the encryption software hard-programmed into the radios.

"How far out?"

The voice designated a vector point in a roughly southeasterly direction, but the military officer kept his eyes fixed on Loggerhead Lake's northern shore.

"Two—maybe three klicks," the voice added.

"Any ID?" Rustman knew the others all watched him, and undoubtedly listened carefully to his softly spoken words.

"Don't recognize the boat, but it sure looks like that damned duck cop to me."

Rustman nodded to himself. "Damned duck cop" was the unofficial designation for Special Agent Wilbur Boggs—the sole law enforcement investigator of the U.S. Fish and Wildlife Service assigned to this beautiful part of southern Oregon. And from Rustman's entirely prejudiced point of view, the sole impediment to unrestricted waterfowl hunting on the Rustman family preserve.

"Is he coming our way?" The question sounded foolish to Rustman even as he asked it. Boggs was a persistent and bullheaded investigator, and he knew the precise locations of Rustman's two VIP blinds. Of course he'd be coming this way. Why else would a federal wildlife agent work on a weekend, and trespass on private property, except to harass Rustman and his very important clients?

You goddamned officious asshole, the lieutenant colonel swore silently. *Why can't you have a price like everybody else?*

"He's been hanging out near the shore with a line out since early this morning. He could've just been fishing, but he acted like he was waiting for something, or somebody. Kept looking around with his binoculars, and I never did see him bait a hook," the voice in Rustman's earpiece reported. "Then he took off all of a sudden, like he intended to loop around and come into the blind area from the south, but I think it's going to be a while before he gets there. Looks like he got his prop caught up in a net real bad, and probably smacked his head pretty hard, too. Want us to make sure he stays put for a while?"

Lt. Colonel John Rustman's lips curled in a taut, thin-lipped smile, pleased at the success of the precautionary additions to his security system. Two days previously, he'd hired a couple of locals to come out at night and string a thousand yards of sun-rotted polyester netting a few inches beneath the water in specific patterns along the outer, lakeside perimeter of the blind area.

Rustman designed the system so that at least ten feet of netting would wrap tightly around an outboard propeller before one or more of the thick hemp ropes holding the net pulled tight and brought everything—prop, motor, boat, and occupants—to a dead stop. And from the sound of things, it had worked perfectly. If all went as planned, it would take Special Agent Wilbur Boggs at least an hour to cut away the netting and rope tightly wound around his prop.

Plenty of time to get Congressman Regis J. Smallsreed out of the area and settled in for a little R&R. No need to make things more difficult now. No need at all.

"Who is it?" His foreman's voice disrupted Rustman's train of thought.

"That damned duck cop again." Rustman made no effort to hide the disgust in his voice.

"Shit!" Eliot swore as he quickly brought a small pair of binoculars up to his eyes to scan the distant shoreline at the four o'clock position. "Are we ever going to get rid of that guy?"

Rustman's smile remained fixed, but the expression in his eyes changed to something far more chilling than amused.

"Colonel, you want us to make sure he stays put?" the voice in his ear repeated insistently.

Rustman continued to stare at his foreman for a long moment with cold, empty eyes before finally answering:

"No, leave him be. Just keep an eye on him and let me know when he cuts himself loose. But send the boats in for a pickup, right now," Rustman ordered in that same subdued voice. Then he turned to his foreman.

"Lou, let's get things cleaned up."

"Yes sir," Eliot acknowledged, tensing in response to the edge in Rustman's voice as the military officer moved toward the other occupants of the blind.

"Hate to be the bearer of bad news, folks," Rustman apologized as he removed the loaded shotgun from Smallsreed's hands, "but it looks like we've got to cut things short this morning."

"Is there a problem?"

Rustman shrugged at his famous guest. "Not really a problem, Congressman. Just a federal wildlife agent poking his nose around private property where he's got no damned business."

Smallsreed stared wistfully at the newly arriving formation swooping low over a distant patch of reeds and cattails, but a trio of small jet boats immediately distracted him.

"I thought you said you had this sort of thing under control, Simon?" he accused his district office manager angrily.

"I thought I did, sir," Simon Whatley admitted. "I'll look into it immediately, as soon as we get back to the office."

"I'd deeply appreciate anything you could do to help, Congressman,"

Rustman declared solemnly. "I'm getting pretty damned tired of being treated like a criminal by a bunch of overzealous, badge-wearing thugs who have the gall to call themselves law enforcement officers. I'm a God-fearing, churchgoing patriot who votes and pays his taxes like every other decent landowner in this county. And I'm all in favor of good law enforcement. You know that. But those fellows are getting out of hand. Somebody needs to rein them in."

"Consider it done," Smallsreed snapped irritably, still staring at the distant reeds and cattails where the formation of covertly released canvasbacks had long since disappeared.

"In the meantime, while Lou and I get things squared away out here," Rustman went on smoothly as he grabbed the bowline of the first boat and tied it up while his foreman quickly began the familiar cleanup routine. "I believe there's a hot breakfast waiting back at the main house."

"And speaking of getting warm" — Simon Whatley's faint leer communicated far more than his words — "I understand that Marla here makes a mean hot toddy."

"Is that so?" The senior congressman arched an inquisitive eyebrow as he appeared to notice the attractive young intern for the first time that morning. She nodded her head cautiously in his direction. Other interns had warned her about Smallsreed's infamous temper, but the shotgun incident had been her first clear view of him as anything other than an extremely calm and powerful — and therefore, from her youthful perspective, strangely attractive — older man who vaguely reminded her of her grandfather.

"In that case, my dear" — Smallsreed wrapped a thick arm around her jacketed shoulders and gave her a firm hug along with a conspiratorial wink — "we'll all agree that the incident with the safety was completely Simon's fault. You are unquestionably and unconditionally forgiven."

The concerned expression of the girl's pretty face immediately blossomed into a warm and dimpled smile that Smallsreed greeted with a wide, predatory grin.

Long accustomed and completely indifferent to the extracurricular antics of his VIP guest, Lt. Colonel John Rustman released the knot on a tie-down line, and pulled an expensive jet boat in close to the blind.

"Congressman?" He gestured with his head, then stepped back to give Smallsreed room to step cautiously into the shallow-bottomed craft.

"John, I've got to be honest with you. I've never seen a hot toddy yet that I'd swap for a daybreak shot at a flight of cans." Smallsreed's conciliatory mood dimmed noticeably as he settled himself into the rear passenger seat and watched Eliot expertly wrap the six bloody canvasback carcasses and expended lead-shot hulls in a camouflaged sink-container, then draw six freshly — and legally — killed mallards and an equal number of expended steel-shot hulls out of a similar dripping container.

"However," he sighed deeply, "if all we're going to see is more of those goddamned horny greenheads, then I suppose I could be tempted to indulge myself a bit this morning."

"In that case" — Simon Whatley played his role to perfection — "why don't you and Marla go on ahead and get those hot toddies ready while I help John and Lou get everything cleaned up out here . . . including that little matter we talked about yesterday," he added meaningfully.

Smallsreed blinked in momentary confusion.

"Oh, you mean the Tisbury — ?"

"Yes, I'll take care of it," Whatley uncharacteristically cut off his superior, an obvious reminder that at least two people in the blind really shouldn't have heard the name that Smallsreed had just blurted out.

For a brief moment, the arrogant congressman's eyes glinted dangerously, and Whatley held his breath, praying that his short-tempered boss wouldn't blow it all, right here, right now.

But then Smallsreed glanced at the young intern — who favored her idol with another naively sensuous dimpled grin — and his fearsome expression dissolved instantly.

Bless you, my dear, Whatley thought to himself. *I owe you more than you could possibly know.*

But it wasn't over yet. No matter how compelling the self-interest, Regis J. Smallsreed had not managed to survive — much less prosper — during his sixteen terms in Washington, DC, by entrusting his subordinates with the truly important decisions.

"Whatever it takes to resolve the matter to everyone's satisfaction, Simon" — the congressman's eyes bored into Whatley's as he spoke — "I want you to make it happen. These people are very important . . . constituents. *Very* important."

These people? What the hell is he talking about? Simon Whatley thought. *This is Sam Tisbury's deal all the way. Who else could he be . . . ?*

"Is that *understood?*" Smallsreed pressed in what Simon Whatley immediately — and correctly — interpreted as a dangerously threatening tone.

"Oh, uh, yes sir, absolutely. I'll take care of everything."

"Fine, you do that." Regis J. Smallsreed's head bobbed approvingly as he moved to the front of the boat and motioned for the young intern to join him. "Now then, my dear, tell me, have you ever been at the helm of one of these infernal machines?"

The young woman's blue eyes grew wide as she took in the smooth curve of the low racing hull, the supercharged engine with the wide blower air scoop, the small steering wheel and thick-knobbed throttle, and the thickly padded cushions. Every inch of the dark green camouflaged boat was a monument to one simple underlying principle:

Power. Pure and sensual.

She shook her blond curls, too awestruck to speak, and the subtle current that zinged through the congressman's crotch verified what he'd already guessed.

First time.

The predatory smile completely engulfed Regis J. Smallsreed's ruddy features.

"Well, in that case, my dear, I think it's about time we expanded your horizons."

Moments later, with the visibly excited young woman at the wheel and one of the country's most influential congressmen nestled close at her side, the powerful jet boat lunged forward, kicking up a long rooster tail as it quickly sped away.

Nodding his head in satisfaction, Simon Whatley watched the small craft disappear around the nearby island.

It's a good thing you're such a lecherous old bastard, Regis, he thought to himself. *Otherwise, this entire deal would be a lot more complicated.*

Then he turned to Rustman.

"I believe we have some business to discuss?"

Rustman shook his head slowly. "Not quite yet."

Whatley blinked in surprise. "What do you mean, not quite yet?" he demanded irritably.

Ignoring the congressional staffer's officious posturing, the military officer turned to verify that two dark-hooded figures now stood in the nearby blind, one of whom—judging from a flash of purple silk barely visible under a dark-cammo collar—was female. Both held identical stainless-steel Mini-14 rifles.

Satisfied, Rustman turned back to his foreman, who was making a last-minute check of the VIP blind.

"Lou, do you have everything under control here? Everything cleaned up and put away?"

Eliot ran through his mental list—the critical items being to wrap and sink the remains of the illegal canvasbacks, and exchange the illegal lead-shot rounds in the guns and ammo bags for steel. Then he took one quick look around before nodding. "Yes sir, all clear."

"John, I'm talking to you! What the hell do you mean . . . ?" Simon Whatley's strident interruption caused Eliot to observe both men curiously.

Rustman froze the congressional district office manager with an icy stare.

"Wintersole," he murmured into the collar mike without taking his eyes off of the political staffer, "put him down."

Simon Whatley's pupils dilated in shock a split second before a single high-velocity gunshot echoed sharply across the lake surface.

Lou Eliot's lifeless body tumbled backwards into the cold water of his beloved Loggerhead Lake and disappeared beneath its dark surface as Whatley watched in horrified disbelief.

"Now then"—Rustman's chilling gaze never wavered from the congressional district office manager's shocked eyes—"what was it you wanted to discuss?"

Simon Whatley could barely force the words through his constricted throat.

"Wha . . . what in God's name . . ."

"You heard your boss," Rustman cut him off. " 'Whatever it takes.' Do you have a problem with that, Simon?" The brutally composed retired military officer deliberately looked over Whatley's left shoulder.

Even though he knew what he would see, the terrified political staffer turned . . . and discovered both of the hooded figures staring directly at him. His heart froze.

"No, I don't," he whispered hoarsely.

"Fine." Rustman smiled agreeably. "Then let's go finish our business before that damned agent manages to cut himself loose."

Chapter Two

Special Agent Henry Lightstone was stretched out beside the trunk of a thick ponderosa pine, staring across an open clearing at a gravel path leading to a small rustic log cabin, and considering some interesting possibilities, when he sensed, rather than heard, movement among the trees behind his back.

He tensed.

It was 6:35 in the morning. Nearly an hour before the much-anticipated exchange. Still a little early for any kind of adversarial sweep or reconnaissance. But that didn't necessarily mean anything, because the people on the other side didn't necessarily play by the rules.

Then a tiny dry branch cracked under pressure, and he distinctly heard a soft curse.

Henry Lightstone smiled.

"You're getting old, Paxton," he whispered as the supervisor of Bravo Team—the most senior of the three covert agent teams assigned to Special Operations Branch, Division of Law Enforcement, U.S. Fish and

Wildlife Service—slid down beside him.

"Don't remind me," Larry Paxton muttered, and then fell silent as both men surveyed the area, searching for any sign of movement or—worse—an active countersurveillance.

But aside from an uneasy pair of geese, which wisely chose to abandon the sanctity of a nesting box under the cabin's back porch in favor of the security of the nearby water, and some unknown species of large snake leaving a visible wake in the tall grass, nothing moved. Or at least nothing that either agent could see through the patchy early-morning fog.

"They're being pretty damned trusting if you ask me," Lightstone finally whispered.

Paxton nodded in agreement. "Yeah, I don't like it either. You check on Woeshack?"

"Uh-huh."

"You double-check his pistol?"

Lightstone smiled. "Relax, Paxton, you're starting to sound like his mother. Woeshack's tucked in tight, loaded and locked, with proper rounds and three full mags in reserve. He's wearing his vest, he knows to keep his head down, and Stoner's keeping an eye on him. He'll be fine."

"Easy for you to say. You're not his supervisor," Paxton muttered darkly. "Eskimos are supposed to be natural-born hunters."

"Yeah, so?"

"So when's the last time you heard about a real honest-to-God Eskimo going out hunting for polar bears and forgetting to bring along any bullets?"

"Probably a self-correcting problem," Lightstone acknowledged. "Besides, I think we can count on Woeshack being an exception to just about any 'genuine Eskimo' definition you happen to run across."

"You know," Larry Paxton went on as if Lightstone hadn't spoken, "only the federal government, in their infinite and mysterious wisdom, would hire a native kid fresh out of Soldotna who hunts polar bears with an empty rifle and is terrified every time he sets foot into a plane, turn him into a Special Agent and a pilot, and then make *me* responsible for his ass."

"Never let it be said that the government lacks a sense of humor."

"Yeah, right."

Paxton fell silent again.

"So what do you think, Henry?" he finally asked.

Lightstone shrugged. "I think it just might work."

"Might?" Larry Paxton turned to face his fellow agent. "Is that the best you can say about a plan that's just one step shy of brilliant, if I do say so myself?"

Lightstone smiled agreeably. "Okay, Paxton, if it'll make you feel better, I definitely think it might work."

The team leader grumbled something unintelligible.

"Hey, come on, man, lighten up. I'm just giving you a bad time," Lightstone apologized softly as he continued to watch their surroundings. "The plan's fine. We're going to catch them by surprise, take them down clean, and nobody's going to get hurt."

"You sure about that?"

"Yeah, of course I'm sure," Lightstone lied reassuringly, but then added, "Just the same, I wouldn't mind having a couple more options to fall back on if we don't get that security team under control right off the bat."

"You still worried about our boy with the big **W** tattooed across his chest?"

"Hell yes. Aren't you?"

"Nope, not my problem," Paxton replied with forced cheerfulness. "My job is to come up with a plan, divide the assignments up all fair and equitable like, and then demonstrate my superior leadership skills by handling the most sensitive issues personally while trusting my subordinates to handle all of the little side details."

"Meaning you get the congressman and the bagman, and we get the goon squad and the little wildcat. You call that fair and equitable?"

"Nope. Fair and equitable would mean you guys getting to have all the fun while I stand back out of the way and keep an eye on things . . . which ain't gonna happen,'cause I ain't gonna *be* standing back watching my supervisory career go up in smoke when one of you guys suddenly get a notion to go ape-shit and blow a congressman's kneecap off."

"You really think anybody'd get mad at us for doing something like that?" Lightstone teased.

Paxton nodded his head glumly. "Shit, my luck, somebody in the DC office would get their shorts in an uproar, decide they want to make an example outta somebody . . . and there I'd be."

"So what are you going to do—say, for example—if Woeshack suddenly goes into some kind of polar-bear-hunt flashback and starts capping off rounds? Throw yourself in front of the guy like a dedicated Secret Service agent?"

Larry Paxton turned his head and stared incredulously at his wild-card-agent partner. "You think I've lost my goddamned mind?" he demanded.

"Just wondering."

"Yeah, well, you can just keep on wondering too . . . and speaking of dumb-shit ideas, I don't want to hear about any of you guys getting careless and falling for some 'sweet-little-innocent-kid' bullshit neither. She may look like she's about fifteen, but that little gal is a wildcat, no doubt about it. You back her into a corner, she's liable to rip your nuts right off if you give her half a chance."

Henry Lightstone observed his superior critically.

"Paxton," he finally said, "did anybody ever tell you that you've got a lousy bedside manner for a raid team leader?"

"All I want you guys to do is be careful, and don't do anything completely off-the-wall crazy," the lanky supervising agent warned in a prayerful whisper. "That's all I ask. Just be careful."

Chapter Three

At precisely 7:20 A.M. on that beautiful Sunday morning, three camouflaged boats cautiously approached an isolated dock on the southern shore of Loggerhead Lake from three directions—one coming in straight from the north, while the other two hugged the shoreline in an easterly and westerly flanking move.

About a hundred yards out from the dock and a nearby cabin, the straight-in driver cut his engines and allowed the pressure of the water to bring the flat-bottomed jet boat to a gentle, bobbing stop.

For five long minutes, Lt. Colonel John Rustman scanned the dock, the cabin, a black Lincoln Town Car parked next to the cabin, and the surrounding trees with his binoculars.

Nothing.

"Tango-one, talk to me, by the numbers," he ordered in a raspy whisper.

The responses from First Sergeant Aran Wintersole's hunter-killer team crackled in Rustman's ear receiver in a crisp, professional cadence:

"Tango-one-seven. In position. No targets, no movement. Out."

The east flank.

"One-six. In position. No targets, no movement. Out."

The west flank.

"One-four and one-five. In position. No targets, no movement. Out."

The cabin.

"One-two and one-three. In position. One target, driver's seat. White male, wire-framed glasses, twenty-five to thirty, brown and brown. No visible armament."

The Town Car.

"One-one. Situation is controlled. Out."

The last voice cold and metallic, even through the scrambling filters. *Wintersole.*

Lt. Colonel John Rustman smiled.

"Ten-four, stand by," he ordered tersely. He set the binoculars aside and observed the trembling man sitting in the passenger seat beside him.

Congressional district office manager Simon Whatley's composure had improved dramatically over the past half hour. He no longer looked like he could throw up or have a nervous breakdown at any moment.

"I hope, for your sake, that boy is alone and knows nothing at all about what's in that trunk." Rustman spoke in a voice that conveyed absolutely nothing in the way of compassion or understanding.

Simon Whatley was furious—at Rustman for placing him in such a horribly compromising position, and at himself for his cowardliness. His pants were soaked with urine, and he knew that Rustman knew the source of the pungent odor as well as he did. The realization that Rustman had been laughing at him during the entire twenty-minute boat trip infuriated the veteran political staffer even more.

Even so, another three or four seconds passed before Whatley could trust his voice to get him beyond the fury, the nausea, and the terror. No matter how hard he tried, he couldn't force those horrible images out of his mind.

Lou Eliot's lifeless body disappearing beneath the water.

The dark-hooded figure.

And those eyes. Those terribly cold, strange, and frightening eyes. *Wintersole.*

Just the thought of the man's name almost made Simon Whatley lose control of his bladder again.

"You don't have to worry about Bennington. As far as we're concerned, he's just a delivery boy," he finally forced out the words, desperate to put every ounce of authority he possessed into them as he turned to face his fellow conspirator. "I told him to stay in the car and wait for me, and that's exactly what he'll do. He knows nothing about the money, and, in any case, he doesn't have the code to open the briefcase." Whatley hesitated, then went on. "But I want an explanation, Rustman. Right now. No, let me put it more clearly. I demand an explanation. What could you possibly have been thinking of, killing one of your own men like that?"

Rustman gazed dispassionately into the terrified eyes of a man who now represented a potential threat to his freedom, if not his life. For a brief moment, Simon Whatley feared that he might have pushed it too far.

But finally the military officer shrugged.

"I had no choice. Eliot compromised the operation."

Simon Whatley recoiled in shock.

"What do you mean, compromised?"

"He knew exactly where that federal wildlife agent got caught in the nets—along the southeastern shoreline, at the four o'clock position," Rustman replied in an unnervingly calm and emotionless voice.

"So?"

"So I was the only one in the blind who heard the vector heading on Boggs from the sentry, and I deliberately faced north the entire time I took the call. Yet as soon as I told everyone in the blind that Boggs was in the area, Eliot immediately put his glasses on the four-o'clock vector. He knew right where to look."

"But . . ."

"He knew exactly where Boggs would be because he'd made arrangements to meet the bastard along the southeast shoreline while the congressman was shooting," Rustman explained patiently. "Which is precisely what he *would* have done if I hadn't changed his schedule at the last minute."

Simon Whatley shook his head in confusion.

"You lost me, Rustman. Why would Lou Eliot want to meet with a federal agent, much less somebody like Boggs? He *hated* Boggs. Hell, he hated the entire federal government, for that matter. Everybody knew that."

"True, but not everybody knew why," the retired military officer responded. "I'd be willing to bet even you don't know that a little over twenty years ago, Eliot's father was forced to sell this land—in fact, this entire shoreline we're looking at right now—to my father when he couldn't come up with the money to comply with some very specific cleanup regs enacted by our very favorite congressman."

Simon Whatley gasped.

"Smallsreed didn't tell you about that, did he?" Rustman smiled. "Ever stop to wonder what else he might not be telling you?"

Whatley ignored the baiting comment.

"Cleanup regs? Twenty years ago?" he countered skeptically. "You're kidding."

"Afraid not. Check your historical files. Assuming that Smallsreed was stupid enough to keep files on something like that, which I seriously doubt."

"You're damned right I'll check," the congressional district office manager muttered threateningly, but Rustman ignored him.

"Anyway, the place was going to hell. The blinds were falling apart, the wheatfields and cornfields hadn't been planted in years, the shoreline was turning into a dump, and the lake was one big oil slick . . . which meant hunting got progressively worse each year, because all the ducks went somewhere else."

Rustman's eyes swept the clean waters and lush shores of Loggerhead Lake.

"Back then, my family owned half the shoreline. With the help of Smallsreed and a few of his helpful contributors who liked to shoot on weekends, my father . . . *acquired* the rest, and began to turn it around. When Eliot's father finally drank himself to death, I talked my father into hiring Lou to help us bring the ducks back. When my father died ten years ago, I made Lou my foreman."

"To make up for what your father did?"

Rustman shrugged. "Yeah, I guess so. I needed somebody I could trust to keep an eye on the place until I put in my twenty and got transferred to the reserves. Lou and I grew up on this lake together. We used to play soldier around that old cabin"—Rustman gestured toward the cabin near where the black Town Car sat parked, waiting—"so it seemed like the right thing to do. But as it turned out, he thought I was rubbing his nose in it."

"So you think he intended to get back at you and your father—and the congressman—?"

"By leading Boggs in through the nets, right about the time Smallsreed cut into that second batch of cans." Rustman nodded his head slowly. "Think about it. It would have been one hell of a pinch. Probably the biggest violation notice Boggs ever wrote in his entire damned career. And you can bet it would have made headlines in every paper in the country within forty-eight hours. Over the limit on a threatened species, illegal lead shot, and an unplugged gun, a sixteen-term congressman . . . and an election year to boot."

Rustman stared straight into Simon Whatley's eyes.

"As the landowner, I'd have been prosecuted, too—probably end up losing my reserve commission, and definitely losing Smallsreed and his industry lobbyist pals as clients—which would've meant trying to fend off those county zoning commission bastards without a shred of political cover." Rustman paused. "You want to take a wild guess who's been seen out drinking and fishing with three of the zoning commissioners over the last few months?"

"Lou Eliot?"

Rustman nodded.

"But even so, did you have to *kill* him? Couldn't you just have . . ." But even as he spoke, the words "election year" set off alarms in the back of Simon Whatley's head.

"What did you want me to do instead? Pat him on the cheek? Ship him out of the country? Offer him a bribe? Threaten him with some sort of crippling injury if he talked to the feds about our VIP hunts . . . or worse yet, connects us to Tisbury?" Rustman added meaningfully.

Whatley remained silent. Rumors that Smallsreed would likely find himself facing a serious challenger this election had already caused him and the congressman to hit the money circuit heavy the last couple of weeks. Not the local circuit, the big show—the major donors who really didn't give a damn what happened in Jasper County, Oregon, as long as they got the votes they needed for their national and international projects.

The ones who'd pull their support back in a second at even the slightest hint of scandal.

Leaving the congressman to dangle in the wind while the opposing team's investigators, sensing blood, started homing in on Regis J. Smallsreed's other extralegal activities . . . like seducing very young women, or helping some of his extremely wealthy backers resolve very touchy personal problems.

Backers like Sam Tisbury, for example.

Simon Whatley suddenly remembered Regis J. Smallsreed's half-spoken comment. The one he'd interrupted and Lou Eliot had almost certainly heard.

Oh, you mean the Tisbury—?

Jesus.

Simon Whatley's eyes widened in horror at the sudden realization.

"He had us, Whatley," Rustman stated flatly. "He had us cold. Even if we managed to find and burn all the evidence, including those pants of his that he rubbed blood on from every goddamned can carcass the dogs pulled out of the water, he still had us. Trip records to snatch up the cans and reds, names of VIP hunters, dates, times. Hell, maybe even photographs of Tisbury out here hunting, for all I know," he added ominously.

The congressional staffer's head snapped up.

"Don't worry, we made a complete search of his house, garage, yard, and vehicles. He wasn't that organized."

"But what if he's already talked to Boggs?"

"What makes you think he hasn't?" Rustman asked. "And even if he has, so what? Eliot didn't know Tisbury by his real name. And if Boggs had had anything useful in the way of evidence, he'd have been on us with a helicopter and a support team of agents the minute Wintersole dropped that last duck. But he was working alone when he got his prop caught, and that tells me he didn't trust Eliot or his information yet. Which means we've still got time to make everything go away."

"But what about the . . . body?" Whatley whispered. "How are you going to make that go away?"

"Body? What body?"

The congressional district office manager blinked in confusion.

"Lou Eliot does a lot of traveling on my behalf," Rustman explained. "Matter of fact, now that you mention it, I believe he took off early this morning, right after the congressman's hunt, on a trip to Mexico. I asked him to check things out in the southern part of the flyway. Not sure when he'll be back. Left it up to him."

"Do you really expect a federal investigator to fall for a story like that?"

Rustman shrugged. "As far as I know, right now Lou Eliot is heading somewhere south of US jurisdiction with an up-to-date passport and a wallet full of cash, fully intending to check out the bars, señoritas, and hunting clubs on my dime. He's a childhood friend and a damned good employee, so I'm not going to kick too much if he stretches things out into a full-blown vacation. Man works hard. Makes me lots of money. He deserves some time off.

"And," Rustman went on, "if the man in possession of Lou Eliot's passport happens to closely resemble that photograph and he's willing to share a big chunk of that cash with the locals, I really don't think anybody down there is really going to worry about him too much, do you? Especially if that passport happens to get lost, and the man with the wallet keeps on traveling with his own passport."

It took Whatley several minutes to digest what Rustman had told him.

"You've thought this all out, haven't you?" he finally asked in an effort to reassure himself.

The military officer nodded his head.

"And what if he *had* given Boggs useful information, and the agents had shown up in a helicopter, what would you have done then?" Simon Whatley demanded.

"Jammed their radio frequencies, shot them down, killed every last one of them as quickly as possible, and then headed straight for Mexico with a couple of passports and a suitcase full of money myself," Rustman replied casually.

Simon Whatley's face turned deathly pale. He felt as if he were about to faint.

"How could you even think about doing something like that?" he whispered hoarsely.

"What the hell's the difference?"

"What's the *difference*?" Whatley's head came up sharply, his eyes practically bulging in disbelief. "Are you serious?"

Lt. Colonel John Rustman smiled pleasantly, but his eyes never lost their coldness. "Whatley, think about what you and Smallsreed and Tisbury want us to do for you. Then tell me what difference five or even ten more deaths would make?"

"But that's not the same—I mean I'm not—" The chief of staff shook his head frantically.

"No, of course not. You're just the bagman. I'm sure the federal prosecutors would take that into account when they divvy up the charges," he reminded his companion sarcastically.

Simon Whatley kept shaking his head and trying to speak, but the words refused to come out.

"Listen to me, Whatley"—Rustman's eyes glittered with cold, purposeful amusement—"the only real difference between yesterday and this morning is that now you and the congressman are directly linked to the murder of a federal witness. I don't feel at all bad about that because my team was fully committed to the job before Eliot made his move. Now you and Smallsreed are, too.

"In military terms," Rustman added with a malicious smile, "that's what we call a controlled situation."

Before the congressional district office manager could find his voice, Rustman glanced down at his watch and spoke into his collar mike.

"Tango-one-one, give me a sitrep."

"One-one," came the metallic reply. "Situation is still controlled."

That's right, Wintersole. It certainly is.

Rustman smiled sardonically as he reached forward and turned the ignition key.

He momentarily listened to the throbbing of the exposed engine, then edged the throttle forward, accelerating the powerful boat over the smooth surface of the water. Moments later, judging distance and wind with practiced skill, he drew the throttle back to the neutral position and allowed the sharply curved bow of the boat to nudge the outermost pillar of the low-lying dock located at the far southern corner of his Loggerhead Lake property.

As his eyes swept the shoreline, searching for movement, Rustman pressed his left elbow against his waist, confirming the positioning of the cross-draw-holstered .45-caliber semiautomatic pistol concealed under his jacket. Then he took a slow, deep, steadying breath.

This is the crucial juncture, he reminded himself. If Smallsreed and his ass-kissing chief of staff had lost their nerve at the last minute and called in the FBI, this was the logical time and place for a team of federal agents to try for a photograph . . . or a takedown.

During the initial exchange. Which was why he'd insisted that Whatley bring the money with him on Smallsreed's hunting trip. So that they could make the exchange at a location where effective surveillance would be extremely difficult, if not impossible.

Wintersole's terse words echoed in Lt. Colonel John Rustman's mind.

Situation is still controlled.

Not "Clear." Controlled.

Translation: Wintersole's team hadn't yet searched the cabin, the car, or the surrounding woods. They had simply placed themselves in position to detect, monitor, capture, or kill any individuals who suddenly appeared in any of those locations. That would, if necessary, include all members of any surveillance or raid team, because Lt. Colonel John Rustman and his people were completely committed now, and he was a realist.

The federal prosecutors wouldn't bargain with him over the death of a federal agent, and he had no intention of spending the remainder of his life in a federal or military prison.

Better to go down fighting than rot in a cell, he thought as he watched Simon Whatley grab a weather-bleached plank with one gloved hand, hold the boat snugly against the thick wooden pillar, and quickly secure the bowline to the dock cleat.

The congressional district office manager turned and started to say something, but Rustman shook his head firmly.

"Go get it," he ordered. "Now. And then tell him to go home. We'll send you back in the Cessna."

The shaken political hack scrambled onto the dock and hurried across the road to the rear of the parked Town Car.

Less than two minutes later—immediately after Whatley closed the trunk and headed back to the dock with a briefcase in his hand—the vehicle started up, made a quick U-turn onto the dirt road, and headed back the way it had come while Whatley awkwardly worked himself back down into the boat one-handed. He hastily untied the craft, then almost catapulted into the water when Rustman slammed the throttle into reverse, backed the boat away from the pier, spun it in a tight turn, and accelerated toward the open water.

Once back at their original surveillance position, Rustman cut the engine and waited for Whatley to open the briefcase and hand over the thick sealed envelope.

"Is this everything?" The colonel automatically turned his back to the shore before slipping the envelope into his jacket pocket.

"Except for the personal information on the agents," Whatley reported, still shaken but determined to carry through his crucial part of the project. "You'll get that soon."

"What does 'soon' mean?"

"Tuesday, at the latest," the congressional district office manager promised.

"Including where to find them, I assume."

"We'll get to that in a moment. First, I want you to understand the money situation. There's five thousand in cash, small bills, for miscellaneous expenses. In addition, there are four separate account books. You've got a total of 2.3 million in one account to equip and fund the operation, which is not to exceed a one-year duration, regardless of what happens. There's eight hundred thousand for basic salaries in the second. Two hundred for Wintersole and a hundred apiece for the others. You have immediate access to both of those accounts with the IDs, linked credit cards, security codes, and other documents in the packet."

"And the bonus money?"

"There's 2.4 million in the bonus account. It's not accessible yet, but it will be—"

"—when the operation is successfully completed," Rustman finished.

"Correct. That money will be authorized for distribution to the survivors, or their designated beneficiaries, if and when the operation is successfully completed," Simon Whatley replied. "We added the beneficiary clause, and the necessary signature cards, based on what I . . . uh, I mean *we* think is a reasonable assumption that you could suffer a few casualties in an operation of this nature, because we don't want any dependents making a fuss."

"We'll expect authorization when the operation's completed, not if," Lt. Colonel John Rustman calmly corrected his companion. "We'll cover any dependents, regardless, but I wouldn't worry too much about casualties if I were you. This is going to be a professional operation. In hard and out fast. I don't anticipate anything more serious than a few minor wounds, at most. You did say four accounts?"

"Your account is separate, of course," Simon Whatley rushed to clarify that particular point. "Four and a half million dollars in designated amounts. Same conditions. One-third down, the remaining two-thirds on completion of the mission. You have to succeed completely, or there's no final payoff. Our client will accept nothing less."

"Complete success defined as the complete destruction of a small covert team of federal wildlife agents?"

"As well as the completion of the aforementioned diversions," Whatley reminded the lieutenant colonel. "Yes, that's correct."

Rustman smiled thinly.

"Just out of curiosity, what exactly did these agents do to piss off Smallsreed and Tisbury? Interfere with their deer poaching?"

"This project has absolutely nothing to do with the congressman!" Simon Whatley forced an indignant edge into his voice. "I . . . we're simply functioning as a go-between to assist a mutual friend. That's all you need to know."

"Ten million dollars is a hell of a lot of money, Whatley." Rustman ignored the other man's ridiculous effort to intimidate him. "I think it's reasonable to assume that these federal agents seriously pissed off somebody. And somewhere down the line, it might be helpful if we knew who . . . and why."

"You can assume whatever you please," Simon Whatley responded curtly, "but you *must* understand one thing very clearly. There have been two previous attempts to eliminate these agents. Both attempts failed. As far as our client is concerned, failure is no longer an acceptable option."

"You know, it amazes me that you've survived this long." John Rustman shook his head slowly.

"I'll have you know I'm perfectly capable of covering my own bases!" the senior congressional staffer retorted hotly.

"Yeah, I'm sure you are." The military officer dismissed Whatley's comment disdainfully. "But let's just make sure I understand all this correctly. We're only talking about five agents, correct? Not soldiers. Not spies. Federal wildlife agents. Basically game wardens with federal badges."

"That's right."

"So tell me something about them."

"Like I said, you'll get the complete dossiers later." Whatley mentally sifted through the briefing data he'd been compiling over the last several weeks. "But in summary, they range in age from twenty-four to thirty-nine. They've worked together as a covert team on two major operations to date."

The congressional district office manager hesitated long enough to organize his thoughts before going on.

"The team's Special Agent in Charge is a black male named Larry Paxton. He's described as well educated, highly intelligent, habitually sarcastic, and occasionally insubordinate. But he gets high marks for motivation and leadership as a team leader. He's also a qualified single-engine pilot, but suffered some fairly serious injuries on the two previous operations. The government pulled his pilot's license, and he may be offered an early-out on a medical disability."

Rustman nodded. "Go on."

"They have a second agent/pilot, a native American Eskimo named Thomas Woeshack, whose skills as a pilot are described as questionable at best. He's been involved in at least two crashes of government planes that I'm aware of. He also barely qualified with his assigned duty weapon—which, I believe, is a nine or ten millimeter auto-loading pistol of some sort—at the last agent in-service training session.

"The team's technical agent is an Asian male, Mike Takahara. Extremely intelligent according to the test scores, top marks on computers and electronic communications, no better than average scores in firearms qualifications, and minimally qualifying scores on tactical exercises, including hand-to-hand.

"Agent Dwight Stoner is an ex–offensive tackle for the Oakland Raiders. He's described as six-foot-eight, 320 pounds, and incredibly strong. He has apparently managed to stay in decent shape, but during the two previous investigations suffered serious bullet wounds to both knees, which required extensive surgery and significantly affected his mobility. He's also being considered for early medical retirement, but . . ."

"Is this some kind of joke?" Lt. Colonel John Rustman interrupted.

Simon Whatley blinked and shook his head in confusion. "I'm sorry, I . . ."

"The people you're describing sound like they need to be put out to pasture while they can still stagger up to the podium to pick up their retirement checks. If this is the team of agents you're hiring us to deal with, your client's wasting his money. From what you're saying, he could probably handle the job himself, or hire a couple of muggers out of New York to do the job a whole lot cheaper."

"I understand your skepticism," Simon Whatley conceded, "but keep in mind that not too long ago these same agents successfully took on a team of fifteen European counterterrorist experts, as well as a professional assassin with an international reputation. They sustained losses, certainly, but they also succeeded — which, as I'm sure you understand all too well, is precisely what concerns our client.

"And then, too," Whatley continued, observing the skeptical look on Rustman's face, "there's one other individual I haven't mentioned yet. An agent named Lightstone who, among other things, is quite proficient in tactics, martial arts, *and* firearms."

"Lightstone? What's that, an Indian name?"

"I have no idea," the senior congressional staffer admitted, "but I can tell you that at least two of his supervisors have described him as a loner and a 'wild card' — whatever that means."

"It means he's unpredictable, difficult to supervise, and not a team player," Rustman explained. "From a military point of view, that can be good or bad, depending on the operation, but it's usually bad. What's his background?"

"Uh, as I recall, he was a police officer in San Diego before joining the federal government."

"What rank?"

"I believe he was a detective in homicide."

"No military background?"

"No. None of these agents has any military experience."

"Then you can tell your client to stop worrying." Rustman smiled calmly. "I'm providing you with First Sergeant Aran Wintersole and a military recon hunter-killer team, one of the most highly trained and lethal units in the US military. Any one of them could easily handle this mission by himself without working up a sweat. As a team, they simply aren't stoppable by anything less than a similarly trained and equipped hunter-killer team . . . although given their tactical advantage of surprise and terrain, I personally wouldn't use anything less than a full Ranger company with air support to hunt them down.

"In other words," the military officer concluded casually, "you can assure your client that those five agents don't stand a chance."

"Actually, we may be talking about six," Whatley added tentatively.

"Oh?"

"As I understand it, an additional agent may be assigned to the team in the very near future."

"Any particular reason?"

"A normal Fish and Wildlife Service Special Operations team consists of four Special Agents, one technical agent, and one or two supervising agents," Whatley explained, "which means Bravo Team is currently short at least one Special Agent. The most likely candidate to fill that slot is a female agent named Natasha Marashenko."

"Russian?"

"In a manner of speaking. Her parents immigrated from Kazakhstan when she was a small child. She received high marks in Criminal Investigator School and Special Agent basic classes. She's a relatively new agent, and normally wouldn't be assigned to a covert operations team until she had several more years of experience. However, I'm told that she asked for and was given an assignment to Special Operations because of her high marks, and the fact that the Fish and Wildlife Service has relatively few female agents in their Law Enforcement program.

"That being the case," the congressional district office manager continued, "we suspect that Special Agent Marashenko could add a very interesting dimension to our project."

"How so?"

"My client has no personal interest in this particular agent, and certainly no desire to see her harmed. However, we do think she would make an excellent subject for the distraction scenario we discussed earlier."

Lt. Colonel John Rustman thought about that for a few moments.

"You don't think they'd sacrifice her?"

"Would you in their position?"

Rustman's eyes took on a distant look. Then he pressed his lips together in a thin smile. "No. In their position, I suppose I wouldn't. Is there anything you can do to encourage her selection?"

"We're trying, but we have to be careful. The last thing we want to do right now is create suspicion or, worse, a link that can be tracked back to the congressman's office."

"That would be an extremely unfortunate situation, for everyone concerned." The malice in Rustman's voice sent a chill up Simon Whatley's spine.

"Yes, of course. Uh, now then," the congressional district office manager went on hurriedly, "there's just a couple more things you need to know. First of all, we want to get an informant situated in close contact with their operation. If we succeed, that person will provide us with some extremely useful real-time intelligence information—which we'll immediately process and pass on to you."

"Anybody I know?" Rustman inquired.

"I sincerely hope not. Because someone could easily tie this informant back to both the congressman and our client, we need to keep that person's identity a closely guarded secret."

"Makes sense." Rustman shrugged indifferently.

"However," Whatley went on, "in the event that it ever does become necessary to link up with Wintersole and his team, the informant will use the code word 'canvasback,' repeated twice, as an identifier."

"Canvasback, repeated twice." Rustman nodded. "Okay, I'll notify Wintersole. What else?"

"Our client has a special interest in one of the targets."

"And which one might that be?"

"Lightstone."

"The ex–homicide investigator."

"Yes. To put it bluntly, it would please our client a great deal if Special Agent Lightstone experienced, shall we say, a heightened degree of suffering during the course of the project."

Rustman raised an eyebrow.

"An interesting phrase, 'heightened degree of suffering,' " the military officer noted wryly. "Just what, exactly, did you have in mind?"

"Our client would be especially pleased if Agent Lightstone were acutely aware of the unfortunate status of his fellow agents before he meets a similar fate."

"In other words, you'd like him to remain conscious, aware of the situation, and, one way or another, in a position to outlive the others by at least a day or two."

"Oh, I don't know about days." Simon Whatley blanched at the thought. "I'm fairly certain our client isn't quite *that* vindictive. I think a few hours would suffice."

"What does Lightstone look like?"

"As I recall, he's a white male, average height and weight. In any case, he's sufficiently distinct from the other members of Bravo Team that you shouldn't have any problem in identifying him. And you'll be receiving a complete set of photos in the briefing materials," Whatley reminded him.

"You do realize that guaranteeing even a couple of hours might be difficult." A thoughtful expression crossed Rustman's face. "Once you engage the enemy in a fluid tactical situation—"

"My client fully understands that such a stipulation would add a significant degree of complexity and difficulty to the mission," Whatley interrupted, gaining confidence when he sensed that his knowledge of the financial arrangements gave him a certain amount of control. "That's why he's authorized me to offer a $50,000 bonus per man, with an additional hundred thousand to you, of course . . . payment based upon the submission of appropriate evidence."

"What kind of appropriate evidence?"

"A videotape of sufficient clarity would be more than adequate."

Lt. Colonel John Rustman stared at Whatley in disbelief.

"Are you out of your fucking mind?"

"We would expect you to edit the tape in an appropriate manner," Whatley continued hurriedly. "I can assure you that our client has absolutely no interest in the identities of your team, and, for obvious reasons, he's the last person who would want such a tape to fall in the hands of a federal agent or prosecutor. He did, however, anticipate that you might object to this provision and asked me to convey his assurances that once he receives the tape, he will review and destroy it immediately.

"I realize we're adding a number of frustrating restrictions to your plan," Whatley added when Rustman remained silent, "but I can assure you that all of this is very important to our client."

The military officer eventually shrugged indifferently. "I'm not that concerned about your restrictions," he informed Whatley gruffly. "They're minor, and civilian interference is a fact of life for any military operation these days. And as it happens, the communications specialist on the team is fully qualified in photo and video surveillance. We'll see to it that she's fully equipped with all the necessary photo and video gear. All I need to know now is how we go about finding these agents."

"I think you'll like that part the best." A smug smile appeared on Whatley's face. "You don't need to find them. We're going to bring them to you."

"And just how . . ." Rustman started to ask, when a barrage of gunfire suddenly erupted across the water.

Chapter Four

The confrontation had been going on for a good three minutes—a flow of events highlighted by an unexpected kiss, a vicious roundhouse left, a countering hip throw, a lunging dive for a discarded pistol, the sharp crack of partially sawed-through support beams suddenly giving way, the muffled pop of an activated tear-gas canister, and an impressive variety of grunts, shouts, splashing, and cursing—when a bloodcurdling scream of terror suddenly and irrevocably destroyed the remnants of what had begun as a calm and peaceful Sunday morning.

For a brief moment, all eyes turned in the direction of the scream.

Which the concussive roar of a 12-gauge shotgun and three rapid eardrum-piercing gunshots from a 10mm semiautomatic pistol immediately drowned out.

Then in rapid succession:

Two figures burst through a pair of ancient attic window shutters and leaped onto a second-story roof.

Rubber-soled shoes frantically scrambled against the incredibly slippery surface.

Two desperately flailing individuals lost their balance and crashed facefirst onto the sun-baked shingles.

A burst of furious curses exploded in two distinct ethnic dialects as both men grabbed the edges of the burning hot gutters with bare hands to keep from sliding off the liquid-soap-covered roof.

And then, finally, a 10mm Smith & Wesson semiautomatic pistol and a Model 870 Remington pump shotgun scraped and slid down the slippery sloped roof, then hit the thick mud with two audible plops.

Shaking his head in visible dismay, David Halahan, Chief of the Branch of Special Operations, Division of Law Enforcement, U.S. Fish and Wildlife Service, muttered a heartfelt curse, and turned to his deputy.

"Okay, I've seen enough. Shut it down before somebody gets hurt."

Special Ops Deputy Chief Freddy Moore nodded in agreement. He stood at the edge of the raised wooden platform, pulled a military police whistle from his shirt pocket, and sounded a single, shrill blast.

The familiar noise caused the eleven field agents to pause in their varying endeavors and glance at the raised instructor's platform that overlooked the entire practical exercise course.

Setting aside the whistle, Moore reached for the bullhorn.

"All right, boys and girls, that'll be all for today," he ordered in a distinct deep, Southern drawl. "Referees will submit all score sheets to the tower, and firearms instructors will collect all weapons and ammunition."

"And Henry," Moore added as an afterthought, "let her go."

Special Agent Henry Lightstone slowly and cautiously released the tight leg lock and nearly secured chokehold on his mud-and-swampwater-soaked opponent—who, in turn, reluctantly stopped struggling to break loose from the carotid choke with one hand while trying to slash, claw, and strike any vital organ she could reach with the other. Instead, she twisted away and then lay there on her back, red-faced, gasping for breath, and glared at Lightstone with furious blue eyes.

"Paxton," Freddy Moore went on in a calm and orderly manner, "would you and Stoner kindly unhandcuff our designated congressman and designated bagman and help them out of the septic tank?"

The tall, lanky Special Agent in Charge of Bravo Team held a handcuff key up in plain view of his sprawled, filthy, watery-eyed, and thoroughly frustrated counterparts. Smiling cheerfully, he let the tiny key drop down into the ankle-deep sewage.

"And Michael," Moore added with a sigh, "if it's not too much trouble, would you and Agent Woeshack mind going back up in that attic, catching that damned snake, and putting it back in its cage before you help Agents Wu and Green to get down off that roof?"

"But they got out there all by . . ." Special Agent/Pilot Thomas Woeshack started to protest. But then he saw the look on Halahan's face and hurried over to the three-story rustic cabin/training structure to help his tech-agent partner cautiously corner and retrieve the hissing twelve-foot reticulated python they'd borrowed from the local zoo.

Moments later, Special Agent Dwight Stoner knelt at the edge of the once-camouflaged septic tank. One by one, he dead-lifted Special Agent/Congressman Donato and Special Agent/bagman LiBrandi out of the slippery, nine-foot-deep concrete tank with his muscular arms, wrinkling his nose at the pungent smell of decomposing sewage and the wispy remnants of the tear gas.

As Stoner thoughtfully directed a stream of water from a nearby hose on the faces of the two olifactorily stunned agents, Larry Paxton walked over to the middle of the practical exercise area and reached down to help Henry Lightstone up out of the mud.

"Made some real nice moves on the lady here, Henry, my man. Real nice," Paxton congratulated his wild card agent in his deep South Carolina drawl as he pulled Lightstone to his feet, then made a show of wiping the mud off his hands. "Can't say as I ever seen anything quite like it. Must be one of them crazy white folk mating rituals my dear ol' daddy used to tell me about. The girl walks up smiling all pretty-like, the boy gives the girl a great big hug and kiss, then the girl proceeds to stomp the living shit outta him. My, my, my."

Paxton paused for a moment to consider the disheveled condition of his Special Agent partner. "Man, I sure do hope she didn't rip off anything you're gonna need later."

"That's good, Paxton." Henry Lightstone winced as he gently probed at his smashed and bleeding nose. "See if you can piss her off just a little bit more by rubbing it in."

"Hell, there ain't no need to be doing any more rubbing. Any fool could see you two already done plenty of that. Tell you the truth, the way you were going with that leg lock, I was kinda thinking we might have to spray you two down with a hose. Which reminds me, Agent Marashenko," the Bravo Team leader added with a cheerful smile as he looked down at Lightstone's sprawled, muddy, and clearly still-furious opponent, "we found this here genuine federal agent pistol down in the septic tank, along with a couple of very sleazy political types who were probably subleasing the place. Don't suppose you might know who could have lost it?"

Paxton gingerly held a wet and grimy 10mm Smith & Wesson semi-automatic pistol with his right thumb and forefinger, carefully moving his feet to avoid the small stream of raw sewage that poured out the barrel.

Ignoring Henry Lightstone's offered hand, Special Agent Natasha Marashenko rose unsteadily to her feet, ripped the dripping pistol out of Paxton's hand, muttered something about idiot macho males under her breath, and staggered away in a visible display of injured pride, barely controlled rage, and almost complete exhaustion. Her muscular legs and buttocks visibly stretched the thin fabric of her tight, water-and-mud-soaked jeans as she made her way over to the water station.

"My, my, my, that gal is definitely an improvement on the standard issue federal agent around here, not to mention a walking endorsement for glasnost," Larry Paxton commented appreciatively as he and Lightstone watched the shapely, dark-haired young agent take the hose from Stoner and then kneel down to help wash the tear gas from the eyes of her fellow covert team members.

"And nice to look at, too," Lightstone agreed dryly as he gently probed some tender areas around his lower abdomen. "If you happen to like blue-eyed wildcats who fight dirty."

"You know, Henry, it kinda looked to me like she almost had you on that last go-around," the SAC of Bravo Team commented thoughtfully. "If ol' Freddy hadn't blown that whistle when he did, that little gal just mighta worked her way out of that chokehold and seriously whipped your scrawny ass. Maybe next time around, it oughta be you who gets to dance around that septic tank, and me who gets to mud-wrestle the pretty young lady agents who come on like the Seventh Cavalry."

Henry Lightstone smiled. "Next exercise, Paxton, she's all yours. But I'm warning you, she kicks and bites, and she doesn't like to lose. You keep trying to piss her off like that, and you're going to find yourself . . ."

"Ah, speaking of being pissed off, gents—" Special Agent Dwight Stoner gestured in the direction of the observation platform as he limped up beside his partners.

The three agents watched silently as Special Ops Branch Chief David Halahan climbed down from the platform, took one final look around the exercise area, shook his head in apparent disgust, and started walking toward the distant training office building.

"Think we mighta gone too far on this one?" Stoner asked.

Larry Paxton nodded his head. "That's a definite possibility, Stoner my man. A very definite possibility indeed."

Chapter Five

Twenty-six hundred miles west of the practical exercise area of the Federal Law Enforcement Training Center at Glynco, Georgia, Lt. Colonel John Rustman listened patiently as First Sergeant Wintersole explained over their scrambled radio communications net why he had believed it necessary to send Simon Whatley's incredibly foolhardy—or perhaps simply incredibly stupid—aide running frantically back to the Town Car by firing a burst of 5.56mm rounds into a nearby tree.

Other than slipping in the mud twice, and undoubtedly creating a mess in his pants if not on the rented Town Car's expensive leather upholstery, they had allowed the aide to escape unharmed.

"What kind of camera?" Rustman asked when Wintersole finished his report.

"Thirty-five millimeter, long lens," the cold, metallic voice responded.

"Did he get away with any shots?"

"Negative."

"Are you certain?"

"Affirmative. We recovered the camera."

"Why did you let him go?"

"He didn't get in very far. Figured it wasn't worth letting him see a face or digging another hole."

Rustman nodded his head in satisfaction. "Good call." He glanced down at his watch. "Maintain your positions for another thirty, and then disengage. We'll link up tomorrow morning at the Windmill, civvies, 0700 hours, for a full debriefing."

"Affirmative. Debrief tomorrow morning, the Windmill, civvies, 0700 hours. Tango-one-one, out."

"One-zero, out," Rustman spoke into his collar mike. Then he turned to confront Simon Whatley, who sat ashen-faced against the far side of the boat.

"Was that your stupid idea, or his?"

If possible, Simon Whatley's face turned even whiter.

"I don't know what you're talking about." He tried to act as though he had no idea what Rustman meant, but failed completely.

Rustman didn't even bother to react. Instead, the retired military officer simply fixed his cold gaze on the senior congressional staffer's watery eyes.

"One more time, Whatley. And this time, I want you to think very carefully before answering. Was the camera your idea, or his?"

Whatley hesitated briefly, then murmured, "Mine."

Rustman shook his head when he received the expected confirmation.

"Let me guess. You thought it'd be a good idea to have pictures in case you ever had to claim that you and Smallsreed were running your own covert investigation?"

The congressional district office manager nodded his head silently.

"But I bet you came up with that brilliant idea yesterday, *before* you understood how completely and unalterably committed you and Smallsreed are to this operation now. And I bet you just forgot to call the kid off when you picked up the money packet, right?"

Whatley nodded again.

"What's his name?"

"Bennington," Whatley barely whispered.

"First name?"

"Uh, uh, Keith, but I can assure you . . ."

The military officer brought his right hand up in a cautioning manner. "Are you capable of convincing Mr. Bennington that something very unpleasant will happen to him if he tries any more of these stupid stunts on his own?"

"Of course." The congressional staffer bobbed his head up and down frantically. "I can assure you that—"

"Good." Rustman reached forward and started up the boat engine again. "Then it won't be necessary to send Wintersole."

Chapter Six

She was exactly as the Sage described.

And more.

Much more.

When she arrived, they all gathered around to greet her, the men and women of the Chosen Brigade of the Seventh Seal who rarely saw a new face or heard a new story in their severely isolated mountainside retreat, let alone two. The men were especially curious and hovered until they got close enough to see for themselves. Then they swallowed hard and quickly moved back a respectful distance.

The women offered her tea, made from a scarce dried herb which she immediately recognized, and the most comfortable seat in the communal meeting place. She accepted both with a natural grace that captivated them all.

The women felt tense, for obvious reasons, but also intrigued . . . and, a tribute to their inherent grace, only slightly jealous.

The children stared wide-eyed and enchanted—especially the older boys.

But the men just stood there, stunned, and mesmerized, and in the fullest sense of the expression, terrified out of their minds.

They all learned, as she sipped at her tea, that she had moved into the old Dogsfire Inn—an ancient house built around an ancient tree about a mile or so down the creek from their isolated community. She had recently purchased it from the estate of the previous owner, an elderly woman of indeterminate age who had operated the inn's small restaurant, held séances, and told fortunes when she wasn't attending her duties as the local postmistress and cursing the government in at least three different foreign languages.

Yes, the woman smiled warmly at them. She, too, had heard the stories about the previous owner being a gypsy whose parents died in a fire way back in 1862. Such interesting stories. Very imaginative.

She took another sip of tea.

Wasn't she scared, a young and attractive woman like her, to live in a place like that, all by herself? They all wanted to know.

She smiled pleasantly and then stretched, unintentionally—perhaps—revealing a taut and slender figure beneath a loose tunic that embodied the very essence of everything sleek and sensual.

Scared? No, of course not. Why should she be scared? She laughed. Such a beautiful location, and such a beautiful old house—or it would be once she furnished it. And, as they could all clearly see, it wasn't as if she lived there alone.

The children bobbed their heads, completely entranced by this once barely imaginable fantasy suddenly there among them in the flesh.

The men gulped nervously and made a conscious effort to hold their bladders.

She thanked them for the tea and stood, causing the men to step back hastily and give her—or rather them—plenty of room.

What was it the Sage had said? Very very dangerous.

Jesus God, yes.

What would she do down there all by herself? one of the women asked.

Well, she wasn't sure just yet. Keep the restaurant open, if it wasn't too much trouble, and perhaps hold séances and tell fortunes when she wasn't busy being the local postmistress and speaking her mind about the sorry state of the government.

She was only fluent in two foreign languages, she admitted apologetically, smiling that warm, charming, and seductive smile one last time. But that was all right.

Her cat would provide the third.

The group parted, and the strange and beautiful creature glided away.

She and the sleek, muscular, and terribly dangerous animal that never moved far from her side.

Chapter Seven

At ten-fifteen that Sunday morning, while the uniformly bruised, muddy, and exhausted federal wildlife agents of Bravo and Charlie Teams worked to dismantle the practical exercise props and untangle their emotions, Deputy Special Ops Chief Freddy Moore entered the building assigned to the Fish and Wildlife Service at the Federal Law Enforcement Training Center, walked down the long hallway, and stood in the doorway to the conference room.

"Well?" David Halahan looked up inquisitively.

Freddy Moore handed his boss the instructor evaluation sheets.

"Pretty much what we expected on the individual batteries," Moore reported as Halahan scanned the pencil-marked pages, "which isn't that surprising seeing as how we handpicked Charlie Team from the last two agent classes. Youthful enthusiasm coupled with superior endurance, speed, hand-eye skills, reaction times, education, and training. You can see the effects all through the combined event scores. The only agent on Bravo Team who even came close to keeping up with these kids on the skill events was Lightstone on the Hogan's Alley and hand-to-hand drills. And he was damned lucky Wu didn't put him into the infirmary with one of those flying-kick combinations," Moore concluded reflectively.

"What about the rest of them?"

Freddy Moore glanced at his notes. "Let's see. Stoner and Riley maxed out on the bench weights as usual, but Stoner lost a lot of time on the agility phase. They both have the upper bodies of a couple of damned gorillas, but Stoner's eyes are getting worse and his lateral mobility's near zero—I think his knees are basically held together with pins and wire. And, speaking of limited movement, Paxton's got so much scar tissue on both arms now, he can't even pass the flight physical to maintain his pilot's license. Fact is, it's about all he can do to hold a pistol steady enough to qualify. Probably ought to retire or deactivate both of them on medicals for their own good. And Takahara's at least six months behind on the latest electronic surveillance and security techniques. He tripped two sensors on one of the entries and never did spot the phone tap in the kitchen."

Halahan raised an eyebrow.

"How'd *that* happen?"

His deputy shrugged. "Not necessarily his fault. The transmitter was molded into the base receiver with its own shielded power source, so there wasn't any line drop. One of our electronic engineers at the forensics lab put it together for us. Takahara had never seen anything like it before—mostly because he missed the last tech-agent in-service class—and there was no way he could've detected it with the gear he had with him during the exercise."

"Even so, I would've expected him to know about the new technology, and be prepared for the unexpected," Halahan commented.

"That's pretty much what he said, too, although he wasn't that polite," Moore agreed. "And as for Woeshack . . . well, I'm still of the opinion that he shouldn't be allowed anywhere near *any* federal government motorized vehicle, much less a goddamned airplane. All things considered, I find it truly amazing that he's still alive."

"He claims he comes from a long line of Eskimo shamans who provide the necessary spiritual guidance when he flies," Halahan explained. "OAS just recertified him, so maybe there's something to it."

"You mean like Paxton's poor black sharecropper ancestors who used to practice voodoo on the plantation?"

"No, that's pure Paxton bullshit." Halahan smiled for the first time that morning. "So what's your take on what happened out there?"

"You mean why does older, slower, half-crippled, and otherwise handicapped Bravo Team take the flag every time, no matter how we stack the deck?" Moore shrugged. "The obvious, I suppose. They watch out for each other. Play off their obvious strengths. Cover their known weaknesses. Continually adapt to the situation at hand. Refuse to give up. And, of course, they cheat."

"You mean the septic tank?"

"One of many examples, as I recall." Moore resisted the urge to chuckle. "In fact, looking back over the past week, I think the only thing they *haven't* cheated on is the restriction on live ammo."

"I thought you said you were going to compensate for the cheating—put more emphasis on the fundamentals?" Halahan reminded him.

"I thought I had." Moore grinned apologetically. "Hell, I even de-signed this last exercise myself, based on some input I got from Boggs."

"Wilbur Boggs?"

"Yeah. He called a few days ago to bullshit and bat around a couple of ideas for a project. He didn't say so directly, but I got the feeling he's hoping to borrow one of the teams for something he's got going out in Oregon."

Halahan's eyebrows rose as he recalled the details of the training sce-nario he'd just witnessed. "Something involving a congressman?"

"That's the way I read it," Moore acknowledged. "Don't you?"

"What did you tell him?" Halahan stopped leafing through the eval-uations and observed his deputy expectantly.

"That I'd get back to him later after we finished in-service."

"Good answer." Halahan nodded his head approvingly. "So tell me more about this exercise that Boggs helped you design."

"Yeah, well, the basic idea was that Lightstone and Paxton would make the contact at the campsite, recognize the congressman and his girlfriend, spot the payoff situation and the illegal dough, then handle the situation in a diplomatic manner that might actually result in a decent case with admissible evidence and a minimum number of follow-up con-gressionals."

"And presumably without getting themselves or their partners killed in the process," Halahan suggested wryly.

"That was the general idea." Freddy Moore smiled. "According to the script, backup agents are available, but radio communications are out. The girlfriend is unpredictable and may be armed and dangerous—Ma-rashenko, by any definition. Donato and LiBrandi were born to the roles of sleazy congressman and lobbyist/bagman. Wu steps onstage as the ever-faithful congressional aide who doubles as a bodyguard, and LiBrandi brings along his own street-smart baby-sitter—a role played to perfection by our genuine Harlem street kid Antone Green—to keep an eye on the money. I figured all that just might make our boys sweat a little for a change."

"You think Bravo Team came up with a legitimate solution to the problem?"

Moore shrugged. "Depends on how you look at it. Starting out by poisoning the opposing team leader's lunch isn't exactly what I'd call a textbook solution."

"They actually poisoned Riley?" Halahan interrupted, blinking in sur-prise.

"Depends on your definition." Freddy Moore failed miserably in his attempt not to grin. "The base nurse suspects a massive dose of a fast-acting purgative, most likely self-administered by the victim through an unfortunate double helping of refried beans and hot sauce. The cafeteria staff claims complete ignorance, and I understand the medical staff declined to investigate the matter any further."

"In other words, you're suggesting it was Riley's own fault?"

"For going about his business in a predictable manner and leaving himself open to a very effective countermove?" Moore shrugged. "I suppose you could look at it that way."

"And as far as the congressional contact issue goes," the Special Ops chief raised the potentially explosive issue calmly, "I guess there's not much point in being overly concerned with diplomatic nuances when your congressman/suspect manages to get himself handcuffed to his lobbyist/bagman buddy, and then ends up getting dragged headfirst into a functioning septic tank when said buddy dives for a loose gun." Halahan shook his head at the memory. "Probably a good moral in there somewhere."

"No doubt."

"Am I being reasonable in assuming that Bravo Team also bribed at least one of the groundskeepers to lay a new pathway to the cabin last night?" Halahan continued, in his methodical manner, to nail down the details of the debacle.

"Yep. Got them to run it right over the nearby septic tank, the top of which the grounds crew and a couple of as-yet-unidentified assistants thoughtfully replaced with a bunch of mostly sawed-through crossbeams and some real thin bender-board, and then covered with gravel." Moore chuckled. "That seems to have been Woeshack's contribution to the overall plan. He claims his ancestors used to hunt mammoths on the Arctic slopes using the same technique."

"Agent Woeshack lacks a firm grip on reality," Halahan reminded his deputy dryly. "He's also believes he's a halfway decent pilot."

"True, but I understand he also came up with the dish-detergent-on-the-roof ploy to supplement Takahara's snake-in-the-box surprise, which you have to admit was a nice touch."

"Effective, if nothing else," Halahan conceded. "Continue."

"Well, with Riley out of the picture, that freed up Stoner in terms of size and muscle. But my guess is that after watching the individual exercises, Paxton figured that Lightstone would have trouble with Wu and those flying kicks of his, no matter how things worked out," Moore postulated. "I imagine he and Takahara did a little research and discovered something in Wu's and Green's backgrounds suggesting that they might be effectively distracted by the sudden and unexpected appearance of a twelve-foot reticulated python."

"Who the hell wouldn't be?"

"Exactly. Which only left one major problem."

"How to deal with Marashenko?"

Freddy Moore nodded.

"Bravo Team knew she could be a significant problem, no matter how they rigged the game," he easily surmised. "They saw her shoot in the simulator courses, and I gather they were suitably impressed. They had to assume she'd either be armed, or have access to a weapon. That meant that if they let her get to her gun—or anyone's gun for that matter—she could take out the entire team."

"Thus the distraction." Halahan sighed.

"Yep." Freddy Moore tried to suppress another grin.

"Think she'll file an EEO complaint against Lightstone?"

"For what," Moore asked reasonably. "The hug and kiss, or the chokehold?"

"I'm not sure one was any more legal than the other."

The deputy chief considered this possibility for a long moment before answering.

"I don't think so," he finally concluded. "Marashenko's a tough gal and a damn good rookie agent. My guess is that she's more embarrassed than anything because she let Lightstone catch her off guard. In retrospect, she should've kissed him right back, smiled, stepped back, drawn her Smith, and threatened to double-tap him—heart and head—if he so much as twitched. Instead, she lost her temper . . . and her gun."

"Not to mention the object of the exercise when LiBrandi dived for the damn thing and dragged Donato into the septic tank with him." Halahan shook his head, still not quite believing what he had seen.

"One of life's finer moments." Freddy Moore smiled cheerfully. "The stuff of which legends are born."

"Legends?"

Moore shrugged. "Pretty much guaranteed in this case. Word is that Takahara set up two concealed video cameras to record the entire exercise. I don't think Charlie Team's going to live this one down for quite a while."

Halahan sighed deeply. "No, I suppose not."

The chief of Special Ops treated his subordinate supervisor to another long silence.

"So what do we do about them?" he finally asked.

"Bravo or Charlie?"

"Charlie."

"They're good young agents, but they got their confidence pretty badly shaken today," Moore replied frankly. "I wouldn't recommend sending them out on their own on anything really serious just yet."

"What about that Oregon deal?"

"What Oregon deal?" Freddy Moore's expression darkened in confusion. "You mean Boggs?"

Halahan shook his head. "Actually, I was thinking more along the lines of that character who's supposedly selling Bigfoot souvenirs. The one who claims to be a direct descendent of Cochise, and therefore immune from federal prosecution."

"I vaguely remember reading the report." Moore's features slowly cleared. "Didn't he turn out to be just some crazy-old-fart white guy, Jim Star or Starrs or something like that, whose great-great-grandmother may have had a part-Indian boyfriend who might have been an Apache, but nobody knew for sure . . . or cared, for that matter?"

"That's our boy." Halahan smiled. "Calls himself the Sage now."

"As in prophet?"

"Or dried-up weed, take your pick."

"Well"—Moore pondered Halahan's remarks thoughtfully—"since we both agree that even the federal government would be a little reluctant to prosecute a certifiably crazy person for selling souvenirs made out of a creature that doesn't exist, am I to assume that the Sage has gone out and done something even more stupid than usual?"

"How would you rate selling genuine Apache battle charms to California tourists?"

"Serves them right for thinking they escaped into God's country," the Special Ops deputy chief commented. "Personally, I happen to be a firm believer in the concept of 'buyer beware' . . . But, by the way, what the hell's an Apache battle charm?"

"Beats me." Halahan smiled. "And I doubt our friend the Sage knows either. But according to the lab, at least one of his offerings included a bald eagle feather."

"Christ, he probably found it on the ground somewhere." Moore snorted disgustedly. "You're telling me you want to put a whole goddamned Special Ops team on a guy like this when we've got a whole shit-pot-full of serious killers and dealers waiting in line to be worked?"

Halahan shrugged. "Like you said, Charlie Team's probably not up to anything too serious right now. Besides, as I recall from the report, our Sage claims to sell bear-claw jewelry, too, and maybe a couple of bear gallbladders that'll probably turn out to be pig or cow. If nothing else, it'll be good practice . . . build up their confidence a little."

"Or destroy it completely if this guy scams them, too," Freddy Moore reminded his boss. "But what the hell, I'm game." He paused for a moment, then looked at Halahan expectantly. "So what about Bravo?"

"That's a little more of a problem."

"There's always those Mexican Mafia types down in Nogales supposedly dealing in hot snakes and red-kneed tarantulas."

"I did give that project some serious consideration, out of pure vindictiveness if nothing else, even before I saw that python stunt," Halahan admitted with a slightly wistful grin. "But then something a bit more interesting popped up on the horizon."

"Really?" The deputy Special Ops chief's eyebrows rose in anticipation. "This ought to be good."

"Oh, it is," Halahan replied emphatically. "I got a call from the Washington Office earlier this morning. Seems they just received a high-priority congressional inquiry asking Special Ops to look into a group called the Chosen Brigade of the Seventh Seal—supposedly one of our friendly antigovernment, outer-fringe, dug-into-the-hillside-crackpot type militant groups based in the Northwest. Washington wants us to find out if there's anything going on there that the congressional delegation should be concerned about."

"Antigovernment militants?" Freddy Moore winced. "Christ, that's just what we need right now. So what did you tell them?"

"The truth. That we have several high-priority projects already in the hopper, and that an inquiry like that really ought to be handled by the local resident agent first. If it turns out that there's something worth digging into, we can always add it to our list."

"Sounds like a perfectly reasonable solution to me."

"That's what I thought, too, but they didn't buy it. They also mentioned that the inquiring congressman—who, they emphasized, is *very* concerned about militant activity in his district, and would like an answer as soon as possible—happens to be a senior member of the House Interior Appropriations Subcommittee."

"Ah." The Special Ops deputy chief considered his superior's remark for a brief moment, then took it to its logical conclusion. "So you bit your tongue, said 'yes sir,' and assured them we'd put our best team on it right away."

"Very intuitive." Halahan smiled.

"Which, at the moment—at least according to all of the scores and assorted paperwork I just handed you—happens to be Bravo."

"That's right."

Freddy Moore closed his eyes and sighed deeply.

"Setting aside the minor issue of budgetary politics, which I do realize is impossible—or at least impractical—just what the hell does a local dug-in, antigovernment militant group have to do with us . . . other than the fact that we are, I suppose, part of the government?" He opened his eyes and stared hopefully at his boss. "I mean, shouldn't something like that get handed over to the FBI as a matter of course?"

"Normally, I'd say yes," Halahan agreed. "Except in this case, apparently there's reason to believe that the members of this cheerful little group make ends meet by running canned hunts in an adjoining national wildlife refuge."

That remark captured Freddy Moore's attention immediately.

"Oh, yeah? Which one?"

"Windgate."

"Windgate National Wildlife Refuge?" Confusion darkened Moore's usually cheerful features. "Don't think I ever heard of it. Where's it located?"

"Jasper County, Oregon."

Freddy Moore blinked in surprise.

"Wait a minute, isn't that Wilbur Boggs's district?" he asked hesitantly.

"That's right."

Then, suddenly, the light dawned.

"Oh Christ, no . . . the congressman and the bagman?"

Halahan nodded his head glumly, and both men sat quietly.

"I don't suppose you happen to know the name of the local congressman representing that district?" Moore finally broke the silence.

"Regis J. Smallsreed."

"Smallsreed? Why do I know that name?"

"Probably because we've got twenty-seven supplemental reports in our files from eight different agents listing him as a possible suspect in several dozen VIP hunt club violations?" Halahan suggested.

"Yeah, that would do it."

Freddy Moore's distinctly unhappy expression made it very clear this news didn't please him at all.

"So what we seem to have here," Halahan continued, "is a high-priority request for an inquiry into supposedly illegal hunting activities by an antigovernment militant group, direct from the offices of Regis J. Smallsreed, Esquire, senior member of the House Interior Appropriations Subcommittee, and suspected killer of anything that runs, swims, or flies, in or out of season, as I believe one of those reports put it . . . who also happens to represent the district where one of the more bullheaded and persistent agents in our outfit—who seems perfectly willing to spend at least some of his free time dreaming up innovative ways for one of our Special Ops teams to go after crooked congressmen—has been assigned for the past three years."

"That is one hell of a frightening coincidence," Freddy Moore whispered.

"Exactly what I was thinking—assuming Boggs's input *was* a coincidence, which I seriously doubt."

"You talk to him yet?"

Halahan shook his head. "According to his secretary, he's out in the field."

"What about his radio?"

"One of the first things she tried. Apparently he shut it off. Probably out on a surveillance."

"She try him on his beeper?"

"She says not to quote her, but she's almost positive Boggs threw it away at least six months ago. She's pretty much given up on trying to get a hold of him out in the field. I guess he checks in often enough, stops by the office every now and then to drop off tapes and sign reports, so nobody worries about it too much."

Freddy Moore sighed. "You think we're ever going be able to drag some of these guys into the twenty-first century?"

"I'm not necessarily sure we want to," Halahan replied thoughtfully. "We need a few of the old-time duck cops in this organization . . . if nothing else, just to maintain our perspective on what we're supposed to be doing out there."

"True, but agents like Wilbur Boggs sometimes forget the nuances of a federal investigation—little things like probable cause," Moore reminded his superior. "And they take shortcuts instead, simply because they *know* they're right."

"Which they usually are . . . but it *is* a problem," Halahan conceded.

"So you really think Boggs is trying to suck us into one of those fly-by-the-seat-of-your-pants deals?"

Halahan nodded his head. "Wilbur's had a bug up his ass about wealthy or influential people who think they're above the law ever since he was a young agent assigned to the Chesapeake Bay. My take on him is that he's an honest man, stubborn as hell, and a damned good investigator when he puts his mind to it. But I don't think he'd hesitate for a second to use any weapon he could get his hands on to take a guy like Smallsreed down, especially if he was absolutely convinced the guy was dirty."

"And you think he'd view us as one of those weapons?"

"If one of our teams were available and properly motivated?" Halahan nodded affirmatively. "I'm absolutely certain he'd try to use us for whatever advantage he could gain."

"And thanks to me," Freddy Moore sighed glumly, "he just arranged for a couple of our teams to be properly motivated."

"That's right."

"But even so, you and I both know that the Washington Office would never give an agent like Boggs free rein on a sensitive investigation like that," Moore argued. "For one thing, they'd never be able to control him—or the investigation—once he got started."

The Special Ops deputy chief paused long enough to organize his thoughts, before continuing.

"And they're not about to turn *us* loose on a player like Smallsreed either, unless they're reasonably sure, number one, that he really *is* guilty, and two, that we'll be able to nail him clean. Because if we don't, the shit is seriously going to hit the fan, and they're not going to want to be anywhere near the blades when it does."

"A little loose on the analogies, but otherwise a fairly decent summary of the situation." Halahan chuckled approvingly.

"Thanks, but only being the deputy around here, I'm still a little confused about how an official inquiry from the office of Congressman Regis J. Smallsreed regarding some loony-tune group of antigovernment militants fits into all of this. If Smallsreed really is dirty, wouldn't we be the last people in the world he'd want poking around his district?"

"Your guess is as good as mine," Halahan confessed. "The obvious answer is that he doesn't crap in his own nest. But that doesn't make much sense if Wilbur's hounding his ass. But then," the Special Ops chief added, "there's always the interesting possibility that we're being handed a fake congressional."

Freddy Moore stared at his boss incredulously.

"I beg your pardon?"

"I can think of at least a couple reasons why a few of our more politically oriented bosses might want us to do a little digging into the situation and see what we stir up. Especially if they weren't going to be held accountable if something went wrong."

"Christ"—Moore shook his head slowly in amazement—"how many years have you spent in the Washington Office?"

"Too many," Halahan acknowledged. "It's called occupational paranoia. And if it's all the same to you, I'd just as soon not dwell on that right now. Let's get back to Bravo Team."

"Hold on a minute," Freddy Moore protested, "You're losing me again. What about Bravo Team? I thought you said you committed them to working the congressional?"

"Think about that for a moment. Do you really want a team that dreams up rerouted gravel paths and bender-board septic-tank covers working a covert investigation on a congressman . . . and especially on a congressman like Smallsreed, somebody they could easily develop a serious disliking for if he's anything at all like Boggs suspects? Keeping in mind," Halahan added meaningfully, "that you and I both have at least two years to go before we're eligible for full retirement."

"No, I guess not," Moore reluctantly agreed with his superior.

"Precisely how I feel." Halahan met his deputy's gaze for a brief moment. "But I think we might have an interesting option. When you said that you didn't think Charlie Team should be assigned to something really serious—I believe those were the words you used—did you mean really serious in terms of complexity . . . or in terms of danger?"

Freddy Moore responded immediately.

"Danger, of course. Charlie Team can handle complex situations just fine, but—"

"I checked into this quasi-militant group while you compiled the scores," Halahan interrupted gently. "From what I can tell so far, the Chosen Brigade of the Seventh Seal consists of a bunch of middle-aged, overweight, underachieving, self-righteous scripture-spouting wanna-bes who came to the brilliant conclusion that if they dug themselves into some godforsaken mountainside unlikely to be a nuclear target, and stayed there long enough, they'd get to repopulate the world after everyone else got fried in a nuclear war."

"Charming idea," Moore commented. "How long have they been at it?"

"According to my informant—a state wildlife officer who's had a number of contacts with them over the years, primarily for shooting deer out of season—they've been tucked away in a little three-hundred-acre canyon that one of their members donated to the cause, in Jasper County, Oregon, for something like twenty years."

"Twenty *years?*" Moore stared at his superior in disbelief. "My God." And then as an afterthought, "How do they make a living?"

"Apparently through a little illegal guiding, hunting, and trapping to supplement their monthly accumulation of food stamps and welfare checks."

"Tell me you're kidding."

Halahan shook his head, a look of disgust appearing on his face. "I get the impression that some of the tax-conscious locals aren't too thrilled about the food stamp and welfare check business, and there seems to be a general sense of uneasiness about what kind of wife- and girlfriend-swapping might be going on in what everybody figures is just an ultra-conservative whacko version of a hippie commune; but other than that, no one seems to pay them much attention. You know the Oregon motto: live and let live."

"Speaking about wives or girlfriends? Have any of them actually stayed around that long?"

"According to the state officer, most of the wives and girlfriends have stayed with the group, although not necessarily with the same husband or boyfriend. Interestingly enough, he thinks the women are starting to get a little disgruntled with the whole program. Probably because they end up doing most of the work while the guys mostly sit around and talk."

"Sounds like your standard, self-serving, lazy-guy scam to me." Moore nodded in amusement. "What about kids?"

"Evidently they take off as soon as they get old enough to make it on their own."

"Good for them. What about weapons?"

"Mostly shotguns, scoped hunting rifles, a few .38s and military surplus .45s. Their ammo is pretty much all reloads now—the state guy said most of the brass he saw looked pretty torn up—but he suspects they haven't been doing all that much shooting anyway the last few years. Oh, and one other thing," Halahan added. "They used to talk a lot about putting the federal government on trial, but they haven't mentioned that much lately, either."

"Cold War came and went, and nobody got around to telling them?" Moore smiled ruefully.

"More likely they didn't want to hear about it." Halahan shrugged. "Probably stuck in a rut and just got used to it. The more relevant question from our point of view is, are these guys likely to be any more dangerous than the average group of hunters our agents run across every day?"

"Anybody with a few screws loose can be dangerous," Moore reminded his chief. "But I don't see these characters as being anything that Charlie Team couldn't handle. If they turn out to be white supremacists, too, which wouldn't surprise me, then they're not going to be real thrilled when they see the team's ethnic diversity. But it would be the same situation if we sent Bravo Team. Personally, I think the kids could handle this one just fine."

Halahan nodded thoughtfully. "We'll hook them up with Boggs, which gives them an experienced agent for moral support, and ideally keeps him too preoccupied baby-sitting to worry much about his congressman. One thing we can be pretty sure about is that Wilbur Boggs isn't about to let a bunch of young agents get into trouble in his district, no matter how badly he wants to use them for something else."

"And even if Boggs *does* talk them into helping him out a little bit on the side, Charlie Team's going to be a hell of a lot more circumspect in dealing with a congressman as a suspect than Bravo," Moore added with a smile. "Among other things, they'd probably follow procedure and ask permission first. I like it."

"So do I," Halahan agreed. "One last question. Do we send them out as is, or do we make the reassignments?"

"Oh, yeah. Marashenko." Freddy Moore stared out the window as he thought about that. "Damn."

"Bravo Team's got one of the open slots, and she wants it. Or at least she did," Halahan reminded his deputy. "But maybe after that incident with Lightstone this morning—?"

Freddy Moore shook his head. "No dice. I talked with her after the exercise. She's pissed at Lightstone, no question about it, but she'd take a transfer to Bravo Team in a second if we offered."

"She say why?"

"No, but I get the impression it has something to do with status."

"Alpha and Bravo being perceived as the starting teams, and Charlie being the reserve?"

Moore nodded. "Something like that."

"You think she's ready for it?"

The Special Ops deputy chief hesitated, recalling how Marashenko let her emotions get the best of her when Lightstone foiled her plan.

"No, I really don't," he conceded finally, "but she's damned close. If we make the transfer now, the guys in Bravo would give her a bad time, but they'd also bring her along. Three months max, she'd belong there."

"Then let her earn it straight, like anybody else," Halahan decided. "We're going to start Charlie Team on this game, and she's an integral part of that team. End of discussion."

"Fair enough. But we still haven't decided what to do with Bravo."

"What do you think about putting Bravo out on the perimeter on a standby basis . . . without telling anyone—and especially not Boggs or anyone on Charlie Team, because this is supposed to be a confidence-building situation, not the other way around," Halahan suggested. "That way they'd be close in case Charlie Team accidentally knocks over a beehive at that Seventh Seal compound, or Boggs gets them into something a little too complicated with his duck-poaching congressman."

Freddy Moore considered the proposition for a few moments.

"Not a bad idea," he finally admitted. "But what about Bravo Team? Do we tell them what's going on?"

"No way." Halahan shook his head emphatically. "If we do, they'll just start poking around and causing all kinds of grief, especially if they link up with Boggs and he gives them an earful about Smallsreed. We're better off just putting them out there and nailing them down with a project that keeps them busy and distracted."

"So what do we tell them?" Moore asked reasonably. "Those guys will spot a bullshit story a mile off, especially if it looks like we're giving them a paid vacation."

The contemplative look on David Halahan's face suddenly gave way to a satisfied smile.

"Oh-oh," Moore groaned. "Why do I get the feeling Bravo Team's not going to like this?"

"Just off the top of your head," Halahan suggested cheerfully, "where's the last place our friends from the Mexican Mafia in Nogales would expect the federal government to run a sting operation on hot snakes and red-kneed tarantulas?"

The smile that blossomed on Freddy Moore's face easily eclipsed that of his boss, then quickly dissolved into a fit of helpless laughter.

"What about the snakes?" he gasped when he finally could speak again.

"What about them?"

"You think they'll be able to handle the cold okay?" Moore asked as he wiped the tears from his eyes. "I hear it gets damn chilly in Oregon in the winter."

Halahan shrugged. "I don't see why not. As long as the warehouse doesn't get too cold, I assume they—and I imagine the tarantulas, too, for that matter—would just stay kind of sluggish. Unless, of course, the agents running the operation foolishly turned up the heat for their own comfort. In that case I suspect the entire team would need to stay alert pretty much around the clock, watching out for escaping poisonous snakes and very large spiders."

"You really think that'll keep them sufficiently occupied so they don't start poking around and spot Charlie Team?"

"I certainly hope so." Halahan's smile faded, and he tapped at his desk pensively. "Between setting up the warehouse, rigging a communications system, establishing their covers, putting out some ads and feelers, making a few purchases and sales from some of the legitimate dealers, and maintaining a reasonable stock of illicit specimens—which reminds me, do we have any good sources?"

"Well, I know the guys in Newark are sitting on a bunch of hot stuff they pulled out of the back of a shipping container an Australian importer abandoned a few weeks ago. About a hundred specimens total," Moore responded. "Mostly African and South America vipers as I recall. Gaboons, bushmasters, puff and mountain adders, fer-de-lances, some bamboo and Russell's Vipers from China, and I think even a pair of death adders and a few brown, black, and tiger snakes from Australia."

"Are the Australian ones poisonous?"

"Oh yeah, definitely."

"Good. That's exactly the kind of thing these Mexican Mafia characters deal in. Exotic and deadly. How about the spiders? Can we get some of them, too?"

"Come to think of it, I heard Miami's still trying to get the Zoo Association to take that last batch of red-knees they seized off their hands."

"How many did they get?"

"Something in the neighborhood of 750 total."

Halahan blinked. "Seven hundred and fifty red-kneed tarantulas?"

"Naw, only about half of them are the genuine article. The rest are either red-legged, or plain old browns . . . along with a dozen baby caiman crocs as a bonus," Moore added. "You want to hear a heart-wrenching sob story, call Jennifer up and ask her what she thinks about feeding those damned things."

"What in the world do you feed 750 tarantulas and a dozen baby crocodiles?"

"Mice, crickets, and chunks of chicken, according to her. Apparently it's not so much *what* you feed them as *how*," Moore explained. "I understand that quick reflexes help tremendously . . . especially with the tarantulas because they fling needle-sharp little hairs into their prey—or at anything they're pissed at. I'm sure Jennifer would be more than happy to give you all the gory details, but I wouldn't call her right before lunch."

"Special Agent Jennifer Granstrom." The Special Operations branch chief's eyes began to gleam. "Don't we owe her for something?"

"The Miami Office has been nice to us occasionally in the past," Moore conceded hesitantly.

"That's what I was thinking." Halahan nodded thoughtfully. "But how in the world would you ship 750 tarantulas from a federal law enforcement office in Miami to a warehouse in Loggerhead City, Oregon, without anyone on the outside knowing what's going on?"

"Beats me." A grin of awareness began to light up Moore's face. "But I'm willing to bet you a steak dinner at the restaurant of your choice that Jennifer either knows how, right off the top of her head, or she'll figure it out in three minutes flat."

"Why don't you give her a call — after lunch," Halahan suggested with a benevolent smile on his face. "Tell her to get the whole batch ready to ship to Oregon, posthaste, along with — what? — all the necessary terrariums, heating elements, and other assorted supplies she's got on hand. Our treat."

"The crocs, too?"

"Oh, hell yes. How can we impress the Mexican Mafia if we don't go all out?"

"David," Freddy Moore's tone bordered on reverent, "remind me every now and then, if you don't mind, to never, ever, piss you off."

"Basic principles of people management." The Special Operations Branch chief shrugged modestly. "If you can't gain the attention of your employees with the standard motivational techniques, try a different approach."

"On second thought, you're not going to need to remind me." Moore shuddered as he tried to imagine several hundred snakes, tarantulas, and crocs all in one warehouse.

"Glad to hear it." David Halahan smiled pleasantly, and then went on. "So you call Jennifer, and then make arrangements with Newark for, oh, say two or three dozen miscellaneous snakes — be sure to include that death adder, and a few of those Australian brown, black, and tiger snakes — along with, say, a two-month supply of mice, crickets, chicken, freezers, holding cages, and the like. I think that should keep everybody on Bravo Team extremely busy, focused, and out of trouble, with the possible exception of —"

"Lightstone?"

Halahan nodded.

"So what are we going to do with him? Ship him down to Nogales to start working on his cover?"

"Not a chance." The Special Ops chief dismissed that option immediately. "I want him there, too, just in case we *do* run into some problems with Charlie Team or Boggs. Lightstone may be a little difficult to control at times, but he's also pretty damned useful when things turn to shit."

"So . . . ?"

"So, while Charlie Team scopes out the militants and everyone else on Bravo Team tries to work out accommodations for seven hundred giant tarantulas, twelve baby crocodiles, and two or three dozen poisonous snakes"—Halahan smiled pleasantly—"I think somebody should take a serious look at our friend the Sage and his Bigfoot souvenir scam, don't you?"

"You know"—Moore paused a moment to savor the Bravo Team's wild-card agent's most likely reaction to his new assignment—"this just might teach those jokers to play fair."

"I doubt it."

"Yeah, me too." Moore nodded in agreement. "But in any case, I think we'd better get them on a plane to Oregon by tomorrow afternoon at the latest. I have a feeling Jennifer's going to have those tarantulas packed up, out the door, and on their way to a certain Loggerhead City warehouse before we have a chance to change our minds."

"Exactly. Which means you'd better get busy putting together a briefing document."

"It will be a pleasure." Freddy Moore smiled in cheerful anticipation.

"Yeah, I'll bet. And in the meantime," Halahan said as he put the stack of exercise evaluations aside, "I'm going to give my old buddy Wilbur Boggs a call. Tell him to break out his big grill and ice chest and stand by, because Special Ops is about to make *his* life a whole lot more miserable, too."

Chapter Eight

It took federal wildlife agent Wilbur Boggs a good five minutes to regain his senses after the accident.

Two or three minutes after that, he discovered that the force of the impact had broken the leather restraining strap on his shoulder holster, thereby sending his old and reliable government-issued Model 66 .357 revolver (he simply couldn't get used to the new 10mm Smith & Wesson semiautomatic pistols that most of the agents in the Fish and Wildlife Service now carried) into at least twenty feet of cold muddy water . . . along with his binoculars, thermos bottle, lunch box, tackle box, fishing rod, ticket book, portable radio, and his badge case.

He would have discovered all of this earlier if he hadn't spent so much time staring in dismay at the bent and twisted mounts of his outboard motor that had nearly been torn loose from the transom, thereby severely damaging the back of his own boat—which he'd opted to use for his rendezvous with Lou Eliot because he knew Rustman's crew would spot his government-owned boat the moment he dropped it into the water.

Then, and in spite of Lt. Colonel John Rustman's optimistic predictions, it had taken Boggs almost four more hours to free his prop from the yards of tightly wrapped nylon netting and twisted ropes for several reasons.

One, the tightened ropes, twisted mounts, and his severely broken right hand prevented him from raising the outboard out of the water or disconnecting it from the ripped transom.

Two, the impact tore open his supposedly sinkproof tackle box, sending his wrenches and pliers and other potentially useful tools—not to mention his wallet—to the bottom of the lake, leaving him with only a pocketknife and the pair of nail clippers on his key chain.

And three, he had to do everything with his merely throbbing and trembling left hand, and he didn't dare drop the pocketknife overboard because he didn't even want to think about how long it might take him to cut all that rope and netting loose with nail clippers.

Boggs spent the first few minutes leaning over the side of the boat in an ultimately futile effort to cut through the tightened ropes that secured the netting and the boat to whatever anchors Rustman and his cohorts had placed in the bottom of the lake. Finally, he gave that up because he couldn't reach all of the ropes, and holding his head upside down made him feel dizzier than ever. So he cursed John Rustman, Lou Eliot, and especially Regis J. Smallsreed for the fifteen minutes it took him to pull off all of his clothes, put the life vest back on, and then awkwardly lower himself into the icy cold water with his forearms, and his one more or less good hand to try to work the ropes and netting loose from there.

Once in the water, he momentarily considered diving to the murky bottom to search for some of his tools, but some still-rational fragment of his mind warned him that if he did, he'd probably get caught in the netting and drown.

A second distinctively sharp, high-velocity gunshot—that didn't sound at all like a shotgun blast, but did sound exactly like the first one that had catapulted him into action at the end of what he assumed was Smallsreed's first round of shooting—caught his attention. He would have tried to pinpoint the location of that second shot if nothing else, but his head and his hand hurt like hell, and his feet and legs ached already in the icy water, so he decided not to worry about it until later.

After he got the boat loose.

It took seven trips into the frigid water before Wilbur Boggs finally managed to free his boat. During each trip, he wrapped his useless right arm around the motor housing, then carefully cut a few nylon strands at a time until his lower body grew numb. When that happened, he carefully slipped the knife into the Velcro-secured pouch on his life vest, heaved himself back into the boat, dried himself off as much as possible with his soggy underwear, socks, and shirt, pulled on his pants and jacket, and sat shivering in the chilly morning air until some feeling returned to his limbs and he could rationalize going back into the water at least one more time.

Several times during this physically and mentally exhausting process, Boggs sensed that someone was watching him. But he forced himself to block that out because he knew if he saw so much as a glimpse of Lou Eliot, or Lt. Colonel John Rustman, or—in a moment of wishful thinking—the Honorable Regis J. Smallsreed himself, he'd forget all about getting tangled in the net and drowning, and dive straight down into that murky, freezing water for his gun and kill the bastards.

For the first time in his life, Special Agent Wilbur Boggs felt that close to losing control completely.

But the worst was yet to come: Once he finally did manage to free his boat, he discovered what he should have expected, had he not been so disoriented and distracted by the combined effects of an almost certain concussion, a broken hand, a smashed nose, missing teeth, the icy cold water, and other assorted aches and pains far too numerous to name.

The motor wouldn't start.

Forcing himself to remain calm, Boggs awkwardly unlatched and removed the engine cover with one hand, checked the fuel lines, switch valve, plug wires, distributor cap, battery connections, and air filter, replaced and latched the cover, and then tried again.

Nothing.

That was when Wilbur Boggs began to laugh.

It wasn't a pleasant laugh. In fact, had any member of Lt. Colonel John Rustman's crew—except maybe Wintersole—heard that laugh, they almost certainly would have given the emotionally and physically drained federal wildlife agent a wide berth . . . because nothing in that laughter indicated the presence of a man with a tight grip on his sanity.

It took Boggs a good three or four minutes to stop laughing and wipe the tears out of his eyes . . . at which point the Fates mercifully gave him a glimpse of the small wooden paddle floating in the distance.

Under anything even remotely resembling normal circumstances, Wilbur Boggs could have retrieved the paddle in, at most, a couple of minutes. But after almost three hours of intermittent exposure to the icy lake water, he now doubted he could swim that far in one stretch, and he knew the life vest wouldn't keep him warm enough if he couldn't. So he used his good hand to paddle to the real paddle instead, stopping only twice to untangle the prop from pieces of rope and netting. Whereupon it all became, in a relative sense, much easier.

Shivering and cursing as he fought to keep the boat on a reasonably straight course, it took the numbed, exhausted, and furious agent nearly three more hours to reach shore. But that was all right, Boggs reminded himself during his rest breaks, because he felt relatively warm and dry now in his damp pants and jacket—but no socks or boots because he couldn't get them on one-handed—and he wasn't going to drown or die of exposure after all. Not only that, he'd discovered that his left hand didn't cramp up quite so much if he stuck the handle of the paddle under his armpit.

Piece of cake.

When he finally did manage to zigzag his way to the shore, dragging several yards of netting and rope and an assortment of miscellaneous lake debris in his wake, Wilbur Boggs simply could have abandoned his boat right there at the base of the launch ramp. No insurance rep in the state would have dared to question such a decision.

But Wilbur Boggs was, above all else, an exceedingly stubborn and persistent man, who refused to admit defeat. Consequently, he spent another forty-five minutes backing his truck down the ramp, cursing his blurred vision and the floor-mounted manual shift, fumbling with the release mechanism on the winch, wading into the cold water one more time to bring the boat around to the back of the partially submerged trailer, stepping on sharp rocks with his bare feet, and then slowly and painfully winching the boat up onto the trailer, cursing Lt. Colonel John Rustman, Lou Eliot, and the Honorable Regis J. Smallsreed with every agonizing turn of the crank.

And then, in the midst of that process, when he rammed his shin into the solid steel tow hitch, recoiled from the effects of the brain-searing impact, slipped on the slippery asphalt, smacked the back of his head against the trailer, and then lay there gasping and cursing on the cold, wet pavement until the pulsating bursts of pain in his shin *and* his hand *and* his head finally evened themselves out into some kind of endurable equilibrium, he still possessed the necessary willpower to pull himself up and go back to the task at hand.

Only when he finally drove toward his rural home nestled an hour away in a quiet little wooded grove, did the federal wildlife agent allow himself to laugh again.

Only this time, no one would mistake the nature of that laugh for madness.

Now, Special Agent Wilbur Boggs was quite furiously—and quite sanely—enraged.

Against all odds, or at least any odds an observant bookie might offer on this star-crossed federal law enforcement officer toward the end of that incredibly disastrous day, Wilbur Boggs managed to get all the way home, all the way up his driveway, and all the way through his front door, without a single other thing in his life going wrong.

Stumbling into his living room in a numbed daze at seven-thirty that Sunday evening, the physically and mentally depleted agent's blurred eyes immediately spotted the blinking red numeral on the glowing face of his answering machine: 1

One message.

Wilbur Boggs turned on the light and staggered forward to rewind the tape as quickly as possible, driven by the thought that Lou Eliot—his best hope in three long years to finally bring John Rustman and Regis J. Smallsreed to justice—had left a message explaining why he failed to appear at the rendezvous point at six-thirty that Sunday morning.

But the instant he heard the familiar voice emanating from the answering machine's cheap speaker, the federal wildlife agent began to comprehend the magnitude of the defeat he'd suffered at the hands of Lt. Colonel John Rustman and Congressman Regis J. Smallsreed.

Stunned and disbelieving, Wilbur Boggs punched the buttons of the infuriating machine again with the swollen, scarred, and quivering forefinger of his left hand—the one that probably wasn't broken—and replayed the message.

That's okay, Halahan, he thought grimly as he stood in his living room—dizzy, nauseous, and trembling with pain, hunger, and almost total exhaustion—and listened once again to the voice of the chief of the Law Enforcement Division's Special Operations Branch advising him that Charlie Team, a new team of covert agents, were being assigned a project in his area and would contact him when they got into town, *you can't make my life any more miserable than it already is . . .*

The answering machine began to swim out of focus.

'Cause that would be pretty damned hard to do.

Wilbur Boggs took a deep breath to steady himself, determined to nail that particular thought down before he lost it.

You just go right ahead and send that brand-new Special Ops team of yours out here, and I'll keep an eye on them, and help you with your congressional problem . . . and then you can help me with mine.

Boggs felt himself starting to go, and grabbed at the wall with his good hand to catch himself, knocking the lamp to the floor in the process, but not giving a damn because it was one of the few things his wife left when she'd moved out and filed for divorce three years ago.

Never liked the damned thing anyway.

However, the lamp's demise plunged the room into darkness — which he considered a more significant problem.

Steady there, Boggs, pay attention. Do something.

He knew he should call somebody. Right now, while he still could. Tell them about Lou Eliot. About how Lt. Colonel John Rustman's foreman had offered to turn over his boss, and the Honorable Regis J. Smallsreed, and some sleazy political bagman named Simon Whatley, and the other one — what was his name? The trained killer Rustman hired to scare the shit out of everyone?

Damn it, what was his name? Something bizarre . . . cold . . . empty. Something about winter?

Wintersole.

Yeah, that's it.

Sergeant Wintersole.

The memory suddenly flooded the federal agent's numbed mind. Gunshots. Loud, high-velocity rounds. Rifle or pistol, not shotgun. Definitely not shotgun. He'd never in his entire career heard of anyone hunting ducks with a high-powered rifle or pistol. And there weren't any deer around the marsh during duck season because the gunfire drove them off.

Two shots, far apart. Execution style?

Christ!

He had to call somebody, tell them about Lou Eliot and Wintersole. Tell them they had to hurry because . . .

Because what?

Because Rustman probably figured out his foreman had turned snitch and shot him, the poor bastard, Wilbur Boggs reasoned.

So there probably wasn't any need to hurry after all. They probably shot him, weighted his body down, and dumped him into one of the deep sections of Loggerhead Lake, where no one would ever find him, even if they used hooks or divers.

Boggs's head started to spin again, and he grabbed the wall in the dark with both hands to steady himself, then choked back an agonized scream. But the excruciating pain in his right hand helped clear his head and reminded him of something important. Something very important.

Charlie Team. Help was on the way.

Only that didn't sound like such a good idea anymore, sending Charlie Team, he suddenly realized. Not a good idea at all.

He had to call Halahan back, right away, and tell him not to send the kids, send somebody else — one of the experienced covert teams — because the situation at Lt. Colonel John Rustman's private hunting preserve for wealthy and influential assholes was a whole lot worse than he'd thought when he'd cheerfully suggested that training exercise to Freddy Moore.

Gotta let Halahan know what's going on. Wilbur Boggs smiled through his split and bloodied lips. *Goddamned stubborn Irishman. He'll take care of everything. Good old Halahan.*

The dazed and nearly unconscious federal agent then tried to decide if he could really drive another five miles to the local hospital, or if he dared to lie down on the couch and go to sleep—which he really wanted to do more than anything else he could think of at that particular moment—in the unlikely hope that he might feel better tomorrow. Or should he just say to hell with it and dial 911 while he still could?

Wilbur Boggs's instinct for survival, more than anything else, told him to forget the car and the couch and call for help.

He clutched the phone and struggled to remember if he'd ever gotten around to programming the automatic emergency button or if he needed to punch in the numbers on the increasingly dim and curiously blurred keypad. But then he felt himself start to fall again and reached out to catch himself. Only this time, the darkness completely disoriented him.

Desperately trying not to hit his broken hand again, he missed the wall and spun, ripping the phone cord out of the wall and wrapping it around himself in the process. He stumbled, pitched forward, and his head struck the lamp table.

Hard.

Don't you worry about making my life any more miserable than it already is, David, old buddy, Boggs mumbled, facedown to the carpet as the darkness overtook him. *'Cause that's gonna be pretty damned hard to do.*

Chapter Nine

A little past a quarter of five the next morning, Special Agent Wilbur Boggs regained consciousness and found himself lying facedown on a carpet in almost total darkness.

A few seconds later, he became aware that he also felt dizzy, nauseous, cold, hungry, thirsty, and, as best he could tell, he hurt in every muscle and bone in his body, from the top of his head to the soles of his bare feet.

Unable to recall what had occurred during the previous twenty-four hours, Boggs initially thought that he must have hit the Jack Daniel's pretty hard the night before and now had the worst hangover he had ever experienced in his entire life.

That meant the best thing he could possibly do for himself was to get something in his stomach—a handful of buffered aspirin for a start—and he attempted to heave himself up into a sitting position to do just that.

Which turned out to be a terribly serious mistake.

However, once he managed to stop screaming and cursing and gently probing his horribly swollen hand, he discovered that his memory of the last twenty-four hours had returned in vivid detail.

And, in fact, the particularly vivid memory of cursing Lt. Colonel John Rustman and the Honorable Regis J. Smallsreed provided Boggs with enough energy to work himself into a sitting position with his more or less good hand and look around for the telephone—which he finally found at the end of the cord wrapped around his hips.

Once his still-muddled mind finally accepted that the phone really *was* dead, he felt his way all the way down to the opposite end of the phone cord, only to discover that he had somehow managed to rip all but the little square connecting end out of the wall when he fell.

No problem, phone in the kitchen, he told himself, only to remember mere moments later that, no, there wasn't a phone in the kitchen, because he'd thrown it out months ago when the third telemarketer had called to solicit his opinion while he tried to eat his dinner.

Which definitely presented a problem, Boggs realized, because that only left the phone in the upstairs bedroom. And even in his muddle-minded state, he realized that he probably couldn't navigate a set of stairs since he could barely stand upright without falling over.

But he could still crawl if that's what it took to get help, he reminded himself. Either up the stairs or out to the truck, didn't matter.

In the end, it came down to pride: He would go for help himself.

After determining by trial and error that he could navigate pretty well using one hand and two knees, Boggs crawled out the front door . . . and fortunately discovered that he'd left his keys in the lock, which immeasurably simplified the process of securing his home. Then he crawled down the steps and across the sidewalk to his truck which he, unfortunately, had locked.

With a great deal of effort, he raised himself enough to unlock and open the cab door, and then hauled himself into the driver's seat.

Exhausted by the effort, the wildlife agent rested his head on the steering wheel until the waves of nausea and dizziness ebbed. Then, after finally managing to pull the door shut, he sat up, looked over his shoulder, and noticed the boat trailer still attached to the back of his truck.

Wilbur Boggs knew that he lacked the strength to climb back out of the truck, unhitch the trailer, move it out of the way, then climb back in the truck again. So he simply leaned forward, braced himself against the steering wheel, fumbled the key into the ignition, started the engine, put the truck in reverse, gave it some gas, eased out the clutch . . . and felt his head snap forward with dizzying speed when his foot slipped off the clutch, his right foot slammed forward on the gas pedal, and the truck shot down the driveway backwards.

A brief flash of blinding pain seared what little remained of his conscious thought processes when his already broken nose slammed solidly into the truck's unpadded steering wheel.

That gave way to a fleeting sense of rapid, uncontrolled, downward motion which then came to a sudden, metal-grinding halt.

Whereupon it all disappeared into merciful blackness.

The paramedics who responded to a neighbor's call at five-thirty that morning found Wilbur Boggs slumped over the steering wheel in the cab of his truck . . . unconscious, covered with blood, breathing erratically, and looking exactly like someone who had just been involved in a violent head-on collision.

Except that made no sense to the highly experienced and observant rescue team because, other than the damage to the back of the boat — apparently the result of Boggs backing his trailer directly into his new neighbor's very sturdy new mailbox post at a fairly high rate of speed, which the neighbor claimed had occurred at about quarter after five that morning — they saw no evidence that the truck had been involved in any kind of accident, recent or otherwise.

A cautious examination of Boggs revealed a grossly swollen hand, a smashed nose, severely split lips, and a wide assortment of head and facial bruises, most of which — judging from the degree of discoloration — he'd sustained at least several hours earlier. And when they finally got him out of the cab and onto a stretcher, they discovered that in spite of the decidedly frosty temperature that morning, their patient was dressed — if that was the proper word — in nothing but a pair of damp jeans and a down jacket. No socks, shoes, underwear, or shirt.

A careful search failed to locate a wallet or any other identification on the victim. However, the truck *was* registered to a Wilbur Boggs at a Loggerhead City address located directly across the street from the now mangled mailbox post. Unfortunately, the reporting party — a new arrival in the neighborhood the previous weekend — had never actually met his neighbor, only saw him come and go in a different vehicle, a Ford Explorer with some kind of government plates, he thought. And though it was hard to tell with all the swelling and bruises, this man did sort of look like the guy he had seen.

In fact, the more he thought about it, the more he decided he hadn't seen his neighbor at all the last couple of days, and the boat and truck had been parked in the carport all that time.

The reporting party's eyes widened when he came to the perfectly logical conclusion that the man who flattened his mailbox—presumably his neighbor—must have had a drinking problem. After all, he reasoned, what else would anybody dressed like that and driving like that—he added, giving his mailbox post a meaningful glance—being doing at five-fifteen on a cold winter morning?

The paramedics had to admit that the reporting party had a point there.

But that wasn't their problem.

The man in the truck obviously had sustained serious injuries in *some* kind of accident. And he equally obviously was in dire need of professional medical attention. At this particular moment, who he was and what he was doing seminaked in the cab of a truck that might or might not belong to him, at five-fifteen in the morning, really didn't matter.

So after carefully strapping him down on the stretcher, taping a series of spinal-cord-protecting pads and blocks around his neck and head, and securing a similar set of pads around his swollen hand, the paramedics radioed the Jasper County sheriff's deputy that they were transporting a John Doe with serious injuries to Loggerhead City Hospital immediately.

They'd leave it for the cops to figure out the who, what, when, where, why, and how.

When a thoroughly fatigued deputy finally arrived at the scene of Wilbur Boggs's accident—almost an hour later, because a frantically waving woman standing in the middle of the road forced him to stop and assist when she couldn't find her child—he found himself in possession of three significant pieces of information:

First and foremost, he now had four calls waiting, including a report of a man with a gun acting suspiciously outside the local 7-Eleven.

Second, the odds greatly favored the "injured party in a vehicle" situation being a simple, single-party-accident insurance claim requiring little if any investigation on his part.

And finally, a note—written by the reporting party to "whomever it may concern at the Loggerhead City Police Department," and taped to the partially destroyed mailbox—had informed the deputy that the reporting party had to go to work and couldn't wait any longer, so he'd backed the vehicle into his neighbor's covered carport to get it out of the street, and locked the truck so no one could steal it or the boat . . . and would keep the keys for safekeeping until someone came for them, if that was all right with the police.

Deciding that was perfectly all right with the police as far as he was concerned, especially since there was no such animal as the Loggerhead City Police Department in the first place, the overworked deputy sheriff quickly scribbled the reporting party's address on the note, folded the scrap of paper, stuck it in his notebook, and decided that was enough paperwork for a single-party accident on this particular morning.

As he did so, the deputy had no way of knowing that the emergency room doctor at the local hospital who examined Special Agent Wilbur Boggs, AKA "John Doe," had just ordered him transported to Providence Hospital in nearby Jackson County, where they were better equipped to handle potentially serious head injuries.

The deputy reached for his mike and notified the dispatcher that he was clear on the "injured party in a vehicle" call, and would respond immediately to the "man with a gun acting suspiciously" call—that was, by his calculation, at least twelve miles and a good fifteen minutes away— ideally with some backup, if any of the other units might possibly be available and in the area.

The dispatcher acknowledged the clearance with a chuckle.

Two units responding to a call for a man with a gun, no shots fired, in Jasper County, Oregon, where pretty much every man, woman, and child owned at least one gun, and the entire graveyard shift amounted to three patrol units when everyone was actually on duty?

That would be the day.

Chapter Ten

At precisely 0700 hours that same Monday morning, eight individuals dressed in jeans, boots, and flannel shirts gathered around a large octagonal table and waited for the waitress/owner to finish putting out the steaming stainless-steel pans filled with scrambled eggs, sausages, fried potatoes, and rolls in the secluded meeting hall.

She examined the buffet table critically, making sure that blue flames still glowed in all of the Sterno cans, and that she'd provided sufficient plates, cups, and silverware to accommodate the group's needs.

"Okay, fellows, here's the way it works," she announced, scanning the buffet one last time. "The coffee's fresh—forty cups and plenty more where that came from—the food's hot, and the bathroom's clean. You want anything else, more food, coffee, cleanup, whatever, pick up that phone and dial '5.' It may take us a while to get here because my husband and I are all by ourselves today, but one of us will come eventually. If it's important, come get one of us. Otherwise, the place is yours until three, when I've got to start cleaning up for a card game this evening. We built this place off by itself, so feel free to make all the noise you want. Just don't break anything, or it comes out of your deposit."

"We'll be fine." Lt. Colonel John Rustman politely dismissed her, then waited until she retreated down the hill to the small bed-and-breakfast lodge before securing the door.

"Okay." He motioned toward the buffet. "Everybody grab something to eat. This may be your last chance for a decent meal for the next week or so."

Rustman waited until the entire team reassembled around the table with filled plates and cups of coffee. Then he walked over to a four-foot-square piece of black cloth covering a section of the far wall, carefully lifted the bottom edge of the fabric, and pinned it to the upper portion of the wall.

The retired military officer's actions caused one of the men to stop eating and stare at the block letters printed at the top of the suddenly exposed map.

"Jasper County?" Wintersole's voice sounded distinctly cold and foreboding. "You're bringing the operation into your own backyard?"

"That wasn't the original plan," the retired military officer replied evenly as he picked up a wooden pointer, "but some opportunities presented themselves which will provide us with some extremely useful advantages—the primary ones being time and terrain."

Rustman indicated a large circular area in the upper-right-hand corner of the map with the pointer.

"You've been conducting training exercises in this area for the past four weeks. You know the lay of the land, the local fauna and flora, the weather and traffic patterns, and the minimal local law-enforcement patrols."

He moved the pointer to a spot just outside the circle.

"The proposed ambush site is located here"—he tapped the map with the end of the pointer—"twelve klicks out from one of your existing hideaways, and within twenty-five klicks of two others and all but two of your reserve ammo and supply caches . . . which means we can simply leave all of that material in place.

"The surrounding mountains are high and close together with superb tree cover, which effectively negates any air-search capability. That's not a particularly relevant issue, because the nearest military base is in Klamath Falls, and the air-search capabilities of the local federal and state law-enforcement agencies are extremely limited and otherwise undependable. But we need to be thoughtful about the escape routes in any case, and local terrain might turn out to be a critical factor if we were ever to lose control of the situation.

"The ambush site is a small, mountainside compound near Logger-head City occupied by an antigovernment, quasi-religious paramilitary group known as the Chosen Brigade of the Seventh Seal. They've been dug into the hills about twenty years waiting for the big curtain to go up. The group consists of approximately fifteen adult males, thirteen adult females, and a handful of kids. None of the adults are known to possess any formal military training, but they've had plenty of time to memorize their library of basic field manuals. All of the adult males hold the self-assigned rank of full colonel, lieutenant colonel, or major. Two young men above the age of fifteen are designated captains, and all of the adult women hold the rank of lieutenant. As far as anyone knows, they have light arms only—shotguns, pistols, and a few scoped hunting rifles—no night-vision gear, a few military surplus grenades that may or may not be functional, and almost certainly some rudimentary traps and trips out on the perimeter, if they haven't all been set off by animals or their own people by now.

"All things considered, I think it's pretty clear that the members of this group represent a minimal threat to our operation."

Rustman paused, pleased to see that not one member of Wintersole's hunter-killer team had cracked a smile.

"And as you may have guessed by now, in addition to being the location of our ambush site, the Chosen Brigade of the Seventh Seal will also function as our primary bait. Any questions so far?"

One member of the team raised his hand, and Rustman gestured for him to speak.

"Colonel, begging your pardon, but it seems to me these people lack the credibility to be bait . . . or anything else, sir."

Lt. Colonel John Rustman nodded thoughtfully. "That *is* a problem, soldier," he agreed. "What would you suggest we do to correct that situation?"

"Arm them properly, sir," came the immediate reply.

"So they become a legitimate threat to your team?"

"I don't think so, sir." The soldier smiled briefly. "Just credible."

Rustman turn to glance at Wintersole, who nodded solemnly in agreement.

"You're going to need a go-between to introduce you to these people." Rustman spoke directly to Wintersole. "I understand there's at least one outsider these people seem to trust enough to let into their compound on a routine basis. Some old codger who claims to be a soothsayer—some kind of fortune-teller—hangs around town trying to sell Indian jewelry and artifacts to tourists. I've seen him down by the pancake house three or four times in the past month. He's about five-ten, one-fifty at most, frizzy gray hair, full gray beard, wears a variety of beaded headbands and jewelry—most of which, I gather, he's perfectly willing to part with if the price is right—and typically dresses in old Vietnam-era cammo gear. He might be worth a try."

"Yes sir. We'll locate and contact him immediately," Wintersole acknowledged the barely disguised order.

"An excellent suggestion, soldier," Rustman congratulated the young man who had posed the credibility issue. "Which, I might add, just goes to prove the basic superiority of the American fighting man—and woman," he added without missing a beat, but noting that the single female member of the team, a very tough, no-nonsense-looking soldier in her own right, acknowledged the comment with a slight dip of her head. "If an American commander is lost in battle, the next subordinate officer, NCO, or grunt is expected to step forward and provide immediate and effective leadership in the field. I expect that premise to apply to everyone in this room. We have a mission, and we will not fail to complete it, no matter what. Are there any other questions?"

Not a single hand went up.

"It's still hunting season," Rustman went on, "so no one outside the community will pay too much attention to gunshots . . . even if we do increase the firepower of our paramilitary associates. In fact, any shooting at all will provide a useful cover for our own activities," he added with a slight smile.

"We have established five primary escape routes"—he indicated these with five quick passes of the pointer—"which will give you access to pre-positioned supplies which we'll also leave in place. A total of one hundred kilos of Semtex *and* twelve claymores, set in rearward-facing, cross-trail patterns at five twenty-yard intervals, protects each escape route. The devices are rigged and armed for remote detonation from your individual transmitters, and the outer ranges are clearly marked in the standard long range reconissance manner. Just make sure you and your teammates are completely clear before you activate and use the system," the military officer added with another one of his thin-lipped smiles.

The team members continued eating with studied indifference. They knew all about the escape routes. They'd spent two full weeks putting the devices and markers in place, and memorizing the kill zones. No problem.

"Your targets—" Rustman went on, and was pleased when every member of the hunter-killer team immediately stopped eating and listened intently—"are five Special Agents of the U.S. Fish and Wildlife Service."

Rustman paused for a moment to let those words sink in.

"For reasons that are not important to you or to your mission, these agents represent a significant threat to our military/industrial readiness. Their deaths, and the subsequent exposure of their activities in the media, will significantly impact the reputations of a number of highly influential people willing to sacrifice the military strength of our nation for the continued survival of a few weak animal species.

"I had hoped to have individual profiles available for you today, but our accelerated timetable made that impossible. However, First Sergeant Wintersole will give you verbal descriptions of these agents which will enable you to recognize and isolate both the primary and diversionary targets. The profiles—which will include photographs—will be delivered to you at the message drop site prior to your interaction with these agents. I can tell you right now, however, that none of these people have any prior military experience, and none are expected to be armed with anything other than their assigned duty weapons, primarily 10mm Smith & Wesson semiautomatic pistols with twelve-round magazines. Like all federal agents, they're trained to shoot for center of mass, a considerable advantage for you, since your body armor will easily defeat a 10mm expanding hollow-point pistol bullet.

"In addition to your superior weapons and firepower," Rustman went on, "you will be equipped with the latest generation of night-vision gear which utilize a phased array of infrared and ultraviolet detectors. The viewscreens provide some interesting computer-enhanced color imagery for hot objects, which turns out to be a major improvement over the old green monotone scopes . . . especially in terms of small objects that are either distant or moving. The effects can be disorienting at first, especially if you're used to the old night-vision gear, so you're going to need to get some practice hours in before we go operational; but as you'll see, the tactical advantage you gain is substantial.

"In other words," the retired military officer concluded, "your adversaries simply won't stand a chance."

Rustman noticed that every member of the hunter-killer team—with the exception of Wintersole, who remained expressionless—nodded their heads and smiled slightly at that last comment. No broad grins. No handslaps or cheerful commentary. Just a quiet and professional display of pleasant anticipation. It was nice that the odds for the impending operation were completely stacked in their favor. Not essential. Just nice.

This pleased Lt. Colonel John Rustman a great deal.

"At 0900 hours this morning, local Caribbean time, a hundred thousand dollars was placed in each of your designated Grand Bahamian bank accounts. At the completion of this mission, an additional two hundred thousand dollars will be added to each account. There will also be an opportunity for each of you to earn a fifty-thousand-dollar bonus," Rustman paused for effect, "in the event that a female agent who is expected to be added to their team is captured alive and utilized for our diversionary ploy. First Sergeant Wintersole will explain all of that to you later.

"Oh, and one more thing," Rustman said. "There is a possibility that we may have an informant working on the outer perimeter of our operation, for purposes of gathering intelligence. In the unlikely event this informant ever needs to make contact with any of you, the code identifier will be 'canvasback,' one repeat, 'canvasback.' Everybody have that?"

All seven heads nodded in acknowledgment.

"If all goes as planned, and it will, make no mistake about that," Rustman emphasized in a firm and confident voice, "this should be a one-day, in-out mission. Once the agents are lured into position, you will move in fast, hit hard, disengage, and get out. Any questions?"

Another member of the team raised his hand.

"Sir," he began hesitantly, "like First Sergeant Wintersole said, you're moving the operation into your backyard . . . or pretty close to it. Won't that make things more complicated for everybody, yourself especially, even if everything goes exactly to plan?"

"It will make things marginally more difficult for me," Rustman admitted, "but not for you. For reasons which I assume are obvious, this is the last time I'll be in contact with any of you until long after the mission is completed. I had intended to hold at least one more briefing before sending you into action, but this new development makes that too risky. I'm too well known in Jasper County, which is why we're meeting here in Jackson County. So, from now on, we'll be relying on the message drop site for routine communications and transfer of materials.

"In fact"—Rustman consulted his notes—"we'll use a little hole-in-the-wall post office off Brandywine Road, right next to Loggerhead Creek, as our primary mail drop point. Name of the place is the Dogsfire Inn. You'll use post office box number fourteen to receive mail, and send any to us using box fifteen." He tossed a ring of six identical keys on the table. "We'll send someone to drop off or pick up mail at 0800 and 1600 hours. You can work out your own pickup and delivery schedules, but try not to be there plus or minus fifteen of those drop times. We want to avoid as many outside connections to you as possible."

"Sir, what about the radios?" the communications specialist and only female on the team asked politely.

"You already know the team comm-net is short range, the transmitters are scrambled, and we've got mountains all around to block or confuse any inadvertent long-range transmissions, so intrateam communications shouldn't be a problem," Rustman reminded them. "But I strongly advise you to stay off the wide-area net unless it's an absolute emergency. The chances of anybody in the area picking up any of your signals and descrambling them are essentially nil. But even scrambled transmitters can be located, and the Fish and Wildlife Service technical agent on the opposing team is supposed to be some kind of electronics hotshot, so there's no sense in taking the risk.

"You have the overwhelming advantages of surprise, terrain, intelligence, and firepower," Rustman concluded. "You will know your targets, your locations, your timetables, and your escape routes. There shouldn't be any need to communicate with me any further once we leave here today . . . other than to signal three simple words," he added with a thin-lipped smile.

"Mission completed. Out."

Chapter Eleven

When congressional aide Keith Bennington returned to Congressman Regis J. Smallsreed's suite of rented offices in Jasper County, Oregon, he found Simon Whatley waiting for him.

"Did you get the congressman off okay?" Whatley asked as he ushered the young aide into his corner office and shut the door.

"Uh, yes sir," Bennington replied nervously. "His plane took off on time, no problem."

"Did he say anything to you on the way to the airport? Any comments about the trip? Anything he wants us to have ready for him when he comes back?"

"Uh, no sir. He just sat in the back, closed his eyes and kind of hummed to himself the whole trip. He didn't actually say anything at all, except 'good morning' and 'good-bye.' That was pretty much it."

"Did he look all right?"

"He did look kind of tired, like he didn't get too much sleep last night."

"I'm sure he didn't. He's a very important man," Whatley reminded the underling. "He works hard, and he plays hard. And it's our job to make sure that he uses his time to his best advantage."

"Uh, yes sir," the young aide agreed, even though he didn't have a clue as to what Whatley was talking about.

"So tell me," Whatley went on casually, "what happened yesterday?"

"You mean about the camera?"

"Yes, that's exactly what I mean." The congressional district office manager nodded his head.

"I . . . I guess I lost it," the young man confessed nervously.

"The camera?"

Bennington nodded silently, staring down at his lap.

"That was a very expensive camera, Keith. How in the world did you manage to lose it?"

"I dropped it," the young aide stammered, and then blurted out: "Because they shot at me. They tried to kill me!"

Simon Whatley closed his eyes and shook his head slowly.

"Keith, what am I ever going to do with you?"

"But—"

"Keith, I can assure you that nobody shot at you . . . and certainly nobody tried to kill you."

"But—"

Whatley put up a silencing hand.

"Keith, that entire area is one huge hunting preserve. Dozens of hunters shoot at hundreds of creatures there every day. But they don't shoot at human beings"—he smiled kindly—"and they *definitely* don't shoot at congressional aides. Especially congressional aides from this office," he emphasized.

"But the tree—" Bennington whispered, his eyes wide and glassy. "The bullet hit the tree right next to me, and pieces of wood hit me in the face, and I . . . I knew you wanted me to get those pictures, but you didn't tell me they might . . ." The young aide looked up accusingly.

"Might what? Shoot you for taking their pictures?" Simon Whatley interrupted with a chuckle. "Keith, those people are very good friends of Lt. Colonel Rustman and Congressman Smallsreed. I wanted to surprise the congressman with a set of candid photos. He likes to put things like that on the wall in his office."

"But—"

"But it was my fault," Whatley went on smoothly. "I should have told you to wear a bright orange hat so that no one would mistake you for a deer."

"A deer!" Keith Bennington exclaimed. "But I don't even—"

"So what you're saying," Whatley interrupted the distressed young man, "is that a stray bullet accidentally hit a tree very close to you, and you panicked, ran, dropped the camera, and then didn't go back to get it. Correct?"

"No! . . . I mean, yes, of course I didn't go back, because I thought that . . ."

"That some of Lt. Colonel John Rustman's dear and close friends were trying to shoot *you*, Keith Bennington, the grandson of Congressman Regis J. Smallsreed's college roommate? Dear and close friends who are expert shots, and who certainly would not have missed if they really wanted to hit you? You do understand how foolish that sounds, don't you?" The congressional district office manager smiled benevolently.

Bennington blinked in confusion and stared down at his hands again.

"Keith, don't worry about the camera," Whatley suggested soothingly.

"I'm sure the congressman would understand, if we ever need to explain it to him, and I'm equally sure we can arrange for a replacement so he doesn't even know how or why it was lost."

"Oh . . . okay, I guess," the young aide reluctantly agreed.

"Good. Now then," Simon Whatley immediately changed the subject, "I want you to focus on that law-enforcement inquiry. We need to get that completed as quickly as possible. Have you heard from Robert?"

Keith Bennington nodded. "I, uh, called him early this morning, before I went to pick up the congressman. He's, uh, not too happy."

"Why not?"

"I guess some of that stuff you wanted him to get is pretty sensitive."

"Of course, it's sensitive—especially to people in law enforcement who don't like the idea of powerful men like Congressman Smallsreed making inquiries into their activities." Simon Whatley shook his head sadly.

"Actually, I think Robert was more concerned about the legal issues," Bennington volunteered. "Something about the files having restricted access, and being afraid he might get caught."

"Robert apparently forgets that we went to a tremendous amount of effort to get him burrowed down into a full-time permanent position," Whatley pointedly reminded his aide.

"I know, and I told him you'd probably say something like that," Bennington replied, then hurriedly added, "since I'd heard you say that to him before."

"And what did he say?"

"He promised to FedEx everything to us tomorrow, so it'll get here Wednesday morning."

"He can't get it out until tomorrow?" Simon Whatley visibly winced.

"I told him it was really important," Bennington hastened to assure his superior, "but he said that was the best he could do."

That wasn't exactly true, but the young congressional aide had no intention of telling Whatley what his congressional aide counterpart from Smallsreed's Washington, D.C., office had really said, because Bennington knew that such a revelation would get them both fired.

Keith Bennington wasn't the smartest congressional aide in the state of Oregon—or in the county of Jasper, for that matter—but he had managed to learn at least that much about big-league politics.

"Okay," Simon Whatley sighed, "here's what you do. The minute that package arrives, you immediately deliver it to the Loggerhead City Post Office out at the intersection of Brandywine Road and Loggerhead Creek, box fourteen. You got that?"

"You want me to send it out by overnight mail to a post office box?" Keith Bennington struggled to control his disbelief at the asinine request.

"No, I don't want you to send it overnight to a post office box, because you can't do that," Whatley explained the obvious impatiently. "Which is why I want you to deliver it to the post office in person."

"Drive all the way out to Loggerhead City?" The young congressional aide looked dismayed. "Why—?"

"Because I told you to," the congressional district office manager interrupted firmly. "Is there anything else?" Simon Whatley's way of dismissing his subordinate staff.

"Uh, no, except . . . uh, do you know if Marla's coming in this morning?"

"I told her to take the day off, get some rest," Whatley reported without the slightest trace of emotion. "It was a tiring weekend for everyone."

Chapter Twelve

"Does this mean we've got to paint red knees on all the giant spiders that just have brown legs?" Special Agent/Pilot Thomas Woeshack asked plaintively, looking up from his copy of the fifty-two-page briefing document Deputy Special Ops Chief Freddy Moore had left with the covert team at seven-thirty that morning, along with specific instructions to read it thoroughly and be ready to discuss options by ten.

"Paint the—what the *hell* are you reading? . . . here, gimme that!" Larry Paxton demanded, lunging out of his chair and ripping the thick document out of the visibly concerned agent/pilot's hands.

"I mean, how could you hold them still long enough do that?" Woeshack asked, turning to Henry Lightstone, who was laughing so hard tears ran down his face as he and the other members of Bravo Team watched their team leader frantically flip through Woeshack's copy of the document. "All spiders have eight legs, don't they? Does that mean four of us would each have to hold two legs while somebody else . . . ?"

"It does say here in the *Wildlife Inspector ID Manual* that unscrupulous dealers will frequently paint the knees of—what?—plain old brown-kneed giant tarantulas, I suppose, to pass them off as the exotic and endangered red-kneed kind to unsophisticated buyers . . . although it also says that the red knees are actually more of a reddish orange," Technical Agent Mike Takahara noted, looking up from the screen of his notebook computer. "Does it say anything in there about us being unscrupulous, too, or do we just get to be unsophisticated?"

"Either way, I'll bet you anything at least one of us is going to get bit," Woeshack predicted.

"Thomas may have a point there, guys," Takahara agreed, as he continued scanning the digitized identification manual. "It also says here, and I quote, 'all tarantulas have fangs, and certain subspecies are more aggressive than others. In fact, some are actually known to stalk and attack humans if they are sufficiently stimulated.' I wonder if that means . . ."

"I am *not* holding any giant spider legs, Paxton," Dwight Stoner, the huge ex–Oakland Raider offensive-tackle-turned-agent warned. "I'll stuff boas and pythons back in their cages all day long if I have to, but I draw the line at tarantulas. That sounds like a team leader's job to me. And not that I really care one way or the other, but just how big are these things anyway?"

"According to the manual, about like this." Mike Takahara spread the fingers of his right hand as far as he could, and then dropped his fingertips down on the surface of the nearby table.

"Jesus."

"You know," Henry Lightstone finally composed himself enough to examine the opened map of Oregon, "there may actually be a bright side to all of this."

"Oh yeah?" Dwight Stoner grumbled skeptically. "What's that?"

"You remember my buddy, Bobby LaGrange?"

"Yeah, sure. He's kind of a hard man to forget, seeing as how we damned near got him killed along with the rest of us on that Cayman Islands deal."

"Well, I got a letter from him a couple of months ago saying that he and Susan were fed up with humidity and cockroaches and drug dealers, and Justin was starting to talk seriously about buying a sailboat and going out looking for that little kid nurse—you remember her, don't you, Paxton . . . the one who thought you were kinda cute?"

"Oh yeah, I remember her all right," Paxton rolled his eyes heavenward. "And how old's that boy now?"

"About thirteen, I think."

"Then Bobby'd better either chain him to the house, take away his bank account, or move the hell away from the East Coast, or he's gonna end up being a grandfather a whole lot sooner than he expected," the Bravo Team leader predicted as he went back to flipping through the briefing document, searching for the part about painting tarantula legs.

"You think Loggerhead City in Jasper County, Oregon's far enough?"

Larry Paxton's lower jaw dropped.

"You're kidding."

"Not if this map's right. Bobby said his place is on the outskirts of a little town called Loggerhead City, and about a half hour drive from Loggerhead Lake, both of which are definitely in Jasper County according to the map. So if I'm reading this thing correctly, it looks like we're going to be setting up shop about twenty miles or so from his ranch. Which means, if nothing else, we've always got a place to hang out, drink beer, and bum an occasional home-cooked meal."

"Sounds like a good deal to me." Paxton nodded approvingly as he went back to his determined search for references to spider knees.

"Wait a minute." Dwight Stoner looked at Lightstone suspiciously. "This is the same guy who invited us out on his brand-new superexpensive yacht, and then got it blown right out from under his ass, right? What makes you think he's gonna let *us* anywhere near him and his family, let alone his brand-new ranch?"

"No problem." Lightstone smiled cheerfully. "Bobby's not the type to hold a grudge. And besides, according to his letter, he and Susan used what he described as a ridiculously inflated insurance settlement to buy what he also described as a piece of God's country, so he ought to be happy about the way things worked out. Especially since now that all he has to worry about are the local Oregon girls getting Justin mutually pregnant."

"Not to mention us coming into town to infest the place with poisonous snakes and giant spiders," Stoner reminded him.

"Wow, that's right!" Woeshack exclaimed. "Say, you know, this whole deal's beginning to sound just like that movie—remember, *Rack-no-phobia*, or something like that—where this young doctor and his family move to this little town in the country, and this really scary tarantula from South America falls out of a tree and accidentally gets smuggled into the town in a coffin, and everybody it bites dies?"

Henry Lightstone collapsed on the floor, holding his ribs and nearly choking in laughter while Larry Paxton stared at his agent/pilot incredulously.

"This is all your fault, Paxton," Stoner muttered ominously. "I told you we went too far on that septic-tank idea."

"*My* fault? What do you mean, *my* fault?" Larry Paxton demanded, looking properly aggrieved. "Who was the one who said 'to hell with protocol, these guys are going down'?"

"Actually, I believe you did." Mike Takahara looked up from his computer screen long enough to correct Bravo Team's leader. "You want to know what it says here about Australian tiger snakes?"

"No, I *don't* want to know what that damned computer says about Australian tiger snakes," Larry Paxton replied testily as he tossed Woeshack's copy of the briefing document aside. "Why should I? If I'm gonna be running this sting operation, and you can bet your badge I am," he added emphatically, "we are *not* going to be buying or selling any damned tiger snakes, whatever the hell they are, based on the simple fact that anything with the word 'tiger' in its name is probably dangerous as hell. And the fact of the matter is, I don't care what Halahan says, we're not gonna buy or sell anything more threatening to my hide than a simple little garter snake. We have to, we'll paint whatever we've got to make it look dangerous. But I'm telling you, that's as far as I'm gonna go on this deal.

"And never mind what I said back when," the covert team leader warned before anyone could respond. "What I want to know is, where did Halahan and Moore ship Charlie Team off to so quick and sneaky-like?"

"Three to one, somewhere warm," Stoner grumbled.

"And I'll bet you ten bucks it doesn't have anything to do with snakes and spiders either," Woeshack added.

"Of course it doesn't," Paxton dismissed the remark irritably. "Halahan wouldn't give the job of running a storefront operation full of god-damned snakes and spiders and God knows what else, in the middle of winter in some God-forsaken part of Oregon, to some rookie covert team who'd probably whimper and whine like a bunch of crybabies the first time something got loose."

"Oh-oh, watch it, guys," Henry Lightstone warned cheerfully, trying very hard to maintain a straight face as he sat up on the floor and leaned his back against the couch, "I think ol' Paxton's about to go motivational on us."

"You're damned right I am," Paxton set his jaw firmly. "That's what us motivational leaders are here for, to inspire the troops. 'Specially when all they do is piss and moan when they draw a piddly-ass rough assignment every now and then."

"I hate to break this to you, buddy," Lightstone pointed out casually, "but I really don't think there was any 'draw' involved in this deal at all. Far as I'm concerned, this whole setup is just a little too bizarre, even for the federal government. I mean, who in their right mind sets up a storefront operation for reptile dealing in the middle of Oregon when they're supposed to be working bad guys down in Nogales? Christ, the airfares alone are going to—"

"Actually, Henry," Mike Takahara interrupted, "I don't think you should worry too much about airfares right away."

"If you think I'm going to let Woeshack fly me a thousand miles from Oregon to Nogales, in the middle of winter, through the, what?"—Lightstone looked down at his map—"Cascade Mountain Range, when you probably can't even see out the window in a damned car, you're out of your—"

"Didn't you read the briefing document?"

"What, fifty-some pages of single-spaced type? Are you nuts?"

"You don't need to read the whole thing. They always put the really sneaky stuff in the middle, because they're pretty sure you'll skip that part." Takahara smiled cheerfully when he located the page he sought. "For example, page twenty-nine informs us that while the rest of us are busy reading snakebite-kit instructions and nailing cage doors shut, Special Agent Henry Lightstone will, and I quote, 'attempt to initiate contact with subject Alistaire Sager, AKA "Sage," for the specific purpose of purchasing wildlife parts and products made from a Sasquatch, AKA "Bigfoot," as well as suspected Apache Indian battle charms.' "

"WHAT?"

Henry Lightstone bolted off the floor and snatched Woeshack's copy of the briefing document.

"Also right here on page twenty-nine," Takahara went on, "it says that 'Agent Lightstone will endeavor to determine subject Sage's source of materials, as well as any links he may have with other illicit wildlife parts and products dealers in the area.' "

"What's a Sasquatch?" Woeshack stared at the others bewilderedly.

"A mythical beast," Larry Paxton replied absentmindedly as he quickly flipped to page twenty-nine of the briefing and began reading.

"More precisely," Takahara expanded on Paxton's meager description, "it's a mythical beast that stands somewhere between seven and ten feet tall, weighs about five hundred pounds, and believe it or not, has feet bigger than Stoner's . . . or at least that's what they say."

"Wow, no kidding?" Thomas Woeshack's eyes grew wide in amazement as he glanced down at his huge partner's oversize boots. "So what does that have to do with Apache Indian battle charms?"

"Better ask Henry," the tech agent advised. "He's the one who's going to be buying them."

"I don't *believe* this shit," Henry Lightstone muttered as he flipped over to page thirty and continued reading.

"Tell you what, Paxton," Dwight Stoner suggested irritably, "you either start exerting some serious supervisory authority around here and get these assignments changed so that Woeshack and I get to buy parts and products made out of eight-foot-tall mythical beasts from the local fruitcake, and Mr. Quick-Reflexes over there gets the spider-knee-painting detail, or you and I are going to go outside and discuss a change in leadership right now."

"What the hell is this?" Paxton demanded to the room at large, ignoring Stoner's threat and tossing the thick document to the floor. "Halahan and Moore must have lost their goddamned—"

"Just out of curiosity, did you get to page thirty-six?" Mike Takahara inquired. "The part about the preauthorized shipping inventories coming out of Miami and Newark?"

Larry Paxton blinked, looked down at the discarded document, and then glared at his tech agent.

"No, I *didn't* get to page thirty-six yet," he whispered menacingly. "So why don't you just tell me what it says about preauthorized shipping inventories, whatever the hell they are?"

"To tell you the truth," Mike Takahara replied seriously, "I really don't think you want to know."

Chapter Thirteen

David Halahan, chief of the U.S. Fish and Wildlife Service's covert investigations branch, looked up when his obviously frustrated deputy walked into his office.

"What's the matter?" he asked.

"They can't find Boggs."

Halahan frowned.

"What are you talking about? Who can't find Boggs?"

"Charlie Team . . . and Boggs's secretary," Moore explained. "Riley just called in. They've been out to his office and his house a couple of times, left a half dozen messages on his answering machine. Checked in at a couple of his favorite watering holes. No Boggs."

"What does his secretary say?"

"Well, apparently it's not unusual for him to be out in the field two or three days without calling in."

"Yeah, but he knew we were sending Charlie Team out there—" Halahan started to protest, but then hesitated.

"Assuming he got the message in the first place," Moore verbalized the thought in both of their minds. "He never did call us back to confirm."

"Yeah, that's right."

"And to make things just a little more confusing, Riley says his house is locked up tight, the government rig's in his garage—they could see it through the side window—and his personal truck and boat are parked in the carport."

"What about the government boats, other vehicles?"

"He's got two boats and a four-wheeler assigned to his office, and they're all present and accounted for in the storage shed next to his office."

"Maybe he went out on a detail with some of the state guys?" Halahan suggested.

"Yeah, Riley's checking on that now. Thing is," Moore went on uneasily, "we don't want to burn the guy or his operation if he's got something going that we're not supposed to know about, but . . ."

"But he's a district agent, not a covert operator, and he's supposed to keep himself available," Halahan finished.

"Yeah, right." The deputy Special Ops chief nodded glumly.

"What's Charlie Team doing now?"

"Riley's got them staying in a couple of the local hotels while they work out vehicles and comm links. The plan is to break them up into three units—Donato and LiBrandi for the hunts, and Riley, Wu, Green, and Marashenko for the two rotating cover units, but we're going to have a problem with transportation if we don't get hold of Boggs pretty soon. We can get by on a rental for Donato and LiBrandi, no problem, because they're acting like they've got more money than brains anyway. But I was counting on Boggs to track down a couple of trucks and a van with Oregon plates for the cover units. Jasper County's a place where you pass your old car down to your kids, then go out and buy a newer used one. Brand-new rental cars won't blend in too well out there."

"Christ, I never thought about that."

"We can always wire them more money to pick up a couple of halfway decent clunkers from a used-car lot," Moore suggested, "but we've got to be careful about buying local. It'll look pretty suspicious if somebody starts poking around, tracks down some sale or registration paperwork, and then starts comparing dates."

"These Chosen Brigade of the Seventh Seal characters don't like *or* trust the government," Halahan reminded his deputy. "You really think they'd walk into the DMV and ask for information?"

"No, but the way our luck's been going lately, Riley'd probably end up buying a car with a countywide history from some Chosen Brigade of the Seventh Seal member's used-car-dealing uncle. Far as we know, all of the members of the group were born and raised in that area."

"Good point."

"So I figure the best thing to do is send them over to Jackson, or even better, Josephine County, where they can spend a little more money and get something only a couple of years old that they can depend on not to fall apart in an emergency."

"And in the meantime," Halahan grumbled to his deputy, "Donato and LiBrandi get to troll themselves through the local bars like a couple of county-next-door idiots looking for a quick and easy way to connect with a big-game trophy hunt. Jesus."

Freddy Moore shrugged. "Yeah, I know, but what else can they do if they can't find Boggs? I sure don't want them trying to approach one of these paranoid Seventh Seal militants out of the blue and try to bring the conversation around to illegal hunting. That's something a guy like Light-stone might be able to pull off, but he's in a different league."

"Just make sure they know to take it slow and easy. I don't want them pushing too fast and blow the whole operation. We've got to respond to that congressional in a reasonable amount of time, but we're not in that big of a hurry."

"Slow and easy are my middle names," the Southern-born deputy Special Ops chief replied with a smile.

"You and Paxton, God help us all." Halahan grinned, but then immediately grew sober again. "Getting back to those vehicles. Another thing to keep in mind is that the more time those kids spend wandering around outside the target area, the more likely they'll run across Bravo Team, or vice versa. We don't need that right now, either."

"Yeah, I know. That's why I wanted to talk to you about wiring the money this afternoon. According to my schedule, the shipments from Newark and Miami should be arriving by air freight"—Moore glanced down at his watch—"right about now."

The deputy Special Ops chief smiled cheerfully at Halahan.

"I figure that by tomorrow morning, our favorite band of renegades ought to be fully occupied with a little matter of unpacking."

Chapter Fourteen

At eight o'clock that Tuesday morning, the Sage was sitting in his accustomed booth adjacent to the rest rooms at the back of the Loggerhead City Pancake House, sipping a cup of hot chocolate, when Sergeant Aran Wintersole suddenly slid into the bench seat opposite him.

The old man jerked back in surprise, then leaned forward and lifted his dark glasses to appraise his uninvited guest with squinted, bloodshot eyes.

Casual clothes: old flannel shirt, old jeans and—the Sage looked under the table—worn boots. Close-cropped grayish brown hair, muscular hands, large military-style watch with a Velcro cover, no rings or other obvious jewelry. But what really got him were the eyes: flat, gray, cold as a winter sky. And there was something funny about them, something he couldn't quite put his finger on. They so unnerved him, he stood and leaned over the table to stare at the stranger's belt buckle—a miniaturized brass replica of the Liberty Bell—then sat back down, returned his dark glasses to their familiar position on his deeply sunburned nose, and continued his evaluation.

"Yes?" the Sage finally asked, when it became apparent the man with the chilling eyes and the disconcertingly relaxed and confident expression on his smoothly shaven face felt perfectly content to be examined in detail.

"I understand you sell Indian jewelry?"

"I might," the Sage acknowledged.

"Might?"

"And might not. It depends."

"On what?"

"What you want. What I've got. Who you are. Who I am. Where I'll be. Because nothing is ever as it seems," the old man rattled off the familiar litany until he sensed it only amused the man sitting across the table.

"Where would you like to start?" Wintersole asked easily.

"I always start at the end," the old man retorted tersely. "It's much easier to predict the future that way."

"And you predict the future?"

"Of course I do."

"I see."

"No, you don't see. I do," the Sage corrected him, hitting his ever-present white walking stick against the wall of the booth for emphasis. "If you did, you wouldn't ask me these questions." Then he set the walking stick back against the wall and chuckled to himself as he sipped his rapidly cooling cocoa.

Wintersole's strange eyes flickered curiously. "In that case, what do I want?"

The Sage reflected on that for a moment.

"You are a hunter," he finally announced. "Not from around here."

"A reasonable assumption."

"You haven't had much luck hunting lately."

"Luck can always be improved," Wintersole acknowledged.

"Which means you need an Apache Indian hunting charm."

"Ah."

"The old way. Guaranteed to bring your prey to you," the old man promised.

"I suppose that could be useful," Wintersole allowed. "Just what, exactly, are we talking about here? I've never seen an Apache Indian hunting charm."

The Sage leaned forward. "Bear-claw necklace," he whispered hoarsely, "to match your spirit."

Wintersole's right eyebrow rose.

"You think I have a bear spirit?"

"Yes, of course you do. It's obvious to anyone who cares to look."

"Are we talking the genuine article here? Bear claws from a real bear?" Wintersole's slightly bemused smile never wavered.

The Sage appeared offended by the implication.

"The mothers of young warriors made these charms to ward off evil spirits during their son's first hunt," he explained patiently. "No Indian woman would send her son out into the wilderness with a fake. That would have been unthinkable."

Wintersole stared at him skeptically.

"Many of these charms have been passed on from generation to generation, treasured by the sons and grandsons of their spiritual ancestors," the Sage rushed on in an obvious attempt to dispel his potential customer's skepticism. "Which, of course, is why they're so difficult to obtain."

"But assuming that one of these genuine Apache hunting charms might actually become available," Wintersole played out more line, "how much could someone expect to pay . . . someone with a bear spirit, such as myself?"

"Money is not the issue here," the old man replied. "A seer has no real use for money."

"Other than perhaps to pay for his hot chocolate?" the hunter-killer team leader suggested dryly.

"I do accept a minimal finder's fee," the old man conceded self-righteously, "but only for the purpose of enabling my physical self to ward off the winter chill."

"Which would bring the grand total for one of these genuine bear-claw necklaces to—?"

"Two hundred and ten dollars," the Sage replied. "I would keep the ten to pay for my hot chocolate."

"Of course you would," Wintersole nodded agreeably. "And if that same person wanted to buy an additional six charms?"

The Sage cocked his head curiously.

"There are seven of us," Wintersole explained. "We work together, and hunt together, and I'm sure that we all could use some good luck. And as you already mentioned," he went on when the old man remained speechless, "money is certainly not the issue here."

The Sage lifted up the dark glasses again to peer intently into the stranger's expressionless gray eyes for a brief moment. Then he nodded in satisfaction.

"I think you are the darkness," he whispered, his dry lips curling faintly upward in a knowing smile, "but I am not altogether certain."

Wintersole recoiled imperceptibly.

"What makes you think that?" He looked curiously detached.

The old man shrugged. "What causes me to see the things I see is not important. What's important is that I *do* see, and that I will find the charms that you and your friends will certainly need." He hesitated for a moment, then went on. "I believe I could talk the tribe into a price of one thousand dollars total for the seven necklaces, if they are to be found—which is by no means certain," he warned.

"That sounds like a very fair price."

"In that case," the Sage added thoughtfully, "my fee would be fifty dollars."

"For more hot chocolate to soothe the spirit?"

The old man didn't miss the sarcasm in Wintersole's voice.

"It's been a cold winter, and the spirit cannot always warm the body," he explained, staring down at his thin hands.

"And what about the taxes?"

The old man brought his grizzled head up sharply.

"What about them?" he demanded.

"Surely you don't begrudge the government their fair share of your, uh, spiritual efforts?"

"I believe very strongly in the separation of church and state, especially when they're both working together to stick their hands in my pockets," the Sage retorted furiously, his graveled voice raising in pitch. Then he glared at the stranger suspiciously. "You wouldn't be one of them damned sneaky federal government tax agents, would you?"

Wintersole smiled. "I don't think they'd want somebody like me in their government," he emphasized the word "their," and the old man picked up on it immediately.

"You don't like them federal government types, either?"

"Let's just say that we have our differences."

"Ah." The Sage nodded his head knowingly. "So it's a good thing you're a man of peace, or you might not take kindly to their evil ways. Is that it?"

"Who said I'm peaceful?" Wintersole countered coldly. "You are right when you said I'm a hunter. But I didn't say what my favorite prey is."

The Sage stared once more into Wintersole's eerie gray eyes.

"You know, sonny," the old man smiled in a conspiratorial manner, "maybe I misjudged you."

"Really? How so?"

"Maybe you ain't so dark as I thought you was."

"What's that supposed to mean?"

"Nothing." The Sage chuckled to himself. "Just something us seers think about when we're not busy helping folks with their problems."

"Speaking of problems," Wintersole returned to his topic of interest, "how soon do you think those necklaces might be available? My friends and I want to begin hunting as soon as possible."

The old man shrugged. "It's possible that I could have them for you as early as this evening, but if I did," he added emphatically, sweeping the small restaurant with one of his sun-wrinkled hands, "I sure as hell wouldn't bring them here."

"No, of course you wouldn't," his companion readily agreed. "Where would you want to meet?"

"There's an old inn built around a great big tree down by Loggerhead Creek, at the end of Brandywine Road, that's pretty much the local community center, a restaurant, and post office. Called the Dogsfire Inn. You know it?"

Wintersole drew in his breath slightly.

"I think I can find it," he assured the old man.

"Meet me there at five o'clock this evening," the Sage ordered. "I like to eat early. Easier on the digestion at my age. The woman who runs the place can feed us—your treat, of course. And if you'd like, she can verify the authenticity of the charms, too."

"This woman can recognize a genuine Apache Indian hunting charm when she sees one?"

"Of course she can." The Sage grabbed his white walking stick, slid out of the booth, and peered down at Wintersole through his dark, protective lenses. "She's a witch."

Chapter Fifteen

Special Agents Larry Paxton, Henry Lightstone, and Dwight Stoner stood in the roll-up doorway of the United Airlines terminal at the Rogue Valley International Airport in Medford, Oregon, and stared numbly at the three six-foot-square pallets of plywood shipping crates stacked head high inside the small warehouse.

From their position, some twenty feet away from the pallets, the agents counted a minimum of seventy-two 2'×4'×1' crates, each drilled with numerous small holes, tightly secured with steel bands, and covered on all sides with bright red warnings labels.

From their position in the doorway, Paxton, Lightstone, and Stoner could easily read several of the labels:

DANGEROUS!
HAZARDOUS CARGO!
LIVE REPTILES!
DO NOT DROP!
POISONOUS SNAKES . . . USE EXTREME CAUTION WHEN OPENING!
And the most intriguing label of all:

FRAGILE

"They can't be talking about the crates being fragile." Stoner stepped forward another six inches to get a closer look. "That's three-quarter-inch plywood, and they must've used a couple hundred wood screws in each one. Man, those things look like they were made to ship artillery rounds."

"We should be so lucky," Lightstone grumbled.

"One of you guys happen to be Larry Packer?" an extremely pale uniformed warehouse attendant asked hopefully as he hurried forward with a clipboard in his hand.

"Uh . . ."

"They told me that a guy named Larry Packer would be here at one o'clock with a Ryder truck and a couple other guys to sign for this stuff." The attendant hurriedly held out the clipboard and a pen. "It's one o'clock, and that sure looks like a Ryder truck, and there's three of you, so if you'll just sign here."

"Don't you want to see any ID?" Paxton stared down at the shipping bill as if it were his own death sentence. Finally, after closing his eyes and shaking his head sadly for a brief moment, he scribbled his name across the face of the form.

"Mister, you want to know the honest-to-God truth?" the attendant asked as he nearly ripped the clipboard out of Paxton's hand, "I really don't care if your driver's license says 'John Smith, Dishonest Snake Smuggler.' You signed for these things, so they're all yours."

Already looking decidedly less pale, the man quickly tore off the bottom copy and handed it to Paxton.

"By the way," he added almost cheerfully, "you want to know what the pilots said when they landed here, after flying all the way from Portland with those damned things like they were crates full of nitroglycerin?"

"No, I don't think so." Paxton shook his head again. "Probably just make us feel a whole lot worse than we already do."

"I doubt that," Stoner muttered.

Ignoring his huge partner, Paxton turned to the now broadly grinning

United Airlines employee. "Uh, seeing as how you probably don't want us to drive our truck inside your hanger here, you want us to just back up to the door so that you folks could . . . ?"

"Hey, don't worry about it. Far as I'm concerned, you can back that truck right up next to those pallets and take all the time you want to load," the warehouse attendant informed them hurriedly. "I'd, uh, be glad to help you guys, but I'm running kinda late. Got a date to meet my, uh, wife for lunch. So go ahead and load up, and then just close the door and shut the gate behind you when you leave. The manager's inside in her office, but to tell you the truth, I really don't think she'll come out until you guys are gone."

The three agents stood at the front of the warehouse and watched the warehouse worker hurry around to the front of the terminal building, hop into a car, and then quickly accelerate out of the parking lot.

"I wonder if he's really got a wife?" Lightstone mused.

"Or if that's really his car?" Stoner added.

"What the hell's the matter with you guys?" Paxton demanded. "You think a guy like that's gonna lie about a lunch date with his wife, then run out and jump into the first car he finds with the keys in the ignition and take off just because he's got a few snakes and spiders in his warehouse?"

"I would have," Stoner said.

"Works for me," Lightstone agreed.

"Well, while you crybabies go in there and start figuring out how you're gonna load them things," Paxton announced, "*I'm* gonna go get the truck."

The two agents waited patiently right where they were until the Bravo Team leader cautiously backed the Ryder truck about halfway inside the roll-up doorway of the warehouse—still a good ten feet from the pallets.

"That's good!" Stoner called out, and then turned to Lightstone. "No sense in letting him get too close."

"Yeah, no kidding."

Paxton hopped out of the truck and stared at his two subordinate agents.

"Well, you two got this all figured out?" he demanded.

"Yep," Stoner replied.

"Good. I'll stand by the door and make damned sure nobody—" Paxton's words ended abruptly when a huge hand closed around the front of his shirt and lifted his entire 185-pound frame a good foot off the floor.

"Don't look upon this as insubordination, Paxton," Dwight Stoner suggested, glaring into Larry Paxton's widened eyes as he relaxed his massive arm enough to allow his supervisor's shoes to touch the ground. "Look upon it as constructive criticism."

"Not to mention a unique opportunity to demonstrate uncommon leadership," Lightstone added.

"Yeah, that too," Stoner agreed. "And besides," the huge agent muttered ominously as he opened his hand and then smoothed out Paxton's bunched-up shirt, "all we'd have to do is show them a copy of that shipping invoice, and not a jury in the world would ever convict us."

Thirty seconds later, having reached a mutual agreement as to the division of labor on this particular assignment, the three federal agents cautiously approached the stacks of crates together.

"Which ones do you think have the spiders in them?" Stoner whispered when they stood about six feet away from the closest pallet.

"If there really are 750 of the damned things, then my guess would be every one that isn't labeled 'poisonous snake,' " Lightstone suggested. "But don't forget," he added thoughtfully, "we could be talking wildlife-agent sense of humor here."

"Bunch of whiny little crybabies, afraid of a few itty-bitty spiders," Larry Paxton muttered as he gingerly moved to within three feet of the pallet and leaned forward, trying to peek through the numerous quarter-inch holes drilled along the upper edge of one of the top crates on the pile.

"See anything?" Lightstone whispered.

"Not a damned thing," Paxton replied nervously.

"It looks like there's some kind of screening on the inside of some of the boxes covering the airholes," Stoner noted, squatting down to examine the pile from a much safer distance. "I wonder what that means?"

"Means whatever's in this one can't get out through a quarter-inch diameter hole," Paxton proposed hopefully.

"Well, you ought to be able to see something through those holes," Lightstone reasoned. "Why don't you move in closer?"

"Don't rush me, goddamnit!"

"Now that's what I call leadership by example," Dwight Stoner grunted approvingly.

Moving very slowly and cautiously, and keeping his fingers well away from the drilled holes, Paxton placed his hands along the lower sides of the heavy crate he was examining, and ever so gently pulled it about two inches toward him.

Nothing.

"See, I told you little crybabies—" Paxton berated them in a soft voice as he carefully lifted the heavy box off the stack . . . and then screamed "SHIT!" when something thrashed heavily inside, sending both the team leader and the box tumbling backwards.

Larry Paxton landed solidly on his back on the concrete floor, forcing most of the air from his lungs in a loud, explosive gasp—followed by another an instant later when the now wildly thumping crate landed on his chest, causing the wide-eyed team leader to scream "SHIT!!!" again in an even louder, higher-pitched voice.

Shoving the heavy container aside with the last vestiges of air in his lungs, Paxton leaped to his feet and staggered behind Dwight Stoner as the huge agent drew his 10mm Smith & Wesson semiautomatic pistol out from under his jacket and aimed it at the crate—which thumped and jerked a couple more times before suddenly becoming silent.

For about five long seconds, only the sound of Larry Paxton's labored breathing filled the warehouse. Nobody spoke a word.

Finally, Henry Lightstone broke the silence.

"I don't know about you guys," he ventured in a hushed voice, "but I sure as hell hope that's not one of the spider boxes."

Chapter Sixteen

Darkness had already fallen when the Sage puttered up the road on his noisy, smoke-belching motorbike. The narrow headlight beam wavered among the surrounding trees as the old man wobbled to a stop next to a pair of wooden benches beneath a brand-new post-mounted wooden sign that said The Dogsfire Inn where First Sergeant Wintersole and the communications specialist of the hunter-killer team awaited him.

"Ah, I see you found the place." The scraggly-bearded old man carefully leaned the motorcycle against a tree, struggled to remove his helmet and backpack, pulled a pair of dark glasses out of his shirt pocket and put them on, then unstrapped his white walking stick from the bike frame.

"At the end of the road, beside the creek. An old house with a tree growing out through the roof." Wintersole shrugged. "It wasn't difficult."

"Who's she?"

"This is one of my associates, named Azaria." Wintersole turned to the young woman. "Azaria, the Sage."

"Pleased to meet you." The attractive but decidedly hard-looking young woman offered a muscular hand.

"Oh, uh, yes . . . pleased also." The Sage grasped the young woman's hand briefly. Then he quickly hobbled onto the spacious wooden deck that extended from the inn and attached screened porch to the dirt road on one side and creek on the other. Several dozen glowing yellow light-bulbs both within and outside the enclosed porch added to the already eerie atmosphere of the old house.

The communications specialist gave Wintersole a puzzled look, but he simply motioned for her to follow the old man into the huge screened area, then sat down at one of the rustic tables surrounding a circular pit with a bell-like brass chimney over a blazing log fire.

"I like to eat outside," the old man explained as he sat in the chair closest to the fire and leaned his walking stick within easy reach against the table. "Gets a mite chilly sometimes, but a good fire warms my bones better than any modern heating system."

"Fine." Wintersole barely glanced at the fire as he and Azaria joined the old man at the table.

"Things are a little slow around here," the Sage advised as he picked up one of the handwritten menus and held it up to the firelight. "Just the new owner and a young feller doin' the cooking and everything else. But that's okay 'cause the hot chocolate's just as good as ever."

"So how did the search go?" Wintersole inquired openly. "Any luck?"

"Hell yes, I had some luck," the old man retorted. "Fact is, I had to sweet-talk a couple of them Indian folks something fierce to round up these beauties." He turned his backpack upside down, and seven ornately beaded and feathered necklaces dropped onto the wood slab tabletop. "Got three from one old woman who planned to save them for her grandsons, but I guess she decided the money meant more to her. Said the kids don't care about the old ways anymore. Guess that's pretty much the way everywhere." The bearded old man sighed deeply.

"But then, too, some would say that children have never cared about such things," Wintersole suggested as his eyes scanned the enclosed porch and surrounding deck.

The old man's dark glasses reflected the warm glow of the fire as he cocked his head curiously.

"What have we here?" he addressed Wintersole suspiciously. "A hunter *and* a philosopher?"

"From my perspective, it's difficult to be a hunter for any length of time without becoming philosophical," Wintersole replied. "At least about death. We humans lack serious teeth or claws, so we make weapons. If we didn't, we'd find ourselves at the mercy of those natural predators who come into this world much better armed."

"Such as the government?" The Sage smiled knowingly.

Wintersole blinked, then chuckled in appreciation while covertly nudging his companion's leg with his boot.

"And speaking of claws—" Wintersole's companion held up one of the necklaces to the light.

"Ah yes, young lady, the charms," the Sage responded immediately. "A very good eye you have, too. That's by far the prettiest—and, who knows, perhaps the luckiest," he added cheerfully. "Are you taking that one for yourself?"

The young woman looked over at Wintersole, who shrugged indifferently.

"Actually, I might need some extra luck on this trip." She briefly fingered the four thick, slightly curved claws before slipping the ornate necklace over her head.

"Then you couldn't have chosen better," the Sage congratulated her. "And as long as we're trying to match charms with personalities," he added as he picked up another one of the necklaces and handed it to Wintersole, "I recommend that our philosopher-hunter wear this one."

"Why so?" The team leader barely looked at the necklace he held in his hand.

"Because the claws came from a grizzly."

That comment caused Wintersole to examine the extremely thick claws that had been strung on a simple knotted leather cord more carefully.

"Really? I thought grizzly claws were a lot sharper than this." The hunter-killer recon team leader fingered the tips that were nearly as blunt as a child's finger and studied the Sage suspiciously.

The old man shook his head. "That's a common misconception. Cat claws are sharp. Bear claws are powerful. Fact is, a bear like that one" —the Sage gestured at the necklace in Wintersole's hand—"could probably rip a car door right off its hinges, if it had a mind to."

The expression on Wintersole's face changed perceptibly as he continued examining the ornament.

"Yes sir," the Sage went on, "all things considered, a grizzly's just about the most powerful animal you're ever gonna ever run across in this life. Unless, of course, you go looking for one of them polar bears. But I don't think you'll be finding many of them critters here in Jasper County." The old man chuckled.

"No, I suppose not." Wintersole reached into his pocket, drew out a band-wrapped roll of money, and tossed it onto the table.

"Eleven hundred dollars," he announced flatly. "I decided to increase our contribution to your hot chocolate fund. I've noticed it gets very cold around these mountains at night."

"And speaking of hot chocolate . . ." The Sage smiled in anticipation.

Wintersole turned around in his chair, then froze . . . as did communications specialist Azaria.

"I thought I heard somebody out here," the woman explained softly. "What can I get for you folks?"

"A large hot chocolate for me," the old man ordered quickly. "Then you can whip me up one of them soy burgers, extra onions."

"Extra onions, you got it." The woman nodded, not bothering to use the order pad in her apron pocket. "And you folks?" She turned to the other two, then quickly realized that neither of them paid her any attention.

"Don't worry, she's fine," the woman assured them, tugging slightly on the thick chain leash—that was hooked to what appeared to be a transmitter collar—to bring the large cat closer to her leg.

Wintersole stared at the dilated pupils in the center of the bright yellow eyes in absolute fascination.

"What an incredible animal," he whispered almost reverently.

"Don't let her hear you say that," the woman advised. "Sasha thinks she's just as human as I am. Or maybe it's the other way around, I'm never quite sure." She smiled. "I raised her from a kitten, and she's very attached, but surprisingly interested in people . . . and pretty good company, too," she added, tugging at the leash again, which caused the large cat to yowl in annoyance, "when she's not being pigheaded."

"You don't think she'll ever hurt someone?" the communications specialist asked uneasily.

"Oh, I'm sure if anyone ever tried to give me a bad time, she'd tear them to shreds in a matter of seconds," the woman declared with certainty. "But that's one of the reasons I consider her good company. So, what will you have?"

"The same," Wintersole responded indifferently, his eyes still fixed on the glowing yellow eyes that observed him with an intensity that seemed far more predatory than curious.

"Me too," the communications specialist added uneasily.

"Okay, the hot chocolate'll be coming right up," the woman announced cheerfully, and disappeared into the main building with the cat following close at her side.

"So, what do you think?" the Sage asked. "Pretty classy dame for a US government postmaster . . . or postmistress, or whatever they call them nowadays. Or maybe you didn't even notice," the old man added with a chuckle.

"No," Wintersole replied, "I didn't."

While they waited for the food to come, the three conspirators sipped hot chocolate, indulged in idle conversation, and watched a few locals wander down the lighted path to the converted garage to drop off mail, check on their post-office boxes, and share a few tidbits of gossip.

However, Wintersole paid very little attention to the conversation. Instead, he leaned back in his chair and stared blankly at the doorway to the converted mill, pensively sipping his drink until the woman finally reappeared with their orders and the cat at her side. Then his cold, gray eyes lit up with intense interest.

This time, however, he paid very careful attention to the woman as well as the cat.

As they ate, Azaria casually questioned the Sage about the origins of the necklaces, and the old man explained how nothing was ever as it seemed, but you could often make sense out of the illusions if you paid close attention.

Only after they finished the soy burgers and exchanged their empty plates for hot cups of herbal tea and chocolate did the conversation turn back to the government.

"You think the people around here are fed up with the way the government runs things?" Wintersole asked casually.

"Oh hell yes!" The Sage nodded emphatically, his reddened cheeks almost glowing beneath his raggedy beard as he launched into a topic clearly dear to his heart. "A lot of folks around here been that way for twenty years or so."

"What do you mean?" Wintersole appeared confused by the old man's words.

"Ever heard of a group called the Chosen Brigade of the Seventh Seal?"

Wintersole shook his head. "Can't say that I have."

"Bunch of people who got fed up with the government telling them what to do, when, where, and how, so they up and moved . . . right out here to these mountains." The Sage's waving hand encompassed much of the surrounding landscape.

"A brigade's a couple thousand soldiers minimum," Wintersole commented casually. "Are there really that many of them?"

"Nah, more like a couple squads at best." The Sage smiled. "Oh, they've got the rank for a brigade. Lord, do they ever! Bird colonel, light colonels, and majors everywhere you look. But the last time I checked, they were a little short on noncoms and ground troops. Fact is, they ain't got any. Guess they figure they'll fill the ranks when the balloon goes up and all locals rally around the flag."

"Sounds like they're running away from reality."

"Sure they are, but the funny thing is"—the old man shook his head sadly—"they really didn't escape at all, because they can't seem to wean themselves off the government tit, and the government's still telling them they can't do this, can't shoot that, can't do much of anything without a permit.

"And they don't like that at all," he added ominously.

"They sound like my kind of people." Wintersole leaned slightly toward the old man. "I don't like being told what I can hunt and where I can hunt, either."

"A lot of people feel that way around here," the Sage agreed, then looked around to see if anyone else was within listening range. "In fact," he added in a lowered voice, "it wouldn't surprise me none if these Seventh Seal folks took it into their heads to do something about it."

Wintersole smiled.

"Like what?" he asked. His eyes made their routine sweep of the enclosed porch. "Picket the local post office?"

"I doubt it," the Sage replied with a sly smile. "Not their style."

"You're suggesting they might take a more direct approach?"

"They just might," the old man acknowledged. "But I don't think they'd get very far," he added glumly.

"Really?" Wintersole drummed his fingers lightly on the table. "Why not?"

The old man shrugged impatiently. "Hell, everybody knows they're just plain outgunned. Bunch of shotguns and hunting rifles won't do them much good against an FBI SWAT team."

"Depends on what you're talking about," the hunter-killer team leader replied. "In the right hands, scoped hunting rifles and shotguns could do a lot of damage against a small police or county SWAT team, maybe three or four men. But you're right," he conceded thoughtfully. "They try to go up against one of the FBI Hostage Rescue teams, that's a different ball game entirely. They'd need modern assault rifles, grenades, and night-vision gear at a minimum, not to mention a whole bunch of trained people with logistics, communications support, trained military leaders, the works. And if they're that big, the FBI's just going to step back and call in one of the National Guard units."

"Well, at least that'd be more of a fair fight, local boys against local boys." The Sage smiled.

"I don't think so." Wintersole shook his head. "Doesn't matter how big, well trained, or well equipped this militant group of yours may be, if they ever went up against something like an air mobile maneuver battalion — 750 trained troops armed with light assault weapons, state-of-the-art communications, air support — they wouldn't last more than a couple of hours, tops. And that's being pretty damned optimistic."

"You sure about that?" The old man peered at him quizzically.

"Positive."

"Sounds like you know something about this kind of business."

"I know how it works," Wintersole replied. "And it's not pretty. Trust me."

"You were in the military, I take it?"

"That's right."

"But you're not any longer . . . retired, maybe?"

"Maybe."

The old man stared intently at Wintersole for a few moments.

"That's an evasive answer," he finally declared.

"Yes, it is," Wintersole agreed.

"Well then," the Sage said after another long moment, "maybe you're just the guy who can explain something I've always wondered about."

"What's that?"

"*Posse comitatus.*"

Wintersole shrugged. "What about it?"

"I want to know how it works. Seems to me I remember hearing that the American military can't be used to do police work."

"They can't," Wintersole replied evenly. "So what? The federal government isn't going to stand for an open rebellion. You can just flat count on that. They'll let the police, FBI, or whatever, take on the small groups, no problem. But the first time an antigovernment organization takes over government property, sets up a perimeter, and plants a flag that says 'come get me if you dare,' you can bet some local National Guard lieutenant colonel will get orders to take his battalion though a live-fire exercise right over the top of that flagpole."

"No shit?"

"None whatsoever," the hunter-killer recon team leader stated emphatically.

The old man sat in silence, apparently disconcerted by this latest bit of information.

"Well, hell," he finally said, "I don't think these people are planning on a full-scale battle anyway. They just want to make a statement. You know, like at Concord right before the Revolutionary War. Show them big boys back in Washington that they can't push true American patriots around forever."

"Now *that's* a different ball game." Wintersole nodded approvingly. "If all these people want to do is make a statement, that can be accomplished with a small tight group . . . assuming they're properly armed, trained, and motivated," he added meaningfully.

"Yeah, well, the way I hear it, it's kinda hard to get yourself properly armed and trained and all that if you haven't had much in the way of disposable income for the past twenty-some years," the Sage responded glumly.

"Sounds like this group needs to find themselves a sugar daddy."

" 'Course they do. But how the hell do they go about finding someone like that?"

"Maybe all they have to do is offer the right person a nice cup of hot herbal tea," Wintersole suggested, tapping his finger lightly against his cup.

The Sage eyed his two guests carefully.

"You know," he lowered his voice, "I've been telling them all along somebody like you would show up someday."

"What do you mean, 'somebody like me'?"

"The forces of darkness and light are coming, just like it says in Revelations. I told them that. Nothing is ever as it seems, but the signs are everywhere." The old man smiled proudly.

"And how did they respond?" Wintersole asked cautiously.

"I don't think they believed me."

The old man stuck a long, gnarled finger into the nearly empty cup and discontentedly stirred the dregs of his now-cold hot chocolate.

"What do you think it would take to change their mind?" Not a trace of sarcasm colored Wintersole's delivery.

The old man hesitated.

"You mean about you being one of those forces?"

"That's right."

"Well, knowing these folks the way I do"—the Sage leaned forward and dropped his voice to a conspiratorial level again—"I'm guessing they'd either want to see the color of your money or the quality of your hardware."

Wintersole smiled pleasantly.

"That could be arranged."

"Then," the old man went on, "I imagine they'd probably want to ask you a few questions."

"Such as?"

"Well, if it was me, 'What's in it for you?' would be right up there at the top of the list."

Wintersole chuckled mechanically.

"Let me ask you something." His eyes again swept the enclosed porch for any sign of eavesdroppers. "How do you think they'd feel about talking to a businessman with an ulterior motive?"

The old man cocked his head curiously.

"Is that the same thing as a hidden agenda?"

"No, it's not." Wintersole leveled his cold gaze at the old man. " 'Hidden agenda' is a term that government bureaucrats use."

"That's kinda what I thought, too." The fire's reflection flickered in the dark lenses of the Sage's glasses.

"You think I'm a government spy?" Wintersole favored the old man with a pitying look.

"Don't matter much what I think. But I can tell you right out, that's the first thing these people are going to think." The Sage nodded slowly. "The very first thing."

"Which means they'll probably want to know more about my business . . . and my ulterior motives."

The old man smiled. "I think you can count on that."

Wintersole stared momentarily at the doorway to the inn before speaking.

"How do you think they'd feel if I told them that my, uh, associates and I share many of their views, but we prefer a much more direct means of carrying forth our message?" he asked.

"And just what does 'more direct' mean?"

"For starters," Wintersole replied, "we have no intention of waiting twenty years to make our statement."

"Ah." The old man nodded, then added suspiciously: "So if you're in such a big hurry, I guess that means you just want to use these people for your own purposes."

"If you know anything about business," Wintersole informed him, "then you know that the most profitable deals result when both sides use the other for their own purposes. That's how the business world works."

The old man appeared to think about that for a while.

"You would supply the weapons —"

"And the ammunition and the training, if they need it," Wintersole completed the statement.

"Right." The old man nodded agreeably. "And they, in turn . . ."

". . . will do whatever they wish with their new resources," Wintersole finished. "Which is precisely what we would like for them to do . . . although perhaps with an additional refinement or two that we might suggest," he added with a tight smile.

"Additional refinements, huh?"

The old man seemed to find those words intriguing.

"However, if this group you describe wants to maintain their purity of spirit, or whatever they choose to call it," Wintersole went on, holding up the grizzly-bear-claw necklace, "then I suggest they set up a savings account and start putting away the profits from their Apache Indian battle charm business. It shouldn't take more than oh, say, the profit on a half dozen of these things to pick up a functional assault rifle through the underground market. Of course, you add a decent supply of ammo, mags, webbing, flak vest, night-vision gear . . . and then take into account the possibility that the ATF may be monitoring your purchases." The hunter-killer recon team leader shrugged.

"You are a businessman, aren't you?" The Sage grinned openly now.

"In a manner of speaking, yes."

"And you want me to introduce you to these people, so you can use each other for your own purposes?"

"For a reasonable fee, of course."

The old man immediately sat upright in his chair and leaned forward.

"How much would you say — ?" he began, but Wintersole cut him off.

"I think we should look upon this as a standard finder's fee situation," he announced curtly. "Perhaps a thousand down, and another two thousand within thirty days — assuming we're satisfied with the manner in which our donated equipment is used, of course."

The old man smiled. "I think —" But then never got a chance to finish that statement either because the woman suddenly approached them.

"You rattling on about the damned government again, old man?" She nudged him playfully as she placed the bill on the table.

"Hey, I didn't have to work real hard to convince these two," the Sage chuckled as Wintersole tossed three ten-dollar bills on the table. "Just like the proverbial preacher reading gospel to his choir. Turns out they don't like the federal government any better'n I do."

"So who does?" She shrugged, then immediately glanced down when the creature beside her started to growl softly.

"She fascinates you, doesn't she?" the woman asked, watching the man with the strange gray eyes stare at the clearly displeased cat while he fingered his bear-claw necklace.

Wintersole nodded his head slowly.

"Most likely because you're fascinated by violent death—probably your own." The woman sighed. "So if I'm going to keep you around as a paying customer, I guess I need to work something out that both you and her can live with."

Her long hair cascaded over Wintersole's shoulder when she reached down and took the necklace out of his hand.

"Is this one yours?" she asked, caressing each one of the claws separately.

Wintersole nodded silently.

"Then here's what we'll do." She unbuttoned her shirt, slowly rubbed the grizzly claws against the exposed curve of her neck and shoulder for a few moments, and then slipped the necklace over his head. "I'm not guaranteeing that's going to help any if you seriously piss her off," she warned as she picked up the three ten-dollar bills and put them in her apron pocket, "but it just might keep her from ripping out your throat someday when she's in a bad mood."

"Can't hardly ask for a better charm than that, can you?" the old man chuckled.

"Next time you come back, let me read the cards for you," the woman volunteered. "Then you'll understand."

"How do you know I'll be back?" Wintersole studied her more carefully.

A faraway look subtly altered the woman's exquisite features for an instant. Then she smiled.

"Because I see it happening."

Chapter Seventeen

"So, guys, what do you think?" Bobby LaGrange stepped back from the smoking grill where a dozen inch-thick steaks sizzled their way toward medium-rare.

From their seated positions around the table, leaning back in their cushioned chairs and smiling cheerfully, Larry Paxton, Dwight Stoner, Mike Takahara, and Thomas Woeshack all raised their wineglasses in salute.

"Gotta hand it to you, Bobby," Larry Paxton congratulated their host, "for an old run-down homicide detective who unfortunately got saddled with Henry for a partner during his formative years in law enforcement, you really do appreciate the finer things in life."

"First-class hut," Thomas Woeshack agreed.

"Yeah, too bad we keep showing up," Mike Takahara observed.

"Actually, I seriously considered locking the gate, barring the door, and calling the sheriff to run you guys out of the county," Bobby LaGrange admitted. "But I figured, what the hell, how much trouble could you get me into all the way out here in the middle of Oregon?"

"You don't want to know," Dwight Stoner warned, glaring ominously at Larry Paxton.

Henry Lightstone stood in the middle of the expansive wooden deck and stared up at the angular face of the towering three-story cedar-log-and-glass structure. Then he surveyed the gently rolling hills, the stretches of bright green pasture, the glistening surface of the two-acre pond, hundreds of scrub oak trees, and the high shale-faced mountains that formed a protective bowl around Bobby LaGrange's brand-new home.

"To tell you the truth, Bobby," he remarked after he completed his inspection, "I didn't know places like this existed except in movies. How many acres did you say?"

"Six-forty on the nose."

Larry Paxton blinked.

"Six hundred . . . ?"

"One square mile, Larry, my man. Otherwise known as a 'full square' among us Oregon rancher types."

"I knew it." Paxton shook his head in wonder. "The man really was running dope off that big yacht."

"Good thing we sank it, huh?" Thomas Woeshack put in.

"Don't remind him," Stoner growled. "We haven't got fed dinner yet."

"I need to sit down for this." Lightstone sought the comfort of one of the thickly padded deck chairs, then he stared up at his ex-partner. "Okay, now let me get this straight. You, Bobby LaGrange, are an honest-to-God Oregon rancher . . . as in cattle ranching?"

Bobby LaGrange smiled cheerfully.

"And those really are cows out there — your cows?" Lightstone gestured in the direction of several dozen tiny black and brown figures scattered across the distant pastures.

"That's right. One hundred and ninety-two heifers, 209 steers, and at least one honest-to-God bull. Four hundred head of genuine livestock, on the hoof, more or less. Actually, less one," he added, glancing down at the sizzling meat. "I believe we're dining on Harold this evening. Or maybe Harriet. I really didn't look all that close."

"You butchered your own cow?" Thomas Woeshack gasped, duly impressed.

"Oh hell no." Bobby LaGrange gave the Native American Special Agent a disapproving look. "I just pointed at one of the damned things and told my foreman we wanted it for dinner."

"Man even has a foreman to do the dirty work." Larry Paxton nodded approvingly. "I like that. Ol' Bobby here's got style, even if he does have questionable taste in his partners and dinner guests."

"Getting back to four hundred head 'more or less,' " Henry Lightstone persisted suspiciously, "I bet you don't have the slightest idea how many of those dark spots out there really are cows, much less how many of them actually belong to you, right?"

"Well . . ."

"Ask him what happened when he took off in his brand-new four-wheel RV and tried to use his brand-new cattle prod to figure out how many of those animals we supposedly own are honest-to-God bulls," Susan LaGrange's voice rang out from the open kitchen window.

Lightstone raised an eyebrow.

"It was an accident," LaGrange muttered. "I was just trying to move its tail out of the way. How the hell was I supposed to know the damned prod was contact activated?"

Henry Lightstone shook his head slowly in amazement.

"I assume you no longer own a brand-new four-wheel recreational vehicle?" Larry Paxton asked cautiously.

"Tell him what the insurance man said, honey," Susan LaGrange's cheerful voice floated through the window. "How he'd never seen a four-wheeler that badly damaged since his tour of duty in Kuwait."

"The woman exaggerates," Bobby LaGrange growled defensively.

"And don't you dare leave out the part where I had to call the neighbors to move the bull to another pasture and get you down out of that tree."

Susan LaGrange walked out onto the deck with a huge platter of baked potatoes. Dwight Stoner immediately lunged out of his chair, took it from her, and placed it in the center of the table in a reverent manner while their hostess disappeared into the house again.

"These would be your genuine Oregon rancher neighbors, I take it?" Lightstone guessed. "The ones who actually know something about cattle?"

"Nice people," Bobby LaGrange commented as he poked cautiously at one of the steaks. "You guys real picky about how these things turn out?"

"Absolutely not," Dwight Stoner declared quickly before anyone else at the table could answer. "They'll eat what they get, and like it . . . or I'm gonna eat it for them," he added, glaring at his fellow agents.

"I'm used to eating raw whale blubber," Thomas Woeshack announced casually, "so any way it comes out is fine with me."

"Did somebody mention raw whale blubber out there?" Susan La-Grange's distressed face appeared at the kitchen window.

"Never mind." Dwight Stoner flashed the diminutive Special Agent/Pilot a threatening look. "One more comment like that and he's not going to be eating with us anyway. Can I help you with something else?"

"Well, I have this big pan of roasted corn on the cob and—"

Dwight Stoner and Mike Takahara immediately disappeared into the house.

"Bobby, do you have any idea what you're actually going to do with 640 acres and four hundred cows, more or less?" Henry Lightstone asked reasonably when Stoner and Takahara reappeared holding two huge foil-wrapped pans and with big grins on their faces. Susan LaGrange followed closely behind with another heaping bowl of salad.

"Well, according to my neighbors, who've been doing this sort of thing ever since God made sunsets," Bobby LaGrange commenced describing the nitty-gritty of ranching, "every year or so, my foreman and I hire ourselves a couple of trusty cowhands, saddle up the horses, ride out on the range, round up everything that looks like a cow, herd them into the corral, separate the big ones from the little ones, whack the balls off all the new guys, brand everything in sight with a bare butt, turn everybody loose, and go back to the house for a beer. Which reminds me" —LaGrange reached into the nearby cooler and pulled out a pair of dripping bottles—"anybody ready for more wine?"

"Allow me," Larry Paxton volunteered, taking the bottles and holding them carefully in his scarred hands.

"Somebody better help him with the corks," Mike Takahara advised. "I don't think he knows how to open anything without a pull tab."

"Have you know I can drink fine Oregon Chardonnay with the best of them." Larry Paxton popped the cork on the first bottle and sniffed appreciatively. "Fact is, I may never leave this place. You real fond of that foreman, Bobby?"

Susan LaGrange stuck her head out of the kitchen window. "Before everybody starts eating," she announced with a grin, "save some room because I've got two apple pies cooling on the deck."

"Forget it, Paxton," Dwight Stoner warned in a deadly serious voice once he spotted the pies. "Anybody around this table gets to retire to this piece of heaven, it's gonna be me."

"I don't know, Bobby." Mike Takahara looked at their host. "If you're gonna have to pay Stoner in free meals, you'd better get that bull back into production real quick-like."

While Paxton poured the wine, they all helped themselves to the corn on the cob, baked potatoes, and salad, while Bobby LaGrange distributed the steaks, thoughtfully dropping two of the huge chunks of mildly charred meat onto Dwight Stoner's plate.

For about ten minutes, only the sounds of clattering silverware and pure unadulterated satisfaction accompanied the disappearance of a sizable amount of food.

Finally, Henry Lightstone put down a thoroughly cleaned ear of corn and turned to Susan LaGrange.

"Susan, I hate to be the one to break this to you, but Bobby and I grew up on fifth-of-an-acre suburban lots in El Cajon. Closest we ever came to livestock was the local meat market and our neighbor's Great Dane. Fact of the matter is, your husband wouldn't recognize a cattle ranch if he tripped over a branding iron and fell facefirst into a cow patty."

"Been there, done—" Susan LaGrange started to say, and then ducked a handful of thrown olives. "Hey, don't blame me, buddy boy," she protested cheerfully. "Who was it who said you were losing your mind when you first started talking about moving to Oregon and buying a ranch and a canoe with the insurance money?"

"All true," Bobby LaGrange admitted. "But the way I look at it, we're a hundred miles from the nearest ocean, and that pond out there is only six feet deep. So if anybody takes it into their mind to try to blow up my canoe with a wheelbarrow full of C-4, I ought be able to wade to shore without having to fight off a goddamned hammerhead shark or damn near drowning in the process. So as long as Bravo Team, Division of Law Enforcement, U.S. Fish and Wildlife Service stays the hell out of Oregon,

I ought to make out just fine. Which reminds me," he added suspiciously, "just what the hell *are* you guys doing in Oregon?"

"You really don't want to ask that question right about now," Dwight Stoner warned as he gratefully accepted another baked potato and a large helping of salad from Susan LaGrange.

"He's right," Thomas Woeshack agreed, waving his half-eaten ear of corn. "Liable to make you sick. I used to eat raw whale blubber for breakfast every morning, and I don't even want to think about it."

"Are you sure you want to hear about this during dinner, with Susan here . . . ?" Henry Lightstone let the statement trail off meaningfully.

"That does it." Susan LaGrange grabbed an ear of corn from the tray and aimed it at Lightstone's head. "I've spent the last twenty years listening to you guys talk about ninety-three different categories of dead bodies and every depraved sexual behavior known to man, woman, and beast, so give. What *are* you guys doing out here?"

"Okay" — Lightstone shrugged agreeably — "you asked for it."

And he told them.

"Mother of God," a decidedly pale Bobby LaGrange whispered after his former partner finished.

"Seven hundred and fifty giant spiders?" Susan LaGrange gasped. If anything, she looked even paler than her husband.

The entire covert team nodded glumly.

"I think that's just . . . horrible." Susan's maternal instincts automatically kicked in. "How can they make you do something like that? If that was me, I'd . . . I'd crawl into my bed and pull the covers over my head."

"Don't think we haven't considered that," Lightstone commented dryly.

"Hey, maybe if you talked to our boss," Dwight Stoner suggested hopefully.

"I take back everything I said about you guys." Bobby LaGrange shuddered. "Give me that hammerhead, any day of the week."

"But what will you do if one of those snakes bites you?" Susan LaGrange couldn't have looked more stricken if she'd found herself serving dinner to a bunch of war orphans.

"Well, since we haven't received any of the antivenins we ordered yet, I guess we'd just drive like hell to the nearest hospital," Mike Takahara replied.

"Oh no, you're not!" Larry Paxton declared emphatically. "Ain't nobody gonna be driving to no damned hospital 'til we get all them things out of those boxes and into those terrariums, I don't care who gets bit by what. I'm telling you, I ain't gonna be the last one standing in that warehouse while all the rest of you crybabies are driving like hell to God knows where just because some little-bitty snake looked at you sideways."

"Got any ideas how to fake a snakebite?" Stoner asked Mike Takahara, pausing halfway down a butter-drenched ear of corn.

The tech agent nodded. "Several."

"Good. We'll talk later."

"But . . . how in the world are you ever going to get those things into all those terrariums?" Susan LaGrange asked.

"We have no idea," Larry Paxton confessed. "Been thinking about trying to feed them through the airholes."

"Actually, that's not entirely true." Dwight Stoner smiled cheerfully over at Henry Lightstone. "One of us happens to be blessed with very quick reflexes, so we figure if the rest of us'll just go outside and nail the warehouse doors shut—"

"Hey, don't look at me," Henry Lightstone protested. "I'm not the one who pissed Halahan off—"

"Oh yes you are," Larry Paxton retorted. "You're the one who kissed that new agent gal and rubbed yourself all over her body."

"Henry, I'm ashamed of you." Susan's eyebrows rose in interest as she turned to Paxton. "I want to hear all the details. Every one of them," she emphasized.

"We're ashamed of him, too," the covert team leader assured her. "Which is exactly why we're not about to let him wander around the town trying to buy up all the Bigfoot souvenirs in Oregon while the rest of us are . . ."

"Bigfoot?" Susan LaGrange blinked. "You're investigating people who sell Bigfoot souvenirs, Henry?"

"And Indian battle charms," Thomas Woeshack reminded his superior.

Lightstone and Paxton nodded glumly.

"But how can you investigate people for killing a Bigfoot?" Susan LaGrange asked reasonably. "They're mythical beasts."

"Actually, it's a long story," Henry Lightstone sighed, "but—"

Susan LaGrange looked over at her husband. "Should we tell them?"

"No, absolutely not."

Henry Lightstone looked back and forth between his two longtime friends.

"Tell us what?" he asked suspiciously.

"It's nothing," Bobby dismissed the subject quickly. "Just rancher stuff. You know, bullshit and cowshit, and crazy old coots you find wandering the back forty. Nothing you'd be interested in."

Lightstone looked back at Susan again. "He knows something about this, doesn't he?"

"Susan, I'm warning you . . ."

"I'll tell you all about that agent gal—especially the body-rubbing stuff," Lightstone promised.

"Deal." Susan LaGrange grinned victoriously at her husband and turned to Lightstone. "What your ex-partner doesn't want to tell you is that tomorrow morning he plans to buy a genuine Apache Indian battle charm, and maybe even a piece of Bigfoot fur to—get a load of this—ward off evil ranching spirits."

Henry Lightstone blinked, then smiled broadly.

"An Apache Indian battle charm, and a piece of Bigfoot fur . . . to ward off *what*?"

"Evil ranching spirits." His hostess grinned cheerfully. "See, I told you he was losing his mind."

"Hey, wait a minute . . . !" Larry Paxton started to protest, but Henry Lightstone waved him off.

"Oh no, I want to hear more about this." Henry Lightstone turned to his ex–homicide detective partner. "Come on, Bobby, 'fess up. Just who do you intend to buy all these spiritual goodies from?"

Bobby LaGrange glared at his wife. "I think I'm gonna need a lawyer."

"Hey, buddy boy, I'm all the lawyer you're ever going to need, and don't you ever forget it," Susan LaGrange retorted. "And to answer your question, Special Agent Lightstone," she said, turning to Henry, "he's meeting some crazy old coot at the local pancake house tomorrow morning at 8:00 A.M. sharp."

"And he really thinks these things will ward off evil ranch spirits?" Mike Takahara asked.

"Ask him." Susan LaGrange shrugged dramatically.

"Hey, if you'd been up in that tree for three hours before anyone bothered to come out and see if you were okay—" Bobby LaGrange retorted defensively.

"I'd be nailing a whole damned Bigfoot hide to that tree, right alongside the bull," Stoner agreed, nodding between mouthfuls of baked potato and steak.

"Us Eskimos usually just nail a walrus penis bone to the door," Thomas Woeshack volunteered graciously. "That usually works pretty good, too, especially once they start getting ripe."

"Uh, this crazy old coot." Henry Lightstone pursued the subject of his greatest interest carefully. "You wouldn't happen to know his name, would you?"

"You mean old Sage, the soothsayer? I'm not sure." Susan LaGrange looked over at her husband. "Do we know his real name?"

If anything, Henry Lightstone's smile grew even broader as he turned to Larry Paxton, who looked totally stricken.

"Tomorrow morning, 8:00 A.M. sharp, at the local pancake house," he repeated cheerfully. "Good old Sage, the soothsayer. Talk about a once in a lifetime opportunity. Can you believe it? My buddy, the illegal wildlife dealer, saves the day again."

"What do you mean, illegal wildlife dealer?" Bobby LaGrange demanded.

"How the hell does he do that?" Mike Takahara asked Woeshack and Stoner plaintively.

"Karma?" Thomas Woeshack suggested.

"Nah, just plain dumb luck," Stoner grumbled.

"Lightstone, if you think you're gonna bail out on us on account of some stupid-ass coincidence," Paxton warned his wild-card agent darkly, "you can just . . ."

"No, no, wait a minute," Henry interrupted, holding up his hand. "Halahan's briefing document, page twenty-nine, and I quote from memory: 'Special Agent Lightstone will endeavor to determine subject Sage's source of materials, as well as any links he may have with other illicit wildlife parts and products dealers in the area.'"

He smiled smugly at his fellow agents around the table. "The way I just heard it, it certainly sounds to me like we just tripped across one of the Sage's primary dealers. A cattle rancher, right in the middle of Jasper County, Oregon. Who would have thought it?"

"Wait a minute, I don't think—" Paxton started to say, but Lightstone quickly interrupted again.

"'Course, I suppose I could always call Halahan and tell him that I'd really like to obey his direct order, but my boss insists that I help stuff a bunch of harmless little spiders into some little glass terrariums instead."

"I am not a crook," Bobby LaGrange muttered darkly.

"Sure you are, honey. Just not a very good one." Susan LaGrange gave her husband a sympathetic pat on the shoulder. "After all, look at the kind of people you associate with."

"Yeah, you've got a point there."

"Now then, Susan"—Lightstone beamed cheerfully at his former partner's wife—"since it doesn't look like I'll need my quick reflexes tomorrow after all, do you think I could have an extra big slice of that delicious apple pie?"

Chapter Eighteen

At precisely eight o'clock that Wednesday morning, Henry Lightstone and Bobby LaGrange entered the pancake house, stood inside the doorway, and looked around.

"You see him?" Lightstone asked.

"Yeah, the guy with the ratty beard and dark glasses in the back booth, next to the rest rooms." Bobby LaGrange nodded toward the rear of the restaurant.

"This the same crazy old fart who's supposedly blind, but rides a motorbike all over town?"

"Uh-huh." A pained expression darkened Bobby LaGrange's tanned features even more. "You sure we've got to go through with this, Henry?"

"You'd rather go over to the warehouse and help Larry figure out how to transfer 750 giant tarantulas and about thirty poisonous snakes into a couple hundred glass terrariums?"

"Yeah, right, never mind," LaGrange muttered as they walked toward the booth.

The Sage greeted Bobby LaGrange warmly.

"You brought a friend?" he noted the obvious as he motioned the two men to the opposite bench where Wintersole had sat the previous morning.

"He's an old school buddy of mine," LaGrange explained as they sat down. "Henry, Sage. Sage, Henry."

The two men nodded at each other.

"I told Henry about how we met at my ranch last weekend, and about those Indian battle charms you said you could get," Bobby LaGrange went on easily. "Figured you wouldn't mind if I brought along another potential customer."

"I'm always interested in trying to help fellow travelers in this terribly confusing world." The old man lifted his dark glasses and appraised Lightstone with his squinting, red-streaked eyes. "Do you believe in ancient superstitions, Henry?"

Lightstone shrugged. "I believe there's a whole bunch of things we don't understand. And my luck's certainly been down lately. Running across Bobby after twenty-some years is about the best thing that's happened to me since my girlfriend took off. So I figured, what the hell, an Indian battle charm might help some, and it sure as hell can't make things any worse."

"Things are never as they seem, but they can always be better than they are," the Sage replied wisely.

"You know"—Lightstone smiled—"my grandmother used to say things like that."

"Really?" The old man leaned forward in the booth with his thin arms wrapped protectively around his cup and saucer. "Was she a seer?"

"A what?"

"A seer—someone who sees glimpses of the future," the Sage explained.

"I have no idea. All I know is that she used to tell me stories about good and evil spirits."

"The ancient stories. Good against evil. Light against darkness," the old man whispered excitedly.

"Yes, that's exactly it," Lightstone replied, instinctively going with the flow of the conversation. "She talked about how the spirits were in balance, harmony—I think she called it—like the day and the night, one following the other into eternity . . . except—"

"Yes?" The Sage leaned forward so eagerly he seemed ready to pounce on Lightstone's next words.

"I don't know. It's been a long time." Lightstone smiled apologetically. "As I recall though, she said some kind of disaster would occur if anything ever destroyed the balance. The darkness could gain strength and overwhelm the light. She called it something, but I can't—"

"The Apocalypse?" the Sage whispered hopefully.

Henry Lightstone smiled, this time in apparent recognition.

"That's it, the Apocalypse. That's what she called it, too." He stared above the Sage's head at nothing, as if remembering something from his distant past. "Man, I'd forgotten all about those stories. You bring back some interesting memories."

"Your grandmother was a seer," the old man stated flatly. "Which means you possibly received the Gift as well."

"Really?" Lightstone eyed the old man skeptically. "I don't have any sense of that—being able to see the future."

"No, of course not." The old man quickly glanced around the restaurant and lowered his voice. "You wouldn't be aware of it, until something—or someone—awakens the spirit within you. And even then, you would only see glimpses. We're never allowed to see the whole truth."

Then, for thirty seconds or so, he seemed lost in thought, leaving the other two men to sit in silence.

"So, you think a genuine Apache Indian battle charm might help me make peace with my ranch spirits, and get my buddy's life back on track?" LaGrange finally pressed the old man gently.

The Sage appeared to rouse himself out of a deep trance.

"Oh yes, without a doubt." He spoke hesitantly at first, but his voice gradually grew stronger. "Unfortunately, my sources at the reservation couldn't talk a very stubborn woman out of the particular charm I wanted for you." He shrugged his narrow shoulders. "It happens sometimes. Most of the Apache women will usually sell their family artifacts for a reasonable amount. But every now and then—" He held his wrinkled hands out as if to say, "What can you do?"

"Do you think she's holding out for a better price?" LaGrange asked.

"I really don't think so, but I suppose that's always possible," the Sage conceded. "If you like, I can offer her more. Would you be willing to go as high as three hundred dollars?"

"For my buddy to change his luck? Hell, yes," Bobby LaGrange volunteered expansively.

"Oh." The old man blinked in surprise. "I didn't realize you intended to buy a bear charm for your friend, too . . ."

Without warning, he reached forward, took Lightstone's right wrist, pulled it toward him, and traced each of the major lines in the covert agent's palm with a wrinkled forefinger.

As Lightstone observed the process patiently, the old man's eyebrows suddenly furrowed.

Mumbling to himself, the Sage quickly retraced three of the lines. Still not satisfied, he pressed his fingertips firmly against Lightstone's knuckles and wrist, as if trying to judge strength and flexibility.

Finally, he released the agent's hand, sat back in the booth, and shook his head.

"I'm sorry, Henry," he spoke with what sounded like genuine regret while staring into Henry Lightstone's eyes through the dark lenses. "Your friend is a generous man, but the bear-claw necklace is not for you."

"Why not?" The federal wildlife agent felt his heart sink as he sensed his link to the Sage—and his miraculous last-minute escape from Halahan's malicious sense of humor—slipping from his grasp.

"You don't have a bear spirit," the old man announced with certainty.

"I don't?"

"Definitely not."

"But what—" Lightstone started to ask, but the Sage cut him off.

"When you were a child, did you have any pets?"

"Ah . . . I recall a dog or two. Tell you the truth, I really didn't pay much attention to them."

"But you have no animals now—no pets?"

Lightstone shook his head.

The Sage closed his eyes behind his dark glasses and rocked back and forth in his bench seat as he apparently digested this information. Suddenly he smiled, opened his eyes, and stared directly at Henry Lightstone.

"Did your grandmother own any animals?" the old man inquired softly.

It shocked Henry when the memory came back so quickly and vividly.

"An old black Manx used to hang around, but I wouldn't say she owned it."

"Then there's your answer." The Sage smiled in satisfaction.

"I . . . don't follow," Lightstone admitted hesitantly.

"You're a cat."

The revelation bothered Henry Lightstone far more than he thought it should.

"I beg your pardon?"

"Not literally, of course." The old man smiled understandingly. "You simply possess a cat spirit."

"I do?"

Bobby LaGrange burst into a brief fit of coughing that Lightstone thought sounded suspiciously like barely controlled laugher.

"Yes, of course you do. Didn't you know?"

"I guess I never thought much . . . about it," Lightstone confessed, starting to wonder if escaping warehouse duty for a day was worth all of the harassment he could expect to receive from his retired homicide detective buddy over the next few years.

"It's nothing you have to think about, or do anything about, for that matter," the Sage explained soothingly. "It's simply there for your use — if you choose to use it. Not everyone does."

"Well, uh, if a bear-claw necklace won't help my friend," Bobby LaGrange made an attempt to keep the conversation focused on the potential evidence, or at least what he thought might be potential evidence, "how about one of those Bigfoot artifacts you told me about?"

The old man cocked his head, stared into Henry Lightstone's eyes again for a few moments, and smiled.

"Do you know how to find the Dogsfire Inn?" he asked. "It's a small restaurant, post office, and community center at the intersection of Brandywine Road and Loggerhead Creek."

Henry Lightstone looked over at Bobby LaGrange, who shrugged, then nodded.

"We can find it," Lightstone replied.

"Not both of you. Just you," the old man insisted emphatically.

"Why would I want to do that?"

"Don't you wish to explore your cat spirit?"

"I'm not sure," Henry Lightstone responded after a particularly uneasy delay. "But I will admit you've made me curious."

"If you want to satisfy that curiosity, be at the Dogsfire Inn at four o'clock today," the Sage ordered as he pulled himself out of the booth. "There's somebody there you should meet."

Chapter Nineteen

At precisely 9:35 A.M., eastern standard time, that Wednesday morning, Simon Whatley hurried into the private sanctuary of Congressman Regis J. Smallsreed, and was surprised to encounter not one but two visitors—one of whom sat in the shadows of Smallsreed's spacious congressional office.

"About time you got here, Simon," the congressman commented dryly.

"Delayed flight," Whatley explained, deciding to save his comments about absurd red-eye flights from Medford, Oregon, through San Francisco and on to Washington Dulles with long stopovers in Chicago. He always hated such flights, especially on short notice, but he particularly hated them when all of their first-class seats were booked, and he found himself crammed in with parents traveling with small children, all of whom spent all of their time screaming, crying, or running up and down the aisles.

All in all, the congressional district office manager had had a miserable night. And given the expression on Regis J. Smallsreed's face, Whatley sensed that the morning wasn't going to be much of an improvement.

"I believe you know Sam Tisbury, Chairman and CEO of Cyanosphere VIII." The congressman waved his hand in the general direction of his two guests.

One of Smallsreed's two visitors—the younger, more visible one—nodded his head in Whatley's direction, but didn't bother to get up.

"I don't believe you know our other visitor, so let's just keep it that way." Smallsreed gestured to an empty chair in front of his expansive desk. "Sit down, my boy."

As Simon Whatley sat, he realized that someone had adjusted the lighting in the room to illuminate him fully from all sides while leaving the other three men in the shadows. In fact, now he couldn't see the other visitor at all.

"I believe you have something to report?" Smallsreed prodded.

"Oh, uh, yes, I do," Whatley replied hurriedly. "I'm pleased to tell you that everything is in place. Our team and, uh—theirs," he hesitated, suddenly realizing that he knew nothing about Smallsreed's other visitor.

"You can speak freely here," the congressman snapped impatiently. "We all know each other."

You do, but I don't, Whatley thought uneasily, but continued on as ordered.

"We're in the process of establishing contact with the militant group. That should occur"—Whatley looked down at his watch—"about eight hours from now."

"Is this group credible?" Sam Tisbury directed his question at Smallsreed.

"Oh hell yes," the congressman responded. "I know several of these people personally, since we were kids. Some of them even kept in touch after they dug themselves into the hills—I get a letter from them every now and then, hoping I'll use my influence to help them with their agenda, I guess—and as far as I can tell, they're all still as rabid as ever."

"They may be rabid as fucking bats, but that doesn't necessarily make them credible," the wealthy industrialist pointed out.

"Sam, I can absolutely guarantee that these people hate the federal government and everything it stands for, and everybody in my district knows it, too," Smallsreed insisted emphatically. "No question about it."

"But do the people in your district consider them capable of taking on a team of federal agents?" Tisbury pressed. "I don't have to remind you, Regis, this whole exercise *must* be completely credible. If any one element looks the least bit suspicious, some goddamned journalist will start digging around asking questions. And if that happens, we're going to have an absolute disaster on our hands."

"Actually, we did anticipate the credibility problem," Simon Whatley offered hesitantly, uncomfortably aware that at least one of Smallsreed's guests had the power to order the deaths of a team of federal law-enforcement agents. He didn't even want to think about where he might stand if something went wrong.

"And?" Tisbury turned to face Smallsreed's underling.

"Well, after evaluating their, uh, offensive capability, we decided to provide them with better weapons."

"Oh really?" Tisbury's eyebrows rose. "Like what?"

"M-16 assault rifles. The earlier military version. Colonel Rustman, uh, 'arranged' the paperwork necessary to prove they disappeared from one of the local National Guard units several years ago. Our team will familiarize the militants with the weapons and let them get in a few practice rounds before we set the stage . . . make sure everything looks legitimate."

"Yes, very good, I like that." Sam Tisbury nodded approvingly. "And you're absolutely sure these agents are in place?"

"Well, uh . . ."

"*Goddamn it!*" the industrialist exploded. "You've got an informant, and it cost us a bundle to put her in place. *Use her!*"

"Uh, yes sir, I am—and, uh, they are. I mean, I know the agents are definitely in Jasper County," Simon Whatley stammered.

Even as he uttered the words, Whatley vaguely recalled some kind of discrepancy in the latest report from his informant. But he'd been racing around his apartment packing—in a hurry to make that damned red-eye—and didn't listen to the recorded messages all that carefully. Something about Bravo Team not working out as planned. But they were definitely *in* Jasper County, Oregon. He remembered that part clearly. That's all that mattered.

"Simon's also got some of his people in a position to provide us with all of the up-to-date intelligence we need," Smallsreed added cheerfully. "They'll make damned sure everybody's where they're supposed to be. Right, Simon?"

God I hope so, Whatley thought, feeling his stomach churn, but he said, "Yes sir, absolutely."

"We're going to need periodic reports, so we're absolutely certain everything goes according to plan. These agents caused the deaths of my father, my son, and my daughter," Tisbury reminded everyone in the room—as only a powerful third-generation industrialist who truly believed that his immense wealth and influence gave him the right to seek out vengeance on his own terms could remind them—"and they're going to pay for that. They are going to pay *dearly*."

"I would also remind you all that we lost six of the founding members of ICER." The unfamiliar, deep, and very foreboding voice that rumbled from the back recesses of the room startled Simon Whatley. "Until we can reestablish the committee with individuals of equivalent power, influence, and ideology, the environmental extremists will continue to run amok. These agents caused us to suffer tremendous setbacks. That must stop, immediately!"

"And it will stop," Regis J. Smallsreed promised. "You have my word on that."

"And the reports?" Tisbury pursued his main point of interest.

"I can fax you a daily briefing, along with—" Simon Whatley began, but Tisbury quickly interrupted.

"No faxes. No written reports. And especially no phone calls," he ordered sharply. "I am not about to find myself in federal prison because of some goddamned wiretap, and I assume everyone in this room feels exactly the same way. I want comprehensive verbal reports every two days, preferably here in this office."

"That's not a problem," Smallsreed agreed affably.

"But—" Simon Whatley tried to protest, but the congressman ignored him completely.

"Simon will be here at, oh, let's say 10:00 A.M. sharp—just in case that red-eye gets delayed again," Smallsreed added with a wink, "every other day, starting this coming Friday. No notes, no reports, no phone calls. Just the four of us in this room. And I can assure you it will be a sorry day if any federal agent ever even thinks about bugging this office."

"But—" Whatley tried again, but no one in the room paid him the slightest bit of attention.

"And keep him out of first-class," Tisbury added. "Make the reservations under different names, randomized locations in the back cabin, inside seats whenever possible, pay in cash, and have somebody else pick up the tickets. I don't want some sharp-eyed stewardess or airport clerk with a good memory for faces wondering why he's making all these red-eye flights to DC."

"No problem." Smallsreed bobbed his massive head agreeably.

"Traveling back and forth like that, will he have enough time to sleep, and still get fully briefed at the other end?" came the ominous voice from the shadows.

"Oh hell yes," Smallsreed replied confidently. "Simon's one of those people you can depend on to get the job done. He'll get all the sleep he needs on the plane."

At 11:30 A.M., eastern standard time, David Halahan, Chief of the U.S. Fish and Wildlife Service's Special Operations Branch, poked his head in his deputy chief's office door.

"Any more word on Boggs?" he asked.

Freddy Moore shook his head.

"We've got everybody on Charlie Team except Donato, LiBrandi, and Marashenko combing the town. Figured we'd better hold those three back in reserve, just in case Boggs doesn't show and we need to make our own contacts with those Chosen Brigade of the Seventh Seal folks."

"What about his house?" Halahan asked. "Anybody look inside?"

"Not yet. I told them to hold off on that on account of the neighbors. Wilbur's got the whole damned place alarmed, and LiBrandi's the only one on Charlie Team who's been through lock school."

"What about at night?"

"LiBrandi's willing to give it a try, but if that alarm goes off, that means dealing with the local cops, any one of whom could have relatives in the militant group. There's a good chance he could badge his way out of it, especially if the locals know Wilbur, but that would still cut us down to Donato and Marashenko for the contact work."

"Okay," Halahan agreed with his deputy, "tell them to keep looking." He started to leave, then turned back.

"What about Bravo Team?"

Freddy Moore looked at his watch.

"Based on the e-mail report they sent last night, I think we can assume that Bravo Team has more than enough to keep them fully occupied for the next twenty-four hours or so."

Chapter Twenty

"I've got a bad feeling about this," Mike Takahara murmured softly as he put down the battery-powered sander and wiped the sawdust off his face.

"What do you *mean* you've got a bad feeling?" Larry Paxton demanded. "You're the one who designed the damned thing."

"Yeah, but—"

"Didn't you ever build things with your dad when you were a kid? You know, birdhouses, Tinkertoys, Legos, things like that?"

"Yeah, sure, but everything we built always fell apart," the tech agent confessed.

Special Agent Dwight Stoner muttered something under his breath, then walked to the rear of the rental car parked next to a huge stack of crates, boxes, and bags containing an assortment of terrariums, specially designed terrarium lids, terrarium lights, extension cords, junction boxes, several dozen rolls of silvered duct tape, boxes of crickets and mice, snake bags, snake hooks, snake tongs, nets, gravel, mouse food, water dishes, four heavy-duty plastic swimming pools about eighteen inches deep and six feet in diameter, and a full-size chest freezer that was delivered earlier that morning.

After grabbing a pair of the long-handled snake hooks, Stoner opened the trunk, removed a Model 870 Remington 12-gauge pump shotgun, a box of shells, a small ice chest, and a fire extinguisher. Then he closed the trunk, walked back over to the mind-numbing stack of seventy-two brightly labeled 2'×4'×1' wooden crates in the middle of the team's leased warehouse, and handed the fire extinguisher to Thomas Woeshack, the ice chest to Mike Takahara, and the snake hooks to Larry Paxton.

The Bravo Team leader eyed the shotgun inquisitively.

"Bird shot," Stoner explained as he fed five of the low-based cartridges into the shotgun's extended magazine. "Way I see it, anything starts to walk, crawl, or slither out of that contraption, one of three things is going to happen. Either you're going to catch it, Woeshack's going to freeze it, or I'm going to kill it. End of story."

"Can we do that?" Thomas Woeshack asked, looking confused as usual.

"Oh yeah, no problem."

The expression on Dwight Stoner's face clearly indicated that any discussions about proper enforcement of the Endangered Species Act—as it applied to poisonous snakes and giant red-kneed tarantulas trapped with him in a warehouse—would have to wait for a better day.

"Well, at least we know Halahan cares about our welfare," Mike Takahara reported after he opened the ice chest and removed a plastic-sealed reference card marked in bright colors.

"Just because the man sends us a whole bunch of expensive snakebite serum by overnight mail doesn't necessarily mean he cares," Larry Paxton countered reasonably. "He's probably just covering his butt in case the Washington Office ever gets wind of this operation."

"Well, according to this, he bought us just about every poisonous snake antivenin known to man." Takahara examined the contents of the chest. "Yep, everything's in color-coded syringes, ready to go. Something goes wrong, all we need to do is figure out who got bit by exactly what kind of snake . . ."—he gestured toward the small library of reference books that came with the emergency snakebite kit—"match up the codes, inject the right syringe in the immediate area of the bite, and we'll probably be okay—provided we get to the hospital in time. Everyone clear on that?"

"Not my problem," Dwight Stoner announced as he dumped the remaining shotgun shells in his coat pocket. "I've got twenty-five rounds of bird shot and twelve rounds of 10mm hollow-points in my Smith. Halahan may need to find some more snakes, and you guys might have to dig bird shot out of your butts, but I'm not getting bit, period. End of discussion."

"Me neither." Thomas Woeshack solemnly nodded in agreement.

Takahara contemplated the jury-rigged contraption that he and Woeshack had spent the morning building with six four-by-eight sheets of three-quarter-inch plywood, six eight-foot-long two-by-fours, approximately 240 drywall screws, two wing bolts, and $1232.00 worth of assorted power tools, all charged to one of Halahan's Special Ops credit cards. In short, they had designed, built, and charged to the government what amounted to a large wooden funnel onto whose top they could lower and secure an unopened crate, hopefully safely open it, and dump its inhabitants into the prepared terrarium below.

"Well, now that we've got the basics worked out," Larry Paxton snorted sarcastically in the direction of the team's visibly nervous tech agent, "you ready to get started?"

"Not really, but . . ."

"Like jumping into a lake of ice-cold water in the middle of winter," Paxton assured him. "If you're dumb enough to do it in the first place, you might just as well hop in and get it over with."

"Was that supposed to be inspirational?" Takahara asked.

"As inspirational as it's gonna get until things start looking up around here," the Bravo Team leader replied. "Okay, Thomas, you pick up one of those terrariums over there, take the lid off, let Stoner fill the bottom with gravel, and then you slide it under the funnel . . ."

Paxton stopped talking while Woeshack carefully set the extinguisher down, removed a terrarium from one of the twelve-by-eighteen-by-twenty-four-inch cardboard boxes, set the lid aside, waited while Dwight Stoner carefully poured a half-inch layer of small gray stones into the bottom, slid the terrarium into the lower slot of Mike Takahara's thoughtfully designed device, locked it in place at both open ends with sections of two-by-four, and then hurried back to the extinguisher.

"Now, Mike, you and I will start with this box, number twenty-three, 'cause it's got screening over the airholes, so we don't have to worry about something getting at us through the holes . . ." Paxton motioned to one of brightly labeled wooden crates on top of the stack.

"First we cut the bands off." He used a pair of metal snips to sever the tightly cross-wrapped steel bands.

"Then we lift it up." Paxton set the snips and cut bands aside, then he and Takahara carefully lifted the heavy crate off the stack.

"And place it in the frame right . . . there."

The heavy wooden crate dropped into Takahara's makeshift apparatus with a satisfying thunk, causing its inhabitants to thrash around in what—as best the agents could tell through the screened airholes—looked like shredded paper.

"I can't believe Newark didn't send us a description of contents," Larry Paxton complained. "You'd think if somebody went to the trouble of numbering the damned boxes in the first place, they could've made a goddamned list, too, while they were at it. You see anywhere on the box where it says what's in this one?" the supervisory agent asked hopefully.

"Not unless they renamed a species Danger, Hot Snakes, or Hazardous Cargo," Takahara replied as he carefully inspected the wooden container from all angles.

"Okay, no problem." Larry Paxton's face had taken on a decidedly glossy sheen in the cold warehouse. "Now we lower the box and the frame just like so . . ."

Working slowly and carefully, Paxton and Takahara carefully released the wing nuts and slowly lowered the jig holding the crate to a point just barely above the top of the wooden funnel.

"All right, now tighten everything back up," Paxton ordered. The two agents carefully retightened the wing nuts. Then Paxton sighed heavily.

"Okay, now comes the fun part."

The sound of a low-based bird-shot round being jacked into the chamber of an 870 pump shotgun echoed throughout the warehouse, causing Larry Paxton to flinch, then glare at his huge subordinate agent. Then he turned to Takahara.

"You ready?"

"Oh sure. Anytime," Mike Takahara croaked dryly.

Stoner set the shotgun within easy reach and leaned forward to hold the top of the crate in place with his two huge hands, while Woeshack moved in with the fire extinguisher. Paxton and Takahara each picked up one of the battery-powered variable-speed drills fitted with Phillips screwdriver bits, and stretched out on the concrete floor on either side of Takahara's makeshift apparatus.

The design allowed just enough room on the outside of the wood funnel to get at the screws that held the bottom of the crate in place . . . which meant a gap slightly in excess of three-quarters of an inch would exist between the sides of the crate and the edges of the funnel when they slid the bottom of the crate out of the way—an issue that generated several hours of emotional discussion until Mike Takahara finally convinced the rest of the team that a three-quarter-inch board couldn't possibly move through anything less than a three-quarter-inch space.

But the unresolved point was whether any of the inhabitants of the seventy-two wooden crates would want to—and more to the point, could—squeeze through a three-quarter-inch space and either escape or attack, rather than cooperatively drop into a nice, clean, gravel-filled terrarium.

Hence Woeshack's fire extinguisher and Stoner's shotgun.

Paxton and Takahara had backed out the first pair of wood screws halfway when the sudden thrashing inside the crate caused both of them frantically to roll away while Stoner lunged for the shotgun.

"I think I'm gonna have a heart attack," Larry Paxton commented to no one in particular as he lay on the concrete floor with his eyes closed.

"Don't forget, I was the one who said somebody's gonna get bit," Woeshack whispered nervously to Stoner, who nodded and glared pointedly at the Bravo Team leader.

Eight minutes and several frazzled nerves later, Paxton and Takahara removed the last two screws holding the bottom of the crate in place, and the last portion of the three-quarter-inch plywood piece dropped a six-teenth of an inch onto the top of the wooden funnel.

"Okay," Mike Takahara murmured softly. "Now it gets interesting."

Larry Paxton glowered at his tech agent. "Well, thank God for that! I was afraid I was gonna fall asleep out of sheer boredom."

Ignoring the sarcasm, Takahara picked up a carefully sanded two-foot-wide-by-three-foot-long piece of plywood. Working cautiously, he used it to push the bottom board of the crate until each covered half of the box.

The inhabitants of the crate stirred uneasily.

"Okay," Takahara whispered to Paxton, "grab the end of the other board, but don't do anything until I tell you."

As Larry Paxton gingerly took hold of the released portion of the crate, he felt the container's inhabitants shifting heavily on it.

Movement continued for several more seconds and then stopped.

Takahara looked at his fellow agents. "Everybody ready?"

The three men nodded with varying degrees of confidence.

"Okay" — Takahara's voice sounded omniously loud in the otherwise silent warehouse — "one . . . two . . . three , . . now!"

In the instant that Takahara and Paxton yanked their respective boards out from under the crate, two huge black snakes with bright red scales on their bellies plummeted into the terrarium with a loud thump and thrashed against the glass, causing Larry Paxton to scream "SHIT!" and lunge out of the way.

"Oh my God," Thomas Woeshack whispered, backing away quickly as he held the extinguisher in front of his body as if to ward off an evil spirit.

Dwight Stoner leveled the shotgun at the terrarium, and then watched uneasily as the huge snakes coiled their thick bodies around each other and began probing the glass with their stubby black noses.

"What the hell *are* those things?" Larry Paxton whispered.

"They kinda look like dwarf king cobras," Mike Takahara suggested uneasily.

"Whatever they are, they're too big for that terrarium," Dwight Stoner noted accurately.

At that moment, a loud pounding on the metal door of the warehouse startled all four agents.

Stoner, Woeshack and Takahara continued ogling the snakes while Larry Paxton cautiously approached the door, looked through the peep-hole, and disappeared outside.

Five long minutes later, he returned with a torn-open FedEx envelope and a clipped stack of papers in his hand.

"We get FedEx delivered to a brand-new covert ops site that *we* could barely find?" Mike Takahara cocked his head curiously.

Larry Paxton eyed them all dangerously as he nodded his head.

"It's from Jennifer. You want to hear it?"

Mike Takahara looked down at the two extremely thick-bodied snakes still probing the thin glass walls of the terrarium, then back up at the Bravo Team supervisor.

"I don't think so," he guessed, "but you'd better go ahead anyway."

" 'Dear guys,' " Paxton began reading. " 'I meant to send this with the shipment, but we got distracted trying to get all those damned things loaded up and out the door before Halahan changed his mind. Hope this gets to you before you open up any of those crates.' "

Paxton looked up to see if his audience was paying attention, and grimly noted that all three of them had immediately moved several feet farther away from Takahara's jury-rigged contraption and the two very large black snakes.

" 'If you've already started to unpack them, I hope you're all okay.' "

The three agents simultaneously closed in around their supervisor, backs to the door and facing the stack of crates and Takahara's snake-transfer device. In addition to Stoner's shotgun, both Woeshack and Takahara had their 10mm Smith & Wesson pistols out and ready.

" 'Knowing you guys,' " Paxton went on, " 'I'm sure you already figured out that the tarantulas go in the small terrariums, and the snakes go in the big ones. And by the way, it's probably a good idea to duct-tape all the lids down because the big snakes can pop them off pretty easily.' "

Paxton looked over at Woeshack.

"Hey, all those terrarium boxes looked the same to me," Thomas Woeshack defended himself as he disappeared behind the pile of boxes. Moments later, his head popped up.

"Good news, guys." The diminutive agent smiled brightly. "There's a whole bunch of bigger terrarium boxes back here, too."

Larry Paxton closed his eyes for a moment, nodded slowly, and continued reading the letter aloud.

" 'The caiman crocs are a separate problem entirely. I personally don't think those swimming pools we sent you are deep enough. The herpetologists we hired assured us they'd be fine for a while, but the damned things kept getting out anyway. I'm sure you'll figure something out. But they're a lot faster than you'd think, and mean little shits to boot, so watch your fingers when you pick them up.

" 'Knowing Mike, I'll bet he's already come up with some really clever way to open those crates and dump the contents into the terrariums without anybody getting bit.' "

Mike Takahara smiled. "Good old Jennifer, I always liked her."

"Yeah, well wait until you hear this part," Larry Paxton growled. " 'Something Mike might not have thought about, though. If you plan to rig the transfers so that the top or bottom part of the crate slides out of the way, remember that the tarantulas can easily squeeze through a three-quarter-inch gap. You'll really need to be ready when they do, because they're really fast little buggers.' "

"Jesus," Dwight Stoner whispered.

" 'Finally, be very careful handling the crates with the screened air-holes. We rigged those for the female snakes because a lot of them look like they're pregnant. That's not a problem with the egg-layers because you've got quite a bit of time before any eggs would hatch, even if they've laid them in the crates by now. But . . . ' " Paxton paused long enough to glower at his agent team meaningfully, " 'you've *really* got to be careful with crates seven and twenty-three . . . ' "

"Oh shit," Mike Takahara whispered.

" ' . . . because,' " the Bravo Team leader continued with a discernible edge to his voice, " 'there's a female tiger snake in crate seven and two female common blacksnakes in twenty-three. In addition to being damned poisonous, they're both ovoviviparous—which means they give birth to live babies instead of eggs—and the two blacksnakes look like they could pop any minute. None of us here know how big a newborn blacksnake is, but we suspect they probably wouldn't have any trouble getting through a three-quarter-inch-wide gap either. According to the literature, the average brood for common blacksnakes is twelve. My suggestion would be to do what we did and hire a couple of professional herpetologists, then go have a beer while they get everything unpacked and put away. But I guess you can't do that and maintain a covert operation in a little place like Loggerhead City, Oregon, huh? Well, good luck anyway. Jennifer.' "

Mike Takahara returned to his snake-transfer apparatus long enough to grab the pile of reference books, then beat a hasty retreat behind Stoner and his shotgun. Mumbling to himself, he rapidly thumbed through one titled *Australian Snakes—A Natural History.*

"Yep, here they are." The tech agent pointed to a photo. "Definitely common blacksnakes."

"That's all she said? 'Good luck'?" Dwight Stoner murmured incredulously.

Larry Paxton shook his head. "No, there's a PS." He handed the letter and the attached pages to Stoner.

"Hey, maybe it's not so bad, guys." Mike Takahara continued scanning the text. "It says here that the venom in the average bite of the most deadly snake in the world—the inland taipan—has a 218,000 LD_{50}, the tiger snake has 15,000, but the common blacksnake only has 700."

"What does that mean?" Thomas Woeshack asked.

"Beats me," the tech agent confessed. "I think the LD_{50} refers to the number of mice that the poison in one average snake bite would kill. But hey, we must have a bigger body mass than seven hundred mice, right?"

"Yeah, I guess," Woesack agreed uneasily. "But what about fifteen thousand for that tiger snake?"

Takahara scrunched his face as he mentally converted mouse to human mass. "Yeah, that might be more of a problem."

Dwight Stoner looked up from the letter and stared at Larry Paxton. "She's *got* to be kidding," he stated flatly.

"You got a better idea?"

"Uh-huh," Stoner volunteered immediately. "Burn the warehouse down and blame it on the gas heater."

Larry Paxton looked around the warehouse. "We don't have a gas heater," he observed.

"I'll install one."

"The problem is," the Bravo Team leader informed his reluctant crew and ignored Stoner's very serious offer, "if those things really *are* pregnant, and they . . . Hey!" A stricken look appeared on Larry Paxton's face. "Those snakes aren't moving anymore!"

"You know," Thomas Woeshack mused aloud as he and Stoner watched their two fellow agents cautiously approach the terrarium where the two thick-bodied blacksnakes now lay suspiciously still, "I wonder what Henry's doing right now."

Chapter Twenty-one

She became aware of their approach as she stood in the greenhouse examining the collection of exotic plants left by the previous occupant.

Two men. The one in the lead plodding, oblivious, doglike and familiar, and of only minor interest. The other fluid, casually aware, catlike, and much more intriguing.

Not to mention dangerous.

The Sage . . . and a stranger.

She deliberately placed herself in their path when she met them at the gate, annoyed because she'd told the old man she didn't want to see any more strangers for a while. Not after the last ones. The visit by Wintersole and his female—what?—companion had left her unsettled.

But not nearly as much as Wintersole's eyes. It took her a while to figure it out, but once she did it unnerved her completely. An unusual pale gray, just as the Sage had said. But more than that, a right eye paler than the left, so much so that the iris merged with the white sclera and the pupil stood out like an infinitely deep black hole. The difference between the two eyes made them appear to flicker and, no matter how hard she tried, she couldn't establish eye contact with him. She always found herself looking at one eye or the other or, much worse, somewhere between the two.

To think that he and I . . .

In spite of the warmth of the sunlight, she shivered.

Sasha doesn't trust him either, she thought as she moved toward the two men. *I wonder if this one will be different?*

To a casual observer, she appeared relaxed and outwardly pleased to see her visitors. However, beneath the loose-fitting tunic, she held her sinuous body tense, ready to strike at the first hint of aggression. After beaming a welcoming smile at the bearded old man, she focused all of her senses on the face and body language of the stranger.

"This is the one I told you about," the Sage declared by way of introduction, then stepped aside in his characteristic, clumsy manner, suddenly leaving her to confront the newcomer directly.

I know you.

The totally irrational awareness momentarily erased every other thought from her mind.

She instantly and instinctively averted her eyes and brought both hands up to control what she sensed was the stranger's dominant, striking hand reaching out toward her — clasping it in a moderately tight grip with her right hand and pressing her other hand firmly around his muscular wrist. In a single graceful motion, she pressed her upper torso against his to neutralize his brute male strength — and then brushed her lips across his cheek.

"I'm pleased to meet you at last." Her soft throaty whisper sounded perfectly poised and confident, as if she'd known him forever. However, her own reaction, as well as his — or rather, his complete lack of one — undermined her self-assurance.

He simply stood there.

But then, he wouldn't feel threatened or mindlessly stimulated, she reminded herself, *because he's not one of them.*

This second instinctive rather than rational thought that simply appeared out of her subconscious told her that this man — whoever and whatever he was — represented a terrible danger.

But also an intriguing opportunity.

For reasons he couldn't explain, Henry Lightstone also found himself instinctively on the alert, something he, too, found extremely confusing and disorienting when combined with his awareness of how much this sleek, sensual, and strikingly beautiful woman attracted him.

When he noticed her staring down at her hands, he glanced down and discovered—much to his amazement, because he had no memory of doing so—that he'd automatically brought his own hand up to encase her firm but much smaller wrist in a move that was somehow . . . defensive.

Confused and uneasy, and vaguely aware that she seemed equally uncomfortable, he looked up . . . and discovered much too late that she had done the same. For the first time during this almost surrealistic interval, his eyes met hers.

The effect was instantaneous and, in a blood-pounding and stomach-wrenching manner, almost hypnotic. He instantly knew that he had never seen—or even imagined—such a woman in his entire life.

What did she say? his mind struggled to remember. *I'm pleased to meet you at last? What does that mean?*

Alarm bells began clanging madly in the back of Henry Lightstone's head.

Who the hell are you, lady?

"Karla. Karla Pardus," she answered his silent question, unfortunately with a split-second hesitation that immediately caught his attention.

"Henry," he countered, instinctively deciding not to put forth a pseudonym just yet. His intuition, honed by years of working covert investigations in which it often served as his primary source of protection, warned him to get away as quickly as he could.

But other more primitive senses—curiosity, opportunity, and erotic fascination—urged him to stay.

"You said 'at last'?" He responded with forced lightheartedness, finding it impossible to turn away from the deeply alluring, gold-flecked green eyes highlighting an intriguing face that was, in some indefinable manner, both outdoorsy tough and sensuously enticing. "Does that mean you've been expecting me?"

"Of course, for some time now." She turned to lead the two men into the screened-in porch, a move that struck Lightstone as leaving her exposed and vulnerable for some unfathomable reason, but it didn't appear to bother her. "After all, I *am* a witch."

They sat at the table, sipped hot tea or chocolate, and conversed about matters of little consequence for almost an hour, allowing the Sage to guide the conversation in and around his favorite topics. As they talked, Henry Lightstone found himself progressively intrigued by the young woman's mannerisms: the way she sat, relaxed yet visibly alert; the way she moved, easily with almost feline grace; the way she smiled, tomboyish yet seductive; and especially the way she maintained contact—with her eyes, and with a light brush of warm fingers against his hand.

It all seemed so casual, warm and open when she did it, and yet she maintained a distance that took it—and her—out of the realm of mere flirtation.

He sensed that she gently probed his past with her occasional questions and brief comments that wove around the old man's rambling discourse. Periodically, though, a vacuum would arise in these parallel conversations that Lightstone felt compelled to fill, sometimes answering her questions, sometimes not. But her questions never threatened him, and she never pressed. Soon he found himself weaving threads of his cover through the fabric of both conversations as the opportunities arose.

He decided that she was the most self-confident woman he had ever met, and yet easily one of the most vulnerable.

Neither that realization nor his awareness of it made any sense at all.

He also became vaguely aware that the old man's ramblings increasingly gave way to periods of quiet mumbling and contemplation of the rough porcelain mug that the woman kept refilling from the thermos of hot chocolate. But because these gaps allowed him and the woman to continue their own conversation with less effort and interruption, he barely noticed.

Finally, the Sage slumped in his chair with his chin resting on his chest.

For a moment, it looked as though the old man had fallen asleep. But then, as if suddenly revitalized by a burst of energy, he sat upright, grabbed for his white walking stick, announced that he was late, and got up and hobbled toward the door.

"Guess I don't need to worry about our soothsayer trying to wrestle the check out of my hand." Lightstone laughed wryly as they watched the old man stagger to the pathway, secure his walking stick to the frame of his ancient motorbike, carefully place his dark glasses in his shirt pocket, strap on the large protective helmet, kick some life into the small motor, and putter down the road, trailing a billowing cloud of smoke.

The woman smiled. "If he ever does, you'd be wise to keep a very close eye on your wallet."

"A pickpocket as well as a con man?" Lightstone smiled, too. "Interesting fellow."

"But not exactly your type," the woman observed candidly. "How did the two of you meet?"

"Through one of my buddies." Lightstone recited a few of the well-rehearsed details related to his fictitious past with Bobby and Susan LaGrange without mentioning their names. "They bought a cattle ranch here a few months ago. Said if I was ever between jobs, I should visit." He smiled again. "I am, so I did."

"You met the Sage on a cattle ranch?" A curious expression swept across the woman's face.

"I didn't, my buddy did. It's kind of a strange deal," Lightstone admitted. "He's under the impression that he's got one of those mythical Bigfoot creatures living on his property."

"And you think the Sage has something to do with that impression?"

"It wouldn't surprise me a bit."

"And you don't believe in mythical beasts, do you?" The woman grinned mischievously.

Henry Lightstone hesitated, trying to decide if she was attempting to bait him.

"I try to keep an open mind about things I don't understand," he explained seriously. "But I also believe in human nature . . . especially the nature of humans like the Sage, who I suspect enjoy taking advantage of people who are more trusting than analytical."

"So you're more analytical?" She observed him with just a little more curiosity than he felt the situation warranted.

Lightstone shook his head. "Not really. I just remind myself that I'll fare a lot better if I cut the cards and count my change. And if somebody like the Sage offers to sell me a genuine good-luck charm made from a genuine mythical beast, I probably wouldn't pay top dollar."

"Yet you claim to maintain an open mind about things you don't understand?"

"I try."

The woman hesitated for a moment. "Do you need to leave now, too?"

The question caught Lightstone off guard, but he recovered immediately.

He smiled easily. "Like I said, I'm between jobs. My friends expect me home for dinner. Beyond that . . ." He shrugged.

The woman stood, the top of her sun-streaked hair rising to the level of his chin as she motioned toward the interior door. "Then come with me."

They walked into the restaurant portion of the house, the woman leading and Lightstone cautiously trailing slightly behind, sensing a certain tension in her walk and trying to ignore the curved and yet slender outlines of her body as her lush, firm thighs, hips, breasts, and shoulders alternately strained against the soft, thin cloth of her tunic . . . a moving vision that embodied, from Henry Lightstone's point of view, the definitive model of sleek and sensual grace.

After following a long narrow corridor lined with smooth logs, they went through a swinging door, turned right, then though another door — this one bolted and bearing a large PRIVATE DO NOT ENTER sign — and then, almost immediately, a second, double-bolted door.

Suddenly, Henry Lightstone found himself in a darkened room that would have been large and cavernous except for the presence of an enormous, ancient black oak growing up through the floor.

As they approached the huge tree, Lightstone realized that the trunk measured at least eight feet in diameter at the base, and its thick branches, beginning just above his head, extended outward and upward in all directions. The only illumination in the room came from a small shaded lamp that directed a small circle of light on a low table surrounded by three cushions, all arranged beneath one of the mammoth lower branches. Looking up, Lightstone realized that he couldn't see the ceiling — it simply disappeared into the tangle of branches extending some fifteen feet above his head.

For some inexplicable reason, that darkness overhead, like the woman, made him distinctly uneasy.

"Sit down." She motioned toward one of the cushions.

Lightstone glanced up at the dark void one last time, and then joined her, sitting cross-legged on the opposite side of the small table, noticing as he did so that the diffused light from the lamp, and the resulting shadows, seemed to enhance the erotic features of her now only vaguely tomboyish face. Once he settled himself, she opened a wooden chest on the table and removed something from it.

The object she placed in the circle of light between them looked like a crudely sawn-off chunk of fence post. On closer examination, Henry Lightstone observed what looked like a tuft of hair caught in a splintered portion of the wood.

"Do you see that?" she asked softly.

"You mean the hair?"

"Yes."

Lightstone paused.

"Are you going to tell me — ?"

"That your mythical beast might not be so mythical after all?" she asked in her soft, husky voice.

Henry Lightstone examined the tuft more closely and noticed the distinct reddish cast to the forty-odd twisted and crinkled hairs.

"How do you know — ?" he started to ask, but the woman had leaned forward to take something else from the chest.

Ignoring his question, she carefully plucked two of the hairs out of the tuft with a pair of forceps, and placed each one in separate small glassine envelopes. She then pressed one of the envelopes into the palm of his hand such that the warmth of her hand seemed to radiate up his arm, and then slipped the second envelope down inside her tunic between her breasts.

"I hate to even ask," he ventured after a long moment.

"Some say that the hair of a Sasquatch protects the one who holds it from the evil ones . . . but *only* if that person possesses a cat spirit and believes that it is so," she added meaningfully.

"And the other one that you—" he gestured in the general direction of her blouse.

She smiled. "Oh, that's just something that we witches do."

"Ah."

"Did you know," she added before Lightstone could comment further, "that the Sage truly believes that the Sasquatch—the creature who left his hair in that fence post—is his pet?"

"I guess he's not the type to settle for a dog, is he?"

A serious expression replaced her smile. "Now that you mention it, you don't strike me as the type who would settle for a dog either."

"Why not?"

"Fortune-teller's intuition."

"Ah."

"Ah, meaning you don't believe in fortune-telling?"

"Ah, meaning I'm always curious to find out how things work. Don't fortune-tellers read palms, or tarot cards, something like that?"

"Sometimes the paranormal takes many forms. I just sense the way things are," she explained seriously. "You look at a person and you know, for example, that they aren't the type to tie themselves down with a spouse, kids, dogs—all of whom require constant attention."

She smiled faintly. "You aren't, are you?"

It was a statement far more than a question.

"No wife or kids," Lightstone agreed, subliminally aware of those warning bells again.

"Of course not," she spoke confidently, as if confirming a well-known fact. "And surely no dogs either?"

Lightstone shrugged. "I grew up with them, and they were okay, I guess. I mean, they were affectionate enough. But they always seemed so dependent—like they didn't have a life of their own."

"So you never got a dog of your own when you left home?"

"Never felt any need to . . . especially since I never seem to stay put in one place for very long."

She nodded her head in apparent amusement, and he felt himself relax . . . only to be jerked back into alertness by her next question.

"Were you ever afraid of them?"

"Of what? Dogs?" Lightstone grinned, but his mind continued to analyze her critically. "Of course not."

"Even big scary ones?" A touch of disbelief edged her sensuous voice.

"You mean Dobermans, German shepherds, ones like that?"

"Or Rottweilers and pit bulls. Dogs bred for strength and aggressive behavior."

"No, not really," Henry informed her after considering the matter briefly. "I see it as a matter of self-confidence more than anything else.

Dogs sense if you're afraid of them. In my experience, if you're not, they usually back off."

"And if they don't?"

"I don't know, use brute force, I guess." Henry Lightstone shrugged. "I've never had that problem."

"What about cats?"

Lightstone cocked his head curiously. "You're asking if I'm afraid of cats?"

She nodded, her gold-flecked green eyes suddenly sparkling with what Henry Lightstone could only define as humor—a vision that effectively distracted him from the persistent uneasiness he'd felt since entering the strange room.

"I guess the truthful answer is that I've never seen one big enough to—" he began. But then a soft (but at the same time very heavy) thump behind his back caused him to whirl his head and shoulders and instinctively bring his hands up into a defensive position—then freeze when he found himself staring into a pair of half-lidded yellow eyes with tightly focused dotlike pupils set terribly far apart hovering in midair.

"—scare me," he finished in a hoarse whisper, as his own pupils dilated from adrenaline-induced shock when he realized why those incredibly hypnotic eyes appeared to hover.

"Don't move," she warned in an amazingly calm and soothing voice.

"Don't worry, I won't," he promised, but he did anyway, slowly, incrementally, relaxing his hands and bringing them down to rest flat on his crossed legs, because that seemed like the right thing to do.

"What is it," he whispered, truly amazed that he could form the words with his fear-numbed vocal cords.

"You'll see . . ."

Slowly his eyes grew accustomed to the dimness and he did see—the low forehead and partially flattened ears, the whitish orange whiskers that bristled on either side of the thick velvety muzzle . . . but most of all, the huge, muscular, silver-tinged blackness.

Oh my God.

Panther.

For a brief moment, Henry Lightstone believed that he was about to die a horrible death. His heart pounded in his chest, and some primitive portion of his mind screamed at him to run, fight, cover up, do *something*, before it was too late. But then, for some reason that he didn't comprehend at all, he sensed that the only partially flattened ears might be significant.

Don't move. No matter what, don't move.

He had no idea if he thought that, or someone—the woman? —actually said it.

But then, in a motion really too fast to see, the cat suddenly moved forward—lunged, actually—and heavy, leathery pads pinned Lightstone's hands to his legs, terribly sharp claws lightly dug into his wrists, and long whiskers brushed against his throat before the huge cat suddenly emitted a deep rumble and rubbed her forehead against his chin.

"Are you all right?" she asked sometime later—moments, hours, Lightstone had no idea—in that same calm, reassuring voice.

"I have a feeling that's completely up to him," Lightstone replied in a very quiet strangled voice.

"Her," the woman corrected him softly.

"Sorry, I didn't notice," Lightstone grimaced when the wickedly sharp claws dug deep into the backs of his hands each time the purring animal flexed her huge paws contentedly.

"That's all right, she did," the woman replied with an underlying edge of sarcasm that—to her amazement—bordered on bitchiness.

"Is it all right if I try to pet . . . her?" Lightstone asked, not at all certain he wanted to do anything whatsoever to disturb the cat's presumably benign behavior, but at the same time, very much aware of his extremely vulnerable position. He knew that at some point, if this cat were like every other cat he'd played with as a kid, it would suddenly and unpredictably do something different—which, he assumed, could easily include biting or clawing. He tried not to think about the impact of those terribly sharp claws on his soft and vulnerable skin.

The truly amazing part, Lightstone realized, was that he didn't feel afraid—at least not in the trembling, whimpering, bowel-voiding sense. If anything, he felt deeply and intensely intrigued. By both the cat, and the woman who apparently owned her.

"I think she'll let you"—the woman's voice carried a barely discernible edge that Lightstone picked up on immediately—"but take it slow. We're in unexplored territory here."

"What exactly does 'unexplored territory' mean?" he asked hesitantly.

"She's never done this before . . . with a stranger," the woman almost grudgingly admitted.

"Is that good, or bad?"

"I don't know. She's usually very predictable. That's why I'm concerned."

The woman grew silent, keeping her own hands firmly on her lap, watching the big cat rapturously rub her face over Lightstone's.

"Your left hand," she suggested softly to her guest. "Can you pull it free?"

"I don't think so."

Not unless I want to lose it, Lightstone thought as the powerful claws continued digging in to the point of not quite breaking through the skin on the backs of his hands.

"When I tell you," the woman directed in an almost hypnotizing voice, "raise your hand—the left one, not the right," she emphasized, "very gently, very slowly, but firmly . . . stay relaxed and maintain contact," she instructed him in that same smoothing voice, "then turn your hand and gently rub the pad of her paw with your thumb. Don't jerk away or make any other rapid movement, no matter how she reacts. Do you think you can do that?"

Henry felt himself relax in response to her voice.

"Yes."

"Then go ahead," she ordered calmly.

"Any suggestions what I should do if she doesn't like it?" Lightstone asked.

"Whatever you do, do *not* make any sudden movements," the woman repeated in that same calm and gentle voice. "She's perfectly capable of killing either one of us in a matter of seconds, if she wants to. But I imagine you already guessed that."

"Oh yeah, first thing," Lightstone whispered hoarsely.

"I have a control collar—a device that I can use to track or sedate her remotely if necessary—which she wears when I take her out in public. But as you've probably noticed, we're not out in public, so she's not wearing it right now."

"So how *do* you control her, if you have to?" Lightstone asked, having a good idea that he already knew the answer to that question.

"If it turns out that I can't control her with my voice, which is unlikely but certainly not impossible, there's a tranquilizing gun on the table about ten feet to your left. It's armed and auto-loading, and the safety's off. One dart will calm her down very quickly, two will put her to sleep, three will kill her. However, you must remember something very important: there isn't a chance in the world that you could get to that gun before she could get to you; and in any case, I don't want her to die unless it's absolutely necessary."

And if she does die, so will you, whoever you are, the woman thought. "Does that answer your question?"

"I . . . don't think we're going to need to worry about the tranquilizer gun," Lightstone responded with a sense of confidence he prayed had resulted from some degree of sanity.

"Just remember, slowly and firmly. Don't forget, she's extremely strong, and very quick."

"I don't think I'll forget that," Henry murmured grimly as he began lifting his hand—and immediately felt the claws digging deeper into the back of it. But he continued to raise his hand until he sensed it supported the cat's paw a couple inches above his thigh, aware that the cat had stopped rubbing him, but still rumbled contentedly.

Maintaining pressure as directed, he slowly rotated his hand and began to rub the soft leathery pad with his fingertips.

The cat paused mid-purr, fixed the federal agent with her two glowing orbs for a brief, heart-stopping moment, and then — to his utter amazement and relief — resumed rubbing and purring even more intensely . . . plus occasionally pausing to lick her elevated foreleg and paw. As she did, Lightstone felt the claws of that paw extend and dig farther into the palm of his hand. Slowly and methodically, he worked his hand up the cat's leg . . . and then her shoulder . . . until, finally, his fingers stroked the deep crevice between her muscular shoulders.

The cat's purring and rubbing increased even more in volume and intensity until suddenly, without warning, she let out a blood-chilling roar and sprang away.

She landed in a crouch, muscles tensed and canines bared, glaring balefully at Henry Lightstone, her black pupils like small black dots in the center of those terrifying yellow eyes.

As Lightstone held his breath, the cat turned and padded out of the room, emitting an eerie sound somewhere between a purr and a high-pitched yowl.

For a long moment, he sat there, aware of the tingling in his arms and the cold chill running up his spine.

Then he slowly let out his breath and turned to the woman.

"What was all that about?" he whispered, not wanting to break the spell.

"She's agitated," the woman replied, standing in one smooth, athletic motion that didn't completely mask her own considerable agitation.

If he'd done that to me . . . she thought, and then forced the disconcerting images out of her mind.

Later, when they stood on the patio squinting in the bright sunlight, Henry Lightstone suddenly became aware of how intensely good it felt to be alive.

Adrenaline response. Just like going in on an armed suspect, he tried to convince himself, but he knew there was more to it than that. Much more.

The woman studied him long and carefully enough to make him feel uneasy.

"She does that to you," she finally remarked in that soft, husky voice Lightstone found increasingly appealing . . . but also threatening for some reason. "And in case you were wondering, yes, the sensation is very addictive."

"I can believe it," he readily agreed, although he was very much aware that he couldn't tell her why he knew about adrenaline addiction. "I know

I have no right to ask, much less intrude on your privacy," he ventured instead, "but—"

"Can you see her—or perhaps us—again?" The woman smiled and nodded knowingly.

"It's been a long time since I was twelve," Lightstone replied in what he hoped sounded like a lighthearted tone.

Fortunately, it turned out to be exactly the right thing to say. She smiled broadly for the first time, a smile that, unfortunately, tore right into Henry Lightstone's heart.

"Yes, I can tell." Her sensuous lips pursed in amusement. She hesitated, and for the briefest of instants, her gold-flecked green eyes gleamed dangerously.

"Please do come back when you can." She held his hand in a grip that was, somehow, soft and yielding but also firm and controlling, and accompanied him to the gate. "I think both of us would like to see you again."

"What about breakfast tomorrow? Would that be pushing my luck?"

The woman nodded slowly.

"Breakfast tomorrow would be fine." She laughed lightly. "We open at six. However, I should warn you: Before I let you interact with Sasha again"—she allowed her eyes to lock onto his for one more brief moment—"I must read your fortune."

"You really think that's a good idea?" Henry Lightstone purposefully lingered so he could maintain contact with her hand.

"Oh yes," she announced firmly as she released his hand and stepped away from him. "It's absolutely essential."

Chapter Twenty-two

Awareness came to Wilbur Boggs in brief flashes.

First, a feeling of being trapped in the ropes and nets . . . struggling in the darkness, unable to move his arms to free himself of the obstructions covering his nose and mouth . . . then drifting away as soothing voices reassured him that everything was okay.

Then, some unknown time later, bright lights, and a horrible dryness in his mouth . . . then darkness again, and then a cold hand holding his wrist.

He blinked his eyes, trying to see who it was.

"Well now," a cheerful voice greeted him, "it's about time you started coming around. We were beginning to get worried about you."

Boggs tried to say something, but his dry tongue and mouth refused to cooperate.

"Thirsty," he rasped in a voice that he didn't recognize as his own.

"I'll bet you are, hon." The nurse dipped a clean cloth into a water flask and wet his lips. "How does that feel?"

"More?"

"Hold on just a minute, there's somebody here who wants to talk to you."

Still lost in a foggy daze, Wilbur Boggs felt the cool hand pat his arm, heard footsteps hurrying away . . . and then a very different, masculine voice jarred him awake again.

"How are we doing?" the voice asked.

Boggs thought about that for a long moment while he tried to sort out all of the confusing images that tumbled through his head.

A boat accident . . . or was it a car accident? Some kind of accident, though, because he remembered being in a great deal of pain. But that didn't make any sense because he couldn't feel anything at all now. In fact, his entire body felt numb, so numb that whatever he tried to re-member kept drifting . . .

The masculine voice again, asking something . . . name?

What name?

No matter how hard he tried, Boggs simply couldn't remember any names. Which was odd, he decided, because a federal agent ought to be able to . . .

"What did he say?" The resident physician looked up at the floor nurse.

"I *think* he said federal agent."

The resident physician's eyebrows furrowed. Leaning down, he whis-pered into Boggs's ear: "Do you want to talk to a federal agent?"

It took every bit of strength that Wilbur Boggs could summon to shake his head slightly.

Remembering the limited nature of the clothing the emergency room staff had removed from her patient, the nurse leaned forward and asked skeptically, "Are *you* a federal agent?"

Boggs tried to nod, but he had no idea whether his head actually moved. So he tried to whisper the answer instead, but it came out a weak hiss.

"You *are* a federal agent?" Boggs heard the disbelief in her voice.

This time he managed to nod perceptibly.

"What's your name?" she pressed, taking his limp hand in hers. "Can you tell us your name?"

The nurse put her ear right next to his mouth, but it still took Boggs three tries before she made any sense out of the sounds.

"Did you say Wilbur?"

He smiled weakly, but the sharp-eyed nurse caught it immediately.

"Okay, Wilbur it is. That's wonderful, Wilbur." The nurse grinned cheerfully and the resident physician made a congratulatory thumbs-up sign, then leaned forward again. "Now, just one more question and we'll let you rest. Can you tell me your last name?"

Boggs thought he could. But when he tried, everything started to drift away again, and he realized how tired he was, and how good it felt simply to lie back and . . . sleep.

"Well I'll be darned." The floor nurse looked up at the attending physician. "Do you believe that?"

"I'd sure like to," he replied as he made a few notations in Boggs's chart. "It'd be nice to have a patient with a real, honest-to-God medical coverage for a change."

The duty agent took the call, listened politely, wrote down the caller's name and number in his official notebook, then walked into the back room of the Medford, Oregon, field office of the Federal Bureau of Investigation.

"Just got an interesting call from Providence Hospital," the young FBI agent reported to the two older agents. "They've got an unidentified patient over there, pretty badly injured, who just regained consciousness, and is claiming to be an FBI agent. They were wondering if we were missing anybody?"

"What did you tell them?"

"That everybody here at the office was accounted for, but I'd put out a teletype."

"Good, that'll keep the hospital administrator and the county folks happy." Senior Resident Agent George Kawana turned to his guest. "You guys missing anyone on your detail?"

Assistant Special Agent in Charge Al Grynard's eyebrows shot up. "I sure as hell hope not," he replied. "Did they give you a description?"

The young agent referred to his notes.

"White male, six-one, two-ten, brown eyes . . ."

"Not one of ours." Grynard shook his head, visibly relieved.

". . . short gray hair, first name possibly Wilbur." The young agent finished.

"I know two or three Wilburs in the bureau, but none of them live around here," Grynard elaborated. "There's Wilbur Collins in the Philadelphia Office, Wilbur Fox in Miami, and . . ."

"You know who that almost sounds like?" A thoughtful look appeared in the senior resident agent's eyes. "Wilbur Boggs, out in Jasper County."

The young agent looked down at his notes again.

"Could be, I suppose," he admitted dubiously.

"Who's he, one of our retired agents?" Grynard asked.

"Nope, Fish and Wildlife."

Al Grynard's eyes snapped wide open.

"What?"

"Did I strike a nerve?" George Kawana cocked his head curiously.

"In a manner of speaking," Grynard admitted. "I had some dealings with a Special Ops team of Fish and Wildlife Service agents a little while back, and the entire experience damned near drove me out of my mind. All things considered, the idea that *any* covert Fish and Wildlife Service agent—much less that particular Special Ops team— might be wandering around this part of the country right now is not a cheerful thought."

"That bad, huh?"

"A walking nightmare would be a very polite description."

"Well, I don't think you have to worry about Wilbur Boggs being part of a Special Ops team . . . or at least not around here," George Kawana offered.

"Really? Why not?"

"For one thing, he wouldn't be able to maintain any kind of cover around this area for more than about fifteen minutes, max. This is hunting and fishing country, and anybody who does either in Jackson, Josephine, or Jasper Counties knows old Wilbur Boggs. Classic old game-warden type. Take an extra fish, duck, or deer over the limit or out of season, and you'll find Wilbur leaping out of the bush with a smile on his face and a ticket book in his hand. And don't even *think* about trying to talk or badge your way out of a violation notice."

"You speaking from practical experience, George?"

George Kawana smiled. "Fortunately not. But I know a couple of local officers who made the mistake of thinking they could roll the gold and bullshit their way past Wilbur. Bad mistake."

"Not exactly your low-key, low-profile, covert-agent type, huh?"

"Hardly." The senior resident FBI agent chuckled. "You know, though, now that you mention it, I think I do recall hearing something about those Fish and Wildlife guys. Didn't some heavy-duty, multinational counterterrorist group working for some political type out of Interior target them, and then those agents wound up whipping a bunch of counterterrorist butts?"

"They lost a couple of good guys in the process, but yeah, they did a hell of a job," Grynard grudgingly conceded.

"It's all coming back." George Kawana smiled. "You got caught up in it when you were working out of Anchorage, following up on the shooting death of that Fish and Wildlife Service supervisory agent. Only the way I heard it, you put a Russian Embassy–level tail on one of those wildlife agents because he kept popping up as your number one suspect. But then he kept on breaking out of the box . . . and eventually led everybody to the bad guys. What was his name again?"

"George, I've got more than enough problems in my life as it is right now, and you're not helping things any," Al Grynard warned.

"Come on, what was his name, that agent who gave you such a bad time?" the senior resident agent pressed.

"Lightstone." A pained look appeared on Grynard's clean-shaven face. "Henry Lightstone."

It was probably just as well that FBI Supervisory Agent Al Grynard had no idea that at the very moment he and Senior Resident Agent George Kawana worked out the final stages of a long-term and exceedingly complex FBI surveillance operation, two of the U.S. Fish and Wildlife Service's three Special Operations teams—eleven agents in total—were actively engaged in supposedly unrelated covert investigations within a hundred-mile radius of the FBI's Medford, Oregon, field office.

All things considered, though, that bit of knowledge probably wouldn't have bothered Grynard anywhere near as much as the realization that the one covert investigator who had caused him the most trouble during the past two years—Special Agent Henry Lightstone—was, at that very moment, less than two miles from the FBI's Medford field office, poised to set events into motion that would cause the supervisory FBI agent even more grief in the days to come.

Ten minutes after Henry Lightstone and Bobby LaGrange walked in through the glass-door entrance to the National Fish and Wildlife Forensics Lab in Ashland, Oregon, and checked in with the receptionist, supervisory forensic scientist Ed Rhodes hurried into the lobby, buttoning up his lab coat as he walked.

"Henry?"

"Hey, Ed! How're you doing, buddy?"

"Great." Rhodes smiled cheerfully as he shook Lightstone's hand. "And, come to think of it, you look a whole lot better than when I saw you last," the wildlife forensic scientist noted.

"The job's a lot more fun when people aren't shooting at you."

"Yeah, I'll bet."

"Ed, this is Bobby LaGrange, my old homicide detail partner from San Diego PD. I'd tell him what you do around here, but I have no idea," Lightstone confessed.

"Today, I'm acting lab director, chief computer repairman, and number two assistant on the mop detail. We just had a water pipe break, which is what took me so long to get out here."

"Acting lab director? You mean the boss is gone again? Doesn't he ever work around here?"

"Not so you'd notice." Rhodes grinned as he shook Bobby LaGrange's hand. "But don't you ever tell him I said that, 'cause then he'll make me go to DC next time."

"This whole place is a crime lab for *wildlife?*" Bobby LaGrange wore a stunned look as he surveyed the modern white concrete and blue-toned glass facility.

"Absolutely," Rhodes boasted proudly. "Like to have a tour?"

"You better believe it." The retired homicide detective nodded affirmatively.

"First things first." Henry Lightstone took a small glassine envelope out of his pocket.

"Well, I guess that means the first stop on the tour is the evidence control unit." Ed Rhodes used a plastic programmable key to enter the secured room, then walked across to the log-in counter, placed his bar-coded ID card into one of the reader slots, then keyed his access code into the case management system computer. "Okay, what've we got?"

Lightstone told him.

Ed Rhodes stared at the federal agent for a long moment.

"You're kidding me, right?"

Lightstone shook his head solemnly.

"Okay." The forensic scientist shrugged philosophically, reached for the nearby phone, and punched in a three-digit intercom number.

"Margaret? This is Ed. Hey, guess who's here? Remember Henry Lightstone, one of the Special Ops agents? Yeah, that's right. Well, he's back again, and you're not going to believe what he brought us this time."

Chapter Twenty-three

Congressional aide Keith Bennington did not enjoy confrontation. Given the choice, he much preferred to leave such unpleasant social interactions to Simon Whatley, and merely enjoy the relatively minor perks associated with his position as a powerful congressman's local assistant while he decided how to pursue his own lucrative political career.

While, at the same time, pursuing the charms of young and vivacious congressional Interns like Marla Cordovian.

A definite perk of the job, he thought with a smile.

But much to his dismay, and for the second day in a row, Marla hadn't shown up this morning.

And Simon Whatley, his normally dependable and available boss, was in no position to deal with this latest confrontational issue either, because he was somewhere over Tennessee on his flight back to Jasper County, Oregon, and, judging from the noise in the background, in very close proximity to a least two screaming children.

And Bennington's news—that the profiles on the agents of Bravo Team had not arrived that morning by FedEx as their deeply burrowed source in the U.S. Fish and Wildlife Service's Washington, DC Headquarters had promised—had done nothing whatsoever to soothe Whatley's simmering sense of frustration, outrage, and betrayal.

Although limited by his surroundings, his barely contained whispered fury came across loud and clear over the plane's satellite relay circuits.

Bennington would track Robert—Smallsreed's deeply burrowed intelligence source in the Department of the Interior—down, right now, from three time zones away, even if he had to use the goddamned FBI.

Robert, if he wished to remain employed anywhere within the legislative or administrative confines of the District of Columbia, would obtain and fax the federal wildlife agents' profiles to Whatley's private office within the hour.

Once the faxed pages arrived, Bennington would lock the door to Whatley's office, put on a pair of gloves, carefully trim the imprinted fax headers off every incoming page, place the wildlife agents' profiles in a plain manila envelope, seal the envelope, address it to Post Office Box Fourteen, Loggerhead City, Oregon, apply the necessary postage without, under any circumstances, using the district office postage machine; and then personally deliver that envelope immediately to the Loggerhead City rural post office at the intersection of Brandywine Road and Loggerhead Creek.

And at 8:45 that evening, Pacific standard time, when congressional district office manager Simon Whatley stepped off his plane and entered the terminal at Rogue Valley International Airport, Keith Bennington—if *he* was interested in future employment of any sort in Jasper County, Oregon, much less the goddamned District of Columbia—would be there to inform him, in person, that every one of those steps had been accomplished.

It took the thoroughly frightened congressional aide nearly an hour of increasingly frantic phone calls to locate Robert, who profusely apologized for his failure to get the profiles out the previous day, but insisted that none of them could imagine how difficult it was to access the personnel files of federal employees. Especially federal law-enforcement employees involved in covert investigations. Didn't they understand what would happen to him—and his girlfriend—if he got caught in the Personnel Office file room using her security keys to access those files? Didn't they understand that the unauthorized copying and removal of restricted law-enforcement personnel information was a felony? Didn't they . . . ?

Numbed and frustrated by the magnitude of his own problems, and in no mood to listen to someone whining who claimed to spend the better portion of his free time dating bright, attractive, and influential congressional staffers, Bennington cut him off with a curt expletive and demanded to know if he had the profiles in his possession.

Yes, as a matter of fact he did, which just went to show how valuable and dependable he was, Robert had replied haughtily. But it was eight-thirty in the goddamned evening, and it just so happened that a rather luscious young House Foreign Relations Committee staffer—a recent acquaintance that his current girlfriend and her friends didn't know about—had agreed to accompany him to a conveniently secluded trendy nightspot for a few drinks and whatever. So Bennington ought to be pretty damned grateful he'd even answered his pager.

And besides, the FedEx offices were all closed now, and there wasn't anything Keith Bennington or Simon Whatley or even Regis J. Smallsreed himself could do about that. So, as far as he was concerned, they could all just take their petty-ass little problems and . . .

It took Bennington another five minutes to convince Robert that Simon Whatley was deadly serious about his threat—which, Bennington noted thoughtfully, would undoubtedly include a discreet call to Robert's current girlfriend, because Bennington wasn't about to hide anything from a man like Whatley—and that everyone would fare much better if Robert simply reined in his overactive libido long enough to fax the damned profiles to Whatley's office ASAP because if he didn't, Bennington's next goddamned phone call would be to Regis J. Smallsreed himself.

Thirty-five minutes later, the temporarily empowered congressional aide received his first inkling of how wretchedly things could go when the cover page of Robert's fax dropped out of Simon Whatley's office machine and informed him that eighty-seven more pages were about to follow.

Fifty-three minutes later, the last page finally arrived, by which time jagged fax header strips covered the floor of Whatley's office and Keith Bennington hovered on the brink of a nervous breakdown.

According to his watch, which he had glanced at two or three times between every faxed page, he had exactly one hour and nineteen minutes to deliver the profiles to the Loggerhead City post office and reach the Rogue Valley International Airport ahead of his boss . . . a total distance, if he added the map segments correctly, of seventy-two miles. He'd already called the airport three times and received the same message. Yes sir, the flight is on time.

Which was probably bullshit, he tried to reassure himself. The flights were never on time.

Except this one will be, he thought sullenly. *Hell, the way things've been going on this deal, it'll probably be . . .*

Early? My God.

The idea numbed his mind.

A mile a minute—that was what, sixty miles an hour?—with seven minutes to spare. Jesus, gotta hurry, he thought as he stuffed the ragged-edged pages into the envelope with his gloved hands, hurriedly licked the seal—cutting his tongue on the sharp-edged flap in the process—and then ran to the postage machine. *All I have to do now is . . . oh Christ!*

He'd almost forgotten Whatley's admonition about the stamps.

Bennington wasted two of his spare minutes tearing Simon Whatley's office apart in a desperate search for the envelope of government-purchased stamps that Whatley used for private mail, and then burned three more ransacking the desks of their four office workers and volunteers. He found dozens of franked mailers and franked labels and franked envelopes. But no stamps.

He was running for the office sedan with the keys and envelope clutched desperately in his hand, vaguely aware—but not really caring—that it was raining, and that he'd forgotten to grab his raincoat and left the office in a shambles and the front door unlocked, when it occurred to him.

Wait a minute. I'm going to a post office. They have stamp machines at a post office!

Another momentary flash of panic brought him to an immediate halt in the middle of the parking lot. The cold rain began to soak through his light jacket as he quickly dug his hand into his pocket and came up with a small handful of change. Two quarters, four dimes, three nickels. He hefted the thick envelope.

Not enough. Not nearly enough.

Shit!

He dug for his wallet, ignoring the fact that his hands trembled.

A twenty, and five—no, six ones!

Yes!

They'd have change machines at the post office, he told himself. Either that or the stamp machines would take ones. They'd have to.

He looked down at his watch. Seven twenty-seven.

Seventy-eight minutes to go seventy-two miles.

Gotta get going . . . right now!

Oblivious to the rapidly deteriorating weather conditions, Keith Bennington ran for the car.

*   *   *

At seven-thirty that Wednesday evening, the woman finally gave up.

For whatever reason, the cat simply refused to come down from her high-limb perch.

"Okay, be that way," she muttered to herself as she firmly closed the door to the ancient-tree-decorated living room and turned the dead-bolt knob.

She knew the cat was agitated. She'd been that way ever since the intriguing stranger—what was his name, Henry something?—had left. And to a limited degree, she even sympathized with her sulking pet.

You and me both, babe, the woman thought irritably. *Just what we need right now.*

After closing and dead-bolting the second connecting door to the living room, the woman walked down the corridor to the door leading to the porch, confirmed that the darkness, the cold, and the now rapidly falling rain had driven away all of her restaurant customers, and returned to the main kitchen.

"Hey, Danny," she hailed the cook over the loud rhythmic sounds of a Cajun fiddler calling out an old bayou tune.

"Yeah?" The music immediately dropped to a low background level.

"It's dead out there, so I'm going to close up and run out to Costco. We're getting low on hamburger, coffee, hot chocolate mix, and a few other things, and I don't want to take a chance on getting snowed in tomorrow."

"Tell you what, if you pick up a couple of ham hocks, too," the young cook suggested after a quick survey of the refrigerators, "I'll brew up a big batch of navy bean soup. That'll keep the customers happy for a few days if we start running short."

"Sounds wonderful," she replied. "But the way this weather's changing, I'm not sure we're going to have any customers at all the next couple of days."

"Great, all the more for us."

The woman laughed.

"Hey, listen," she warned, "I left Sasha in her room. She's in one of her moods, so don't go in there."

"Don't worry. I wouldn't go back there even if I thought she was in a *good* mood."

The woman smiled, then placed the CLOSED sign in the window and turned off all the outside lights except those illuminating the pathway and the post office.

"I'll be back in a couple of hours. Don't forget to lock up when you leave."

Danny agreed, and as she closed the door behind her, she heard the plaintive voice and music of a Cajun fiddler slowly rose in volume.

The brief interchange with the young cook improved the woman's mood greatly, and she began humming to herself as she hopped into her small four-wheel-drive Toyota pickup truck with the strange-looking tracking device mounted on top of the cab, strapped herself in, and headed toward the distant shopping complex in Medford.

At exactly seven minutes after eight, Keith Bennington turned onto Brandywine Road and accelerated the heavy sedan down the dark, narrow, and extremely wet and slippery backcountry lane.

A steady rain had accompanied the panicked congressional aide ever since he left Regis J. Smallsreed's district office, and he'd almost gone off the road twice already, so he knew better than to push his luck.

But it was getting terribly late, and the Rogue Valley International Airport was a good thirty-five minutes away — thirty, if he really pushed it — and Bennington didn't even want to think about how Simon Whatley would react if his congressional aide wasn't there in the lobby waiting to take his briefcase and carry-on luggage the instant he walked off the plane and into the terminal.

Why am I doing this? Bennington asked himself for perhaps the twentieth time that evening as he gripped the vibrating steering wheel tightly, trying as best he could not to drive beyond the safe braking distance defined by the car's intersecting headlights as he peered through the water-streaking sweeps of the windshield wipers into the increasingly violent downpour.

It was a meaningless and useless question because he already knew the answer.

Like all too many of his peers, Keith Bennington was already addicted to the rush of high-level political power. Worse, the man who had led him into that addiction, the man who showed him exactly how to ride the coattails of a political powerhouse like Smallsreed to the maximum benefit of all concerned, was also the man who could take it all away in a heartbeat.

Clash with Simon Whatley just once, and Keith Bennington knew he'd spend the rest of his life in some dreary, meaningless job, remembering the taste of power that had been his . . . if only for one brief and tantalizing moment.

The thought proved more than the congressional aide could stomach, and he pressed down just a little more on the accelerator as he entered the sweeping turn.

And suddenly, there it was.

The sight of the darkened inn at the end of the long, narrow dark road almost caused Bennington to lose whatever remained of his lunch right there in the car.

No, it can't be closed. It can't be!

But then he saw the lighted path that led to the makeshift post office at one end of the rambling structure.

Bennington accelerated the sedan into the parking lot, skidded to a stop that sent mud and water flying across the wooden deck adjacent to it, and was running up the path and into the rustic post office before the car stopped vibrating on its sorely abused shocks.

The first thing he saw when he entered the office — or more to the point, the first thing he didn't see — was the stamp machine.

This can't be! he thought as his eyes frantically searched every inch of the small area. *This is a post office. It says so right there on the wall. There must be a stamp machine here somewhere.*

But there wasn't.

He pounded on the roll-down, but no one responded.

A brass slot next to the window smirked at him. DEPOSIT STAMPED MAIL HERE the sign above it said.

What if I put it in there without stamps? He asked himself. *Wouldn't they put it in box fourteen anyway, along with a postage due notice, if there wasn't any return address on the envelope?*

Because he didn't know for sure, he didn't dare risk it.

He even tried the door on box fourteen, praying that whoever opened it last hadn't closed it fully. But the door remained tightly shut, and no matter how hard he tried, he couldn't pry it open.

Only when the increasingly desperate congressional aide staggered outside, searching for someone, for anyone at all who might know where he could buy three or four dollars' worth of stamps in the next two minutes, did he notice the door.

The sign said PRIVATE, EMPLOYEE ENTRANCE ONLY, but Keith Bennington, long accustomed to the ready access that came with his proximity to Congressman Regis J. Smallsreed, easily ignored it.

Nobody responded when he knocked loudly.

No alarms went off when he turned the knob and the door clicked open.

So he went in, telling himself that it was clearly an emergency, and he only wanted a few dollars' worth of stamps . . . which he intended to leave the money for, so it wasn't like he was entering a private residence to steal something, for God's sake. By the time he convinced himself of all that, he barely noticed the PRIVATE, DO NOT ENTER! sign when he turned the dead bolt on the door.

But the third door did catch his attention.

The one with *two* dead bolts.

Something about them caused congressional aide Keith Bennington to wonder if he shouldn't go straight to the airport, right now, pick up Whatley, explain the situation, take him home, find an all-night market that sold stamps, and then drive all the way back to the Loggerhead City post office to mail the envelope as instructed.

That would be the smart thing to do, he told himself, as his hand paused on the first heavy dead-bolt knob that gleamed dully in the meager light shed by a single, distant wall source.

But then Bennington remembered Simon Whatley's voice over the Airphone. So Keith Bennington took a deep breath, turned the two hefty bolt knobs, cautiously opened the door a few inches, and whispered, "Hello?"

No answer.

If anything, the room on the other side of the door was darker than the hallway, and the congressional aide felt a terribly sick feeling in the pit of his stomach.

But the luminous dial on his watch reminded him that his vindictive employer would land in precisely twenty-eight minutes, so, in a burst of mindless courage, he pushed open the door and stepped inside the room.

Keith Bennington became aware of the acrid smell immediately. Unfortunately, he wasn't an animal person, so he had no way of knowing that the pungent aroma far exceeded anything that emanated from the average household pet.

Thus it wasn't until his pupils dilated . . .

And he saw the ancient tree in the center of the large room . . .

And he stepped forward in awe to touch its huge trunk . . .

And heard the soft, heavy thump behind his back, whirled, and found himself staring at a pair of half-lidded yellow eyes with tightly focused black pupils set terribly far apart that hovered in midair . . .

That he understood the enormity of his error.

He tried to say something that would give credence to the idea that that creature couldn't *possibly* be in this room, but the words simply froze in his mouth.

When the eyes began to move toward him, Keith Bennington did the only thing that he could think of at that moment. He held the envelope containing the eighty-seven faxed pages that had consumed his life for the past six hours in front of his body in the ludicrous hope that it might somehow, miraculously deflect the attack of the terrifying creature and allow him to live a few seconds longer.

He felt the whiskers of the terrifying beast brush against his hand, and tensed — even as his mind went mercifully numb — for the searing impact of extended claws ripping open his throat and chest and stomach . . . then stood stunned as the huge panther ripped the envelope out of his hand instead, turned, and then leaped upward and disappeared into the darkness.

Waves of adrenaline flooded Keith Bennington's frozen muscles, but it took the sound of paper tearing high above his head to finally galvanize the terrified young man into action.

Less than three seconds later, and with no memory of how he did it, Bennington stood in the dark hallway fumbling with the heavy dead bolts.

It took him fifteen more seconds to close and dead-bolt the second door, exit the house, get into the car, start the engine, launch the heavy sedan into a tire-spinning U-turn onto the dark, narrow, and extremely wet backcountry road . . . and another twenty-seven minutes and thirty-two seconds to pull into the entrance of the Rogue Valley International Airport parking lot, take a ticket, park the car, run into the terminal, and plant his trembling body in front of the ARRIVING PASSENGERS door.

The clock over the door read 8:54.

He still stood there twenty-three minutes later, numbed and glassy-eyed, when Simon Whatley's late-arriving airplane finally touched down and taxied to the terminal.

But only much later that night, as he lay in bed trembling under his electric blanket, did Keith Bennington finally realize that his equally numbed, glassy-eyed, and completely exhausted superior had simply handed him his briefcase and carry-on luggage, followed him out to the car . . . and during the entire trip home, never once asked about Robert, or the delivery of the agent profiles, or the reason that the district office staff car—not to mention Keith Bennington himself—reeked of human urine.

Chapter Twenty-four

When Henry Lightstone and Bobby LaGrange turned into the small industrial park a little after nine that Wednesday evening, they drove through the dimly lighted complex and pulled into the parking area in front of Bravo Team's rented warehouse.

When Lightstone shut off the engine, they could hear Dwight Stoner's distinctive booming voice, and Larry Paxton yelling something in reply.

"You call this a covert operation?" LaGrange commented as he and his former partner stared at the intensely bright light streaking out from under the roll-up door, around the drawn window and door shades, and through the fairly impressive gaps in the aluminum siding beneath the roof. Compared to this display, the rest of the warehouses in the small industrial complex appeared abandoned.

"Yeah, me too. I guess they're arguing over who gets to put the neon sign up," Lightstone commented sarcastically as he and LaGrange walked up to the small metal door and knocked.

When Larry Paxton opened the door, a blast of brilliant light nearly drove the two men backward.

"Jesus Christ, Paxton, what the hell—" Lightstone shielded his eyes to keep from being blinded.

"Get your butts in here before the damned thing escapes," the Bravo Team leader muttered as he yanked the two men into the warehouse and slammed the door.

"Before what escapes?" Bobby LaGrange's blinking eyes immediately focused on the red warning labels covering several of the wooden crates stacked in the middle of the warehouse floor. Around them, he saw an incredible assortment of haphazardly scattered cardboard boxes, bags, cans, power tools, and lumber that covered most of the concrete floor.

"The goddamned snake," Larry Paxton replied in a voice that gave the distinct impression of rapidly approaching hysteria.

"You guys let one of those things get loose?" Bobby LaGrange instantly moved to an open section of concrete and began scanning the surrounding piles of cardboard and assorted debris for movement.

"One?" Dwight Stoner's deep booming voice echoed across the cavernous warehouse. "Yeah, right, that's a laugh."

Larry Paxton glared at the ex–Oakland Raider turned agent.

"Hey, what happened to the rental car?" Lightstone asked, noticing the shattered windshield and the huge dents on the top of the hood.

"Go ahead, Paxton." Dwight Stoner waved the snake net in his massive hand encouragingly. "You're the team leader around here. You tell the man what four highly trained covert federal agents have been doing here the last couple of hours."

"Things got a little bit out of hand for a while, but we've almost got it under control," Paxton started to explain when Thomas Woeshack's head popped up from the other side of the pile of terrarium boxes.

"Yeah, you should have been here, Henry. It was awesome! We were trying to hurry and get them all in the terrariums 'cause we don't them to die of hunger or thirst when all of a sudden, we had snake babies! A whole ton of them. And then Mike starts yelling 'Tape the lid shut!' and Larry's screaming 'Oh shit!' over and over again. But before Stoner and I could find the tape, the babies were everywhere. Must've been a hundred of them!"

"You guys let a hundred baby snakes get loose in here?" Henry Lightstone shook his head in amazement as he ran his hand over the huge dents in the car hood.

"Yeah!" Woeshack's eyes gleamed with delight. "Common red-bellied blacksnakes. Really evil-looking! And man, you should've seen Stoner. Soon as those little snakes started coming out through those gaps in Mike's transfer contraption, he jumped right up on that stack of crates, and then the whole stack started hissing and thrashing around like crazy, and he screamed and jumped all the way over there to the rental car and—"

"I think I get the picture."

Henry Lightstone nodded his head thoughtfully as he picked up a couple of the snake hooks littering the floor and walked back to where Paxton and Bobby LaGrange stood.

"There wasn't no hundred baby snakes." Larry Paxton switched his supervisory glare to Woeshack. "According to Jennifer, common red-bellied blacksnakes only have about twelve babies in a batch—"

"I think you mean 'offspring in a litter,'" Lightstone corrected his superior as he handed one of the snake hooks to LaGrange. "Twelve offspring in a clutch, if they're egg-layers, or twelve offspring in a litter if they're live-bearers. I assume common blacksnakes are live-bearers?"

"Yeah, whatever," Paxton acknowledged absentmindedly. "Anyway, we've already found twenty-three of the little buggers, which means— Hey, wait just a minute now! How come you know so much about snakes all of a sudden?" the Bravo Team leader demanded.

"You mean like this one?"

Henry Lightstone suddenly thrust the snake hook down behind Larry Paxton's feet, squatted, and stood holding a small, frantically wiggling black-and-red snake just behind its head with his thumb and forefinger.

"What the hell!" Larry Paxton's eyes bulged as he hurriedly searched the floor around his feet.

"Just gotta know where to look, Paxton." Lightstone glanced around the floor again and casually brought the wiggling snake up to eye level.

"What the hell are you doing, holding a poisonous snake like that in your bare hand?" Larry Paxton demanded, his eyes still round as he watched the tiny reptile furiously try to work itself loose enough to bite its captor.

Henry Lightstone examined the snake's gaping mouth critically. "Come on, Paxton, a little guy like this can't do much damage. Little baby fangs like that, it probably would've taken him a good thirty seconds just to chew through your sock. And even then, he probably wouldn't have given you much of a jolt. They like to save their venom for something that looks good to eat.

"Which reminds me," Lightstone went on, "you really don't have to worry too much about food and water for a few days with reptiles at this temperature, but it'll be a lot easier to get all the snakes into the terrariums before the babies hatch out. And another thing," he added, glancing down at Paxton's low-cut tennis shoes, "most professional snake handlers wear high-topped leather boots. Cuts down on the number of trips to the emergency room."

"I ain't no professional snake handler!" the Bravo Team leader snapped irritably.

"Yeah, no kidding." Henry Lightstone scanned the surrounding floor again. "Anybody got an extra snake bag handy?"

"Right here!"

Mike Takahara ran up with a long, narrow canvas bag and held it open as Lightstone thrust his hand deep into it. As Henry removed his hand, the tech agent clamped his own around the neck of the bag and tied it shut with the attached canvas straps.

"Twenty-four!" Takahara's voice echoed in the cavernous warehouse holding the snake bag up triumphantly.

"Thank God," Dwight Stoner tiredly agreed as he and Woeshack came up beside Paxton. "We've been looking for that damned thing for the past hour." Then a puzzled frown crossed the huge agent's face. "Hey, wait a minute." He looked at Henry suspiciously, then glared at Paxton. "How come *he* found it so fast?"

"And caught it with his bare hands, too," Thomas Woeshack reminded them.

"The bastard knows something about snakes." Larry Paxton looked like someone who had been thrashing in a pond convinced he was about to drown at any moment, only to discover that the person sitting on shore observing him was an off-duty lifeguard.

Henry Lightstone shrugged. "Bobby and I were interested in herpetology when we were kids."

"But that was before we discovered girls." Bobby LaGrange smiled helpfully. "I take it you guys are still working yourselves up to that stage?"

Larry Paxton stood momentarily speechless.

"You mean you—" It took the nearly apoplectic Bravo Team leader several seconds to finally get the words out. "You left the four of us here— four people who don't know shit about snakes, in a freezing warehouse full of some of the most poisonous snakes in the whole damned world—to try to figure out how to put snakes that are too big into terrariums that are too small . . . with nobody bothering to tell us that some of the damned things might be pregnant and start squirting out baby snakes right and left . . . while you and your ex-partner here—"

"Were out risking our lives purchasing Bigfoot evidence?" Henry Lightstone finished with an innocent look on his face.

"Actually, that's not exactly true," Bobby LaGrange pointed out. "I didn't risk anything except my reputation and my bank account. And the way you explained the situation to me, you really didn't buy anything from her, Henry. It was more like a gift, wouldn't you say?"

"Yeah, good point."

"*Her?*" Four voices practically howled in unison.

"The witch," Bobby LaGrange explained helpfully. "Personally, I think Henry's in love. I've seen that look in his eyes before, but he won't admit it."

"You let him buy Bigfoot evidence from a *witch?*" Dwight Stoner demanded. "What happened to the old fart soothsayer?"

"Wow." Thomas Woeshack looked duly impressed.

"What does she look like, Henry?" Mike Takahara asked.

"Well, *I* think she's pretty attractive . . . as far as witches go, anyway," Lightstone added with a cheerful smile as he looked around the warehouse. "I would've called and told you guys all about her, but I gather you haven't installed the phones yet?"

"Next item on the list," Mike Takahara promised.

"And while we're on the subjects of lists," Lightstone interrupted. "You guys need to cut down on your lights in here, or do a lot better job in sealing off under the roll-up door, around the window and door shades, between the aluminum siding and the roof. Looks like a carnival show out there."

"Door, window, and roof seals, check," the tech agent muttered as he made a few cryptic notes.

"Another thing," Lightstone went on. "Looks like I'm going to need some halfway decent ID after all."

"Okay." Mike Takahara looked up from his notebook. "What do we know about you so far?"

Lightstone paused for a moment. "Let's see, I'm in between jobs, my girlfriend took off on me a few weeks ago, and I'm out here to look up Bobby—a guy I went to school with when we were kids."

"Any particular discussion on location where you two went to school?"

"No."

"What about your name?"

"I'm locked in on 'Henry,' but no last name yet."

"Okay. Bobby's got a pretty strong Southern accent for somebody who grew up in San Diego. Why don't we see if we can get you away from the West Coast. Maybe somewhere back East. How does North Carolina sound?" The tech agent looked over at Bobby LaGrange.

"Why don't you make it South Carolina," Bobby LaGrange suggested. "I've got relatives down in Beaufort, so I can fill Henry in on the appropriate local color. And as far as the local people around here are concerned, all they know about us is that we moved here from Miami."

"South Carolina's fine with me," Lightstone agreed. "Just get it as soon as you can, and make sure whatever name you come up with can stand up to a half-decent background check."

"Yeah, that's right, you never know what a witch can find out if she really puts her mind to it," Thomas Woeshack pointed out.

"I think I need to sit down." Larry Paxton fumbled for one of the overturned boxes.

"Uh, not there, Larry." Lightstone quickly reached past the Bravo Team leader with the snake hook, knelt, and stood with another tiny wiggling black snake. "Kinda cute little critters," he remarked to Takahara. "Got another bag?"

"Don't worry, Larry, he always did that when we were kids, too. Used to drive me crazy." Bobby LaGrange smiled sympathetically as he watched the visibly shaken Bravo Team leader gingerly kick at the box, move it out into a bare patch of concrete floor, then look around once more before finally sitting down uneasily.

"That's twenty-five, Paxton," Dwight Stoner pointed out with a menacing edge to his deep voice. "What about that 'two-times-twelve is twenty-four' bullshit you've been handing us all evening?"

"Actually, those clutch and litter numbers are usually plus or minus a whole bunch," Henry Lightstone pointed out. "At least that's the way it worked for all the North American snakes Bobby and I raised, and I'll bet it's pretty much the same thing for Australian snakes, too. So if I were you guys, I'd keep my eyes open, just in case."

Larry Paxton gave him a venomous look.

"And just what, exactly, makes you think any of us intend to have any part of our anatomy anywhere near this place from now on, now that we know about you two junior herpetologists?" he asked reasonably.

"Hey, Bobby and I'd be glad to help. Honest. Giant spiders give me the willies, but snakes are cool. But as it turns out, I've got a date with the witch for breakfast tomorrow, and unfortunately" — Lightstone looked down at his watch — "I told the folks at the forensics lab to call me at Bobby's house around ten to tell me what they found out about the Bigfoot hair we dropped off this afternoon."

"Those lab folks must not have much of a social life," LaGrange observed. "But then, I suppose if they started hanging out with people like you and your witch friends instead of working all night" — he poked his ex-partner good-naturedly — "they'd probably end up having to exorcise the whole lab on a regular basis."

"Which reminds me," Henry Lightstone added after he dropped his latest captive into Takahara's snake bag, "Bobby and I probably should keep our distance from this place for a while. We're pretty much linked together now as far as my cover goes, and with all the bright lights, yelling, and screaming going on here, you guys are about as covert as a carnival. If anybody like the Sage or the Witch spots Bobby and me out here, they're liable to think we're a couple of federal wildlife agents running a snake scam on some poor Mexican Mafia gang down in Nogales. Then they'll never show us their mythical beast."

"Or offer to sell us any of their genuine mythical souvenirs," Bobby LaGrange added.

"Which probably wouldn't make Halahan very happy, although why he could possibly care, one way or the other, completely escapes me." Lightstone admitted.

"However, he is the boss." LaGrange reminded his ex-partner.

"Exactly. Which means we'd better get going." Lightstone looked around one last time. "You guys going to be okay out here on your own for a couple more days?"

"Oh hell yes." Larry Paxton stretched his arms to take in the expanse of Bravo Team's assigned warehouse operation. "We've only thirty deadly poisonous snakes, a dozen man-eating crocodiles, and 750 giant tarantulas to transfer into 120 terrariums in the middle of a freezing warehouse which we can't warm up because if we do, everything in the crates will go bat-shit . . . and if we don't get them into the terrariums pretty soon, we're going to be up to our butts in thirsty baby snakes, and probably baby spiders, too, for all I know.

"Plus," he went on dramatically, "it only took the four of us twelve hours, $2800.00 in tools and lumber and shit, one squashed rental car, two rolls of duct tape, and a down payment on my nervous breakdown to unload one whole crate, which means we've only got seventy-one measly crates to go. So don't you worry none about us. We'll be just fine."

"See," Henry Lightstone assured his dubious former partner as they headed back to the truck, "I told you they'd be okay once they got a system going."

Chapter Twenty-five

At precisely 4:00 that following Thursday morning, Congressman Regis J. Smallsreed placed a call from his Virginia estate to Simon Whatley, waking the physically exhausted district manager out of a sound sleep to demand a verification that the "sensitive material" on their project had been delivered as ordered.

Having no idea what Smallsreed was talking about, Whatley mumbled something to the affirmative . . . and immediately fell back to sleep after the congressman snarled "good," and hung up without any further comment.

Smallsreed immediately called Lt. Colonel John Rustman to advise his field project leader that everything was back on schedule and a "go" as far as he and his clients were concerned.

Much later that morning, a more or less rejuvenated Simon Whatley would not remember receiving Smallsreed's call.

At precisely 7:00 A.M. the six youthful wildlife special agents of Charlie Team met for breakfast at a small diner a few miles outside Loggerhead City to decide what to do next.

After considerable discussion, they came to the very logical conclusion that their first field operation wasn't likely to go anywhere at all until they found and talked with the elusive Special Agent Wilbur Boggs.

At precisely 8:32 that Thursday morning, the floor nurse at Providence Hospital took her fingers off Wilbur Boggs's wrist, made a notation in the chart, then looked up as the resident physician entered the room and quietly shut the door.

"Any changes?" he asked in a soft voice.

She shook her head.

"How long has it been this time?"

The resident nurse looked at her watch and consulted Boggs's chart.

"Almost twenty hours since he last regained consciousness," she replied.

Pursing his lips in concern, the resident physician took the chart and quickly scanned the last series of notations.

"If his vital signs weren't so steady, I would seriously consider another CAT scan," he muttered mostly to himself as he handed the chart back to the floor nurse. As he did so, he noticed the chart still read John Doe "Wilbur."

"Any more luck on tracking him down?" he asked.

The floor nurse shook her head again. "Nothing so far."

The resident physician sighed tiredly.

"Well, I suppose someone is bound to come looking for him eventually. Keep me posted, and have someone notify me right away if anything changes in the next twenty-four hours," he said as he walked back into the hallway to continue his rounds.

Chapter Twenty-six

"You seem surprised to see me," Henry Lightstone remarked when the woman placed a menu on the place mat, and filled his cup with steaming coffee. "Did I give you the impression I was unreliable already?"

She had dressed for the colder weather that morning: soft white cotton long johns with hand-crocheted trim edging at the ends of the long sleeves and scooped neckline, faded small-bib denim overalls with a hand-stitched panther head — complete with bright yellow eyes — over the left breast, and a pair of well-worn, low-cut hiking boots. A self-assured woman dressing for herself who made no particular effort to show off her taut, curvaceous, and yet slender figure.

Yet to Lightstone, everything about her appeared sleek, sensual, and alluring.

"You may not have noticed, but nine o'clock's a little late for most working people around this town." Karla lightly tossed her head and her long hair fanned out toward the empty tables. "And besides, predicting the future isn't always an exact science," she added with a mischievous grin.

"That's the advantage of being between jobs — every now and then, when your rancher buddy isn't dragging you out to some cow-related project, you get to sleep in." Lightstone picked up the hand-printed menu. "And speaking of predicting the future, I don't suppose you checked out the cook's tea leaves this morning?"

She shrugged, causing the soft cotton fabric of the long johns to stretch invitingly across her full breasts.

"Sorry. You really can't tell much from a short-order cook's coffee grounds, especially the way this one makes coffee. But Danny's pretty good with scrambled eggs — if you like them with lots of chopped green onions and China peas. On the other hand, his hash browns definitely need help. He claims he's working on the problem. But his jambalaya is fantastic — except not for breakfast, unless you're real adventuresome."

"The scrambled eggs sound fine. Extra onions and peas, if that's an option . . . but I think I'll skip on the hash browns — probably forever — and the jambalaya for now."

"Good choice."

Lightstone made a show of looking around the enclosed porch. "I don't see your helper today."

Karla gave him a cool, appraising look. "Apparently this was one of those mornings all the 'between-job' types decided to sleep in."

"Ah."

She opened her mouth as if to say something, but then suddenly turned and retreated to the kitchen.

When she returned about thirty seconds later, she carried an ornate ceramic cup. Wordlessly, she pushed Lightstone's coffee cup aside, set the steaming cup in front of him, walked around to the opposite side of the table, sat down with her chin resting on her interlaced fingers, and commanded, "Drink."

Henry Lightstone's brows furrowed in confusion as he stared into the woman's gold-flecked green eyes for a brief moment, then into the cup.

"Tea?"

"That's right."

He smiled in sudden understanding. "Are you serious?"

"Very," she answered in a voice that offered no compromise.

After shrugging agreeably, Lightstone cautiously brought the steaming cup to his lips, and winced.

"It's hot."

"Drink it anyway."

He allowed his gaze to settle on those seductive gold-flecked green eyes for another brief moment. Then he obediently brought the cup to his lips, drank the hot tea in several long sips, and set the ornate cup back on the table.

He felt the warmth of her hand radiating across his when she reached across it to slide the ceramic cup to her side of the table.

As Henry Lightstone watched in fascination, the sensuous young woman scrutinized the remaining contents carefully, stuck her index finger into the cup, stirred gently, waited a few more seconds, and then apparently considered results for a very long time.

Finally, she released a deep sigh that caused Lightstone's heart to thump in his chest.

He waited for her to say something, but she simply sat there with her chin resting on her interlaced fingers, staring down into the small cup.

"What's the matter?" he asked cautiously.

Startled, she looked up, shook her head as if to clear it, and fixed Lightstone with a long, appraising stare.

"Do you *really* want to see her again?"

Henry Lightstone hesitated, intuitively aware that whatever he said could significantly affect many things . . . his future among them.

Finally, he nodded his head. "Yes, I do. I wanted to see both of you again."

As Lightstone watched, Karla briefly closed her eyes, then looked down into the cup one last time, took in a deep breath, released it slowly, then silently got up and disappeared into the inn.

Two minutes later, she returned with the panther at her side, the cat's eyes seemingly unfocused and her ears partially down as she swung her massive head slowly from side to side.

In the daylight, she looked even more stunning . . . *and* more intimidating.

They both do, he thought, and then recoiled subliminally when the alarm bell in the back of his head started up again. He continued considering the possible implications of that subconscious reaction as the woman and cat approached him.

"She has her collar on, but take it easy anyway. She's acting a little weird this morning," Karla warned.

The panther stayed close to her human mistress's side until they came within a half dozen feet of Lightstone. Then, the big cat suddenly stopped, turned her velvety head sharply in his direction, emitted a spine-chilling yowl, and lunged.

Once again, Henry Lightstone found himself pinned by a mass of claws, muscle, and gleaming fur while two huge glowing yellow eyes stared intently into his own. He could feel her breath—and her coarse, bristly whiskers—tickling his face. Although the daylight made her appear visually intimidating, this time he didn't feel anywhere near as startled or frightened.

Some analytical portion of Henry's brain tried to correlate the initial visual data he'd accumulated about the big cat—her close attachment to the woman, her head swinging slowly back and forth, partially flattened ears, and eyes seemingly unfocused—with the fact that now the panther's ears stood erect and her eyes *definitely* focused on his. But he knew little about animal behavior, and even less about a predatory creature like this.

But then the huge cat began to rumble contentedly, dug her claws into his arms, and rubbed her muzzle hard against his chin and jaw, and suddenly all of the data fell into place.

"My God," he whispered, "she's blind."

"She has spots," Henry announced in surprise when the panther lost interest in him a short time later and he noticed the dark patches in what he'd originally thought was a solid black coat.

"Panthers are part of . . ." Karla hesitated for a split second, ". . . the leopard family. She's actually a very very dark brown leopard with even darker brown spots.

"What's wrong with her eyes?" Henry asked as he studied the cat with the hidden spots lounging in the sunlight next to the table, her head resting on his boot.

"The zoo vets had no idea how it happened," she explained as she sat beside Henry Lightstone at the table and observed her fearsome companion. "There was no sign of trauma to the outer or inner eye structures. The skull X-rays look fine. All of the neurological data were unremarkable. The most likely cause was a spontaneous mutation that occurred prior to birth."

"You got her from a zoo?"

Karla nodded. "Her mother wouldn't feed her. A lot of captive animals have lousy maternal instincts. Or it could've just been one of those instinctive reactions. You know, don't waste any effort on a defective cub. The zoo director was a family friend, and I'd spent a lot of time in the nursery when I was a kid. He told me they planned to put her down because they couldn't afford to keep her, and none of the other zoos wanted her. So he offered her to me."

"Sounds like a lot of work."

"I already had my wildlife rehabilitator's certificate and was . . . between jobs"—she smiled evasively—"so I took him up on it. Sasha was still young enough to imprint on me, and now she thinks I'm her mom. Well, her queen, really." Karla smiled at Lightstone, obviously relishing the scientifically correct term for a mother cat.

"I'm surprised that no one around here complains," Lightstone commented.

"You mean like to the government, for example?"

Lightstone nodded.

"The State Fish and Game people weren't exactly thrilled. I was fortunate that the zoo director was well connected . . . but I guess that's pretty much how government operates anyway, isn't it? It's always who you know, not what you know," Karla added with a cynical twist to her voice. "However, I guess I should be grateful because they finally did give me a permit, as long as I agreed to keep her collared and within my range of control whenever she's out of her enclosure."

"I'm not much of a fan of government, but you can kind of see their point. A creature like this is bound to terrify people if she's running around loose," Lightstone remarked, feeling the cat's rib cage rhythmically rise and fall against his outstretched leg. Even asleep, she was such an awesome creature, he couldn't imagine her unable to defend or feed herself.

"And then, too," he added thoughtfully, "I suppose it probably goes both ways. A blind panther probably wouldn't stand much of a chance out in the wild."

"She'd have a rough time on her own, but if she could get close

enough to the prey before she attacked . . . or had a protective mate."
Karla shrugged as if to say "Who knows." "But the fact that I raised her,
rather than another panther, would probably undermine her chances as
much as her limited sight."

"Then she's not really blind?"

"Not totally. Like most cats, her vision is more motion- than detail-
sensitive. But as best we can tell, anything beyond two or three feet probably looks like a blur to her."

Lightstone frowned. "That's strange. I got the impression she saw me
from farther away than that."

"No, I think she smelled you." Karla smiled again. "It may have something to do with your friend's cattle ranch."

"So what should I do, rub up against one of Bobby's cows every morning before breakfast just to keep her happy?"

"I couldn't even begin to advise you on *that* subject," the sensuous
woman replied cryptically.

Interesting answer, Lightstone thought uneasily.

But before he could follow up on that curious remark, Karla suddenly
responded to the young cook's appearance at the doorway to the dining
room.

"Say, speaking of eating," she changed the subject completely. "Want
to give it one more try? I forgot to warn you that Sasha considers Danny's
scrambled eggs with onions and China peas one of her favorite snacks.
But from the looks of things"—she glanced down at the loudly snoring
animal—"I'd say she's sacked out, and I know Danny's got more."

The event so captivated him, he'd completely forgotten he hadn't
eaten.

"That sounds real good to me," he gratefully accepted Karla's offer.

She relayed the order to the young cook, who smiled and returned
to his kitchen.

"So what . . . ?" Lightstone started to ask, when the exterior door to
the enclosed porch suddenly opened behind them.

"Uh-oh, time to work," Karla automatically reacted to the familiar
sound. She started to get up, but hesitated when she remembered the
blissfully sleeping panther.

"That's okay, leave her," Lightstone assured her, "she'll be fine."

"I don't know . . ."

"I won't move. Just don't go too far way, in case she wakes up and
decides she wants another snack."

It was obvious that Karla still felt uncertain, but Lightstone's relaxed
smile reassured her. Then she glanced back over her shoulder and saw
who had entered the restaurant.

"All right, you stay here. I'll be right back," she agreed with a subtle
but distinct edge to her voice.

* * *

"May I help you?" Karla asked as she approached the two men—Wintersole, whose eyes had given her cold chills, and another, younger one she'd never seen before. She noticed Wintersole still wore the bear-claw necklace.

"I was expecting a letter this morning, but it's not in my box." Wintersole's eyes flickered toward the lone diner sitting at the nearby table.

"I'm sorry, but all the mail is in the boxes. Next delivery will be in late this afternoon."

"This would have been a personal delivery to the post office," Wintersole persisted. "Sometime yesterday morning."

Karla shook her head. "I'm sorry, but everything's in the boxes, and no one dropped off anything this morning."

"Would you mind checking, just to be sure?"

He probably intended it as a question, but it came out as a direct order.

"We don't get that much mail here." The young woman forced herself to control her irritation and stare directly into those disconcerting gray eyes. "You have box fourteen, correct?"

The hunter-killer team leader hesitated a split second, then nodded.

"Then there's no need to check. I'm absolutely certain there's no mail for you."

She started to turn away, but a strong, restraining hand suddenly grabbed her arm.

"The sergeant asked you to check." Wintersole's younger companion glared at her. "I suggest you do that. Now."

"Take your hand off . . . !" Karla started to exclaim, when the younger soldier let out a startled yelp and went down on his knees, hard.

"I believe I heard her say you don't have any mail in this post office. Perhaps you misunderstood that?" Henry Lightstone held the young soldier down on his knees with the painful, single-handed wristlock, but his eyes transfixed Wintersole's.

"Hey, knock it off, you two, I don't want . . . !" Karla stepped in fast, but not fast enough.

The young well-trained soldier relaxed, seemingly giving in to the wristlock. Then, when he sensed the opportunity, he dipped his shoulder, brought his feet around, and started to come up with a knuckle strike to Lightstone's exposed groin.

But the martial-arts-trained ex-cop had anticipated the move.

A high-pitched scream immediately masked the sound of crunching wrist bones.

"Oh, shit!" This time Karla made no effort to disguise her true feelings as she quickly reached into her apron pocket.

Responding instantly to the enraged look in Wintersole's eyes, Henry

Lightstone released the young man's broken wrist and was shifting into a defensive stance when the enclosed room suddenly reverberated with a spine-chilling feral scream.

Wintersole, already in motion with his hand clenched for a crippling strike, and Lightstone, instinctively set for the block and counterstrike, both turned.

"SASHA! NO! TO ME, NOW!"

The cat was already in mid-lunge, her hind legs driving her claw-extended forepaws within striking range of the two blurry targets, when the familiar, reassuring, and commanding tones of the woman's voice caused her to abort her lethal charge. She twisted midair, sprang in the direction of the woman's voice, and then—once she made physical contact with her queen—spun toward the others with bared teeth and let out a defiant, rafter-shaking roar.

"Don't move, any of you!" the woman spit out angrily.

She needn't have bothered. All three men were frozen in place.

"Just stay where you are, all of you," the woman ordered again, her eyes blazed with fury as she slowly dropped her right hand—the one clutching the small transmitter—to her side. "I'm taking her out of here."

The young soldier, shaken by his eye-level view of imminent and savage death, remained on his knees while the woman and the cat disappeared into the inn. But Lightstone and Wintersole automatically moved apart, even though both of them still mentally reeled from the shock.

Lightstone recovered first.

"I'm terribly sorry," he apologized, turning to face the man he immediately—and instinctively—recognized as a trained and experienced killer. "I had no business interfering. I thought—"

The sound of Henry Lightstone's voice appeared to snap Wintersole out of his trance. He looked down and saw that his left hand tightly clenched the bear-claw necklace. He smiled when he looked at Lightstone with his strange pale eyes.

"No, it was our fault, entirely our fault." Wintersole briefly glanced down at the injured soldier. "We were expecting a very important letter that involved . . . a great deal of money. It wasn't her fault—or yours—that it didn't arrive. We were out of line, and I apologize," he added, as he extended his hand.

Lightstone accepted the peace offering, aware of the extraordinary, controlled strength in the man's handshake as he did so. Then he looked down at the still-sprawled younger man.

"I'm really sorry about his wrist." Lightstone shook his head regretfully. "I'll be happy to pay for his medical treatment."

"That won't be necessary." Wintersole reached down and brought the younger man to his feet. "You're not hurt bad, are you, David?"

"No sir," the pale-faced young man spoke with surprising calmness under the circumstances.

Another one just like him. Muscular, trim, short-haired, and intense, but younger and nowhere near as cold ... or dangerous, Lightstone decided, surprised to see disciplined obedience in the young man's face rather than anger. *Who the hell are these guys? Cops?*

To Lightstone's absolute amazement, the young man extended his uninjured right hand. "My sincere apologies, sir. It was my fault for grabbing the woman. That was inexcusable. You had every right to come to her defense, and I had no call to go at you like that."

"To tell the truth," Lightstone chuckled as he accepted the young man's hand, "I'm not sure she *needed* defending . . . at least not from me."

"Man, that's sure the truth."

For a brief moment, the terrorizing aftereffects of the panther's near-lethal charge flickered across the young man's face.

"I don't believe this."

The three men turned at the sound of Karla's voice.

"When I walked out of here with Sasha a couple minutes ago, all three of you were ready to go at each other's throats, and you damned near got yourselves killed because of it. I come back and find you shaking hands like the whole thing was just some kind of male-bonding ritual. What the hell is it with you guys anyway?" she demanded angrily.

Wintersole stepped forward before Lightstone or the younger man could respond.

"Ma'am, I'm *extremely* sorry for the way my associate and I acted," he graciously apologized. "I was completely out of line. That's no excuse at all, but as I was explaining to your friend, that letter's crucial to a very important project we're working on. It didn't arrive, which means we lose a great deal of valuable time. But that's not your problem . . . and we had no right to take our frustration out on you."

Karla appeared unimpressed, but Wintersole soldiered on.

"To tell you the truth, I'm so embarrassed that I'm reluctant to ever show my face here again, except"—he averted his eyes momentarily before meeting her gaze again—"that letter really *is* important to us, and"—the team leader paused for effect—"we really do like the food and the company here."

It was such an inspired performance that Henry Lightstone almost felt like applauding.

Karla peered at Wintersole's strange eyes for several seconds. Then, without a trace of warmth in her voice, she asked: "Where are you from? Georgia?"

"No ma'am, South Carolina."

"I knew it. That goddamned Southern male charm." She shook her head, then sighed. "Unfortunately, much as I hate to admit it"—she flashed him a slight smile that made Lightstone feel inexplicably jealous—"it works on us dumb Southern women every time."

"I'd never call a lady from the South dumb, ma'am, especially you. Does that mean we're forgiven?" Wintersole peered at her hopefully.

"Yes, apology accepted."

"Well, that being the case"—the hunter-killer recon team leader breathed a visible sigh of relief and distractedly ran his fingers over the bear-claw necklace—"would I be pushing my luck if I asked to buy a piece of paper, an envelope, and a first-class stamp?"

Karla cocked her head curiously.

"You didn't get a letter today, so now you want to send one?" She smiled at him.

"Yes ma'am."

"I think that can be arranged."

Three minutes later, Wintersole handed her the sealed envelope. She glanced down at the address.

"P.O. Box fifteen? Not going very far, is it?" she remarked pleasantly. "Almost hate to charge for the stamp."

"That's all right, ma'am, I'm sure the government needs the money." Wintersole motioned the younger man toward the door. "Unless you change your mind, we'll see you tomorrow, same time."

Karla waited until the two men got into their pickup and started backing out of the parking space. Then she turned to Lightstone, who stood next to her, his eyes fixed on the departing vehicle, which was painted in an unusual mottled green color.

Almost like military camouflage, but not quite. Interesting.

"Would you care to explain to me what the hell just happened in here?" the sensuous young woman asked pointedly.

"I'd love to, except I haven't the slightest idea," Henry Lightstone replied truthfully as he watched the younger man give one final glance at the restaurant before driving off. "You get some interesting customers."

"That's putting it mildly."

"Uh, listen, uh . . . Karla, I think I've probably caused enough trouble around here for one morning. Would you mind if I—?"

"Came back tomorrow . . . for breakfast?" she finished his question for him.

Lightstone nodded.

"That's probably a good idea," she agreed, massaging her neck. "I think we all need to cool down a little."

He started to say something, but simply nodded again.

The sensuous young woman with the gold-flecked green eyes concealed herself behind the kitchen door and watched Henry Lightstone walk across the porch, look back briefly, then run to his truck when he thought no one observed him.

Okay, Henry, Karla thought as she watched him start up his truck and accelerate out of the parking lot in the same direction as the other vehicle, *I give up, just who are you?*

And more importantly, what the hell are you doing here?

Chapter Twenty-seven

As directed, the other members of the Army Ranger hunter-killer recon team awaited Wintersole when he returned to the rented KOA campsite. All except one.

"Where's one-seven?" Wintersole demanded as he and the younger, injured soldier joined the other casually dressed members of the team around the small cook fire.

"Unable to leave his position at this time, First Sergeant," the team's communication specialist and medic responded immediately. She had immediately noticed the fresh cast on one-four's left wrist under his jacket, but like the others, knew better than to ask. First Sergeant Aran Wintersole would tell them what he wanted them to know, when and if he wanted them to know. End of discussion.

"Why?"

Wintersole's brief coded message, transmitted from his truck over the secured long-range comm-net, directed the entire team to regroup at campsite Foxtrot at 1300 hours, sharp. While it wasn't unheard-of for a member of an elite, handpicked Ranger hunter-killer team to disregard a team leader's directive—as opposed to disregarding a team leader's direct order, which simply was unthinkable—the circumstances that might justify such an action were extremely limited.

And the fact that an Army Ranger first sergeant of Aran Wintersole's caliber and reputation led this particular hunter-killer recon team, instead of a more customary buck sergeant, made one-seven's decision all the more intriguing.

"Unknown, First Sergeant. His entire signal was 'one-seven, unable to disengage, out,' " the comm specialist responded.

Wintersole nodded.

"Okay, we'll debrief him when he arrives. Let's have the status reports—weapons first."

"One-five and I picked up the weapons for the militia group this morning, First Sergeant." One-two, the team's weapon specialist and ranking corporal, pulled a small notebook out of his pocket and began to read from his list. "Twenty refurbished M16A1s—one assault rifle each for the fourteen adult males and two teenage males in the group plus four spares; one hundred thousand rounds of five-five-six ball ammo; two hundred twenty-round magazines; two magazine loaders; twenty sets of Nam-era web gear, complete with canteens and first-aid kits; a used reloading outfit rigged for five-five-six military ball; sufficient supplies— bullets, powder, and primers—to reload an additional fifty thousand rounds; and twenty cleaning kits. All weapons, magazines, ammo, loaders, reloaders, supplies, and kits manufactured prior to 1976."

"Where are they now?" Wintersole asked.

"We established a temporary supply dump two klicks south of the militant compound. The site's camouflaged with rocks and local vegetation, but we were limited on the latter." The soldier shrugged. "You can only lay out so much fresh-cut pine before it starts drawing attention."

"Will it be okay out there until Saturday?"

"Yes, First Sergeant. No problem."

"Okay, good job, soldier. Next status report—recon."

One-three and one-six both reported essentially the same thing: they had cruised the local motels, bars, grocery stores, restaurants, and gas stations all morning. Neither of them had seen any sign of the Special Ops agent team Lt. Colonel John Rustman had described—federal wildlife agents who, according to their informant, supposedly had been operating in the general area for the past three and a half days. As far as they knew, one-seven would likely report the same situation. Neither soldier had any idea why their teammate suddenly found it impossible to disengage from the recon assignment.

It was left to one-three to state the obvious.

"It'll be a lot easier to spot these people once we get their profiles, First Sergeant," she offered hesitantly.

"The profiles weren't there when we checked a little while ago," Wintersole announced matter-of-factly.

No one seemed surprised. Simon Whatley was a civilian and a politician, and his young aide was an easily frightened wanna-be. That said it all.

"However, we did run across something interesting at the Dogsfire Inn, where we also suffered our first casualty: one-four's broken wrist."

Wintersole turned his attention to the injured soldier. "Give them a sit-rep," he ordered.

One-four, also known as David for any civilian purposes, presented his situation report in clear, precise, and dispassionate detail, describing his error in grabbing the woman, the response and subsequent actions of the woman's apparent boyfriend, his own failed attempt to counter the wristlock takedown, the disruptive role played by the woman's pet panther, the careful disengagement of the three men, and the brief stop he and the first sergeant had made at the local hospital for a quick set of X-rays and a cast. The injury was inconvenient, he conceded, but it would not impede his effectiveness as a member of the team. Per the first sergeant's orders, he would switch to sidearms, and trade duties with one-three for the duration. He would camouflage the white plaster cast for any fieldwork. End of report.

Wintersole nodded his head approvingly, then looked at the other members of the team.

"Questions?"

One-five raised his hand. "Do you think the boyfriend could be a cop or a federal agent?"

The injured soldier thought about the question for a long moment.

"I suppose either one is a possibility," he responded hesitantly, "but I don't believe so. If he was, he probably would have pulled a badge instead of going for the wristlock. He's martial-arts trained, no doubt about that, but at a higher level than most cops—I'm guessing third or fourth Dan—and he's definitely in competition shape. He let me think I could power out of the wristlock and put him down, then he snapped my wrist one-handed. And he stayed pretty damned cool when confronted by the first sergeant," the soldier added meaningfully. "Way I saw it, if that damned panther hadn't popped out from under that table, I think we would have had our hands full."

One-four's last statement told the other attentive members of the Ranger hunter-killer team a great deal.

One-four, the Ranger Reserve company's secondary hand-to-hand instructor, held a brown belt in judo, and a first-degree black belt in the Army Rangers' lethal version of contact karate. The black cloth belt that Company First Sergeant Wintersole wore while instructing hand-to-hand drills at Fort Bragg was worn and faded. He never mentioned his black belt rank, and no one ever had the nerve to ask. But the entire team had seen Wintersole work—on the mats, at the range, and in the live-fire Hogan's Alley exercises. The idea of an experienced and deadly senior noncom like Wintersole "having his hands full" with any single individual—with or without the backup of a fellow combat-trained Ranger—was an eye-opening concept, to put it mildly.

"I agree with one-four," Wintersole stated flatly. "The man's been in his share of scraps, no doubt about it. But he maintained control and, more importantly, made no effort to push weight. I'm guessing he's just one of the local good-old-boys, but he may have a military background.

We can't discount that possibility. I suspect he works an evening or night shift, instructs at one of the local dojos, wants to maintain a good reputation in the community, but won't back off if somebody gives his girlfriend a bad time. We won't repeat that mistake," he added meaningfully. "We need that drop point."

"Uh, one thing, First Sergeant," one-four ventured hesitantly.

"Go ahead."

"That damned cat came out from under the table where the boyfriend was sitting. I'm sure no expert on panthers, but it seems to me that might mean this guy's either real comfortable around wild animals, or has something to do with wildlife."

"That's a good observation, soldier." Wintersole nodded his head thoughtfully. "The next time we . . ."

However, he never completed that statement because at that moment, the missing member of the Ranger hunter-killer team came roaring up on his motorcycle.

All six members of the team turned and watched as the combat rifleman designated one-seven (the seventh member of Fire Team One, First Squad, Second Platoon, Delta Company, Third Battalion of the 54th Army Ranger Reserves) set the kickstand on the motorcycle and ran toward them.

He turned to Wintersole and announced breathlessly, "One-seven reporting, First Sergeant. I think I found them."

It took the Ranger hunter-killer recon team almost an hour to camouflage themselves appropriately and work their way along the low, tree-filled ridge overlooking the designated site.

"I spotted the black guy first, coming out of the local 7-Eleven," one-seven explained, speaking softly into the short-range radio mike mounted on his shirt collar as the spread-out team members focused their field glasses and spotting scopes. "It's not all that unusual to see twenty-to-forty-year-old black males walking around town, so I didn't necessarily think too much about it until I saw him hop into a beat-up car with an Asian dude. We know local real-estate figures classify this as a pretty much white, conservative, working-class community—say 3% Asian, 1% black and Hispanic combined—so I figured the odds real quick, decided I might be on to something, followed them out to a warehouse just outside town, and dug myself in deep."

"Understood." Wintersole acknowledged the soldier's perfectly valid justification for ignoring his "disengage and report back to Charlie Foxtrot immediately" directive.

"The third guy, the smaller one in the long-sleeved red shirt and vest there in the back of the booth, kinda fit the profile the colonel gave us—male, white, six-foot, one-eighty—but I wasn't convinced until I saw the big guy. He should be . . . wait a minute, there he is, coming back from latrine duty. Right side, gray plaid shirt, big belt buckle. Looks like a goddamned Abrams without the gun, don't he? I figure six-seven, six-eight, maybe three-twenty. Looks like he's done his share of weight lifting, probably even played a little pro ball back when. That's when I decided, hey, these have gotta be our boys, and reported in."

"Good job, soldier," Wintersole spoke softly into his collar mike, and then: "One-three, do you have them all?"

"Negative, First Sergeant. Two more to go," the comm specialist replied as she made a slight focus adjustment, dropped down a half stop, snapped one more quick telephoto shot, and then shifted the viewfinder of her camouflaged, telephoto-lensed and tripod-mounted camera to the next figure in the restaurant.

"Take your time," Wintersole directed her. "Let me know when you finish. We need them all for verification. Tango-one-one out."

First Sergeant Aran Wintersole smiled as he put down his field glasses.

Very good job, soldier, he thought to himself. *Now we can get down to the serious work.*

Henry Lightstone remained in place a good fifteen minutes after the camouflaged surveillance team packed up and moved off the ridgeline . . . and gave thanks that he did so when he sensed movement to his left, waited another five, then observed another camouflaged figure come up to a kneeling position in the concealing brush before moving out.

Spotter. Covering the back door, just in case. Jesus.

Lightstone felt extremely unhappy with himself, knowing that he probably wouldn't have played it safe—that he more likely would have opted to follow the group—if he hadn't been watching for the cast. When the first six figures appeared to use their left hands freely as they moved out, Lightstone had remained in place . . . and discovered that his young, muscular, trim, short-haired, intense, and ever-so-disciplined and obedient new friend with the cleverly camouflaged cast was the one who had been given—or, more likely, volunteered for—the tail-end-Charley detail.

What was I waiting for, a goddamned salute? The experienced covert agent chastised himself as he watched the camouflaged figure disappear over the ridgeline.

So that makes seven, he thought as he shifted his field glasses back to the interior of the restaurant and mentally ticked off the very familiar faces in his head.

As he did, he tried very hard to ignore the cold sick feeling in the pit of his stomach that slowly yielded to a burning, protective rage. A feeling accentuated by several pertinent overriding questions: *Just who are these people working for?*

And what the hell are they doing here?

Chapter Twenty-eight

It took Henry Lightstone a good forty-five minutes to work himself back to his truck, and another hour slowly and methodically to make a 360-degree search of the surrounding area until he felt as certain as he could that they—whoever they were—hadn't posted another spotter on the vehicle.

No reason at all why there couldn't be more than seven of them, he reminded himself.

What's the smallest mobile operating unit in the military. A squad? And how many men in a squad? Staff sergeant in charge, two buck sergeant team leaders, and what, four or five riflemen in each of the two fire teams? Eleven minimum? Nine more like those two?

Shit.

And that's being optimistic, he reminded himself. *They could be part of a maneuver platoon—four squads, forty-six minimum with a lieutenant and a platoon sergeant. Or worse, a whole damned company—a minimum of three platoons along with a captain, executive officer, and a first sergeant. Shit.*

But anything that big implies an official assignment, especially if there's a lieutenant or captain involved. But who says they have to be military? Just because they look like soldiers and act like soldiers?

Nobody.

Especially when they're using a two-way drop box to communicate with somebody. Box fourteen and box fifteen at a remote, rural post office. What else could that be? And since when did the United States Army, or United States Marines, or whatever, start communicating with their military teams by drop box?

And besides, United States government soldiers aren't supposed to be running around the county surveilling federal agents, Henry Lightstone reminded himself as he tried to decide just how paranoid he could afford to become at four o'clock on a bright and chilly Thursday afternoon when he needed to do several things very quickly.

In other words, how much time could he spend checking his truck for some kind of device?

He answered that question ten minutes later when he worked himself under the bed of the leased pickup and found the first transmitter. Or at least what he assumed was a transmitter.

Aluminum box, one-by-two-by-five inches, magnetic base, long spring steel antenna, dark green camouflage paint. What the hell else could it be?

Oh yeah, right.

Military thinking.

Why bother to track something or someone when it's a hell of a lot easier just to blow it or them into small pieces? Saves a lot of wear and tear on boot leather.

Christ, Mike, Henry Lightstone thought wishfully, *why aren't you ever around when I really need you?*

He found another device very much like the first under the engine block—except that this one had a recessed, two-pole switch on the side and spring steel antennas of different lengths sprouting from either end. He managed to get close enough to verify that the switch was set to the ON position. Then he decided to hell with it.

The first device probably *was* a transmitter, he guessed as he quickly maneuvered himself out from under the truck. But he couldn't think of any reason why a perfectly simple device like a tracking transmitter would need a protected on-off safety switch and a pair of antennas rigged for two different frequencies, assuming he read the electronics situation cor-rectly.

He could, however, think of a lot of reasons why a receiver might come equipped in such a manner. Especially one filled with C-4 and an electronic detonator.

One to activate, and one to touch it off.

Wonderful.

Okay, guys, he thought as he cautiously reached under the driver's seat, removed a small cell phone and a Velcro-secured nylon pouch, checked the contents of the pouch, slid the cell phone and the pouch under his jacket and belt, and then cautiously closed the driver's side door, *what did we step into this time?*

By a quarter to six in the evening, Henry Lightstone had finally hiked back to the center of Loggerhead City—a little bit of an exaggeration as names went, he decided, since Loggerhead City was, at best, a small town. However, the long walk gave him plenty of time to consider a number of relevant issues . . . the most important being that he had no intention of going anywhere near the warehouse where Bravo Team was busy doing God knows what. Not now. Not until he found out what was going on.

In the meantime, however, he had to warn everyone.

But not through a land line, because Takahara hadn't installed the phones in the warehouse yet.

And not through the cell phones, because people capable of playing with dual-frequency remote detonators were perfectly capable of monitoring cell-phone conversations.

Have to wait until they get back to the motel rooms, Henry decided, uneasy because he knew Paxton would keep everybody at the warehouse until they accounted for every loose snake. And that could take a while.

But could he wait that long?

He thought about that specific question all the way back to the center of town, and he finally came to the conclusion that he could. If time were critical, then one of those surveillance characters would have hung around the truck with a pair of binoculars and a transmitter set to the activating and detonating frequencies, waiting to ID the driver and blow him to bits if necessary. The fact that the team walked away from the truck implied a long-term situation: They obviously felt they had plenty of time to set off the charges under his truck if he got in their way somewhere down the line.

So, Lightstone decided, that meant he could afford to take the extra precaution of staying away from the warehouse for a few more hours, until he had a better sense of the situation, rather than risk drawing whatever attention he'd attracted to the rest of Bravo Team.

But in the meantime, he had no intention of going back to Bobby and Susan LaGrange's ranch house either, even though he felt fairly confident that no one had followed him from the ridge or his abandoned truck. However, nothing said those hard-ass characters—whoever they were, and whatever they were doing surveilling a team of covert federal agents—hadn't been tagging him, too, the last couple days.

Which means they could easily have other members of their team in place, waiting for me to show, so that they can pick up the tag . . . or split it off if I try to hand something to a messenger. And that would be real easy to do if I don't find another means of transportation pretty damned quick.

Shit.

Lightstone checked his watch and kept walking, hurrying now because the shop he remembered probably closed at six if he was lucky, or five-thirty if he wasn't.

As he walked, his thoughts returned to the transmitter and receiver. Someone could have put them on his truck earlier in the week, but he doubted it because Bravo Team had only arrived—what?—four days ago, and the only local people they'd had any significant contact with, outside of the warehouse owner and a couple of deliverymen, had been Bobby and Susan, the old coot, Sage . . . and the woman. So that didn't make much sense.

And besides, he'd found a couple of boot prints around the truck only partially wiped away by what looked like pine branches, judging by the few bright green pine needles he'd found scattered around the truck.

Which meant the camouflaged figures probably worked their way back to their vehicles, spotted his truck off the road, remembered seeing it, or—unless they were good at remembering license plates—a truck just like it back at the Dogsfire Inn.

And then went ahead and rigged it with a transmitter and detonating device, just for the hell of it? Some random truck parked on the side of the road?

Yeah, right, that makes a lot of sense.

Lightstone mentally put the past day's events in chronological order.

Bobby finds an old coot wandering around his ranch supposedly looking for Bigfoot who offers to sell him a genuine Apache Indian hunting charm. We show up at Bobby's place for dinner. Susan tells us about the old coot. Bobby and I meet him at the pancake house the next morning. Then the old guy takes me to meet a very attractive woman who seems unsure of her name and who has an overgrown house cat for a pet. The goons show up the next morning, one of them wearing a bear-claw necklace, looking for their letter, and get seriously pissed at the woman when it's not there. And I end up out in the woods with a truck rigged to squeal . . . or blow, depending.

So what kind of trail is that?

And more importantly, what do I do now?

That's reasonable.

And explainable.

And useful.

The big cardboard sign in the shop window said CLOSED, and the small block lettering on the inside of the window confirmed that 5:30 was the customary closing hour.

I need to do something that makes sense, maintains my cover, and allows me to put Bravo and Charlie Teams on notice.

And something that allows me to move about, communicate, and track back on these characters.

But at the same time, something that nobody really expects me to do.

Henry Lightstone blinked.

A helpful, smiling face appeared before his eyes.

And at that moment, he knew exactly what he was going to do.

The owner had closed the shop at five-thirty as advertised, but business was slow this time of year, he explained when he noticed Henry and opened the door. Besides, his wife never had dinner ready until seven at the earliest, so he certainly didn't mind opening up again for a serious customer.

Lightstone assured him he was quite serious.

The new models tempted him, but the image was all wrong, so he reluctantly shifted his attention to the used ones the owner displayed in the back of the store.

"What's the story on this one?" Lightstone pointed to a red-and-white Honda with visible dents in the gas tank and numerous gouges and scrapes on the fenders, exhaust, and chrome.

"That's a real sweet little machine. Honda XR 250L. Five years old, thirty-two thousand and change on the odometer. Owned by a real nice local fellow who used to play around with it on weekends. Rode it hard, but took real good care of it. But then one night he took it to a bar, had a couple beers too many, wound up in a ditch, and decided he'd probably live a whole lot longer if he stuck with four-wheeled vehicles."

"Smart man."

"Yeah, I guess that's pretty much what his wife said, too, among other things. Anyway, my son—who's a pretty decent bike mechanic—took it all apart. He says the bike's solid, no internal damage, just looks a little rough around the edges. I've listed it at twenty-five hundred for quite a while now, but as you can see, it's still here." The owner looked thoughtful for a moment. "Guess I could let her go for twenty-one," he offered hopefully.

"What would you say to twenty-five hundred even for the bike, plus one of those used leather jackets, a pair of halfway decent leather gloves, like maybe that pair in the display case, and one of those new two-hundred-dollar Bell helmets?"

"I'd say 'cash, check, or charge?'" The shop's proprietor grinned broadly.

"Cash, if you don't mind." Lightstone withdrew the nylon pouch from behind his back and counted out twenty-five one-hundred-dollar bills. "I'm not much for credit cards or checking accounts," he explained as he pushed the pile across the counter. "Lot easier to keep track of your money when you can actually see and feel it."

"A man after my own heart." The owner quickly recounted the notes, his sharp eyes automatically noting the worn condition of the bills and the widely varying serial numbers. "Tell you what," he looked even more cheerful once he dropped the folded bills into the safe slot under the cash register, "why don't you pick out your jacket, gloves, and helmet while I work out a receipt, and we'll get you and that Honda on your way."

At nearly eight o'clock that evening, the woman was clearing the last of the tables when she heard a motorcycle rumble into the parking lot.

She glanced up through the screen door and vaguely noticed the dark, leather-jacketed figure stepping onto the porch with his helmet in hand.

"Don't turn everything off yet, Danny. Looks like we've got one more customer," she called out to the cook.

She continued wiping the last table with her back to the door while the motorcycle rider entered the dining area and pulled out a chair.

"Welcome to the Dogsfire Inn," she greeted him without looking up. "Be with you in just a second."

"No hurry," the rider replied.

The sound of his voice caused her to freeze. Then Karla turned slowly and stared at him for a good ten seconds.

"Never mind, Danny," she called out toward the kitchen. "Go ahead and shut down." Then she walked slowly toward Henry Lightstone.

"Does that mean dinner's out of the question?" Lightstone asked.

"I thought . . ." She stopped and shook her head. "I thought we decided we all needed to cool off for a while. You, me, Sasha, your macho playmates."

"I don't know about anyone else, but I'm so cooled off right now, what I really need is to thaw out." Lightstone gestured toward the helmet, leather jacket, and gloves resting on the nearby chair. "And those yahoos weren't my playmates. I never saw either one of them before today."

"Do you do that a lot?"

"What?"

"Make such violent first impressions on people?" Her gold-flecked green eyes locked onto his.

The covert agent met her gaze squarely. "I was raised in a fairly strait-laced household. My mom insisted I say 'yes, ma'am' and 'no, ma'am,' and be polite to my elders, you know, help ladies cross the street whether they really need help or not."

He deliberately emphasized the word "ladies" just to see how she'd react. When he saw her hand ball into a fist, then almost immediately relax, he figured he had his answer.

"You ever call me 'ma'am' again, or try to help me cross a street, you're going to be picking up your teeth," Karla warned. "But as long as we're on the topic of your mother's influence, did she also teach you to break people's wrists when you get into conflicts?" She looked at him suspiciously.

"That was my dad's influence," he admitted, trying not to notice the way her hips flared out from her trim waist.

Uh-oh, watch yourself. You don't know who she is, or how she's related to the guy with the funny eyes . . . this is the drop point, he reminded himself.

"Dad believed in being polite, too, up to a point." Lightstone spoke cheerfully, hoping to diffuse her suspicions as well as his own, increasingly physical, thoughts.

"And then what?" She continued looking more defiant than amused.

"You stand your ground," Henry replied, making it quite clear he didn't intend to budge an inch in that particular situation either, in spite of how much his plan depended on her cooperation.

"I see."

Karla stared down at her interlaced fingers for a few moments. "You know, back in junior high my girlfriends and I used to get a kick out of watching the younger boys—probably kids just like you—in the playground standing up to the older boys—probably kids just like those two this morning."

"Let me guess. The younger ones usually got their butts stomped?"

Karla nodded her head solemnly. "Just about every time."

"Did you or your girlfriends ever notice that after one of the younger boys finally managed to win one—or at least keep standing until one of the teachers finally got there and broke it up—the older kids didn't pick on him very much anymore?"

"As I recall, we classified you XY-types into four basic groups even back then: the perpetual bullies, a pretty disgusting lot at best; the perpetual victims, who weren't much better; the ones smart enough to avoid the fights—we figured they'd be the ones who ended up rich and famous; and then"—she gave him a barely perceptible smile—"those few 'white knights' who—once they finally learned how to stay upright for the entire thirty-second fight without most of their blood running out their noses—started sticking up for their friends or the perpetual victims. But sometimes they just went for the bullies, period."

That's right, lady, you always confront the bastards right away, get right in their faces, because that's the only way you'll ever keep them off your back, Lightstone thought to himself. *So who the hell are you?*

She stopped and stared at Lightstone with those lovely gold-flecked green eyes until he felt compelled to say something.

"And the white knights kept on getting their butts stomped on a fairly frequent basis, since they usually fought out of their weight class?" Lightstone guessed.

"That's right." She continued staring at him, but he refused to look away.

"Ah," he said instead.

"You know what we used to call them?" she pressed, clearly determined to make her point.

"Not white knights, I bet." He tried another half smile, but Karla was obviously in no mood to be placated.

She shook her head firmly. "That just would have encouraged them . . . and probably gotten several of them half-killed," she added thoughtfully. "We called them the idiots."

Henry Lightstone nodded his head sympathetically.

"Why do I get the feeling you and your girlfriends cared just a little more about those poor 'idiots' than you want to admit, in spite of your better judgment?" he teased her.

"Probably because I had a couple of older brothers who had the white-knight act down cold, and a younger brother who thought they were heroes—and damned near *did* get himself killed because he tried to be just like them," she retorted hotly.

"I take it your brothers came to his rescue?" Lightstone asked, more than aware that something was going on between him and the woman, but not at all sure if it would give him the opening he so desperately needed.

Careful, he reminded himself. *Like the old fart said, nothing is really as it seems.*

"No, my brothers didn't come to his rescue," she informed him crisply. "*I* did."

"Ah."

Lightstone tried to shake the feeling that he was trapped in a very small room with a very edgy cat.

"If you don't mind my asking," he finally asked, hoping to soothe her and keep her talking because he definitely needed to use her telephone within the next few hours, "just what did they call a young girl with a white-knight complex in those days?"

"Nothing polite."

"I can imagine."

"No, I don't think you can." She outlined the edge of the place mat with a slender finger. "You're assuming I fought like a boy. Fists, knees, brute force, that sort of thing."

"Didn't you?" Henry Lightstone's eyebrows came up inquisitively.

"Of course not." The gold-flecked green eyes grew distant for a moment. "Fighting like that is a good way to get yourself hurt. I found it much more efficient—and effective—simply to scare the little bastards half to death."

Henry Lightstone smiled, and felt somewhat gratified to notice at least some of the tension leave her very tight and totally feminine body.

Whoever you are, you're one hell of an interesting lady, he thought, more aware of her increasingly physical effect on him than ever.

"I'm thinking you were probably a little young for the direct approach—you know, razor blade against the throat, that sort of thing." He tapped his fingers lightly on the table as he considered the new data, and the way her thick hair nestled in the curve of her neck. "I bet you used fear of the unknown."

"Something wrong with that?" She challenged him levelly.

"Not at all," he hastened to assure her. "A very effective way to deal with unpleasant characters, especially if you happen to be a witch—and equipped with your very own black cat," he added thoughtfully.

"Exactly." Her eyes momentarily looked far away again. "Even then."

She paused. "You know something about that, don't you?" Her question sounded more like an accusation.

"What, witchcraft?" He flashed her another friendly smile, well aware that what little tension had left her body had returned.

Who are you? Come on, lady, open up, give me a hint.

"You do that a lot, don't you?" Her gold-flecked greenish eyes impaled him with a merciless glare, and he had to fight the sensation that he dangled helplessly.

"Do what?"

"Evade serious questions."

Henry Lightstone watched his fingers lightly tapping against the rough table as though they belonged to someone else.

"In my experience, the only effective way to deal with fear of the unknown is to seek it out and confront it," he volunteered in an effort to dissipate his own increasing tension as well as hers. "If you don't, it can work its way in around the edges of your mind and become overwhelming if you're not careful."

"You worry about that sort of thing a lot in your line of work?" She continued to pinion him in place with her enticing eyes.

Oh, and by the way, would you happen to be a cop? Lightstone's covert agent instincts heard instead.

His pulse quickened.

"If you call trying to get by on a day-to-day basis a line of work, sure." He searched the sensuous young woman's face for whatever clues her expression might offer. "Like I said, I'm between jobs. But I don't think I'd like to have to worry about that sort of thing on a professional basis," he added casually. "Sounds like a good way to have a real short life."

"I'm sure it is."

Henry Lightstone couldn't even begin to interpret the edge to the woman's voice.

Why do you want to know if I'm a cop? And more to the point, why the hell would you possibly care?

They both remained silent for a good thirty seconds.

"So it turns out we have something in common after all." The corners of her lips turned up in an ironic smile.

Lightstone cocked his head curiously, wondering where this highly unpredictable woman's thoughts were taking her now.

"Fear of the unknown," she elaborated. "I'm forced to create it, and you feel equally compelled to confront it. You see the problem?"

"Sounds like one of those classic 'short-life' situations, if you ask me. Sort of like the one the male black widow faces when his mate starts taking an unhealthy interest in his whereabouts?" Lightstone suggested.

Karla gave him a penetrating look.

"Although, come to think of it, that's probably not a real good analogy," he hurriedly corrected himself, thinking, *What the hell did I say
that for? Christ sake, be careful. You don't know who she is or how she's
connected to those damned devices under your truck . . . that were put there
for the specific purpose of blowing you into small pieces. Pay attention!*

"No, not a good analogy at all."

Her smile shifted slightly, but to Lightstone's amazement *and* discom-
fort, it was still there . . . and he could feel his heart starting to beat faster.

Don't look into those goddamned eyes! Stay focused on the job, he
warned himself, but then her eyes locked on his, and he felt himself
being drawn into their depths.

Another period of contemplative silence that Lightstone felt powerless
to break enveloped them.

"So"—she stood up and glided toward him—"setting aside the self-
serving viewpoints of those black widow spiders, male or female, where
does that leave us?"

"Well, actually, I was going to suggest dinner." Lightstone hesitated.
"But all things considered, I'm not sure . . ."

The lovely gold-flecked green eyes so completely engulfed him, he
forgot what he wanted to say.

"I agree," she replied, undoing the clasp on the strap of her overalls.
"That's not a good idea at all."

Larry Paxton stared pensively at his watch.

"Okay," he addressed his crew, "that ought to do it."

After glowering fiercely at the Bravo Team leader, Dwight Stoner
opened the chest freezer, reached in, lifted a one-by-two-by-four-foot crate
out of the bottom, pivoted around, and thrust the crate deep into a plastic
wading pool full of ice.

Then, as the Bravo Team leader stood over the pool with the pump
12-gauge and Thomas Woeshack stood ready with the fire extinguisher,
Stoner and Takahara quickly backed all of the screws out of the top of
the crate using the two battery-powered multispeed drills.

"Okay, you two ready?" Paxton asked.

"I am." Mike Takahara rested his hands on the crate top and looked
at his huge partner.

Stoner nodded grimly.

"All right, one . . . two . . . three . . . now!"

At Larry Paxton's command, Takahara pulled the lid off the crate and
lunged out of the away so Stoner could flip the heavy crate upside down
on the ice.

All four agents stared wordlessly at the overturned crate, which initially moved a little, but eventually grew still.

Larry Paxton glanced down at his watch again. "Okay, thirty more seconds, just to make sure." The team leader counted down the time, then nodded to Stoner and stood ready with the shotgun.

The huge agent looked up to confirm that Mike Takahara had the snake hook ready. Then, in one quick motion, he leaned forward, grabbed the crate, lifted it up, and leaped back.

"Shit!"

KA-BLAM!

The edge of the crate caught Paxton's shoulder, causing him to stagger backward and accidentally trigger a round of bird shot off into the warehouse ceiling. The spreading pattern of small pellets narrowly missed one of the high-intensity ceiling lamps as they punched through the thin aluminum panels.

"Jesus Christ, Paxton!" Dwight Stoner screamed as he dropped the crate and grabbed his ears. The other three agents appeared equally disoriented and deafened by the incredibly loud and reverberating blast.

It took the stunned agents several seconds to regain their senses and return their attention to the wading pool.

To their amazement, two extremely thick-bodied creatures, each approximately sixteen inches long, with broad scales arranged in alternating reddish brown and tan rings, lay immobile on the six-foot-diameter bed of ice.

"Are they dead?" Concern clouded Thomas Woeshack's boyish features.

"Who the hell cares? Get those damned things into that terrarium, now!" Larry Paxton ordered, still squinting from the effects of the unexpected, close-proximity shotgun blast as he first gingerly rubbed his throbbing shoulder then racked another round into the smoking shotgun's chamber.

Using the snake hook, Mike Takahara quickly transferred each of the snakes from the bed of ice into an open terrarium nestled into an identical bed of ice in the adjoining plastic wading pool. As soon as he completed the transfer, Stoner quickly snapped one of the specially designed feeding lids in place, held the terrarium—staring nervously at the two still-immobile snakes now mere inches from his face—while Takahara hurriedly wrapped duct tape around both ends of it to make *sure* the top stayed on. Then he carefully placed the terrarium at one end of the bottom shelf of a long three-tiered plywood-and-stud-beam rack of shelves that the agents had constructed along the back wall of the warehouse.

All four agents then breathed an enormous sigh of relief.

"Which ones are these?" Thomas Woeshack asked as he brought his nose close to the glass.

"Common death adders," Mike Takahara replied.

"Far as I'm concerned, there ain't a goddamned thing *common* about a snake with death for a middle name," Larry Paxton commented as he snapped the shotgun's safety back on and set the weapon aside.

"Hey!" the team's Eskimo agent/pilot exclaimed excitedly. "I think they're starting to move!"

"Well, thank God for that," Larry Paxton muttered sarcastically as he looked down at his watch, then back up at his fellow agents. "It's now nine o'clock. A mere thirteen hours since we started this job, and we've already unloaded a whole two crates. The way I calculate it"—the team leader added, glaring over at the two duct-tape-wrapped terrariums at the far end of the long shelf, "at this rate, it shouldn't take more than oh, say, two months, tops, to unload the rest of the damned things."

"You really think this system will work for those tarantulas, too?" Thomas Woeshack asked skeptically.

"I think we need bigger wading pools, and a *lot* more ice," Dwight Stoner commented darkly.

Larry Paxton favored his subordinates with a withering glare.

"It may be necessary to modify our system to deal with the situation at hand," the Bravo Team leader acknowledged. "If we need to, we will. That's why they call us Special Agents."

"Speaking of Special Agents, I wonder what Henry's doing right now?" Mike Takahara asked his exhausted colleagues.

"I don't know." Larry Paxton snorted as he rubbed at his aching shoulder again. "But whatever it is, I hope the hell he's in some serious pain."

"And scared out of his mind?" Dwight Stoner offered.

"Oh yeah." Paxton nodded his head agreeably. "That too. Definitely."

Henry Lightstone gasped in both fear and pain when the sharp claws dug into his leg.

"Quit ... complaining," the sensuous young woman responded in a breathless voice. Her entire body gleamed with perspiration and her gold-flecked green eyes smoldered with a seemingly endless supply of passion and desire. "My nails aren't ... that long."

Every muscle in Henry Lightstone's own glistening body tensed as he fought to fend off a combination of physical and emotional sensations that seemed—from his highly stimulated point of view during those few uninhibited hours—determined to overwhelm him absolutely.

"Not you—her!"

"What?"

Karla raised her upper body to peer over her shoulder, and then arched her back and moaned as his hands roamed over her slick swollen breasts gleaming in the glow of the night light.

"When did ... she get here? Supposed to be ... locked up!" She briefly tried to control herself, but then abandoned that in favor of fully enjoying her fully aroused if slightly distracted partner.

"No idea . . . never saw her come down." Lightstone gasped, torn between passion and self-preservation, when every shred of his awareness converged on the woman's increasingly focused, heated, and frantic movements. "I wasn't paying . . . any attention."

"Good!" She began to kiss him passionately while rubbing her sweat-slickened breasts against his heaving chest.

Realizing that all sense of control had rapidly deserted him, Lightstone growled deep in his throat, and then flipped them both over so she lay on her back with her long silky legs tightly wrapped tightly around his waist and her arms around his neck.

You're insane, Lightstone, he told himself. *Absolutely fucking insane.*

He sensed, in the midst of absolute bliss, the force of the panther's head butting hard against his own and, without thinking, he shoved the huge cat aside, then proceeded to ignore both the subsequent roar and the sharp pain across his arm as he gave in to an ancient and ultimately irresistible urge. . . .

Only later, as he lay on his back, trying very hard to control both his breathing *and* his emotions—Karla snuggled tightly against his right shoulder and sighing sleepily, and the panther snuggled in tight against his neck and other shoulder rumbling contentedly—did Henry Lightstone finally realize that a goodly amount of the glossy sheen on his chest, arms and shoulders was definitely not sweat.

"Hey," he whispered to the sensuous creature laying against his right shoulder, while trying to ignore the other one rumbling against his neck.

"Hummf?"

"I think I'm bleeding to death."

"Just some scratches. Don't be a wimp," Karla mumbled. "Betadine in bathroom. Fix you up in the morn . . ." Her voice trailed off into an exhausted sigh that almost immediately gave way to the sound of soft, regular breathing.

"What do you *mean* . . . ?" he started to demand, but quickly shut up when the cat jerked awake, her bright yellow eyes suddenly appearing in the darkness and focusing on his for a brief moment before they closed again.

Moments later, the deep feline rumbling against his neck and left shoulder resumed.

Lightstone remained unmoving in the semidarkness for another ten minutes until the breathing of the enchanting but dangerous creatures on either side of him evened out into a deep-sleep rhythm.

Then, ever so carefully, he slid out from between them. When he did, the panther gracefully rolled over into his abandoned spot next to her sleeping mistress, and with equal grace the woman wrapped her body around the big cat's.

He remained motionless, silently watching the two of them until the deep rumbling slowly evened out again. Then he picked up his clothes and slowly worked his way to the bathroom door.

After carefully pulling the door closed behind him, Lightstone turned on the bathroom light, squinted, and then stared in disbelief at his right forearm, where blood oozed from four deep parallel slashes.

"Christ, no wonder it hurts," he muttered as he quickly confirmed that most of the blood covering his torso had apparently come from the wounds on his arm.

After muttering a few other things under his breath, Lightstone turned on the shower, walked over to the mirror, then winced as he examined the various wounds that corresponded to numerous tender areas on his shoulders, back, hips, and buttocks. Even though they paled in comparison to the deep gouges that crisscrossed his calves and his right hand, to say nothing of the four outright slashes into his right forearm, a few of the human-induced scratches were deep enough to have bled slightly.

You may have short nails, lady, but you sure as hell know how to use them.

The warm shower felt wonderful, but the rivulets of diluted blood swirling around Henry Lightstone's feet reminded him of the real reason for his visit.

He tried not to curse as he rubbed soap into the wounds, reminding himself that it would get a lot worse in a few minutes. He rinsed off, dried himself as best he could with the single large bath towel on the rack, used some folds of toilet tissue as a temporary compress, opened the medicine chest . . . and sighed.

The antiseptic spray caused him to blink a few times when he awkwardly applied the stinging mist to the scratches that crisscrossed his shoulders, back, hips, butt, calves, and hand. But he knew that cat bites and scratches could be highly infectious, and he could think of no reason why panther claws would be any different.

Which meant he needed something stronger.

Must be out of my goddamned mind, he told himself as he reached for the small brown bottle on the top shelf of the medicine chest.

Without thinking about it any more than absolutely necessary, he quickly removed the makeshift compress, firmly placed his right hand palm down against the bottom of the porcelain sink, poured the Merthiolate down the full length of the first deep slash in his forearm . . .

And then sprayed the rest of it all over the bathroom wall when he slammed his left hand against the sink while trying—with only minimal success—to contain an anguished scream.

He was still trying to regain his senses when the door behind him burst open.

"What in the world are you . . . oh my God!"

"Sorry, didn't mean to wake you," he mumbled thickly, blinking back the tears as he tried to will away the agonizing pain in his forearm that knifed all the way up into the center of his skull.

"I thought—Jesus, never *mind* what I thought," the woman muttered as she grabbed his arm, quickly examined the deep slashes, and then observed the empty Merthiolate bottle in the sink and the bright red spray pattern all over her bathroom wall.

"I swear I don't understand you males," she continued muttering as she squatted down and removed a brown plastic bottle and a large tube of ointment from the cabinet beneath the sink, along with a handful of large gauze pads and a roll of medical tape. "Every damned one of you seems to go into arrested development the moment you turn twelve.

"And by the way," she added absentmindedly as she removed the top from the larger bottle, "didn't I tell you to use the Betadine solution?"

"What's that?" Henry Lightstone's glazed eyes slowly began to focus, a process that rapidly accelerated when he realized that she was stark naked, and that he was actually seeing her that way—in the light—for the first time.

"Tamed iodine," she explained. "Works just as well as Merthiolate, but doesn't make your eyeballs pop out of your head." Working quickly and professionally, she stoppered the sink, pushed his hand back down onto the bottom of the porcelain sink, then lathered and rinsed the bloody slashes in his forearm repeatedly.

"There, isn't that better?"

"Much." Lightstone nodded gratefully.

"I don't know what got into her," the sensuous young woman apologized as she gently blotted the wounds dry with a clean cloth, smoothed a thick layer of antibiotic ointment over them, and neatly bandaged his arm.

"If it's anything like what got into you, I don't want to know about it."

Karla blinked, started to say something . . . then thought better of it.

"You may be closer to the truth there than you think," she admitted, giving him the full benefit of her gold-flecked green eyes. But before Lightstone could say anything, she began examining his other wounds.

"Hey, what's that all about?" she demanded, pointing to his shoulder.

"As I recall, that's where you bit me." Lightstone tried very hard to ignore the sensual impact of the woman's close and naked presence, and failed miserably. "I guess some women reach for a cigarette afterward, and others just try to rip a guy's shoulder off."

"No, not those little things, I mean *these*, right here," she persisted, running her fingers lightly over the patch of ragged white scar tissue on his shoulder. "I sure as hell didn't do that . . . and these either," she added as she moved behind him to examine his back. "What caused all this?"

"Well, uh . . ."

"You know, several of these scars *do* look an awful lot like claw marks." She moved closer to examine the scar tissue and, in doing so, unconsciously pressed her breasts against his arm and back. "But I don't think a cat made them."

"Bear," Lightstone mumbled, thinking, *Jesus, I've got to get out of here!*

"What?" She pulled him around by his shoulders and stared into his pain-dulled eyes.

Careful.

"Bare. Naked. We're both standing here bare-ass naked—"

His comment momentarily confused her until she looked down at herself.

"Oh."

"That's right, 'oh.' And it would be a lot easier," Henry Lightstone went on halfheartedly, "if you'd go get dressed before—"

"Before what?" she deliberately lowered her voice to a sultry whisper and pressed her body firmly against his.

"This isn't what it looks like."

"It certainly looks like it to me."

"That's not what I meant."

I don't know what I meant, but that wasn't it, Lightstone tried to tell himself. *And if it was, I don't want to know about it.*

"I know." She ran her fingers lightly over the irregular pattern of scar tissue on his shoulder again, and let them trail slowly and gently down his chest. "Just shut up and let me take care of it."

Oh Christ.

She was still moving her warm hands over his lower torso, thirty seconds later, when the sudden sound of sharp claws digging into the outside surface of the bathroom door, immediately followed by a loud and demanding yowl, jarred them both.

"Ignore her," the woman ordered in that same sultry whisper.

"Yeah, but what if—"

"Don't worry, she can't get in here." She nibbled his earlobe.

The sound of shredding wood grew louder and the yowling more insistent as the door rattled on its hinges.

"Are you sure?" The look and feel of her warm and smooth body wrapping around his made it difficult for him to think clearly.

"Trust me. It'll take her a while," she murmured, pressing her soft warm lips against his.

Chapter Twenty-nine

By eleven o'clock that Thursday evening, Wildlife Special Agents Mark LiBrandi and Gus Donato of Charlie Team figured they had their surveillance system down pat.

It's simply a matter of timing, Donato explained to LiBrandi as they drove into the parking lot of the Creekside Bar. Go in, find the closest thing available to a dark corner table, let the waitress take her own sweet time getting there, order a pair of drafts, put a few wrinkled one-dollar bills on the table—enough to cover the two beers plus a minimal tip, to discourage any further interest on her part—milk the beers as long as possible, then order a couple of coffees at the precise moment her patience finally runs out.

With any luck at all, they could stretch that whole process out for at least an hour—ideally an hour and a half—thereby maintaining their surveillance for a reasonable time at each bar in town without undue risk to their covers, their covert per-diem limits, their sobriety, or their waistlines.

"Hope that Sally gal isn't on duty tonight," Donato remarked as they approached the entrance. "I think she's getting kinda sweet on you. Must've come by our table at least a half dozen times the other night."

"Maybe you tipped her too much?" Librandi suggested.

"Fifty cents on a couple watered-down two-seventy-five beers?"

"No, you're probably right," the young covert agent conceded. "She must be hot for my bod."

"Well, try to keep it in your pants tonight. I don't think I can stand more than one cheap beer at this place, and I don't even want to think about their coffee."

As it turned out, Sally was off on Mondays and Thursdays. And while several of the easily recognizable regulars slumped in the cheap, Naugahyde-covered booths or hovered around the pool table, the booth in the darkened far corner of the bar was available. Accordingly, the pair of agents ordered their beers, took their turns at the pool table, tried to ignore the necking couple in the adjoining booth, engaged in a few casual conversations that never quite worked around to the local militia groups, and finally ordered two cups of the bar's predictably bitter coffee at twelve-fifteen.

Ten minutes later, having dumped a good three-quarters of their coffee in the fake potted fern behind their booth, Donato and LiBrandi departed, trying to decide whether to finish the evening at the Gopher's Hole—a seedy sports bar with no apparent relationship to any kind of mammal, much less a gopher, but which offered an impressive collection of Confederate battle flags and other Civil War memorabilia—or go all out and splurge at the more upscale Gunrack Saloon, locally known for its decent beer and equally impressive collection of deer antlers.

Busy arguing the investigative merits of the two local watering holes as they walked toward their rental car, the young and inexperienced covert agents failed to notice that the necking couple had followed them into the parking lot.

A few minutes after one in the morning, Henry Lightstone slowly and carefully worked himself out of bed for the second time that night.

It was much easier this time because the panther had retreated to her tree loft, and—judging from the audible snoring—slept soundly. He and the woman had finally managed to distract the big cat by retreating to the shower. While Lightstone held his bandaged arm high above the spray of water, the woman quickly rinsed off then ran dripping to open the partially shredded door. The panther leaped into the bathroom, padded to the shower, stuck her head around the curtain, and stared bleakly at Henry Lightstone through the spray for a few moments. Then she pulled her head back out, shook off the water, and exited the bathroom with a shrug of feline indifference that left Lightstone feeling inexplicably disappointed.

And getting out of bed was also easier because Karla had fallen into a deep sleep within moments of her head hitting the pillow.

Henry Lightstone could have duplicated that trick without the least difficulty, but he needed to do something very important before he allowed himself the luxury of a good night's sleep.

It took him a few minutes to locate his clothes and put on everything except his shoes. Then he slowly worked his way through the adjoining tree-room, down the hallway, and into a small room he'd identified earlier as the postmistress's office.

He didn't dare risk a light, but rather felt his way carefully in the dark until he located the old dial phone on the standard-issue metal desk. It had been so long since he'd used a dial phone, he had to open one of the window shades to let in some moonlight so he could see well enough to dial the number of the motel that Bravo Team had chosen as a home base.

"Holiday Inn."

"Larry Packer's room, please."

"One moment."

Lightstone heard the distant phone ring eight times before the operator came back on the line.

"I'm sorry, sir, your party doesn't answer. Would you like to leave a message?"

Yes, I would, Lightstone thought, *but I wouldn't know where to start.*

"Could you try Dwight Stanley's room, please?"

"Just a moment."

This time the operator cut in after only seven rings.

"Neither of your parties answer, sir. Would you care to leave a message?"

"No, that's all right."

Henry Lightstone pulled his watch out of his jeans pocket, then frowned at the 0132 digital display. Under normal circumstances, members of the covert team still could be out at this time of night, either working on some phase of the operation, or eating a late dinner.

But nothing about this entire operation has been normal so far, he reminded himself as he glanced down at his bandaged forearm.

He felt tempted to call Halahan or Moore, figuring a 4:30 A.M. wake-up call was the least the two Special Ops branch supervisors deserved for the red-kneed spider business. But he also realized that local post office managers often checked the phone records of the small rural locations, to discourage personal use of official phones by the resident postmasters. The last thing he needed right now was the woman getting called in to explain a 1:30 A.M. phone call to an unlisted number on the East Coast.

Nor could he use the cell phone because even if those real or fake soldiers didn't monitor calls in the middle of the night, he'd left it in the saddle bag of his motorcycle, and he couldn't get it because Karla had activated an alarm system after locking the outside doors and shutting off the lights in the restaurant. It was always possible that some of the windows weren't alarmed, but that would be difficult to determine in the darkness, and a triggered alarm would be equally difficult to explain.

Using the little available moonlight, it took Lightstone another five minutes to confirm his suspicion that an old-time wildlife officer and resident agent like Wilbur Boggs wouldn't list his home phone in the directory. The local office number for the Division of Law Enforcement, U.S. Fish and Wildlife Service was listed, but not knowing anything about local arrangements, or the backgrounds of any other employees who might have access to the answering machine there besides Boggs and his secretary, he decided to save that option until things became a bit more desperate.

Ditto for the local FBI, DEA, and sheriff's offices. While Lightstone didn't question a local federal agent or sheriff's deputy's ability to relay a carefully worded message, such a request—especially at one-thirty in the morning—would almost certainly require a personal display of his credentials or, at the very least, more of an explanation than he was willing or able to provide at that moment.

Which only left one more option, and a very interesting question.

If these military—*or militant, that's always a possibility in this area of the country,* he reminded himself—characters could tag a supposedly alert team of covert federal agents to what Lightstone assumed was Charlie Team's operational warehouse, what were the chances that this group had also tagged all of Bravo Team to Bobby LaGrange's ranch?

The more he thought about *that,* the less he liked it.

The phone rang three times before a very familiar voice answered in an equally familiar, grumpy manner.

"You never did like getting called out at one-thirty in the morning, did you?"

"What?"

"Without mentioning my name," Henry Lightstone directed carefully, "do you know who this is?"

The wild-card agent could easily visualize his ex-partner snapping wide-awake.

"Yeah, you sound vaguely familiar. What's up?" LaGrange's voice carried a discernible—and dangerous—edge.

"We may have a problem." Lightstone briefly described the sequence of events starting from the confrontation at the restaurant and ending with his purchase of the motorcycle.

"Christ," the ex–homicide detective whispered. "Do they know about it?"

"No, not yet."

"You want me to make contact with them?"

"No, too dangerous. You were the link to the old coot with the genuine Apache Indian hunting charms," Lightstone reminded him. "If everything else connects, we could easily be on a party line right now."

"Yeah, right." Bobby LaGrange fell silent for a few moments. "Shit."

"Exactly," Henry Lightstone responded, knowing what kind of thoughts raced through his ex-partner's mind. "Can you two camp out somewhere?"

A pause.

"Yes."

In the background, Henry Lightstone heard a drawer opening, then the familiar sound of a semiautomatic pistol slide slowly being drawn back.

That's right, buddy, he thought approvingly, *Susan's number one, no matter what.*

"Then you'd better do it, just to be safe. What about Justin?"

"He's with his . . . relatives for the rest of the week."

"Can you keep him there?"

"Sure, no problem. What about you?"

"I'm staying put. If I've got a tag, there's no point complicating things at your end."

"Yeah, right," LaGrange acknowledged. "Are you secure?"

Translation: do you want help? Just say so. I'll get Susan tucked away somewhere safe, and then be there with the cavalry ASAP. Lightstone smiled. *Good old Bobby. Hell of a partner.*

"I'm fine, but I'm out of contact with everyone else right now, so if Larry calls, tell him what's going on, and that I'll connect up with them sometime tomorrow morning."

"Will do. Anything else?" Bobby's question came out a little faster than usual.

In a hurry to get Susan out of there. Good thinking.

"Still got your beeper?"

"Yeah, somewhere. I'll find it."

"Okay, get going. I'll be in touch."

Lightstone was in the process of hanging up the phone when he sensed a presence in the doorway.

He turned around slowly, trying to decide what he could say, and then saw—to his immense relief—what, under any other circumstances, would have absolutely terrified him: a pair of glowing yellow eyes hovering at about waist height.

"Christ, you scared the hell out of me, Sasha," he whispered.

The panther responded with a deep-throated growl that sounded more like a cough.

It occurred to Lightstone that he'd never been alone with the fearsome animal for any significant period of time before, and that the panther might consider his presence in the woman's office an unacceptable transgression.

But then the big cat made another noise that sounded both familiar and demanding.

"What do you want? Something to drink?" Lightstone hazarded a guess.

The panther immediately turned, walked down the hallway, and waited patiently for a disbelieving Henry Lightstone to open the secured door to the restaurant's kitchen.

"We could both get into serious trouble for this," he whispered as the cat proceeded to rub the side of her head against the edge of the commercial refrigerator. "But you don't care, do you?"

Apparently deciding an answer to such a dumb question constituted a waste of a perfectly good growl, the panther sat silently and waited patiently for Lightstone to open the refrigerator, find an already-opened half gallon of milk, and locate a bowl.

He poured about a half pint of milk into the bowl, put it down on the vinyl floor, and stared expectantly at the panther. She stared right back at him, unmoving.

"You want more?"

He poured another half pint or so in the bowl and got exactly the same response.

"Christ, what are you, picky or — ?"

At that moment, it occurred to Henry Lightstone that a hundred-pound panther probably wasn't all that much different from an eight-pound Manx . . . especially in terms of self-serving attitude.

Accordingly, he opened the refrigerator, rooted around until he found a quart of cream, glared at the panther once more, dumped the milk into the nearby sink, and replaced it with the cream.

He barely managed to get the bowl on the floor before the panther butted him aside and began lapping happily at the cream.

Muttering to himself, Lightstone returned the milk and cream to the refrigerator, noticed a partial loaf of pumpernickel and a plastic-wrapped plate of sliced turkey on one of the upper shelves, and realized he was hungry.

Five minutes later, as he chewed a first large bite of the thickly stacked turkey sandwich, something else occurred to him.

The letter.

It took him another two minutes to find his way past the public rest room to the door of the back room of the tiny post office, which the woman apparently had forgotten to lock.

Fortunately, enough moonlight came in through a skylight to illuminate the area.

Lightstone found two envelopes in box number fifteen, a manila one about an inch thick, and a second plain mailing one — identical, as best he could tell, to the envelope Karla had sold the man with the strange eyes — that felt like it contained a single, folded piece of paper. The addresses on the envelopes, each obviously written by a different individual, were both block-printed. And even more interesting, Lightstone thought, both individuals used the adjacent Dogsfire Inn Post Office Box Number Fourteen as a return address.

The covert agent momentarily considered opening both envelopes, but then immediately rejected the idea. Tampering with US mail was a fairly serious felony, and he well knew that the probable-cause information he possessed was circumstantial at best — and certainly far less than any federal judge would require to issue a search warrant for a subject's private mail. Which meant—among many other things—that any leads he might obtain as a result of opening and reading those letters would inevitably fall under the "fruit-of-the-poisoned-tree" rule.

In all, three very good reasons to put both envelopes right back where he found them.

Lightstone started to do exactly that, but then noticed an assortment of letters and flyers in box thirteen. A quick check confirmed that mail had been accumulating there for several days.

Smiling maliciously, he put the thick envelope back into box fifteen, but slipped the thin envelope—the one he was almost certain the man with the cold gray eyes had addressed and sealed—into the middle of the mail stack in box thirteen.

Then he hurried to the nearby counter, pulled a sheet of paper and an envelope out of the supply stacks, picked up one of the available US government pens, block-printed five words, folded the paper and placed it into the envelope, block-printed the appropriate P.O. Box Fourteen and P.O. Box Fifteen addresses on it, tore a first-class stamp off one of the available sheets, put the appropriate change in the stamp tray, and was looking around for a cancellation stamp and ink pad when he heard footsteps.

Lightstone quickly tossed the envelope upside down into box fifteen and was heading for the door when he heard a voice outside.

"Henry?"

He barely had time to duck behind the counter before the door opened and the light came on.

He sensed Karla moving toward him, then heard a loud yowl that also caught her attention.

"Sasha?"

Another yowl, this time louder.

"What did I do, forget to lock up out here, and forget to feed you, too?"

If anything, the third yowl sounded even more insistent and demanding.

"Is that right? So what did you do with your buddy? Stash him up in the tree house?"

Henry waited until the sensuous young woman stepped back into the hallway and began walking toward the restaurant kitchen. As she did, he quickly and quietly stood up, slipped around the partially opened door and into the darkened hallway, and cautiously nudged the public bathroom door open. Then he lunged for the urinal, hit the flush lever, ran some water over his hands in the sink, wiped them with a paper towel, and hurried out into the hallway and around the corner . . .

"There you are!" Karla yelled as she stepped into view.

Lightstone froze, his eyes wide-open in surprise.

"Christ Almighty, that's a good way to give a guy a heart attack!" he complained as he stared down at the enticing body that was barely concealed by the thin cotton nightgown.

"Good. You deserve one."

"Oh yeah? How come?"

"I thought you might try to sneak out on me, which is about what I can expect from men these days. But then I find out you're even more devious."

"You call taking a leak in a portion of a house not inhabited by a bathroom-door-shredding panther *devious*?" Lightstone tried, uncertain of how much of his movements Karla had actually seen.

"No, *this* is what I call devious." She slapped the partially eaten turkey sandwich into his hand.

"Oh, that. Well, uh, I can explain *that*," he began hesitantly.

"Go ahead. Explain to me why you only made one, and then didn't bother to wake me up to share it?"

"Well, uh, you looked tired." He looked down at the sandwich. "Hey, wait a minute, I only took one bite out of this."

"I was tired, and I still am, but I'm also hungry." She gracefully led the way into the kitchen. "You ought to be grateful I only took the one bite and gave it back. And speaking of lucky," she added as she turned on the lights, "I'm amazed you found your way through this maze in the dark."

"I had help." Lightstone glanced meaningfully at the panther.

"So I see." Karla nodded as she watched the panther stare back at Lightstone, and then emit a much softer, protesting yowl.

"She complains a lot, too," he added.

"Life's tough when the men in your life won't cooperate."

Lightstone's brow wrinkled in confusion. "What do you mean by that?"

"She likes you."

"Yeah, so?"

"I mean she *likes* you. As in *a lot*."

Henry Lightstone blinked.

"You're kidding."

"I don't think so."

"You mean . . . ?"

"Uh-huh."

"But I'm . . . I mean, she's . . ."

"Nobody ever accused us females of being smart or practical in our relationships, Henry. However," she added thoughtfully as she glanced down at the sandwich in his hand, "we *can* be distracted."

Taking advantage of the thoroughly stunned expression on Henry Lightstone's face, Karla snatched the sandwich out of his hand, took another large bite, handed it back, went into the refrigerator for a gallon jug of water and a half gallon of milk, and then noticed the bowl on the floor.

"I see she conned you into letting her into the kitchen."

"Uh, yeah, as a matter of fact, she did," Lightstone admitted. "Is that a problem?"

"Only if the county health inspectors find out." She smiled. "Grab that bowl, hang on to these, and we'll get her out of here."

She handed him the jugs of water and milk, got the sliced turkey and pumpernickel from the refrigerator, and picked up two empty glasses. Then she led him into a private employee's lounge consisting of a wooden table, two chairs, and an ancient refrigerator.

Kneeling, she poured about a quart of the chilled water into the bottom of a large stainless-steel bowl, then nodded in satisfaction when the panther quickly thrust her muzzle into the bowl and began lapping away.

"What?" the woman asked when the stunned expression on Henry Lightstone's face shifted to one of total disbelief.

"Let me guess, she conned you out of the milk, didn't she?"

"Uh, well . . ."

"Don't tell me. You gave her cream?"

Lightstone nodded glumly.

Karla closed her eyes and sighed. "Henry, do you have any idea what can happen when you feed a cat milk or cream?"

"I vaguely recall my grandmother saying it wasn't a good idea," Lightstone volunteered tentatively. "Will she be all right?"

"You mean Sasha? Oh, she'll be fine. You may not be, though, after you get done cleaning up."

"That bad?"

"A panther with the runs is an impressive sight, my friend. So much so, I strongly suggest you cross your fingers and pray to whatever gods you think might take an interest in your problem."

"Seems to me that sort of problem would probably rate pretty low on the old deity-response list."

"If I were a god, that's certainly the way I'd see it," the sensuous young woman admitted agreeably as she filled the two glasses with milk. "But then, too, I always thought you XYs were too damned gullible for your own good . . . especially when it comes to double-Xs."

She opened the ancient refrigerator, took out a large butcher-paper-wrapped package, unwrapped its contents, deftly hacked the hindquarters of a good-sized deer in several chunks with an ominously sharp cleaver, and dropped them into the large stainless-steel feeding pan next to the panther's water bowl.

"That's an interesting perspective," Lightstone commented as he watched the panther tear into the hide-covered meat with her teeth and claws.

"Don't *ever* forget what she is, Henry. A hundred-pound panther with very deep-seated predatory instincts," Karla reminded him very seriously. "And speaking of self-preservation," she added, looking down at the significantly reduced stack of turkey slices, "it's a good thing you left some of this for me, or you'd have to fight both of us for what's left of that sandwich."

"I think I'll stick to fighting the human XYs, if it's all the same to you two," Lightstone replied, eyeing the temporarily distracted panther uneasily.

"Good idea. You'll probably live a lot longer." Karla quickly built herself a sandwich just as thick as Lightstone's, then tossed the remaining scraps of meat into the panther's bowl.

"As long as we're on that topic," Lightstone ventured as they sat down at the table and started in on their sandwiches, "you got any suggestions about how I should deal with *my* problem?"

"By 'my problem,' I assume you refer to the common male fantasy of having two adoring females on your hands at one time, both of whom happen to live in the same house . . . as opposed to *her* problem, of course?" Lightstone could see a glitter of pure amusement in the young woman's eyes.

"Uh, no, that's not exactly what I meant."

"Well, Henry my friend" — Karla handed him the last two bites of her sandwich — "as one of the interested parties, I'm not sure I'm the best person to advise you on how to handle your 'problem.' However," she added, "I would say that I'm probably the best person around here to advise you on what you *shouldn't* do."

"Which is?" Lightstone asked warily.

The woman glanced fondly down at her pet snapping the deer femur like a toothpick with her powerful jaws, "you really shouldn't go wandering around with Sasha at night all by yourself anymore. Unless, of course, you take along a nice big picnic basket full of deer meat and turkey sandwiches."

"A picnic basket?"

"Like I said," she added with an ambiguous smile as she picked up her glass of cold milk, "we *can* be distracted."

Chapter Thirty

First Sergeant Aran Wintersole met with his team at an all-night coffee shop some ten miles distant from the Gopher's Hole, where Wildlife Special Agents Mark LiBrandi and Gus Donato of Charlie Team had finished their Thursday evening shift of barhopping.

"Did you send the photos?" he asked the team's communications specialist after the waitress had departed.

The young female soldier nodded her head solemnly. In a public restaurant, surrounded by civilians who might easily overhear any scrap of conversation, they automatically dropped the use of military demeanor and team-member designations.

"I had the negs processed and printed in Ashland, four-by-five color, and dropped them off at the post office at" — she hesitated briefly as she translated the military time — "a little after seven this evening. I included the primary subjects and the secondaries. Figured the Colonel might want to see who these people have been contacting. The package should go out in the . . ." she paused only briefly this time, ". . . 8:00 A.M. pickup."

"Did you include the ones of the subjects at the drop point, including that character with the truck?"

"Yes."

"Good. We need verification, and I'm tired of waiting for those profiles." Wintersole nodded approvingly, then looked at the other team members. "How did it go this evening?"

"One thing for sure, those two at the Gopher's Hole were definitely trolling," one-five reported.

"For what?" Wintersole leaned forward expectantly.

"That I don't know," the civvies-dressed soldier admitted, "but the one time I talked with them, it was pretty obvious they wanted the conversation to work its way around to the local militant groups."

"They ever ask anything directly?"

"Never." One-five shrugged. "Just my impression."

"I agree with John," one-six added. "They brought up — or responded to — just about every related topic: right-wing politics, fundamentalist religion, guns, the federal government, you name it."

"So what do they want?" Wintersole addressed the entire group.

"Wilbur Boggs, for one thing," the communications specialist volunteered softly.

That brought Wintersole's head up in surprise.

"Are you sure?"

The communications specialist nodded. "David and I"—she nodded toward the injured member of the team—"managed to get close enough to dangle one of the pickup mikes over the back of their booth."

"And?" Wintersole pressed her for details.

"Putting a bunch of things they said together, I got the impression that everybody on their team—except for the three we keep seeing," she emphasized, "go out looking for Boggs every day."

"That doesn't make any sense." Wintersole lowered his voice as he looked around at the members of his hunter-killer team. "Why would an undercover team of federal wildlife agents try to make contact with the local resident wildlife agent—a man so well known throughout the county he could easily blow their cover—when they're supposed to be covertly working their way in on the Chosen Brigade of the Seventh Seal?"

"Maybe they think he could help them pinpoint specific members of the group—the ones who might be more approachable?" one-seven suggested.

"If that's the case, then why can't they find him?" Wintersole asked reasonably. "He lives only a few miles from his office, and we know he was out at the lake last Sunday."

"And we also know his vehicles are still at his house, both government and personal," one-three added.

"And so do they," one-five reported. "They were out there this evening and sure acted like they knew the place. One of them just jumped out of the car, ran up to the front door, knocked, tried the knob, and then took a quick look through the garage window. Didn't even bother going around to the back."

"You think they checked his office?" one-three asked.

"First thing," one-four responded confidently. "If he was there, all they would've had to do was make a simple call-in asking for a meet at a remote location. Which means Boggs probably isn't out on assignment or on leave," he added.

"Maybe he just took off without telling anyone," one-three suggested. "You think he'd be allowed to do that?"

"Pretty damned loose outfit if he could," one-two commented.

"According to Rustman, the man doesn't take real vacations," Wintersole reported thoughtfully. "Spends his days off out on the lake fishing. But that brings up an interesting point," the first sergeant added. "If those agents have checked his office and his house—probably more than once from the sound of it—and they're still looking for him instead of doing what they were sent out here to do, they must have a real good reason for wanting to talk with him. Which could help us, because we need some way to bring them all together at one location at a specified time."

"So if we find Boggs first, we can use him as bait," one-three came to the obvious conclusion.

"Exactly." Wintersole nodded grimly. "The question is, how do we do that before they do?"

"Man likes to fish, but he probably won't want to do much of that for a while," one-two suggested with a smile. "Last time we saw him at Rustman's place, he was bleeding from the nose real bad, and it looked like at least one of his hands was broken. He must have spent at least four hours in the water cutting all that rope and netting loose."

"He did look pretty wiped out by the time he got that boat back to shore," one-seven confirmed. "Gotta hand it to him. He's a tough old bird. If I'd been hurt that bad, I'd have called for a medic straightaway."

Wintersole turned to the team's communications specialist/medic and smiled thinly.

"The hospital," she whispered softly, when the realization hit her suddenly. "I'll bet that's exactly where he is right now."

Chapter Thirty-one

At 8:05 that Friday morning, with his heart pounding in his chest, Congressional Aide Keith Bennington stumbled into the Dogsfire Inn Post Office, fumbled with the key, and then blinked in surprise when he saw the inch-thick manila envelope lying sideways in box fifteen with another much thinner envelope.

"Christ, it's about time somebody finally put something in the damned thing," he muttered, heartsick because the presence of the envelope would make it even more difficult to convince his boss that there wasn't much point making two trips a day out to the rural post office — at 8:00 A.M. and 6:00 P.M. — to check on an empty mailbox.

This was Bennington's third trip to the Dogsfire Inn since that fateful night when his attempt to deliver the federal-agent profiles resulted in his horrifying confrontation with the nightmarish creature whose hovering—

and glowing—yellow eyes still haunted his dreams. And it hadn't gotten any better. In fact, it took every ounce of resolve that the young congressional aide could muster just to get out of his car and enter the post office.

He had hoped to talk Marla Cordovian into taking over—or at the very least sharing—the drop-off and pickup runs, but the strikingly attractive young intern hadn't spoken three words to him since the weekend hunting trip at Rustman's, and office rumor hinted that Smallsreed wanted her to fill an open slot at his DC office.

Bennington tried not to think about the other—more lurid—aspects of that rumor.

Not that Whatley would listen to me anyway, he thought morosely as he pulled the envelope out of the mailbox, quickly relocked the small metal door, and hurried back to his car.

Ever since his red-eye flight to DC the previous Wednesday, Simon Whatley's mood had vacillated wildly between rabid dementia and manic-depression, a fact not lost on any member of the congressional district office staff.

And that was after just one flight, Bennington reminded himself, breathing easier once he locked all the car doors and turned the key in the ignition. *God, what's he going to be like tonight?*

Probably either homicidal or suicidal, Bennington decided as he hurriedly started up the car, gunned the engine, backed up, and accelerated out of the parking lot . . . then pinned his hopes on "suicidal" as the better option of the two.

Chapter Thirty-two

"You two planning on getting out of bed sometime today?"

Henry Lightstone blinked slowly awake . . . and immediately found himself staring into a pair of adoring bright yellow eyes.

The shock of waking up six inches from the muzzle of a fully grown panther still surged through his nervous system when he became aware that his right forearm throbbed painfully.

The panther rumbled a greeting. And all of the relevant pieces began to fall into place in his sleep-starved mind.

"What time is it?" he mumbled as he cautiously turned over and looked up at the slender woman leaning in the doorway with her arms folded across her chest.

"According to my watch, about twenty after eight."

"How long've you been up?"

"Since about five-thirty this morning. I've got a restaurant and a post office to run, a government to curse, and fortunes to tell, remember?"

Lightstone blinked some more, heaved himself up on his elbows, and then looked at the panther, stretched lazily out on the bed with her eyes closed, her head resting against her right shoulder, and her right forepaw pressing against his arm. Then full awareness struck home.

"You left me alone in this bed with her . . . for three hours?" he sputtered.

"Sure, why not?" Karla shrugged, although a hint of a smile appeared at the corner of her lips. "It's common knowledge you men are pretty useless once you fall asleep."

"And a cheerful good morning to you, too."

"Although come to think of it," she added thoughtfully, "from the looks of that bed, I'm not sure how much sleeping the two of you did after I left."

Henry Lightstone stared in disbelief at the patterns of dried blood that covered what little remained of the torn sheets.

"Jesus Christ," he muttered as he sat up in the bed and looked around.

"Mother warned me about letting strange men in my bed," Karla commented, "but I think this particular situation far exceeds anything she possibly imagined. Maybe I should send her a copy of the photo. Better yet," she smiled brightly, "I wonder what the *National Enquirer* would pay?"

"You took a picture of me lying here?"

"I can just see the headlines now," Karla went on, ignoring his question, " 'FEMALES SCORNED. CATFIGHT LEAVES BOYFRIEND WITH HURT FEELINGS.' "

"Is there some purpose to this visit, other than to give me a bad time about your sheets?" Lightstone inquired tersely.

"As a matter of fact, there is. I came to let you know that breakfast will be on the table at nine sharp . . . unless, of course," she smiled brightly again, "you'd like it served in bed?"

At ten minutes to nine, Henry Lightstone entered the screened dining area with a tight-jawed look on his face, the panther following closely at his side.

"And how are we doing this fine morning?" Karla inquired cheerfully as she put a bowl of water on the floor for the panther, attached the control collar around her neck, and poured Lightstone's coffee.

"I have to go to the bathroom," the covert agent muttered irritably.

The sensuous young woman cocked her head.

"Is this one of those 'my boyfriend has this really bizarre problem' situations they write about in *Cosmo*?" she whispered hopefully. "Or are you just asking permission?"

Lightstone leaned toward her until their heads almost touched.

"What I'm asking," he hissed through gritted teeth, "is for you to keep that damned cat here, and distracted, so that I can go into the bathroom, unzip my pants, and take a leak without having a hundred-pound panther nuzzle at my crotch."

"I don't know, that sure sounds like a bizarre guy-problem to me." She smiled brightly and glanced down at her watch. "However, I think I can guarantee you a maximum of nine minutes, following which your breakfast will be placed on the table and all bets are off."

"Deal."

Three minutes later, Lightstone emerged from the public rest room, and entered the back room of the post office—determined to find a cancellation stamp for the letter he'd dropped in box fifteen the previous evening. However, he then noticed that box fifteen was empty, heard footsteps, and was in the process of pulling the door to the back room shut behind him when a FedEx agent hurrying down the hallway with a package almost knocked him over.

"Excuse me, my fault," Lightstone apologized.

"Oh, uh, no problem." The uniformed deliveryman offered a brief but harried smile. "Say, uh, you wouldn't happen to know if the postmaster . . . or postmistress," he corrected himself, looking over Lightstone's shoulder at the not-quite-shut office door with a hopeful expression on his face, "is around anywhere?"

"Last time I saw her, she was heading toward the kitchen. She should be out in a few minutes."

"Oh . . . uh, do you work here?"

"Well . . ."

No, of course I don't work here, you idiot. I'm just snooping around the back office when the postmistress isn't looking, Lightstone thought to himself, willing the man to go away before the woman showed up and started asking questions he didn't even want to think about trying to answer.

"Look, I'm running kinda late, and all I need is a drop-off signature. If you don't mind?"

"Sure, no problem." Lightstone accepted the pen and clipboard. "Say," he asked as he scribbled an illegible signature in the designated block, "when did FedEx start doing pickups and deliveries at post offices?"

The driver shrugged. "I deliver wherever it says on the address, and pick up just about anywhere in town . . . even the local girly-joint if they've got something to go." The driver smiled as he accepted the clipboard and handed the package to Lightstone.

"So you guys deliver at the industrial complex out on the west side of town?" Lightstone asked as an idea suddenly occurred to him.

"Sure do. In fact, that's where I'm headed now."

"You have time to pick up another package for delivery out there?"

"Always time to pick up new business. But it won't get there until tomorrow."

"Why not?"

"It has to go through one of the central routing points first."

"You mean you guys would actually fly a package all the way to Memphis or San Francisco, fly it *back* to Medford, and then truck it all the way back to Loggerhead City?"

"You bet." The driver smiled again. "That's what you pay for — twenty-four-hour guaranteed service. Not necessarily efficient service, but definitely guaranteed."

"What if I offered you a hundred dollars for a *one-hour* guaranteed delivery?"

"A hundred dollars?" The driver gasped. "Are you serious?"

"I am as long as the package gets there before ten this morning."

"Well, I don't know . . ."

"Listen," Lightstone quickly pulled out his wallet, "if it makes you feel better, send another empty package the long way around through Memphis, full fare . . . just as long as the first one gets to the warehouse by ten this morning." He handed the driver a hundred-dollar bill and a ten-dollar bill. "Deal?"

The driver looked at the money, hesitated once more, then directed Lightstone to follow him out to his truck.

Five minutes later, Bravo Team's wild-card agent hurried back into the restaurant with a FedEx package in his hand and sat down at the table just as Danny came out of the kitchen with a steaming tray balanced on his shoulder.

"That was close," the woman commented, looking down at her watch. "Only fifteen seconds to spare."

"Figured I'd better do something worthwhile to earn my keep around here," Lightstone explained, handing her the package as the cook set the tray on a nearby table.

"Don't tell me you're angling for a job with the post office?" The woman's eyes narrowed slightly as she glanced at the package before she set it aside.

Lightstone laughed. "Not hardly. I don't think I'd make a very good federal employee."

"Oh really? Why's that?"

"The federal government and I don't exactly see eye to eye on a lot of things," Lightstone told her truthfully. "Fact of the matter is, until I met you, I kinda figured they were all just a bunch of lazy good-for-nothings pigging out at the government trough. You know the type. Too lazy to go out and get a real job."

"As opposed to your standard, skinny, hardworking, good-for-nothing male who just happens to be—how did you put it—'between' real jobs?" Karla smiled.

"Exactly," Lightstone nodded agreeably. "Man has to know his place in this world."

"Actually," the slender young woman studied him thoughtfully, "I bet you'd be a perfect candidate to give some of those higher-ups in Washington a few well-deserved coronaries."

"That's been mentioned before," Lightstone admitted.

"Yeah, I'll bet it has." Karla chuckled, making no attempt to restrain her good-natured sarcasm. Then she smiled in gratitude when the cook placed a steaming plate of scrambled eggs with minced China peas and sliced mushrooms, and one of toast, on the table in front of her.

"Danny, you are a gem. Remind me not to ever let the federal government steal *you* away from here."

"Yes, ma'am, that I am . . . and no, ma'am, there ain't no chance of *that* ever happening." The young cook smiled cheerfully. "Added the mushrooms for a little variety." He gestured toward the contentedly sleeping panther. "Figured y'all might need your strength this fine morning."

The cook then deliberately glanced down at Lightstone's bandaged forearm, shook his head, smirked, placed a second steaming plate in front of the covert agent, and walked back into the kitchen humming a cheerful Cajun tune, seemingly oblivious to the glares the two diners aimed in his direction.

Chapter Thirty-three

"Why the hell didn't you think of something like this in the first place?" Larry Paxton asked reasonably after he examined Mike Takahara's latest construction project.

"Lack of perspective," the team's tech agent replied.

"What's that supposed to mean?"

"A couple days ago, I wouldn't have thought that building something this elaborate just to drill a four-inch-diameter hole into the side of a shipping crate would have been worth the effort."

"Chasing little baby poisonous snakes around a frozen warehouse for eight hours straight tends to give you a whole different perspective on a lot of things," the Bravo Team leader commented grimly.

"Amen to that."

"Yeah, no shit," Dwight Stoner agreed as he and the other three agents watched the first red-kneed giant tarantula step cautiously into the twelve-inch segment of four-inch-diameter clear plastic tubing that now connected one of the wooden crates to ten feet of flexible black irrigation pipe and the feeding tube of one of the special terrarium tops.

As the covert agents watched, fourteen more giant tarantulas followed each other into the thin, opaque, corrugated plastic pipe.

"Well, it looks like *this* contraption just might work," Paxton commented with a decided edge of skepticism in his voice.

They waited patiently—for one minute, a second, and then a third—for the tarantulas to drop into the terrarium.

Nothing.

"Now what the hell's going on?" Paxton finally demanded.

"They're not going into the terrarium," Mike Takahara observed.

"I can see *that*," Larry Paxton retorted as he knelt down by the terrarium and turned his head sideways to try to see inside the black corrugated pipe. "What I want to know is why."

"I don't know, maybe they're afraid of strange new environments," the Tech Agent suggested as he gently tapped the thin, flexible four-inch-diameter pipe. They heard the whisper sound of scurrying feet within the tube, but not a single tarantula ventured into the terrarium.

"Bullshit," Paxton muttered. "Spiders are the primary reason everybody else is afraid of strange new environments."

"Maybe they don't see it that way," Thomas Woeshack offered.

"Hit it harder," Stoner suggested.

Takahara cautiously shook the flexible pipe, causing considerable more scurrying but no giant spider appearances. The terrarium remained empty.

"No, no, not like that. Like this." Paxton grabbed the pipe and gave it a hard shake.

"Wait, Larry, don't . . . !" Mike Takahara tried to warn his boss, but it was too late.

To the horror of all four agents, the ten-foot length of thin, corrugated black pipe pulled loose at both ends.

"Oh SHIT!"

Larry Paxton and Dwight Stoner instinctively lunged for an end of the pipe. Without stopping to think, they lifted the ends off the floor and quickly covered the four-inch opening with their free hands.

The enormity of their error struck the two agents simultaneously as they both looked down at their exposed hands, and then back up at each other. But Stoner—whose reflexes had been honed by twelve years of diving for loose footballs—reacted first.

Reaching out, the huge agent yanked Paxton's hand away from the end of the pipe, slapped it around the pipe end he was holding, used his overwhelming strength to bring the two open ends of the pipe in his supervisor's resisting hands together, and then quickly stepped back.

Larry Paxton was still staring at the closed loop of four-inch-diameter corrugated pipe in his hands—his eyes bulging with shock as the sound of rapidly moving giant tarantulas caused him to clamp the two pipe ends tightly together—when someone knocked loudly on the warehouse door.

Immediately, four sets of eyes focused on the door.

"Who that hell is that?" Dwight Stoner whispered.

"Can't be Henry," Woeshack reminded them. "He said he and Bobby were going to stay away from here for a while."

"I don't care who it is, I want somebody to get me some . . ." Larry Paxton started ranting, but then fell silent as Stoner quickly brought his forefinger up to his mouth.

As Paxton remained frozen in place by the frantic scurrying inside the ten-foot closed loop of pipe, Stoner drew his semiautomatic pistol from his concealed shoulder holster. Taking a protected barricade position against one of the warehouse pillars, he directed Woeshack to the far side of the rental car and nodded to Mike Takahara to open the door.

Paxton, Stoner, and Woeshack all tensed as they watched the team's tech agent cautiously approach the door, pull back the curtain on the small window, then open the door and go outside.

Four minutes later, Takahara returned with a FedEx envelope and a single piece of paper in his hand.

"You know," he announced thoughtfully as he approached Larry Paxton, who had a decidedly dangerous expression in his dark eyes, "the next time we set up a covert operation, we probably ought to pose as FedEx agents. Save everybody a whole lot of time and effort . . . not to mention a certain amount of grief," he added, glancing meaningfully down at the loop of plastic pipe in his supervisor's shaking hands.

"I . . . don't . . . care.   Get . . . me . . . some . . . goddamned . . . duct tape . . . right . . . now," Larry Paxton ordered through clenched teeth.

"Who's it from, Jennifer again?" Dwight Stoner asked, ignoring his team leader's furious glare. "What did she do, suddenly remember another piece of crucial information she forgot to tell us?"

"No, this one's from Henry." Mike Takahara handed the paper to Stoner to read while he rummaged through a nearby storage box.

"Oh yeah, what's he doing now?" Thomas Woeshack asked as he tried to read the paper over Stoner's muscular arm.

"I'm not really sure," Takahara confessed as he retrieved a roll of duct tape and began to examine the ends of the corrugated pipe clenched in Larry Paxton's shaking hands, "but if I read that note correctly, I'd say he's trying to tell us that we've got a serious problem on our hands."

Chapter Thirty-four

At a little after one that Friday afternoon, Larry Paxton, Dwight Stoner, Mike Takahara, and Thomas Woeshack stood in the hallway as the assistant manager opened the door to a three-bedroom suite located at the far end of the top floor of their hotel.

"I think you'll find our executive suites to your liking, Mr. Stanley," the assistant manager assured Dwight Stoner as he motioned for the four men to enter the suite, then followed with the luggage cart.

"Actually, I kind of liked our old rooms," Stoner remarked wistfully as he examined the luxurious furnishings, not at all surprised to discover a set of upright wooden chairs of some indeterminate European vintage instead of the less formal overstuffed chairs that had decorated their previous, more comfortable but much less elegant rooms. "Unfortunately, though, our corporate director has developed more refined tastes in his declining years."

"Damned right he has," Larry Paxton muttered under his breath.

"I beg your pardon?" the assistant manager turned to Paxton.

"I said I can't wait to see how the boss likes these rooms," the covert team leader replied cheerfully.

"Ah, yes. Well, I think he'll be pleased. And your suite, of course, connects through this doorway." The hotel executive banged his knuckles lightly on a dead-bolted door. "Almost an exact duplicate, and just as nice, really."

"I'm sure we'll all be very happy here. Think you could rustle up a half dozen barbecued beef sandwiches and some chips from that little slow-cook place down the street?" Dwight Stoner asked. He slipped four twenties to the assistant manager, who scanned, folded, and pocketed the money in an admirable show of one-handed dexterity.

"Would a half hour be soon enough?"

"Perfect." Stoner nodded agreeably as he gently guided the young man toward the door.

They waited until the assistant manager's footsteps died away. Then, while Stoner and Woeshack searched the adjoining suite and Paxton watched out the window, Mike Takahara reached for the phone and punched in a local number.

"Room 1012, top floor, end of the hallway to your right."

Fifteen minutes later, there was a knock at the door.

Mike Takahara checked the peephole, opened the door, stepped aside to let Henry Lightstone enter, then bolted the door behind him.

"You clear?" Larry Paxton asked as Lightstone pulled a bottle of cold beer out of the open ice chest, briefly examined the high-backed wooden chairs, and then sat down on the floor with his back against the wall.

"Far as I know." Lightstone took a deep, satisfying swallow of the cold beer, then looked around. "I see we're spending Halahan's money with our normal indifference to government rules and regulations."

"You have any idea how hard it was to find two adjoining rooms at the end of a hallway in this place?" Paxton asked irritably. "Considering all the shit we've gone through on this operation so far, the government auditors can kiss my ragged butt."

"Spoken like a true bureaucrat." Lightstone nodded approvingly as he turned his attention to the team's tech agent. "Did you check the place out anyway, just to be sure?"

"Absolutely." Mike Takahara nodded. "Telephones, lamps, outlets, switches, and electrical lines are all clear. Nothing in the overhead that I can spot. The walls are solid, the room below us is occupied by a sales rep for a pharmaceutical company, and I disconnected the radio and TV.

Add what I assume was a random move on our part to the picture and we're as clean as we're ever going to get in a public hotel . . . unless, of course, we've got a seriously professional technical type on our ass, in which case all bets are off," he added thoughtfully.

"I'll settle for that." Lightstone accepted the tech agent's assessment of the situation. "Sorry if I sounded overly paranoid in the message, but the last twenty-four hours have been pretty bizarre." His eyes swept the room again. "You guys got anything to eat around here?"

"Sandwiches are on their way," Stoner informed him, but studied Lightstone's bandaged forearm. "What the hell happened to your arm?"

"Never mind his arm. We'll get to all that later." Larry Paxton surveyed the team with a no-nonsense look in his eyes. "First thing *I* want to know is what the hell's going on with Charlie Team."

Between sips of beer, Henry Lightstone described his initial contact with the two apparent soldiers at the Dogsfire Inn and the subsequent military-like surveillance of Charlie Team at the restaurant, leaving out only his personal involvement with the cat woman.

He paused when someone knocked at the door, waited for Stoner and Takahara to collect the sandwiches from the well-tipped assistant manager, and finished with a description of the devices he'd found under his truck.

For a long moment, the five Special Agents looked at each other.

Mike Takahara broke the silence.

"Can you draw me a rough sketch of that second device?" He tossed Lightstone a pencil and pad of paper.

Bravo Team's wild-card agent made a few quick passes with the pencil, thought for a minute, added a few more details, then handed the pad back to Takahara.

"You sure about these holes at the base?" the tech agent asked after studying the sketch.

"Yeah, they were definitely there. I'm pretty sure four on each side."

"How big?"

"Maybe a quarter of an inch in diameter."

"What about this rectangle above the holes?"

"It looked like some kind of cutout. There was one on each of the two long-dimension sides, about one inch by three inches, with some kind of seal that definitely attached from the inside. Based on the slightly irregular surface, I'm guessing the seal was foil or some kind of metallic-coated paper. I didn't want to poke it to find out."

"Good thinking." Takahara nodded approvingly. "What about the base? Magnetic?"

"I don't think so. As best I could tell, some kind of adhesive pad, maybe an eighth of an inch thick, held the device in place. Looked like one of those peel-off-strip kinds of systems, but I didn't find any of the strips in the immediate area."

"Only the really dumb ones leave their trash around. Unfortunately, these guys don't sound like dummies," Mike Takahara commented dryly. "How was the device camouflaged? Standard military green?"

"Right."

"Any insignia, markings, numbers?"

"No. Or at least none that I remember."

The tech agent nodded and looked around the room at his companions.

"Okay, what I *think* Henry found is an MTEAR-42 device. Military, training, explosive, arm-switch, remote." He rattled off the military terms. "The crucial word is 'training.' The military uses a lot of these for their war games. What they do is mount these things under all the tanks, armored personnel carriers, trucks, Humvees, then the referees set them off whenever they want to indicate a hit or disabled vehicle. A small charge blows out those foil seals to create a decent concussion and a nice loud bang, then red smoke pours out of those quarter-inch holes, basically to let the crew know they're either on fire or dead . . . or both. It's a very instructional little device."

"So these things aren't real explosives?" A look of relief crossed Henry Lightstone's tanned face.

"Depends on your definition of 'real,' " Mike Takahara responded. "There's certainly enough of a charge in an MTEAR-42 to give that little truck of yours a good bounce, and all that red smoke pouring out of the engine compartment probably wouldn't have done much for your nerves, especially if you didn't know what it meant. But it wouldn't spread pieces of you and your truck over a couple of acres . . . assuming, of course, that what you saw wasn't a modified MTEAR," the tech agent added after a moment.

"What would they modify it with?" Thomas Woeshack asked.

Mike Takahara shrugged. "I don't know. Probably a standard detonator and a half pound of C-4."

Another long moment of silence ensued.

"Is there any way to tell if the one I saw had been modified?" Lightstone asked.

"One good way, if you don't mind the obvious drawbacks." The tech agent grinned wryly. "Just drive your truck over to the warehouse, and I'll take a look . . . after maybe an hour or two."

"Ah."

Yet another moment of silence filled the elegantly furnished room, this one finally interrupted by Larry Paxton's barely audible voice.

"It's a game. It's *gotta* be a game."

"What?" Lightstone and the other three agents all turned to stare at the Bravo Team supervisor.

"Think about it," Paxton insisted. "First, there's the obvious factor: Charlie Team isn't ready to work anything serious yet. They know it, Halahan knows it, and we certainly proved it beyond a shadow of a doubt. So how likely is it that Halahan would send a rookie team that isn't ready out on something serious—not just somewhere in Oregon, but in the exact same Jasper County, Oregon, we're assigned to—without putting us on standby just in case they run into some kind of trouble?"

"Not very likely." Lightstone admitted, and the other three agents nodded in agreement.

"Okay, so stay with me on this," Paxton went on patiently. "We know that Halahan and Moore went to a lot of work to set up that series of training exercises for Charlie Team—using us as the crash dummies— and what did we do?"

"We won." Dwight Stoner smiled pleasantly.

"But we cheated," Thomas Woeshack added.

"Okay, we won *and* we cheated," Mike Takahara compromised. "Both fair and square, more or less."

"Yeah, but wait a minute." Henry Lightstone didn't look at all convinced. "Do you really think Halahan would go to all the effort to set up something—a game, exercise, whatever—*this* complicated, just because he's pissed at us?"

"Hey, look at the assignment he gave us," Larry Paxton argued. "You tell me that the brilliant idea of shipping us thirty deadly poisonous snakes, a dozen crocodiles, and 750 giant spiders didn't come from the twisted mind of a supervisor bent on revenge."

"That *is* pretty convincing, Henry," Dwight Stoner conceded.

"Damned right it is. And keep in mind, not only did we seriously piss off Halahan and Moore, but we also embarrassed the hell out of Charlie Team in the process," Larry Paxton went on, "which specifically includes that little wildcat, Marashenko, who, if you ask me, is definitely the type to hold a serious grudge."

" 'Destroyed their team spirit, set them back at least a month in their training,' was the way Halahan put it," Mike Takahara reminded them.

"Right." Larry Paxton looked around at his agent team. "So what better way of rebuilding that team spirit, and putting them right back on track . . . ?"

". . . than by setting Charlie Team up in a position to embarrass the shit out of us?" Thomas Woeshack finished.

"Exactly. See, even Woeshack recognizes a case of pure treachery when he sees it." Larry Paxton smiled approvingly at the young agent. "Halahan puts us in a godforsaken warehouse in the middle of Oregon with seventy-two shipping crates from hell, knowing we'll be too busy watching out for our own asses to look around and see what's going on . . ."

". . . and then works it out so that Henry makes contact with that blind soothsayer . . ." Dwight Stoner added.

". . . who links him up to some crazy woman post-office worker who's really a fortune-telling witch in disguise. Wow, that really *is* devious planning." Thomas Woeshack's eyes widened in amazement.

"And speaking of curious events, that reminds me," Larry Paxton interrupted after briefly staring at Woeshack in dismay, "just what *did* happen to your arm, Henry?"

"Uh . . . nothing, just a little scratch."

"You're trying to tell us you bandaged your whole damned arm because you got a little scratch? Come on, give me a break." Stoner glared at Lightstone skeptically and reached for his arm. "Let me see that thing."

"Hey, wait . . . AGGHHH!" Henry Lightstone's eyes bulged as Stoner trapped his wrist in an inescapable grip and yanked up one side of the taped bandage loose, ripping out several hundred of his fellow agent's forearm hairs in the process.

"Jesus Christ, Henry," Stoner whispered reverently as he and the others stared at the exposed wounds.

"You trying to tell us a woman did that?" Larry Paxton demanded, his eyes widening with disbelief as he inspected the deep, encrusted wounds on Lightstone's forearm.

"No, her cat did," Lightstone muttered as he hurriedly pressed the taped bandage — now covered with dozens of pulled hairs — back in place.

"Must be one hell of a cat," Mike Takahara offered dubiously.

"She's pretty good-sized," Lightstone acknowledged as he glared at his fellow agents.

"You know," Larry Paxton remarked thoughtfully to Stoner, "something about this whole deal just doesn't smell right."

"I know what you mean." The huge agent nodded. Then, before Henry could react, the huge agent reached behind Lightstone and yanked up his shirt, pinning the lanky agent's long, muscular arms over his head and exposing his bare back.

"Bingo." Stoner smiled and turned his futilely struggling partner so the other agents in the room could see the evidence.

"Now *those* look like they were done by a woman," Larry Paxton announced approvingly. " 'Less, of course, you'd like to try to convince us that the lady's cat climbed all over your body and tore it up like that," the Bravo Team leader added with a pleasant smile on his face when Stoner returned Lightstone to his place on the floor, released his arms, and handed him a cold bottle of beer.

"I was lucky to survive the night," Henry muttered as he struggled to straighten his shirt, "and that's the unvarnished truth."

"You all do realize what this means, don't you?" Mike Takahara asked.

"Henry spent the last two days getting laid while the rest of us froze our nuts off in that warehouse collecting a lifetime supply of nightmares?" Dwight Stoner suggested.

"Well, yeah; that, too," the tech agent agreed, "but don't you think Bobby must be involved in Halahan's scam, too?"

Larry Paxton's brows furrowed. "How do you figure that?" he demanded.

"Simple." Takahara smiled. "Halahan needs a twist on Henry, some way to control or direct his movements. So he finds out where Bobby and Susan live, knowing that if Henry ever gets reasonably close, he'll track them down first chance he gets. Then our dear Machiavellian Special Ops chief works out a deal with Bobby for . . . what? What would it take to get an ex–homicide detective with a warped sense of humor like LaGrange in on this deal?"

All eyes turned to Henry Lightstone.

"Not much," Lightstone conceded, a thoughtful expression appearing on his face as he finished tucking in his shirt. "Bobby and I pulled some serious shit on a few people when we worked together in San Diego. He really gets into that sort of thing."

"Like that time you floated your drunk supervisor—the one who couldn't swim and was deathly afraid of sharks—in San Diego Bay in an open coffin in the middle of the night, and then woke him up with a string of firecrackers?" Larry Paxton reminded in a mildly threatening voice.

Lightstone nodded silently, his eyes taking on a distant look as he began to drum his fingers lightly on the floor.

"And we did pretty much destroy Bobby's boat out there in the Bahamas, Henry," Mike Takahara pointed out. "So Bobby, and probably Susan, too—you have to figure they were in on it together—tag-team you onto this Sage character, who links you up to this post-office seductress with the big cat . . . or was it a little cat with the big claws?"

"Which, in any case, probably made it real easy to rig a confrontation scene with Henry and this military character, since—knowing our buddy here—he might as well have been wearing the lady's scarf on the end of his lance." Larry Paxton smiled in satisfaction.

"Nicely put," Dwight Stoner commented.

"Thank you."

"I don't understand . . ." Thomas Woeshack turned to Mike Takahara, looking confused again.

"Knights of the Round Table analogy, Thomas," Mike Takahara explained. "Henry happens to be cursed with a white-knight complex. Can't resist rescuing the fair maiden, no matter how many dragons come popping out of the woodwork. It's a genetic defect. I'll explain it to you later," the tech agent promised.

"You know, we *could* be stretching ourselves a little too far on this Halahan-scam business," Henry Lightstone cautioned.

"But think about how they'd work it, Henry," Paxton argued. "They set it up so you trip across these military characters at the restaurant, you follow them and spot their surveillance, you warn us, we notify Halahan, he tells us to stand by — let Charlie Team handle things themselves — we ignore him like we usually do, ride to the rescue . . ."

"Hey, their side even gets a fair maiden too — Natasha!" Thomas Woeshack interrupted, grinning widely. "I'll bet she'll be surprised when Henry rides in wearing the witch's scarf on his lance!"

"Yeah, that's putting it mildly," Stoner chuckled.

". . . and we find ourselves surrounded by video cameras and up to our butts in red smoke when the referees — presumably Halahan and Moore — set off all the MTEARs they've probably been tagging us with ever since we landed in Medford," Paxton finished after giving the team's Eskimo agent/pilot a sadly sympathetic look.

"You've got to admit, Henry, the whole thing tracks real nice," Mike Takahara added.

"Yeah, I know . . . it sounds good, it really does. But for Christ's sake, I broke that guy's wrist!" Lightstone continued to look perplexed in spite of the other's comments. "I *know* I did. I heard it snap. And the other one — that pale-eyed guy the kid called Sergeant — is definitely a dangerous s.o.b. I can tell you that much for sure, whoever or whatever else he may be."

"Okay, so these particular militants are tougher than the average bear." Larry Paxton shrugged indifferently. "You telling me Halahan couldn't get his hands on a team of marines out of Quantico, or even some Army Rangers out of Fort Bragg? Guys who wouldn't think any more about a broken wrist than you would a sprained toe?"

"The FBI's Hostage Rescue Team trains at Quantico," Mike Takahara reminded Henry. "And I hear they hire a lot of those guys straight out of the military. Halahan would know that . . . and a training scenario like this would be right down their alley, too."

"There you go." Paxton nodded his head in satisfaction.

"But what if we're wrong?" Lightstone pressed, still not fully convinced.

"You mean what if Charlie Team really *is* being tagged by a bunch of hard-as-nails characters, for whatever reason, and they don't know it?" Paxton asked.

Lightstone nodded his head.

The Bravo Team leader paused for a moment. "Then they could be in deep shit."

"Exactly."

"So what can we do to make sure . . . before we go turn things around on Halahan and Moore again?" Stoner asked.

"I think—at a minimum—we have to report what I saw." Lightstone looked over at Paxton for confirmation. "How could we word it? In the process of making contact with subjects linked to suspect Sage, special agent Lightstone observed members of Charlie Team in the area of Jasper County, Oregon, under active surveillance by individuals who appear to have military backgrounds. Request further instructions."

Larry Paxton stared pensively at the floor for a few seconds. Then he nodded his head and consulted his watch. "Henry's right. We've got to be sure. But it's two o'clock now, which makes it five o'clock East Coast time on a Friday night."

"No problem. Halahan and Moore both wear beepers," Mike Takahara reminded.

"Yeah, but for emergency messages only." Paxton scrutinized his troops carefully. "The question is, do we really have an emergency here? Or just a situation?"

"If that surveillance is for real, I sure wouldn't want those guys following *me* for very long," Lightstone announced firmly, then hesitated. "But as far as an emergency goes, I guess I can't say they did anything especially threatening . . . outside of leaving that MTEAR device on my truck."

"Which could have been put there by someone from Charlie Team just as easily," Mike Takahara reminded him. "Donato, LiBrandi, and Marashenko are all tech-trained. Fact of the matter is, for all we know, they could've put those things on your truck right after you rented it."

"That's a point," Lightstone agreed.

"So how do we go about reporting all of this to Halahan in a timely manner, without making it sound like we're panicking out here?" Larry Paxton asked his team.

"I can send an e-mail message to Freddy—to the office and to his home computer—along with a couple of 'tell dad to check his e-mail' notes to his son and daughter," Mike Takahara suggested. "I know he spends a lot of time with his kids on the Net. Probably at least one of them will be on-line this evening, and he'll get the message within the next three to four hours. Worst-case scenario is he doesn't get it until he gets to work Monday."

Paxton nodded his head. "Okay, do it, then keep an eye out for any return mail this evening. I really want to see what Freddy has to say about all this."

"No problem. I'll set up an audio alarm so the computer beeps us if we get any incoming messages," the tech agent proposed as he reached for his nearby computer case.

"In the meantime" — Henry Lightstone rubbed his sore arm distract-edly — "I've got an idea how we just might be able to find out what's going on around here."

"Yeah? What's that?" Paxton demanded.

"What's the first thing they teach covert agents to do on a new as-signment?"

"Check in with the local resident agent," Thomas Woeshack re-sponded immediately.

"You think those characters on Charlie Team would actually *do* some-thing like that?" Dwight Stoner asked skeptically.

"Oh hell, yes. Rookie agents are like that." Larry Paxton smiled cheer-fully and turned to Mike Takahara, who was busy hooking up the modem line to the back of his notebook computer.

"Mike, who's the closest resident agent in southern Oregon?"

"Just a second."

Thirty seconds later, Takahara looked up from his screen. "Looks like Wilbur Boggs."

"Good old Wilbur. The terror of the Chesapeake Bay when he was a young agent. I remember hearing he'd gotten transferred out to Oregon. Pissed off more duck-poaching congressmen than . . ."

A startled look suddenly appeared on Larry Paxton's face. Then he looked around at his fellow agents. "You guys thinking what I'm think-ing?"

"Oh yeah," Henry Lightstone murmured softly, his eyes lighting up with amusement as he and Stoner and Takahara all nodded their heads. "Halahan, Moore, Charlie Team, Glynco, Bobby, Susan, the soothsayer, the witch-lady . . . and now good old Wilbur. One big happy game-playing family."

"You mean they're *all* working together to set us up?" Thomas Woe-shack asked. "Wilbur Boggs, too?"

"It sure does look that way." Lightstone shook his head slowly, trying to ignore the apprehension that continued to plague him as the pieces of the puzzle apparently fell into place. "One big game, and we're the target."

"You mean we *were* the target," Dwight Stoner corrected him.

"Exactly." Larry Paxton smiled again. "So where do we find Special Agent Wilbur Boggs these days?"

"You'll love this part," the tech agent predicted.

"What?"

"If I remember my map correctly, we're about twenty minutes from his office right now."

Chapter Thirty-five

Awareness, when it came to Wilbur Boggs again, freed him from the stupor that enveloped him like a dank, impenetrable cloud.

The vague feelings of fighting the ropes and nets, struggling in the darkness, or trying to work himself free of obstructions trying to cover his nose and mouth vanished.

Instead, he awoke to a sense of freedom, and brightness, and general well-being marred only by the persistent dryness in his throat, the gentle numbness that didn't quite mask the pain which emanated from several parts of his body, and most unsettling of all, the confusion regarding where he was . . . and why.

Because of this, it took the federal wildlife agent several long moments finally to understand that the wires and tubes attached to his arms probably signified something important.

Monitors? IVs? Bright lights. Must be in a hospital. No wonder everything feels numb. Probably giving me drugs.

In that case, he decided, in order to figure out what happened, he needed to stop the mind-numbing flow.

Accordingly, Wilbur Boggs carefully reached around with his left hand — for some reason his right hand felt heavy and immobile — followed the thin plastic tubing with his numbed fingers until it ended under a strip of medical tape attached to the inner elbow of his right arm, peeled up the tape, then slowly pulled the IV needle out of his arm.

For reasons he couldn't quite grasp, he'd expected alarms to go off, and people to come running . . . and felt momentarily confused when nothing happened.

Supposed to happen, because that's what always happens on TV, he finally managed to reason out, but with no idea why that bit of knowledge might be important, much less true. *But they wouldn't need to rig any kind of alarm on the IV, because they've already got me connected to at least four or five other electronic doodads and that big monitor over there . . . with the big ON/OFF switch . . . right next to the bed.*

Ah.

Special Agent Wilbur Boggs slowly sat up with his legs dangling over the side of the bed, after finally deciding it might be a good idea to make sure he was more or less okay *before* he disconnected himself from the monitor. However, then his tongue felt an unfamiliar empty space in his mouth.

What happened to my front teeth?

He brought his right hand up to feel for his missing teeth — and saw the cast on his right hand for the first time. When he did, the memories began to trickle into his head.

Boat.

My boat.

All tangled up and broken, goddamn it, because they. . . .

They?

His eyes grew wide as he continued staring at the thick plaster cast on his right hand. *What the hell . . . ?*

Rustman.

Whatley.

And Smallsreed. That goddamned sleazy . . .

Wait a minute. Sleazy what? Congressman? No, something else.

Sleazy bagman. That's it. Political bagman named Simon Whatley. Smallsreed's man. Him and who? The new guy Eliot said scared the shit out of everybody at Rustman's place?

Eliot? Who's that?

Something about Eliot's name made Boggs feel anxious.

Oh yeah, that's right.

Got to tell them about Lou Eliot.

The memories came faster now.

Gotta warn them.

Them? Who's 'them'? And why do I have to. . . .

And then the flood gates opened, and the entire day's events surged through the agent's dazed mind.

Shots fired.

Two shots, far apart, execution style.

Gotta warn them. Tell them about Lou Eliot . . . he never showed up . . . and the new guy. The one Eliot was afraid of. Sergeant somebody.

Somebody cold and empty, just like win—

Wintersole.

Sergeant Wintersole.

He knew he had it now — almost within his grasp — and Wintersole was the key. If he could just get a focus on that last murky element drifting around in the back of his mind. Something about help. Needing help. Calling for . . .

Was that it? Calling for help?

No.

He felt a cold chill start up his spine.

He didn't have to call for help because . . . why?

Because help was already coming.

That's right. They're already on their way, thanks to good old Halahan. Goddamned stubborn Irishman. He'll take care of everything.

But . . .

But what?

Got to warn them. Gotta tell . . . Charley?

He blinked again, then immediately felt dizzy and sick to his stomach as the spine-chilling awareness hit home.

Charlie Team. The kids.

Oh Christ.

Boggs fumbled for the phone on the monitor table, but he immediately gave that idea up when he realized he couldn't remember a single phone number. Not a one. He thought about asking someone for a phone book, but the door to his room was almost shut, and he didn't feel strong enough to yell. Instead, he simply reached over, shut the monitor off, ripped the rest of the electronic sensors off his head and arms, then staggered to the nearby closet.

And discovered, to his amazement, nothing but a pair of white hospital pajamas, a white bathrobe, and a pair of flat cloth slippers.

Wait a minute. What happened to my clothes?

He tried to remember how he'd wound up there, but the only memory he could dredge up out of his aching head had something to do with crawling toward his truck on his hands and knees, which didn't make any sense at all.

So lacking a better plan, Wilbur Boggs pulled himself out of the open-backed hospital gown, worked himself into the pajamas, robe, and slippers—trying, as he did so, to ignore the cast on his hand—retaped the IV needle to his arm, and then did what he vaguely remembered seeing someone do on TV.

He got up and staggered out the door of his room and into the wide hallway, dragging the IV rack in his wake.

Incredibly, he made it all the way to the lobby, and then through the wide automatic door and across the covered entryway before anyone reacted to his presence—and appearance—with anything other than a brief, professional smile.

"Mr. Boggs?"

Wilbur Boggs blinked in the unaccustomed daylight.

"That's right," he replied in a raspy voice, trying to remember if the muscular yet attractive young woman standing in front of him was his nurse.

"Are you going somewhere?" she asked hesitantly.

"My office," he mumbled, wondering if he could muster the strength to shove her aside and make a run for it, or find a taxi before she called the security guards to drag him back to his room.

No, probably not, he told himself glumly.

"Oh really?" The young woman smiled. "Do you have a ride?"

He looked around the entryway. Except for a single truck parked at the far end of the driveway, it was empty.

"Uh, no, I guess not."

"Well then," she beamed at him, "may I offer you one?"

Chapter Thirty-six

Mike Takahara had based his time estimate for locating Wilbur Boggs on rough distance and the clearly marked speed zones through town, rather than the speed and mobility of the small Honda.

And the uneasy determination of Henry Lightstone.

Consequently, it took Lightstone five minutes less than the tech agent's estimate to find Boggs's office. But he then spent another ten slowly circling a four-block area—until he felt reasonably certain he hadn't been followed—before he risked entering the small office building through a door that opened into the back alleyway.

It took him another five minutes to properly identify himself as a federal agent of the United States Fish and Wildlife Service, and get the relevant information out of Boggs's secretary. No, she hadn't seen Wilbur since last Tuesday. Yes, she was worried, but she felt confident that the other agents who also were looking for Wilbur would find him soon. The names of the other agents? She paused for a moment to scan her notebook. Oh, yes. Gus Donato, Mark LiBrandi, and a young woman agent whose name escaped her at the moment.

Gus Donato, Mark LiBrandi, and Natasha Marashenko. Henry Lightstone smiled to himself. *The offensive players of Charlie Team, scene two, sleazy congressman and bagman try to make a deal.*

Bingo.

Fifteen minutes later, using directions provided by Boggs's eager-to-help secretary, followed by a good half-hour spent on the back-track, searching for any sign of an active or passive surveillance, Lightstone stood in the covered carport next to the resident wildlife agent's home, wondering what out-of-place element had triggered his mental alarms.

He'd done the standard things first. Rang the door bell, and received no response. Then he carefully examined all the doors and windows—house and garage—and found everything securely locked with no sign of forced entry. A cursory search of the yard led him next to the carport, where he'd stood studying the backed-in pickup truck and boat trailer for a good two minutes now.

Then it finally hit him.

The boat trailer.

It was still attached to the truck.

And not just the bumper hitch, but the safety chains, trailer brakes, and electrical hookup, too.

Not an unusual situation if you planned to go on a trip, or left everything hooked up for a quick run out to the lake; but hardly the way a wildlife agent would leave his personal truck and trailer when working twelve-hour patrol duty shifts with a government truck and trailer. Lightstone moved in closer . . . and then immediately went on the alert when he saw the blood splatters on the boat's windshield.

What had Boggs's secretary said? Something about the other agents checking Boggs's home every evening?

Which made as much sense as anything else, he decided as he cautiously moved to the rear of the carport—where the back of the boat trailer nudged the back wall—because if Mark or Gus or Natasha had checked the house during the day, at least one of them should have noticed the blood splatters on the windshield . . . or at the very least, the damage to the back of Boggs's boat.

Pretty hard to miss, guys, even in the middle of the night, Lightstone thought as he knelt and surveyed the external damage sustained by the small watercraft.

Okay, Wilbur, let's hope for your sake this isn't what it looks like.

Alert for the slightest movement, Henry Lightstone cautiously approached the near side of the boat, looked over the railing, then breathed a small sigh of relief.

No body.

But more than enough blood for a body to have been here, Lightstone decided as he carefully stood up on the trailer, eased himself into the boat, and began to examine the scene like he'd done so many times when he and Bobby LaGrange had worked homicide investigations together.

Yeah, you do like to play, Bobby, Lightstone smiled to himself as he made a cursory examination of the damage sustained by the outboard engine, then furrowed his brows in concentration as he turned slowly—watching where he stepped, carefully avoiding any potentially latent-fingerprint-bearing surfaces with his bare hands—and began methodically to work through the cause-and-effect aspects of the blood splatter patterns around the windshield . . .

And I can see you and Susan hooking up with Halahan to have some fun with Bravo Team, Bobby.
     . . . the instrument panel . . .
Problem is, though, I know you too well.
     . . . the steering wheel . . .
You were scared when I called last night because you were worried about Susan.
     . . . the seat cushions . . .
And you wouldn't have been worried about her, or pulled out that old .45 of yours, if you knew the whole deal was a setup.
     . . . and the flooring.
So that cuts you and Susan out of the grand conspiracy theory, leaving me to hook up with Sage the soothsayer on my own . . . however and whenever that might have happened. But not . . . uh oh, what's this?

Lightstone reached down under the driver's seat, came up with a bloody front tooth—and then another one under the cowling—sat down on the front passenger seat to consider this latest bit of evidence for a few moments, then moved to the back of the boat to reexamine the damaged transom and outboard motor.

Only when he began a detailed examination of the outboard motor shaft did Henry Lightstone notice the rope fibers and fragments of nylon netting. That discovery led him to the prop and the protective skeg, where he made another interesting discovery—which caused him to reexamine the damaged transom with a decidedly different perspective.

Boat's traveling at a high rate of speed, gets caught up in nets, rope, something like that, and comes to a sudden stop, causing Wilbur Boggs's face to smash into the steering wheel, knocking out a couple of his front teeth, and sending blood all over the place. Wilbur cuts the boat loose, tries to fix the engine—getting blood all over the cowling—but never gets it running again because there's still a bunch of netting wrapped around the propeller shaft, and finally ends up paddling to shore. Easy read. Trouble is, judging from the damage to the motor skeg and some—but not all—of the damage to the transom, the boat was going backwards at a fairly high speed at the time of impact.
Hell of a trick, Wilbur my man.
Unless . . .

Then Lightstone noticed the truck's broken rear window.

Ten minutes later, after expanding the scope of his search and placing several more very intriguing pieces of the puzzle at least within reasonable proximity to each other, Henry Lightstone walked across the street, rang the doorbell, and waited.

This time, to his amazement, he got a response.

"Yes?"

"Hi, I'm a friend of Wilbur Boggs, your neighbor across the street," Lightstone began.

"Oh, I'm so glad you stopped by. How is he?"

"Well, we think he'll be all right," Lightstone replied hesitantly, "but I was examining his truck and boat trailer just now, and happened to notice your mailbox . . ."

"I planned to talk to Mr. Boggs about that once he got home from the hospital. I'm sure the entire situation was simply an accident on his part. As you can see, we don't have many streetlights around here, and it's pretty hard to see anything that early in the morning anyway. My homeowner's policy should cover the repairs just fine, but to tell you the truth," the neighbor paused, "I was hoping . . ."

"That's why I stopped by," Lightstone interrupted, reaching for his wallet. "Wilbur's terribly embarrassed about the entire incident, and doesn't want you inconvenienced any more than you've already been, so he asked me to try to set things right if I can."

Lightstone pulled three one-hundred-dollar bills out of his wallet and extended them toward the man. "Will this cover the necessary repairs?"

"But that's . . . exceedingly generous," the neighbor protested as he accepted the money after only the briefest hesitation.

"No, not at all. It can take a lot of time to locate a contractor, and then oversee the work. Besides," Lightstone added with a wink, "this way, neither you nor Wilbur need to bother your insurance agents, fill out all that paperwork, or more importantly, run the risk that they might raise your rates. You know how those things always seem to work out in the insurance company's favor."

"Don't they ever," the neighbor nodded his head vigorously.

"Anyway," Lightstone went on, "I know Wilbur would be grateful if you'd consider the money as his apology until he can get back home and apologize in person."

"Of course," the neighbor assured the agent hurriedly, trying very hard not to smile. "And please, if there's anything else I can do for Mr. Boggs . . ."

"Well, there is one thing." The wildlife agent smiled. "I'm trying to help Wilbur get all the paperwork together on the accident, and we're having trouble locating the people who took him to the hospital. I was wondering . . ."

"I'm afraid you'll find that's pretty typical for local government around here," the neighbor smiled apologetically. "If our fire department's records are anything like those at city hall . . ."

Henry Lightstone nodded his head. "I understand completely."

It took the persistent ex–homicide investigator an hour and a half to determine that the extent of Wilbur Boggs's injuries got him transferred to Providence Hospital in nearby Medford . . . and the better part of another two hours to finally track down the supervising floor nurse at Providence Hospital, where he learned that patient John Doe — now positively identified as U.S. Fish and Wildlife Service Resident Agent Wilbur Boggs — had disappeared.

Chapter Thirty-seven

After the unnerving arrival of the woman and her terrifying pet, the men of the Chosen Brigade of the Seventh Seal could come to no agreement about how to respond to the Sage's most recent pronouncement.

Or more to the point, even if they should respond at all.

Some of the men thought it unwise to violate their long-standing security policy and allow any more strangers into the compound, no matter how compelling the reason.

Others questioned the wisdom of allowing the crazy old seer into the compound any more either.

But these naysayers comprised a very small minority, and in truth, didn't feel entirely convinced by their own arguments.

So, at eight o'clock that Saturday morning, it came to pass that when the Sage's ancient motorbike finally puttered up the narrow, winding dirt path, all sixteen of the ranking officers of the Brigade (after ordering the women to prepare for a sudden and immediate evacuation to the back-canyon caves with little or no warning) waited nervously at the forested entrance to their well-concealed mountain-canyon training grounds, weapons at the ready.

Much to the Brigade members' surprise, five camouflage-garbed men riding atop five new, heavy-duty, camouflage-painted, four-wheel RVs — each with several wooden crates strapped to the back carrier — immediately followed the old man in a single file.

The Brigade's elder, a white-haired man of indeterminate age who proudly displayed the rank of colonel on his faded and tattered cammo gear, waited uneasily until all six men had disembarked from their vehicles.

Then, when it became apparent that the Sage cared more about cleaning his sunglasses than in making proper introductions, the group elder sighed, took in a deep steadying breath, and stepped forward.

"Good morning, gentlemen, I'm Colonel Rice, commander of the

Chosen Brigade of the Seventh Seal." He made a deliberate effort to conceal his anxiety by speaking in a slow, deliberate voice as he extended his hand. "Welcome to our compound."

"Thank you, Colonel. Glad to meet you, sir." Sergeant Aran Wintersole came to attention, snapped a proper salute, then stepped forward to clasp the Brigade commander's hand.

The salute took the militant commander by surprise. For a moment, he wondered if he should release the other man's hand and return the salute, or simply continue on as if nothing unusual had happened. That became a moot point, however, when he established contact with cold pale gray eyes of the man standing ramrod-straight before him, and felt a sudden, terrifying pressure on his bladder.

"And you are?" He struggled valiantly to keep his voice from breaking.

"First Sergeant Aran Wintersole, sir."

The group elder's eyes flickered down to the small, black, first sergeant's insignia on Wintersole's camouflaged collar, and then to the small unit patch on the man's left shoulder.

"Army Rangers?"

"Yes sir. Third Battalion, 54th Army Ranger Reserves, sir."

The militant group leader immediately recognized that the professional soldier standing before him undoubtedly possessed far more military skills and experiences than he had ever dreamed about. And the fact that this man — *a first sergeant in the Army Rangers, for Christ sake!* — was visibly unarmed, as were the other four soldiers who accompanied him, made him all the more intimidating and dangerous. A most unnerving realization.

"And what brings you here, Sergeant?" the group elder asked uncertainly, uncomfortably aware that, in addition to having possibly committed a grave error by allowing these men to see the entrance to their training facilities, he'd done absolutely nothing in his life to earn the pair of black eagles sewn into the collar of *his* field uniform.

"Resupply, sir."

"Resupply?"

In typical fashion, the Sage had told the Brigade little in his latest pronouncement, beyond that the battle between light and darkness could not commence until the Brigade was properly equipped . . . and that one of the chosen ones — the fearsome warriors who would lead the forces of darkness and light into battle (although the Sage's rambling commentary hadn't made it clear which side this newcomer might represent) — would arrive tomorrow morning, at 0800 hours sharp, to equip the Chosen Brigade of the Seventh Seal for battle.

"Be there or prepare to disband the Brigade in shame!" the Sage had yelled out over his shoulder as he gunned the motorbike and disappeared in a cloud of rancid blue exhaust.

But the Brigade leader didn't recall the old man saying anything at all about resupply.

"That's correct, sir. Your brigade is scheduled for resupply from existing National Guard reserve unit stocks. Your allotment consists of twenty each refurbished M16A1 assault rifles; one hundred thousand rounds of five-five-six ball ammo; two hundred twenty-round magazines; two magazine loaders; twenty sets of web gear, complete with canteens and first-aid kits; a reloading kit for five-five-six military ball; sufficient supplies—bullets, powder, and primers—to reload an additional fifty thousand rounds; and twenty cleaning kits. Sir."

The militant colonel's mouth fell open.

"The ..." It took him a few tries to get the words out. "... National Guard is providing us with M16s?"

"That's correct, sir."

"But ..." The militia colonel shook his head several times, trying to rearrange the incomprehensible facts in his mind.

"I take it this was unexpected, sir?" Wintersole smiled politely.

"Uh, yes ..." The group elder nodded his head, a dazed expression apparently frozen on his face.

"If I may say so, sir, you might be surprised at the number of people— and the positions they hold—who strongly advocate and support the efforts of patriot groups such as yours."

A sudden glimmer of comprehension lit up the group elder's dull eyes.

"You mean ..."

"It's not my place to speak for these people, sir," Wintersole informed the older man. "My orders are to deliver the weapons and supplies to your unit, and to provide any additional training that you and your men may require in their use."

"Training?" The militant colonel simply couldn't keep his lower jaw from dropping.

"Yes sir. My men and I are prepared to demonstrate current fire-team assault tactics, and to run every member of your Brigade through a basic familiarization course on the M16A1. The course consists of two hours of basic weapon familiarization; two hours of range work, selected fire, prone position; and two hours of fire-team assault tactics, select and auto. I understand you have training facilities and firing ranges we could use?"

"Uh ... yes, we do," the group elder somehow managed to choke out the words.

First Sergeant Aran Wintersole looked down at his watch. "Then with your permission, sir, perhaps we can begin."

"You mean *now?*"

Wintersole settled his cold pale gray eyes on those of the militant colonel, who trembled at the mere thought of the idea.

"Yes, sir," the hunter-killer team leader replied evenly. "My men are ready to begin the demonstration and the training whenever you are, sir."

Thirty minutes later, the sixteen highest-ranking members of the Chosen Brigade of the Seventh Seal—who were already sweating and out of breath from unloading the four-wheel RVs—gathered around a cluster of picnic tables, where Wintersole's men arranged twenty black-matte-finished assault rifles, stacks of cardboard ammunition boxes, magazines, and webbing gear before putting on their own black nylon web gear.

The Brigade members then watched warily as one of the Rangers walked to the end of their target range and randomly set a total of eighteen sand-filled tin cans on the ground, on top of large rocks, and on varying flat surfaces of the six crudely welded target holders. Then they all stepped back and drew in their breath in unison when Wintersole picked up one of the lethal-looking rifles and casually drew and released the bolt-retracting lever with a loud CLACK! to verify an empty chamber.

"Gentlemen," he began in a voice that carried the authority of hundreds of instructor hours at Fort Bragg, "the weapon you will be training with today is the United States Army M16A1 assault rifle chambered for 5.56mm ball ammo. The M16A1 is gas-operated, magazine-fed, and equipped with a selective-fire lever for semi- or full-automatic fire. It is capable of delivering firepower at a target, at a sustainable rate of seven hundred high-velocity rounds per minute, to a maximum effective range of three hundred yards. In the hands of a properly trained soldier, the M16A1 can accurately place rounds on target out to five hundred yards. Today, however, we will focus on the capabilities of this weapon at standard close-combat distances."

After verifying that everyone wore ear protection, Wintersole picked up one of the loaded magazines, automatically tapped the base of the aluminum magazine against the tabletop to properly seat the rounds, and then walked to the middle firing position of the small range at the twenty-five-yard marker.

At the direction of the other four Army Rangers, the visibly intimidated militant Brigade members formed a loose semicircle around the formidable-looking first sergeant.

"Until you are told differently by your range instructor, you will leave the selector lever of your weapon set to the SAFE position." Wintersole spoke in a loud instructor's voice as he snapped the magazine into the receiver of the assault rifle, then drew and released the bolt with his left hand to feed the first round into the chamber, keeping his right index finger across the outer edge of the trigger guard and away from the trigger.

"When you are instructed to do so, you will use the thumb of your right hand to move the lever to the upright, SEMI-AUTO firing position." Wintersole snapped the small firing lever into the indicated position, then brought the weapon around one-handed with the barrel pointing straight up in the air so that everyone could see what he had done.

"You should never have to look to verify that your weapon is in the semiauto firing position," Wintersole told them emphatically. "You will keep your eyes downrange on the target, and verify the firing status of your weapon with your thumb. Is that clear?"

Sixteen heads nodded vigorously.

"The rear sights of the M16A1 are adjustable. However, I cannot overemphasize the fact that a properly trained soldier should be able to combat-sight his weapon with two rounds."

Turning to face the downrange paper targets, Wintersole brought the M16A1 up to his shoulder and squeezed off two quick shots.

The first bullet struck approximately two inches to the right of the center-of-chest mark. A second bullet hole appeared dead center in the black silhouette target's forehead.

"Based on the impact points of those rounds," Wintersole went on calmly, "you ought to be able to correct your aim and hit your target."

In one smooth motion, the hunter-killer team leader brought the weapon up to his shoulder and—with legs and hips steady, and rotating only his shoulders—began rapidly firing single shots . . .

BLAM-BLAM-BLAM-BLAM . . .

. . . sending expended casings, ruptured tin cans, and explosions of sand flying in the air in all directions until the M16A1's bolt finally snapped against an empty magazine.

A moment later, the last of the eighteen shattered tin cans rolled to a stop in the projectile-softened dirt.

Every member of the Brigade stood paralyzed with shock as Wintersole casually redirected the barrel of the M16A1 back up in the air, thumbed the select lever to the SAFE position, and then handed the still-smoking weapon to one of his men.

"Now then, gentlemen"—he turned and addressed the stunned militants—"if you'll move over to your pop-up target range, my men will demonstrate how to utilize the M16A1 properly in fire-team assault tactics. Please pay close attention. As you will see, things can happen very quickly in a combat situation."

Chapter Thirty-eight

Thirty miles from the Chosen Brigade of the Seventh Seal's hidden training grounds—where Wintersole's men prepared for the fourth stage of their eye-opening demonstration of modern small-fire-team assault techniques, and the two covering members of Lt. Colonel John Rustman's rogue hunter-killer recon team quietly shifted to new concealed positions with their telescopic-sighted sniper rifles—Henry Lightstone entered the hotel using his now-customary rear-alley approach, jogged up the rear stairs, checked to make sure no one lurked in the hallway, and knocked on the door.

Mike Takahara checked the peephole and quickly unlocked and opened the door.

"How's it going?" the tech agent asked as he closed and rebolted the door.

"It's not," Lightstone grumbled as he walked over to the window and checked the street. "Where's everyone?"

Takahara glanced at his watch.

"It's three o'clock on what any normal person would consider a beautiful Saturday afternoon, so assuming everything's proceeding in a reasonably uneventful manner, which is pretty unlikely, all things considered," the tech agent added ruefully, "Larry and Thomas should be transferring 750 giant tarantulas into forty or so terrariums as we speak."

"How'd you and Stoner manage to escape that detail?"

"In my case, I was saved by predictable bureaucratic inefficiency." Takahara smiled as he walked over to the coffee table, picked up a rubber-band-wrapped packet of papers, and tossed them to Lightstone. "However, before we get to that, and speaking of bureaucratic efficiency for a change, there's your ID packet. Congratulations. You're now officially Henry Randolph Lee."

"Henry Lee?" Lightstone blinked in disbelief. "That's the Washington Office's idea of a Southern name that can pass a casual background check?"

"Actually, I do recall something about Lee being a reasonably famous Southern surname," Takahara looked at the ceiling pensively.

"Yeah, well, there's a reasonably famous Taiwanese-American forensic scientist named Lee who's been in the news lately, too. You don't think it's going to draw attention when I start calling myself Henry Lee?"

"Hey, don't look at me. I'm Japanese-American. What do I know?" Mike Takahara shrugged. "I thought I was doing good when I only had to threaten them three times to get them to send us a pair of guaranteed noninterceptable encrypted cell phones."

He held up the phones, then tossed one of them to Henry.

"That *is* efficient," Lightstone agreed as he slipped the phone into his back pocket.

"It's not great, but it sure beats the phone company," the tech agent groused. "I can't get anyone to install a phone line in the warehouse yet. Now they tell me Monday morning at the earliest, and I wouldn't bet much on that. Meanwhile, Larry asked me to hang around here and monitor the phone until I heard from you and Halahan."

"What about Stoner?"

"Larry's got him staked out on Charlie Team's warehouse, trying to keep an eye on things until we find out what the hell's going on."

"Any sign of my military buddies?"

"Not as of a half-hour ago."

"So what's Charlie Team doing?"

"According to Stoner, still making a serious effort to connect up with anybody who might be running illicit guided hunts out here in Jasper County. The way he put it, about the only thing they haven't tried so far is putting Marashenko out on a street corner with a short skirt and small purse."

Lightstone's features darkened in confusion. "Is she the only one they're trolling?"

"No, actually, it looks like they're sticking pretty much to a script. Marashenko, Donato, and LiBrandi alternate as the bait in varying combinations, with Riley, Wu, and Green on rotating surveillance duty when they're not out looking for Wilbur Boggs."

"Wait a minute. Why use LiBrandi for bait instead of Green? Shouldn't the team's tech agent stay focused on the monitoring chores?" Lightstone asked reasonably.

"That's the standard procedure," Mike Takahara acknowledged. "But according to Stoner, Riley's added an interesting twist. He's got both LiBrandi and Marashenko taking pictures of each other all over town. Even using a flash for some evening shots."

"Setting the stage for either one of them to have a camera either in their hands or within reach to snap off a covert picture or two with infrared film if somebody starts nibbling at the bait." Lightstone smiled appreciatively.

"You got it. In fact, Stoner's pretty sure they're using one of the new

30–70 zooms with an extra wide setting. If they watch out for the incidental lighting and work the angles right, the bad guys will never know they've been shot."

"They'd better be careful," Lightstone muttered. "I sure wouldn't want to be in their shoes if one of those military characters got his hands on that camera and found it loaded with sneaky-type film. And speaking of that, does Marashenko know how to use infrared film?"

"She should. She monitored the photo surveillance course at FLETC on her own time, and from what LiBrandi told me, she's a pretty accomplished amateur photographer. I don't think we need to worry about her on the technical end even though LiBrandi's definitely got more training and experience, but I'm not sure that's the only reason why Riley decided to use him instead of Green."

"Why not?"

"I'm thinking that even though it makes sense to pair Marashenko up with an accomplished street actor like Green, our buddy Riley may have felt a little uneasy about an interracial couple walking around town in conservative Jasper County."

Lightstone thought about that for a moment.

"I guess that could be a problem, depending on the circumstances. But it could also work to their advantage . . . if they played it right."

"Sure it could," Mike Takahara agreed. "But Green came to us straight out of the Refuge program—basically a uniformed, public image type of law enforcement—so he's still pretty new to covert investigative tactics. And Marashenko's still a little unsure of herself, which makes her a wild card as far as her temper is concerned—which, as I recall, you got to experience firsthand, so to speak," the tech agent reminded Lightstone with a smile.

"Yeah, that is a point," Lightstone conceded.

"Anyway," Mike Takahara went on, "knowing Riley, I bet he thought the whole thing out and decided it'd be a lot easier for Charlie Team to make contact with these militant assholes if they didn't piss them off first."

Henry Lightstone blinked.

"Hey, wait a minute. That's the second time you used the word 'militant' instead of 'military,' " he pointed out his friend's critical change in terminology.

"About time you started paying attention." The tech agent smiled as he handed Lightstone a piece of paper. "Take a look at this."

"What is it?"

"E-mail message from Freddy Moore. Came in a few minutes ago."

Henry Lightstone scanned the paper quickly.

" 'Charlie Team was assigned to observe and infiltrate a local militia group known as the Chosen Brigade of the Seventh Seal in Jasper County, Oregon,' " he read out loud. " 'That being the case, it's not surprising that members of the Brigade might monitor their movements; however, the group as a whole is believed to represent a minimal threat. Accordingly, Bravo Team will continue with its assigned project, and shall avoid contact with Special Agents assigned to Charlie Team unless so directed.' "

Lightstone looked up at the team's tech agent in disbelief. "Minimal threat? What the hell's he talking about?"

"You got me," Mike Takahara confessed. "The way I read that message, we're dealing with one of two likely situations. Either this whole thing really *is* a game, like Larry said—which probably means your tripping across that spooky sergeant spoiled some aspect of the surprise, but Halahan still wants to keep the scam going—or there's something going on here that's a lot more serious than either Halahan, Moore, or Charlie Team understands. Which reminds me," the tech agent added, "what did you find out about Boggs?"

"Nothing that makes me feel any better about option number two," Henry Lightstone said as he tossed the paper down on the couch.

"How so?"

"As best I can put it together, sometime before five A.M. last Monday, Boggs got into some kind of accident with his boat—his personal boat, not the government one," he clarified—"that probably involved getting the motor caught in some fishing nets. I'm not positive about the net angle, but what happened almost certainly occurred at a fairly high speed, because he managed to knock a couple of his front teeth out on the steering wheel and left a lot of his blood all over the instrument panel, windshield, and deck."

Mike Takahara's eyes widened. "You sure it was Boggs who got hurt?"

"Oh yeah, I don't think there's much doubt about that."

"Why not?"

"Well, mostly because at five A.M. last Monday, a neighbor found him unconscious in the cab of his truck, wearing only a pair of jeans and a down jacket—no socks, shoes, underwear, or shirt—after Boggs backed that very same boat into the neighbor's mailbox directly across the street, again at a fairly high rate of speed."

"What the hell was Boggs doing dressed like that and driving crazy at five in the morning?" the tech agent demanded. "Drunk?"

"Possibly." Lightstone shrugged. "At least that might explain the driving and clothing parts. But from then on, things get a little more complicated."

"How so?"

"Well, first of all, the paramedics who responded to the scene transported Boggs to the local emergency room here in Loggerhead City. But the attending physician immediately medevacked him to Providence Hospital in Medford, where they're better equipped to treat head injuries."

"Makes sense." Mike Takahara shrugged. "So?"

"So Boggs gets checked in to Providence as a John Doe," Lightstone went on, "because he wasn't carrying any identification, and the paperwork from the traffic-accident investigation—assuming there even was one—never caught up with him. He regains consciousness at least once, starts mumbling to the floor nurse and on-duty resident about being a federal agent, and then goes out on them again before they can get a name. In the meantime, the resident continues to treat Boggs for a concussion, broken nose, broken hand, loosened teeth, assorted cuts and scrapes and bruises on his hands and feet—including one really good bruise on his right shin—and exposure."

"Exposure? So whatever happened with his boat occurred real close to the time of his truck accident."

"That's how I read it. But it also implies that Boggs was running his boat at high speeds in the middle of the night, which doesn't make a hell of a lot of sense for a guy who's spent the better part of his life on the water," Lightstone reminded the tech agent.

"No, it doesn't," Mike Takahara agreed.

"But according to the emergency-room physician's notes," Lightstone went on, "Boggs's overall condition—which specifically included reduced mean body temperature, bluish fingernails, severely wrinkled skin, weed and algae fragments in his hair, etc.—was consistent with a person who had been exposed to very cold lake water for several hours."

"Several hours?"

"Right. But then," Lightstone went on, "before anyone at Providence Hospital can put all of this together and get a few answers out of their John Doe patient, he regains consciousness when no one's around—as best anyone can tell, sometime after the floor nurse made her rounds at about two o'clock yesterday afternoon. Shortly thereafter, he—the hospital staff is assuming Boggs did this all on his own, because no one saw him with anyone else—shut off his monitor, removed his IV and a set of electronic sensors, exchanged his hospital gown for a pair of hospital pajamas, slippers, and robe, walked out of his room using the IV rack as a prop, and managed to get all the way out the front entrance of the hospital without anyone asking who, what, or why. Then, in some as-yet-undetermined manner, he effectively disappeared."

"In Medford? Wearing pajamas, slippers, a bathrobe, assorted bandages and a cast on one hand, and dragging an IV bottle rack down the street?" The tech agent raised his eyebrows skeptically.

"They found the IV rack at the curb."

"Meaning somebody probably picked him up?"

Henry Lightstone brought his palms up in a who-knows gesture.

Takahara observed his companion pensively.

"So how does all this link up with Charlie Team and those militant idiots we think slapped a MTEAR on your truck?"

"That's the jackpot question," Lightstone admitted. "We know Charlie Team's been looking for Boggs in a very low-key, behind-the-scenes manner, which is exactly what they ought to be doing if they're really working a legitimate assignment and want to pick up some hints on the local environment. And whatever Boggs is up to sure as hell isn't a game, unless he's got a serious masochistic streak."

"Speaking of games, that reminds me." Mike Takahara walked over to the small desk, where he'd connected his computer notebook and small portable printer to the telephone jack, and picked up another piece of paper. "Take a look at this."

"What is it?"

"Preliminary examination report on those supposed Bigfoot hairs you and Bobby dropped off at the lab last Wednesday."

Lightstone quickly scanned the report, his eyes furrowing in confusion. He read it a second time, much more slowly and carefully.

"Did you look at this?" he asked.

Mike Takahara nodded.

"So what do you make of it?"

"Makes about as much sense as everything else," the tech agent replied, dusting off his keyboard with his sleeve.

"Which means damned little," Lightstone muttered.

"It's just a preliminary report," Takahara reminded him. "Which, I guess, does make some sense, when you stop to think about it. Obviously not the kind of thing a forensic mammalogist runs across every day."

"I guess not. But what does it mean, technically?" Lightstone pressed.

"Well, among other things, I'd say it means your new playmate is deeply involved in this, all the way up to her pretty little eyeballs . . . either way you look at it."

"Exactly." Henry Lightstone tossed the report down, looking thoroughly disgusted with himself.

"Hey, it could be worse," Mike Takahara attempted to console his teammate.

"Yeah? How?"

"Well, if it really is a game, then the rest of us could just as easily be involved in it, too. You could be out on the limb all by yourself on this deal . . . with the possible exception of Larry, who's suffered more than anybody," the tech agent added thoughtfully.

"Yeah, I guess." Henry Lightstone nodded his head slowly, then suddenly looked directly at his friend. "You know what really bothers me about this whole deal?"

"What?"

"Bobby."

"Bobby LaGrange? Your ex-partner?" Mike Takahara blinked in confusion. "I don't follow."

"Unless he's become a lot better actor in his retirement years, I got the distinct impression his blood turned to ice water when I suggested he and Susan might be targets. Bobby's a pretty laid-back guy, and it takes a lot to get him riled, but going after Susan or Justin would definitely do the trick. I really don't think he was faking it."

"Unfortunately, that takes us right back to the rather frightening idea that none of this has anything to do with Halahan wanting to get back at us for screwing up his training program," the tech agent pointed out.

"That's how I see it."

"Which takes us back to the equally frightening idea that Charlie Team may have put themselves right in the crosshairs of some whacked-out militants, and not know anything about it."

"Exactly."

"So what do we do about it, given the fact that Halahan and Moore just gave us direct orders to stay the hell away from Charlie Team?" Mike Takahara asked reasonably.

"Like I've always said, the only way to deal with bullies is to stand your ground, confront the bastards right away, get in their face . . . or they'll go right over the top of you."

"Sounds like useful advice for a ten-year-old schoolboy," the tech agent commented. "But how does that apply to Halahan . . . let alone those militants?"

"I'm not sure it does, but I think it's worth a try. Got a plain piece of paper, a plain envelope, and a first-class stamp handy?"

"I think so."

Two minutes later, Mike Takahara peered over his partner's shoulder as Henry block-printed twelve words in the middle of the sheet of paper.

"You really think that'll draw them out?"

"I think it'll draw *someone* out," Lightstone promised as he addressed the envelope, folded the paper, sealed it in the envelope, applied the stamp, then handed the envelope to the tech agent. "The relevant question is 'who?' "

"Not to mention when, where, and how," Mike Takahara added thoughtfully.

"Oh yeah; that, too." Henry Lightstone smiled pleasantly. "You know how to find the post office?"

"Dogsfire Inn, at the intersection of Brandywine Road and Loggerhead Creek?"

"That's the place."

Mike Takahara looked at his watch. "I can be there in a half hour, no problem. Then what do we do?"

Henry Lightstone shrugged. "After that, we go back to doing what we always do when things go to shit on us."

"Oh yeah, what's that?"

"We stop playing by the rules."

Chapter Thirty-nine

At almost 1830 hours — six-thirty in civilian terms — that Saturday evening, Lt. Colonel John Rustman's rogue hunter-killer recon team finally regrouped at a hidden campsite approximately eight miles northeast of the Chosen Brigade of the Seventh Seal's training grounds.

Concerned but not totally surprised by the events of the day, First Sergeant Aran Wintersole maintained a thoughtful silence while his team went through the practiced motions of stowing their assault gear for ready access; establishing a concentric pair of perimeter trip wires, heat sensors and motion detectors; setting up camp; tending to their prisoner; preparing hot water, coffee, and a composite MRE combat ration meal with three dug-in, Sterno-fueled burners; consuming the high-protein, high-carbohydrate rations; then washing the team's cooking and eating utensils and burying the resulting trash before he finally brought them all together.

The campsite was far removed from the militant's compound, the town, rural homes, popular camping sites, and all of the established hiking trails in the area. And the outer-perimeter detection system would alert the team to the presence or movement of any warm-blooded creature larger than a medium-sized dog. So they could have built a small fire to fend off the evening chill without adding any significant risk to their security if they so desired.

But the desire for creature comforts held little appeal for any of these rigorously trained, professionally alert, and highly motivated soldiers.

In the last seventy-two hours, the team had made several forays into enemy territory; spotted, monitored, and photographed members of the opposing team; suffered a casualty; taken a prisoner; and established a very useful aura of superiority over a group of supposed "allies" who ridiculously described themselves as a "paramilitary organization."

In effect, Lt. Colonel John Rustman's rogue hunter-killer recon team had engaged with the enemy.

And until the team accomplished all of the essential steps to disengage safely from that enemy and return to home ground, an after-dinner pot of hot coffee would serve as the highest luxury these soldiers would allow themselves.

"Give me a status report," Wintersole ordered the team seated around him in the growing darkness. "Start with the prisoner."

"The prisoner has been fed, allowed to relieve himself, resecured, sedated, and put to bed, First Sergeant," one-seven reported.

"Is there a chance that he could hear us talking?"

"No. We plugged his ears and taped them closed."

"What are you using to keep him quiet?"

"Sodium phenobarbital, injected," one-three, the team's communications specialist and medic responded.

"What's his condition?"

"His external injuries are relatively minor, with no obvious signs of infection. Or at least none that I can see. However, to play it safe, I'm giving him some broad-spectrum antibiotics, as well as some decongestants to deal with a mild cold." The young female soldier hesitated. "It's his internal injures that concern me. Based on the extent of his facial injuries and the amount of time we know he spent in the water, we can assume that he suffered a fairly severe concussion as well as from exposure. He's stable, and I'm keeping him warm and quiet, but I don't think he'll be up to any serious movement for at least a couple more days."

Wintersole nodded his head. "No problem. We can transport him if necessary."

The team members all nodded agreeably.

The Army Ranger hunter-killer recon team leader then scanned the group.

"Anybody have anything else to add regarding the prisoner, our targets, resources, intel, tactics, or anything else, before we discuss the merits of our new associates?"

Nobody responded.

"Okay." Wintersole nodded, then turned his attention to the team's heavy-weapons specialist. "One-two. How do you see the situation?"

"Not good, First Sergeant," the muscular young soldier with the corporal's chevrons on his collar replied evenly.

"Explain."

"Of the sixteen men we trained today, less than half qualified on the paper targets at twenty-five yards. Two qualified at fifty yards, one just barely, and none of them topped out higher than marksman on the overall scores. That was the good part. The assault exercises were a complete disaster. Teamwork and fire discipline were nonexistent. Not one Brigade member qualified on the pop-ups, and only two of them—the two youngest ones—made it all the way up the hill to the final set of targets. I saw four of them leaning on their weapons, and damned near every one of them with their fingers in the trigger guards while running. By my count, there were at least seventeen incidents of accidental discharge—three of which went cyclic in spite of direct orders to stay on select fire—and I'd guess at least that many more I didn't see. From my perspective, it was an absolute miracle they didn't sustain any friendly-fire casualties."

"How do you assess their capability for accomplishing their portion of our mission?"

"Poor . . . and that's really giving them the benefit of the doubt," the sturdy weapons specialist concluded. "If these people actually went up against a professionally trained and properly equipped adversary—these federal wildlife agents, for example—I estimate they'd take one hundred percent casualties within a matter of minutes. One-four said it exactly right at the Colonel's briefing, First Sergeant. They're not credible. They're just not."

Wintersole sighed.

"So how do we make them look credible?" he asked after a long moment.

"Additional training's not the answer," one-five volunteered. "Even if we had the time, which we don't, we wouldn't accomplish much. Maybe with the two young kids if we ran them through a serious basic, instilled some discipline, got their minds straight. But the adults are too far gone. They're wanna-bes, and that's all they'll ever be."

"I concur with one-five, First Sergeant," one-seven added. "Those people aren't combat troops—much less high-ranking officers. They're just lazy, overweight, and underexercised barflies with delusions of grandeur. Give any one of them a pair of lieutenant's bars, a real platoon, and a serious combat mission, and you'd end up with fifty dead troops . . . and a blown mission."

Three of the other four Rangers solemnly nodded their heads in agreement.

Wintersole turned his attention to the one man on his team who didn't agree with one-five's assessment.

"You see it differently, one-four?" the hunter-killer team leader inquired.

"No, First Sergeant."

"What's the matter then?"

"I was just thinking . . . maybe what those clowns need has nothing to do with weapons, training, or motivation. Maybe what they really need is some new blood. Somebody on their team who would be a credible threat to these federal wildlife agents."

"You have somebody in mind?"

"Oh yes, First Sergeant." A slight smile formed on the young Ranger's face as he held up his broken wrist. "I certainly do."

At ten-thirty that Saturday evening, East Coast time, Special Operations Chief David Halahan's beeper began to vibrate against his hip.

Sighing inwardly, he excused himself from his understanding wife and late-evening dinner companions, went out to the lobby of the Japanese restaurant, and was directed to a phone.

"Hello?"

"This is Halahan. What's up?"

"I'm not sure," Freddy Moore replied. "I received an interesting e-mail message from Bravo Team a few hours ago. I didn't want to disturb your evening, but the more I thought about the whole deal, the less I liked it."

Halahan's deputy chief went on to describe the message, and his reply.

"So what do you think?" Moore finally asked.

Halahan was silent for a few moments as he considered some of the possible implications.

"I think you were right the way you answered them," he said finally, "but I'm a little uneasy about the number of individuals involved in the surveillance of Charlie Team, and I don't like that business about Lightstone finding a device under his truck at all. How did Takahara describe it again?"

"As a switched tracking device. Lightstone's description was consistent with a military MTEAR device," Moore read from the printout in his hand.

"What's a MTEAR device?"

"Simulated explosive, magnet- or adhesive-based, remote-triggered, generally rigged as a combined flash-bang and a smoke grenade. The army uses them for war games," Freddy Moore explained.

"Are they something these militant characters could pick up through military surplus?"

"Wouldn't surprise me," Moore replied. "I remember we used to get some batches with a high frequency of duds. Pretty soon, we'd just survey the entire batch and open a new shipment."

"No wonder my taxes are so high," Halahan grumbled as he considered this new bit of information. "Was Takahara able to make a confirmation ID?"

"Negative. They decided to leave the truck where it was for a while."

"What's Lightstone using for transportation?"

"He bought a motorcycle out of his emergency funds."

"Bought a motorcycle?"

"Yeah. According to Takahara, Lightstone wanted to stay mobile, and maintain his contact with Sage and the woman innkeeper. A new car would have been a little more difficult to explain. I approved it after the fact, and wired them some more cash." Freddy Moore sighed audibly.

"What's the matter, something bothering you?"

"Yeah, a couple of things, I guess." The deputy Special Ops chief hesitated for a moment. "I still think it's a good idea to keep Bravo Team out of Charlie Team's way. Those kids have enough problems with self-confidence as it is. And I still don't see these Chosen Brigade of the Seventh Seal idiots as representing any kind of a serious threat to a team of highly trained and moderately experienced field agents. And Riley's still there to keep an eye on them. But this business with Boggs has definitely got me worried."

Halahan's eyebrow came up.

"What's happening with Boggs?"

"Nothing. That's just it. They still can't find him."

"That doesn't make much sense."

"No, it doesn't," Freddy Moore agreed. "Think we ought to notify the regional office?"

"And possibly get Boggs in trouble if it turns out he went off on a fishing trip with some of his state fish-and-game buddies without bothering to tell his boss?" Halahan finished.

"That's one of the problems," Freddy Moore admitted. "You know Boggs. He never was much for paperwork and following standard protocols, but he sure gets the job done when he puts his mind to it."

Halahan hesitated for another long moment.

"Let's give him another day or so," he finally said. "If he hasn't checked in by close of business Monday, we notify his boss that we can't find him."

"Okay, fair enough."

Halahan could sense the uncharacteristic hesitation in his deputy's voice.

"You think we're leaving Charlie Team a little open, cutting off their liaison with the regional agent like that?"

Freddy Moore chuckled.

"No, not really. I guess that's part of the second problem."

"You think Bravo Team's disobeying your directive to stay away from Charlie Team?" Halahan guessed.

"I don't think they'll make contact. And from what Takahara said—and didn't say—in his e-mail message, I get the impression that they've got their hands full with that warehouse situation. But I wouldn't be a bit surprised if they put somebody out on the perimeter to keep an eye on things."

"You mean someone like Lightstone?"

"Uh-huh."

"Why so?"

"You know Lightstone," Freddy Moore replied. "How likely is it that he's so concerned about maintaining contact with some demented old fart who rides a motorbike while pretending to be blind, and an innkeeper slash post-office employee who thinks she's a fortune-telling witch, that he goes out and buys a motorcycle an hour after he abandons his truck — and before he checks in with the rest of his team?"

"As opposed to him wanting some immediate and fast transportation, such as a motorcycle, because he didn't take well to being tagged like that?"

"That's right."

"You want to pull them out?"

Freddy Moore snorted with amusement.

"Which team?"

"Either one, or both," Halahan replied. "You call it."

"Gut feel tells me to pull Charlie Team, and leave Bravo in place. Logic says leave them both in place and see what happens. I'd like to go with logic, but I'm not sure that my gut's going to leave me alone for the next couple of days."

"What, no bureaucratic intuition?" Halahan teased gently, wanting to get the measure of his deputy's sense of uneasiness. He had chosen Freddy Moore as his deputy because the ex–military officer and experienced wildlife agent was a skilled survivor as well as a top-notch field supervisor.

"If I had any bureaucratic sense at all, I'd pull everybody back to DC and put in for Boggs's job myself," Freddy Moore replied, laughing.

"Okay," Halahan said, "let's leave them out there for a while. And in the meantime, let's see what you and I can do about trying to find Boggs."

Chapter Forty

At almost nine-thirty that Saturday evening, Henry Lightstone walked into the dining room of the Dogsfire Inn with a brown paper grocery bag in one arm, and went directly to an empty table.

His alert and cautious eyes located her immediately, setting bowls of hot berry cobbler and ice cream in front of the only two diners in the restaurant. She turned, saw him, turned back to her youthful customers, said something apparently amusing to the young woman, and patted the young man on the shoulder.

Then she walked casually over to Lightstone's table with one of the hand-printed menus in her hand.

"Nice to see repeat customers," she greeted him in a neutral voice as she placed the folded menu in front of him. "Can I start you out with something to drink?"

"Actually, I was thinking of starting you out with something, my treat," Lightstone replied, staring up into her gold-flecked green eyes.

The woman hesitated, maintaining a careful distance—mentally and physically—and looked at him suspiciously.

I'll bet you'd be real good at verbal judo, lady. Probably a natural, Lightstone thought to himself, sighing inwardly as he continued to leave himself wide open in an attempt to penetrate the protective barrier she'd erected around herself.

"Somehow I didn't think flowers would work on you." He shifted his gaze to the grocery bag sitting on the adjoining chair.

Her eyes followed his . . . and considered the bag for a moment.

"So just what, exactly, did you think might work?" she finally asked.

"Actually, it was a pretty tough decision. I finally decided to try a couple bottles of homegrown Oregon wine, some homemade tofu from a little place in Ashland, five pounds of top sirloin for any serious carnivores in the house, and a sack of fresh shrimp supposedly flown straight in from the Gulf. I thought maybe I could talk Danny into making some of that fantastic jambalaya you told me about . . . especially if we're willing to share it with him."

"You really think that'll work?"

Lightstone allowed himself to glance into those gold-flecked green eyes long enough to ascertain that they no longer seemed quite so aloof.

"I seem to recall you saying something about double-Xs being easily distracted by picnic baskets."

This time, a slight smile appeared at the corner of her lips.

"I don't know." She played with her pen and order pad. "Danny can be a little overly protective at times."

"I've heard good cooks can be like that . . ." Lightstone paused long enough to give special meaning to his next words, ". . . about their special recipes."

"Certainly seems that way." She smiled almost wistfully.

"Well, that's okay." Lightstone shrugged. "Like I said, I'm willing to share."

"Can you see them from there?" Larry Paxton whispered softly into his headset microphone more than an hour later.

"Uh-huh," Mike Takahara replied.

"Well, what the hell are they doing?"

"Eating dinner."

"That's all?"

"No, they're drinking, too. Some kind of white wine—looks very expensive. Probably spent our entire per diem on that bottle."

"Not mine, he didn't," Dwight Stoner warned over the scrambled short-range communications system.

"I don't give a shit what they're drinking," the Bravo Team leader retorted. "Who's that with them?"

"Looks like the cook." The tech agent shifted his spotting scope and refocused. "Holy shit, look at that thing," he whispered.

"Where?" Stoner and Woeshack's voices echoed in the headsets.

"Down and to the left, next to Henry's chair."

"What the hell are you talking about?" Larry Paxton demanded. "I can't see anything with these damned binoculars."

"Jesus," Stoner whispered.

"That must be the panther Henry told us about. Wow, isn't she something." Thomas Woeshack's awe-filled voice sounded childlike over the scrambled communications system. "Hey, what's it doing now?"

"Looks to me like it's nuzzling Henry's crotch."

"What? Gimme one of them scopes!" Larry Paxton demanded.

"No, wait a minute, I guess that was just to distract him. Looks like she really wanted his shrimp. Hell of a move for a supposedly dumb animal," Dwight Stoner chuckled.

"Who said cats were dumb?" Woeshack asked.

"Probably not anyone with a full-grown panther sitting in his lap," Mike Takahara guessed.

The four agents all focused their spotting scopes and binoculars on the slightly blurred image of the huge black cat bracing her front paws on Henry Lightstone's lap as she licked his plate clean.

"Uh, oh, looks like the lady's pissed," the tech agent observed.

"Yeah, and there goes the cook with the panther in tow," the young Eskimo agent/pilot spoke excitedly into his mike. "Man, this is really neat! I wonder what's going to happen next."

The four of them waited silently.

"Looks like the lady's about to make a move on Henry's shrimp, too," Dwight Stoner commented.

"Yeah, but she's too late," Thomas Woeshack reminded him. "The panther already licked his plate clean."

"Doesn't look like that's going to stop her any," Mike Takahara observed dryly.

"Henry either," Dwight Stoner added. "Think maybe he's going after her plate now?"

"No, probably not. It just hit the floor, along with her silverware . . . *and* the expensive wine," Bravo Team's tech agent noted.

"Hey," chirped Woeshack, "I don't think they're after each other's shrimp at all!"

Larry Paxton lowered his binoculars, closed his eyes, and slowly shook his head.

"You ask me, you're running a pretty loose ship around here, Paxton," Dwight Stoner commented into his headset mike. "I think us peon agents could make a pretty good case for discriminatory treatment on the part of our field supervisor. Like, for example, how come we get to deal with all the poisonous snakes, the giant spiders, and the baby crocodiles—and then have to hang around out in the cold all night as the standby rescue team—while Henry gets to play on the table with a very sexy lady."

"Who may or may not be a witch," Mike Takahara added.

"Hey, yeah, wow! That's right!" Thomas Woeshack exclaimed.

"Still looks like a very sexy lady to me," Stoner commented as he refocused his spotting scope.

"But Henry *does* tend to get bitten, scratched, beaten up, and shot at a whole lot more than we do, which probably does sort of even things out," the team's tech agent reminded them. "Speaking of which, I think she just bit him."

"Yeah." Stoner sighed sadly.

Another interval passed during which the four men continued to monitor their colleague.

"I don't know about you, Larry, but I'm starting to feel like a Peeping Tom," Mike Takahara finally announced. "Think it's about time to get Thomas out of here and go back to keeping an eye on Charlie Team?"

"Yeah, I suppose so." The Bravo Team leader sighed sadly, too.

"Fine with me," Dwight Stoner commented. "I don't think Henry would be real appreciative if we tried to rescue him now anyway."

Two hours later, as the members of Bravo Team moved onto the second shift of their all-night surveillance, and as the huge panther stretched her sleek body then snuggled in closer to the limp, naked form of Henry Lightstone, the woman who called herself Karla sat up in bed and stared down at the two figures who—much to her dismay—now shared her heart as well as her bed.

It wasn't supposed to work out this way.

Chapter Forty-one

Henry Lightstone woke up at seven-thirty that Sunday morning with a throbbing head, an equally tender forearm, long bristly whiskers in his face, and the claw-studded paw of a gently snoring hundred-pound panther draped across his chest.

What?

Indistinct images flickered through the covert agent's momentarily disoriented mind. Bizarre, sweaty, muscular, clawing, and undeniably erotic post–dining room images that he immediately—and prayerfully—hoped had nothing whatsoever to do with the huge predatory cat beside him.

But then the images sorted themselves out, and Lightstone recalled how the panther had yowled and raked at the door of her cage with her razor-sharp claws until the temporarily sated Karla finally groaned in surrender and staggered to the adjoining room to release her.

"We need to get one thing absolutely clear here," Lightstone had pronounced emphatically when the naked woman gracefully tumbled back into bed with the enthusiastically bounding feline close behind. "I like cats. I really do. But I don't care what you say—or what either of you do, for that matter—I am *not* going to get romantically involved with a completely different species."

"You explain the biology to her, I'm tired," Lightstone remembered Karla mumbling before cuddling up next to him, pulling the sheet and blankets over them, and immediately falling into a deep sleep.

He also vaguely remembered the panther's diesel-like purring, her claws rhythmically digging into his skin as she happily kneaded his other shoulder, and her bewhiskered head rubbing his for what seemed like a very long time, until finally—after thinking how odd it was that the idea of lying in bed next to a predatory creature who was perfectly capable of tearing him apart with either her teeth or her claws no longer frightened, or even seriously unnerved him—he, too, fell into a deep, exhausted sleep.

This entire situation is getting out of hand, Henry Lightstone told himself as he carefully extracted himself from the sheet, the blanket, *and* the paw, ignored the bright yellow eyes that blinked open momentarily and slowly closed again, staggered into the bathroom, then considered the haggard face that stared back at him in the mirror.

Gotta get a grip.

Not to mention some sleep.

And . . . wait a minute, what time is it?

He fumbled in the pocket of his jeans for his watch.

Shit. Gotta get dressed.

Ten minutes later, shaved, showered, and dressed, Lightstone hurried down the hallway toward the post office and dining room, hesitated at the small intersecting corridor, looked around, tried the post office door, smiled when he once again discovered it unlocked, and quickly entered.

The first thing he did was check the contents of box fifteen.

Two letters. He immediately recognized the one on top as being the envelope he'd asked Mike Takahara to deliver the previous afternoon.

Good job, Michael, my man. How does that old saying go? Neither rain nor sleet, nor warehouse full of loose snakes and giant tarantulas . . . ?

Lightstone smiled, wondering for a brief moment how Larry Paxton was dealing with the latest emergency, whatever that might be.

He was about to reach into the box, to examine the other letter, noticing as he did so that the box thirteen—the one that had been full of mail the other day, and the one he'd slipped Wintersole's letter into—was now empty, when he heard a key rattling in a lock. Then he saw a hand reach into box fifteen and remove its contents.

For a brief moment, Henry Lightstone simply stood there, stunned.

Then, realizing fate had just presented him with a wonderful opportunity to track back on the militant sergeant's drop-box system, he hurried back out of the office, and pulled the door shut behind him . . . only to find himself staring into the cold pale gray eyes of First Sergeant Aran Wintersole.

Completely unaware of the sudden, unexpected, and potentially violent confrontation that had just occurred within a few feet of his back, congressional aide Keith Bennington walked out of the small post office and over to the staff car with the latest batch of messages in his hand.

Emotionally and physically exhausted, and thus oblivious to the lethal nature of his surroundings, Bennington had no idea that only a matter of seconds had prevented a fiercely protective federal wildlife agent named Henry Lightstone from tracking him back to his mentor, Simon Whatley, and worse, to Whatley's ever-so-powerful boss, Congressman Regis J. Smallreed.

Which, for Keith Bennington, turned out to be a very unfortunate situation indeed.

For had the young congressional aide possessed even the slightest sense of the impact his actions were about to have on the impending clash between terribly powerful and violent foes, he would have deposited those two letters in the nearest Dumpster and run for his life.

That would have been the smart thing to do.

But Keith Bennington had no idea of the importance of his role in this gathering battle between the forces of darkness and light; and in spite of his quite impressive IQ test scores, he wasn't especially smart.

So he simply drove away from the Dogsfire Inn and rural post office with the two fateful letters lying next to him on the front seat, wondering instead if he really, truly coveted the job of his mentor, Simon Whatley, or if he should set his sights a little bit higher.

After all, he reasoned as he turned off of Brandywine Lane, heading back into town, Regis J. Smallsreed wouldn't be a congressman forever.

And for the first time in several days, Bennington actually smiled.

Henry Lightstone sipped from the mug of hot coffee in his hands as he continued to stare at the muscular, pale gray–eyed man seated across from him who, oddly, appeared uncertain about what he should do next.

It's your move, buddy-boy. I've got all the time in the world—especially where you and your sneaky, cammo-wearing friends are concerned.

Lightstone completely ignored the younger man with the cast on his wrist because the older one definitely posed the greater threat.

You can see it in his hands, and in his body language, the experienced covert agent reminded himself, *even if you can't see anything in those damn eyes of his.*

"If I seem hesitant, Henry," the hunter-killer recon team leader finally began formally, "it's because we don't wish to . . . How should I say it? . . . offend your sensibilities any more than we already have."

Bullshit. You didn't give a rat's ass about my "sensibilities" when you and your friends slapped that MTEAR device under the transmission of my truck, Lightstone thought to himself.

Outwardly, he simply smiled politely and continued sipping at his coffee.

"On the other hand, it turns out that your response to David's un-questionably misdirected enthusiasm put us in a rather difficult situation."

Lightstone cocked his head curiously, but remained silent.

"My associates and I were hired to provide some advanced training to a group of—What should I call them: dedicated survivalists? militants?—located just outside of Loggerhead City," Wintersole went on smoothly. "One segment of that training included basic hand-to-hand defensive tactics. Unfortunately, David is our only qualified martial-arts instructor. And now he's going to be on limited duty for a while . . ."

"So you're looking for a substitute instructor," Lightstone finished helpfully, making a mental note of the term "limited duty."

"Exactly."

"I'm curious to know what makes you think I'm qualified to instruct hand-to-hand tactics, or that I'm available."

"Well, first of all, you strike me as a fellow who's spent a few hours in a dojo."

Lightstone shrugged. "A reasonable assumption. But that doesn't necessarily make me a qualified instructor."

"No, it doesn't," Wintersole admitted affably. "But to tell you the truth, Henry, we'd be perfectly happy if you only taught these guys a couple of basic wristlock techniques. They really aren't what you'd call action-oriented types. As far as your availability, it simply occurred to me—since you don't appear to work an eight-to-five shift—that some part-time employment might appeal to you."

"I could be working a swing or graveyard shift," Lightstone pointed out.

"Well, yes, that's true, although . . ." The hunter-killer recon team leader made what Lightstone considered a poor attempt to look embarrassed.

"Although you and your associates are also under the impression that I don't go to work at night either?" Lightstone finished, smiling slightly.

"We do have a couple of people on our staff qualified to teach basic surveillance techniques," Wintersole conceded. "And, for what I hope are understandable reasons, your qualifications are of great interest to us at the moment. We try to be discreet, and would be the first to acknowledge your right to privacy. But given the, uh, rather sensitive political orientation of our clients, and the fact that we don't know much about you—your surname, for example—we thought it wise at least to get a sense of your politics—not to mention your views regarding the federal government—before we made you an offer."

"So what did you find out?"

"As it turns out, not much. For obvious reasons, we believe you were trained—and have stayed active—in some contact form of martial arts. You don't appear to be employed, although you may just be on vacation. And we know almost nothing about your political leanings . . . other than the fact that you appear to have a close relationship with a woman who is certainly very vocal about her views of the federal government, which, I might add, are surprisingly negative for someone presumably employed by the federal government."

"Karla's pretty open about expressing her opinions," Lightstone agreed. "I find that a refreshing trait in a woman . . . in anyone, for that matter."

"No argument there."

"So who are your clients?"

"They call themselves the Chosen Brigade of the Seventh Seal," Wintersole replied casually. "Ever heard of them?"

Lightstone nodded. "It's a small town."

"Yes, of course." The hunter-killer recon team leader hesitated momentarily. "What do you think of them?"

"Personally, from what little I know or have heard, I think they're a bunch of flakes, losers, and lazy idiots. But being what passes for a typical Oregonian around here, I also believe they have every right to live like flakes, losers, and lazy idiots if they so choose . . . just as long as they don't intrude on anyone else's right to live the way they want to."

"A commendably open-minded attitude." Wintersole nodded his head approvingly.

"Us Oregonians are like that." Lightstone smiled briefly. "And to answer a couple other questions you haven't gotten around to asking me yet: First of all, My name's Lee. Henry Randolph Lee."

"Good Southern name," Wintersole nodded approvingly.

"My grandmother thought so. And secondly, I'm not the least bit interested in politics or the federal government."

"When you say you're not interested . . ."

"I mean I'm not interested in working for the feds, or being recruited by a federal agency."

Wintersole blinked.

"Then you think I . . ."

"That's right." Lightstone nodded, meeting the hunter-killer recon team leader's gaze.

"If you don't mind my asking"—Wintersole appeared genuinely surprised by the accusation—"why do you think that?"

"I don't know. I guess it occurs to me that the federal government might want to keep an eye on these Seventh Seal characters, no matter how incompetent and disorganized they may be." Lightstone shrugged. "And, I recall reading somewhere that certain federal government agencies like to recruit—what do they call them? Operatives?—from the local community."

"If you're talking about the CIA, I believe they call the local people they recruit 'agents' or 'resources,' " Wintersole replied. "I have no idea what the FBI calls them."

"You have some practical experience with the CIA?"

"In Vietnam," the team leader explained. "The spooks pretty much ran that war. Every now and then, one of them would suit up and go out on recon with us."

" 'Us' being . . . ?"

"U.S. Army Rangers. At the time, I was a combat infantryman, buck sergeant, in charge of a long-range recon team," Wintersole tossed out casually. "I retired as an E-8, first sergeant. I'm not a spook, Henry. Just a thirty-year man trying to get by on a military pension."

Lightstone gestured toward the young man seated to his left. "Your associate looks a little young for retirement," he noted, watching to see if the comment caused the quasisoldier with the cast on his wrist to lose any of his polite, respectful, and attentive demeanor.

He didn't.

Wintersole smiled pleasantly.

"David's a classic example of all the highly trained and extremely dedicated young men who, sadly, are being tossed aside—wasted, actually—by the current downsizing of our military forces," the hunter-killer recon team leader explained. "But then, too, I suppose our nation's loss is my gain. Once I decided to go into business for myself, I found it very easy to put together a small team of highly qualified instructors."

"Your business being a civilian version of basic infantry training?"

"That's right."

"And you want to add me to that team?"

"Only temporarily." Wintersole nodded. "I won't insult your intelligence by making any promises I can't keep, Henry. David's an excellent hand-to-hand instructor, and I expect him to recover very quickly. However, if things work out in the manner in which we hope . . ." The hunter-killer team leader shrugged.

"And for whatever it's worth, I want you to know I don't hold any grudges." Wintersole's young associate spoke for the first time. "I would personally welcome you on board as an associate. Only thing I ask is that you walk me through that wristlock sequence a few times . . . ideally after I get this thing off." He held up the cast and smiled.

"That's the least I owe you, whether I work for you or not." Lightstone nodded agreeably.

The young man grinned openly. "Fair deal."

Lightstone searched for some hint of anger or frustration beneath that controlled smile, but saw nothing.

Where in the hell do they get these guys? he wondered.

Shrugging internally, Henry Lightstone turned back to the supposedly retired Army Ranger first sergeant.

"So what are we talking about in terms of hours and pay?"

"I've scheduled eight hours of hand-to-hand instruction per student, broken down into two four-hour blocks. We've got a total of sixteen students, and we're training them in four-man teams. Figure thirty-two hours of instruction, eight hours for prep and grading, which makes it a full forty-hour week. I'm offering two grand even, payment in cash at the end of the week, if you handle your own taxes."

"Pretty decent pay," Lightstone noted casually.

Wintersole shrugged. "We're interested in generating repeat customers and picking up more through word of mouth. You don't accomplish that by providing your customers with second-rate instruction. These are unusual circumstances; however, I do expect you to earn your pay. Any questions?"

"Just one. When do I start?"

"How about tomorrow?"

Lightstone hesitated briefly. "Tomorrow's as good a day as any, but there's one thing about me you probably need to know."

"What's that?" Wintersole's eyes narrowed slightly.

"In spite of my Southern heritage, I'm not very good at saying 'yes sir' to people."

"That won't be a problem, Henry." Wintersole smiled. "The very first thing we teach raw recruits in the army is never to call a sergeant 'sir.' We like to think we work for a living."

"I take it that goes for retired first sergeants, too?"

"*Especially* for the retired ones," the hunter-killer team recon leader replied, his cold gray eyes glistening with a sense of amusement that Henry Lightstone couldn't even begin to interpret.

Henry Lightstone was still sitting at the table, sipping his nearly cold coffee, when Karla came over and sat down beside him.

"So what was that all about?" she asked softly.

"I seem to have stumbled into a temporary employment situation."

"With them?"

Lightstone nodded solemnly. "Looks that way."

"Would you care to explain what the hell is going on?" A half-troubled, half-dangerous glint brightened her gold-flecked green eyes.

He described the retired army sergeant's job offer.

"They want you to teach hand-to-hand combat techniques to the *Chosen Brigade?*" Her expression suggested that she couldn't quite believe her ears.

"Apparently."

"Are they serious?"

"I guess so. At any rate, two grand for forty hours of work sounds pretty serious to me."

"But why you? I mean, no offense, my friend, but it's not like you go around waving a 'Don't Tread On Me' flag. And you may not have been around here long enough to notice," she added, "but these Chosen Brigade folks are pretty paranoid about newcomers."

"I have no idea why they chose me," Lightstone confessed. "Maybe they figure it's my fault their martial-arts instructor got hurt."

"They're lucky I managed to get Sasha stopped in time, or that broken wrist would have been the least of that kid's problems," Karla muttered darkly.

"Yeah, well, she definitely put the fear of God into those two," Lightstone smiled, remembering the expression on the retired Army Ranger sergeant's face. "And besides," he added, "it's not like I'm going to teach them something dangerous."

"You're not?"

"In eight hours? Not hardly. If these guys are anything like I've heard, I'll be doing good to teach them how to fall down without getting hurt. And besides," he added with a smile, "I can use the money. Two grand is two grand. Might even be able to make a dent in my restaurant tab."

She dismissed his teasing comment with an aggravated wave of her hand.

"You do realize that these future students of yours advocate the violent overthrow of the federal government?" she asked after a long moment.

"So what? You do, too," he reminded her.

"All I'm doing is exercising my First Amendment rights to express my opinion," she argued irritably. "There's a big difference between mouthing off and taking action, Henry. A very big difference."

"I'm not going to wave flags, or march in any parades, or throw any bombs," Lightstone explained patiently. "At best, I'm just going to teach those idiots how to survive a fistfight. And if that's all it takes to overthrow the federal government these days, then the government's in a hell of a lot worse shape than I think it is."

"You're really determined to do this, aren't you?" She tapped her slender fingers on the table.

"I'm not sure that 'determined' is the right word. I just can't see any reason not to do it. But if the idea really bothers you . . ." he added to see how she'd respond, "I'll reconsider. I'm not that hard up for money."

The woman sat quietly for a while, then suddenly got up. "I'll be right back," she murmured softly, and disappeared into the Inn.

Four minutes later, she returned with a claw necklace in her hand which she draped over his chest and tied securely behind his neck.

"What's this?" Lightstone asked as she sat down opposite him again.

"A cougar-claw necklace."

Henry Lightstone looked down at the eight sharp claws surrounding what appeared to be a thick light green jade medallion with a cougar carving on its face, all of which was strung on a beaded leather cord.

"Cougar claws? Why a cougar?"

"Because you're a cat, Henry," the sensuous young woman explained with a sigh. "A bear-claw necklace would do absolutely nothing for you."

"But where did you . . . ?"

"We witches have our sources," she replied cryptically. "Do you still have that Bigfoot hair I gave you?"

Lightstone nodded, and felt distinctly uneasy when he lied to her.

"Good. Keep it on your person at all times. And no matter what happens," she insisted gravely, "*don't* take that necklace off until you finish that job and come back here."

"I don't understand." He peered inquisitively into the woman's intense gold-flecked green eyes as he gingerly fingered the sharp claws. "What's it supposed to do?"

"It's an ancient Indian battle charm."

"Battle charm?" He cocked his head, his lips forming a slight smile.

"It's coming, Henry. Right here to Jasper County. A major conflict between darkness and the light. Maybe you can't sense it, or maybe you don't even realize you're part of it . . . but you are," she emphasized, making no effort to conceal the half-worried and half-angry look in her eyes.

"If you insist on confronting your demons, Henry, the least I can do is try to keep you alive."

Chapter Forty-two

Simon Whatley woke up at a little past ten that Sunday morning with a queasy stomach and a massive headache . . . the predictable aftereffects of far too many hours spent in cramped airplanes eating lousy food and surrounded by obnoxious children, not to mention sitting in noisy airport lounges filled with more obnoxious travelers and equally lousy food.

Only the alcohol had saved him, the congressional district office manager now remembered, remorsefully rubbing his aching head.

Whatley's primitive survival instincts told him to roll over and go back to sleep. But his stomach continued to churn, and his head continued to throb, so he finally got up and rummaged through the medicine cabinet for anything that appeared remotely like a proper antidote and consumed it in large quantities.

A half hour later, he felt good enough to get up again. This time he managed to shave, shower, and brush his teeth before his churning, throbbing hangover drove him back to the soothing stability and comfort of his bed.

Whatley knew he had things to do—important things, like reviewing the drop-box messages—that he simply must get done. But the mere thought of another mind- and body-numbing red-eye flight to Washington, DC, that evening proved more than he could bear.

"It's not right!" he ranted to himself. "I'm a goddamn congressional district office manager. A person of power and influence who controls a wide range of congressional office perks and privileges. One phone call from me, and a friend or associate of Regis J. Smallsreed—or someone who desperately wants to be a friend or associate of such a notoriously powerful and influential congressman—and . . ."

Simon Whatley blinked at what began as a frustration-relieving diatribe ended with a brilliant idea.

He smiled and rubbed his aching neck.

So many special perks and privileges that a congressional district office manager could hand out for services rendered, even in a rural enclave like Jasper County, Oregon . . .

But the special services of René Bocal rank right up there at the top of the p-and-p list, Simon Whatley thought to himself, resting his throbbing head gingerly on his pillow as he dialed the familiar number, identified himself, then provided the address and necessary details.

Whatley felt vaguely guilty as he hung up the phone. A call to René Bocal constituted an expensive perk, one generally reserved for Smallsreed himself or one of his most favored clients. He wavered. Maybe he should call back and cancel the reservation. But then Whatley remembered the remark made by Sam Tisbury, one of Smallsreed's most favored clients and certainly most favored political donors.

. . . better keep him out of first-class. Make the reservations under different names, random locations in the back cabin, inside seats whenever possible. . . .

Simon Whatley closed his eyes, wincing at the memory.

Oh yes, he thought, *I do deserve this. Matter of fact, I damned well earned it.*

So by the time the very professional-looking young woman in the very professional-looking business suit arrived at his door with the thin, executive-style briefcase in her hand, the congressional district office manager no longer felt the least bit guilty about adding a fifteen-hundred-dollar charge to Smallsreed's special account.

And by the time the senior congressional staffer stretched out facedown on his bed, and the young woman kneaded his narrow and decidedly tense shoulder and neck muscles, her carefully oiled breasts and thighs sliding deliberately but distractingly against him, Simon Whatley could not have cared less about the important work he must get done.

There would be plenty of time for that on the plane, this evening, when he would feel much better . . . and much more up to the task at hand.

At one o'clock that Sunday afternoon, the first trace of a smile finally broke the tense contours of Bravo Team leader Larry Paxton's face.

It had been a long time coming.

Given the very same circumstances, Paxton decided as he glared down at the finally cooperating arachnids with no little satisfaction, even a potential saint like Mother Teresa undoubtedly would have allowed disparaging remarks to escape her lips.

Christ, what the hell do they expect? The Bravo Team leader immediately abandoned his holy thoughts in favor of a more practical one as he waited patiently for the last of the fifteen giant red-kneed tarantulas to venture out of the jury-rigged clear-plastic tunnel and drop into the waiting terrarium, where fourteen of his or her fellow tarantulas investigated a clear plastic box filled with scurrying crickets. *I'm sitting here in an unheated warehouse in the middle of Oregon, freezing my ass off with a kid-agent-pilot who's afraid to fly, thirty deadly snakes, 750 giant spiders, and a dozen baby crocodiles that attack anything that moves; I've got a rookie covert team that isn't even supposed to be here being tagged by a bunch of militant idiots who may or may not be attaching bombs to our vehicles; I've got two of my best agents tagging the rookie team and the taggers in direct violation of direct orders from Halahan, instead of helping Woeshack and me figure out how to move the goddamned spiders into the goddamned terrariums; and I've got a wild-card agent who's supposed to be out buying Bigfoot evidence running around with a blind-man soothsayer who rides a motorbike, and shacking up with a beautiful post-office worker with a goddamned panther who thinks she's a witch.*

And if anything goes wrong with all that, anything at all, Larry Paxton reminded himself, *it's gonna be my fault.*

And they wonder why I get upset?

Shit.

Then, to Paxton's absolute amazement, the last red-kneed tarantula dropped into the terrarium with a barely audible thud.

The Bravo Team leader's face broke out into a beaming smile.

Hot damn, he thought, as he quickly disconnected the tubing, pulled the string to open the small plastic box—sending dozens of crickets scurrying in all directions, pursued by fifteen apparently ravenous tarantulas—and hurriedly duct-taped a piece of cardboard over the ragged hole in the stamped-aluminum terrarium top.

"Hey, Thomas, how you coming with that next cricket box?" Paxton yelled across the warehouse.

"Not too good," the team's quasipilot confessed. "It's really hard to make a hundred crickets go into a box this small all at the same time. A lot of them are getting loose. You sure we need a hundred?"

"Whatever." Paxton dismissed the younger agent's question with a wave of his right hand. "Just hurry it up. I'm on a roll over here."

"You mean your invention works?"

The young special agent/pilot's head popped up in surprise.

"Hell yes, it works. What did you expect?" A pained expression flashed across Paxton's face. "You think I need an electronic genius like Mike to come up with something simple like this?"

"We always did before," Woeshack pointed out truthfully.

"Well, you can forget what happened before, 'cause from now on, things are gonna be different around here," the Bravo Team leader predicted as he worked his jury-rigged device into the crude hole drilled in the next aluminum terrarium cover. "Seeing as how I'm the boss around here, things are gonna go my way for a change."

Which, coincidentally, was exactly what Simon Whatley was thinking, too, until the phone next to his bed rang.

Chapter Forty-three

At 6:35 that Sunday evening, Keith Bennington handed a numbed and glassy-eyed Simon Whatley his suit bag, briefcase, airline tickets, and the pair of letters that he—Bennington—had picked up from the drop box at the Dogsfire Inn post office.

He then watched his boss toss the two letters into the briefcase, on top of what Bennington immediately recognized as the other packets and letters that he'd collected from the designated drop box over the past two days . . . all of which clearly appeared unopened.

Christ, the young Congressional aide thought, *hasn't he even looked at that stuff yet?*

Then, deciding that the contents of those drop-box messages definitely didn't concern him, Bennington hurried on with his briefing.

"Don't forget, sir, you transfer from the Horizon flight from here to the United flight in Portland which will take you to San Francisco, where you'll catch the American red-eye to Washington Dulles. They're getting ready to board now, so you better go through security."

Simon Whatley looked at the line disdainfully.

"Wait a minute. Why can't I check my luggage?" he demanded petulantly. "This damned suit bag's heavy. Christ, I'm only going for the day. Why did you pack so many clothes?"

"Sir . . ."

"And why the hell do I need to fly all the way to Portland in one of those damn little puddle-jumpers, and change planes and fly all the way back over Medford, to get to San Francisco? What happened to the goddamned 737 direct flight?" the congressional district office manager whined in a decidedly childlike tone of voice.

"Sir, I . . ."

"Why can't I fly direct into Washington National instead of landing all the way out in goddamned Dulles and spending a goddamned hour driving through the goddamned rush-hour traffic?" Whatley stopped, visibly out of breath and dangerously flushed.

"That's what I tried to tell you when I called earlier, sir," the aide explained patiently for the third time, hoping that his boss was more alert now that he'd had some time to recuperate in the car.

A frantic Keith Bennington had passed the brightly smiling, heartachingly attractive, and all-too-familiar young woman from the René Bocal Agency at the door to Simon Whatley's expensive apartment. Trying not to think about what the young woman wearing the professional-looking business suit and carrying the executive briefcase had actually done in Whatley's apartment, Bennington had hurried inside and found his exhausted, bleary-eyed boss in the shower, trying with minimal success to wash off what looked like a great deal of lipstick and body oil from various parts of his pale, slender body.

For some incredible reason that defied logic — or at the very least, Keith Bennington's limited imagination regarding such sordid events — Whatley's hair lay in a mass of slippery, oil-soaked and soap-resistant tendrils atop his slightly pointed head. It took the congressional aide almost two hours to get his boss properly scrubbed, rinsed, dried, dressed, packed, into the staff car, and to the airport.

Like bathing a damned dog, he thought ruefully as he glanced down at his watch. *Thank God I left early.*

"The direct flight from Medford to San Francisco was canceled because of a mechanical problem," Bennington repeated for the third time. "I busted my butt to get you on this flight . . . which is boarding right now," he reminded Whatley firmly. "And as soon as you get off this plane, you've got to grab your luggage and run because even if you make it to Portland on time, you've only got twenty-three minutes to make your next flight. And don't forget, the United terminal's up that long ramp and way over on the far side of the terminal."

"Twenty-three minutes?!" Whatley squawked. "But tha . . . that isn't even legal!"

"No sir, it's not." Bennington leaned forward and lowered his voice. "In fact, they didn't even want to issue me the tickets. I had to mention Congressman Smallsreed's name twice before they agreed to make an emergency exception. Even then, they wouldn't promise to hold the plane in Portland. *That's* why you can't check your luggage, sir, because if you do, it simply won't make the connection in Portland."

"*But then why the hell do I have to fly on three goddamned different airlines?*" Whatley continued raging hotly, resisting his congressional aide's firmly guiding hand and ignoring the other people in the small airport terminal who were now staring at them curiously.

"Because only these two flights can get you to San Francisco in time to make that flight. And if you don't get going right now, you will definitely miss the last commercial flight that can get you to Washington, DC, in time for your meeting tomorrow."

"But what about United or . . ."

"Sir"—Keith Bennington continued firmly to guide his boss toward the security checkpoint, knowing full well that if Whatley missed this flight, someone would pay dearly . . . and he could easily guess who that someone would be—"this time of year everyone's looking for cheap fares. If you're willing to travel first-class, I can easily get you on a later red-eye, and I can *always* get you on a special military flight," he reminded Whatley, having no clue why his boss suddenly rejected the standard congressional travel perks available to the members and staff seated on the right appropriation subcommittees. "But if you insist on traveling coach, this is it . . . and that was the final boarding call, sir. If you don't get going right now, sir, *you're going to miss the goddamned plane!*"

Either Bennington's use of profanity, or his amazingly loud and insistent voice when he said it, ignited some survival-oriented circuit in Simon Whatley's fevered brain and galvanized him into action.

Cursing to himself, Whatley hurled his luggage and briefcase into the gaping maw of the X-ray machine, bolted through the metal detector, screamed at the approaching security guard when the warning bell began to sound . . . then turned and ran back through the detector, frantically pulled his wallet, keys and coins out of his pocket, flung them between the metal detector and the X-ray machine—where they ricocheted off the equipment and nearly hit the security guard in the process—lunged back through the metal detector, scooped up his wallet and keys, snatched his waiting briefcase and carry-on bag, ran for the doorway, fumbled for his boarding pass, and then frantically raced across the tarmac toward his distant plane.

Gasping for breath, Whatley finally staggered up to small plane, handed his suit bag to the impatiently waiting baggage handler, and stumbled up the stairway . . . only to discover—as he hunched over to walk down the narrow, low-ceilinged aisle—that only the middle seat in the back row of the tiny plane remained unclaimed.

Only as he wedged himself into his seat between a very large man and his equally large wife who had claimed the two back window seats, strapped himself in, and stared wistfully up the narrow aisle toward the cockpit, did Simon Whatley realize there wouldn't be any flight attendants on this flight.

And no comforting and numbing booze either.

At 6:55 that Sunday afternoon, as a truly distressed Simon Whatley contemplated the cruelty of fate, Larry Paxton was on a roll.

Working at a feverish pitch, the Bravo Team leader frantically drilled hole after hole in the wooden sides of the shipping crates and the tops of the aluminum terrarium covers, sending slivers of wood and aluminum flying as he urged Woeshack—his ever-loyal and faithful Eskimo special agent/pilot assistant—to move faster between temporarily plugging up the holes in the sides of the crates, connecting sections of clear-plastic tubing between the holed crates and terrariums, filling small plastic boxes with crickets, and securing the aluminum covers to the filled terrariums with long strips of duct tape.

In fact, only after the two Special Agents taped the sixteenth terrarium cover to the sixteenth filled terrarium did it occur to Paxton to ask a relevant question.

"Thomas, how are we doing on duct tape?" he inquired as he wrapped his chilled and slightly trembling hands around the blissfully warm drill.

"No problem." The diminutive agent smiled cheerfully. "I bought sixty-two rolls—every one left in town, far as I could tell."

"Sixty-two, huh?" The nearly exhausted Bravo Team leader surveyed the warehouse, noting uneasily that in addition to approximately fifty duct-taped terrariums now lining the three-tiered shelf, sticky clumps of the easily tangled adhesive now covered a good portion of the warehouse floor. "How many have we got left?"

"Uh . . . just a second." Woeshack disappeared behind a pile of crates, then popped back up a few moments later. "Looks like at least forty or so."

Paxton smiled.

"Thomas, my man," he announced cheerfully, "in my humble opinion, I believe the crucial elements of this insane operation are finally starting to come together."

Thanks to a slight head wind, the pilot of the bumpy flight from Medford to Portland touched down on the long PDX runway four minutes behind schedule.

It was all that Simon Whatley—who had frantically checked and re-checked his watch every fifteen seconds throughout the entire flight—could do to keep from unbuckling his safety belt, running down the aisle, ripping open the flimsy barrier to the cockpit, and screaming at the pilot and copilot who, from Whatley's fevered and biased viewpoint, barely looked old enough to qualify for a driver's license.

Christ Almighty, the congressional district office manager raged to himself, *whatever happened to the idea of taking a goddamned plane to get somewhere faster?*

Simon Whatley continued checking his watch every ten seconds or so as the pilot taxied toward the terminal, knowing full well he was hope-lessly trapped by the sixteen people in the eight rows of seats in front of him, who undoubtedly would use those few first deplaning minutes to dawdle or suddenly decide to share photos of their latest grandchild with a perfect stranger. Suddenly, the idea of unbuckling his safety belt and running down the aisle seemed like a perfectly reasonable thing to do.

Accordingly, Whatley waited until the plane almost reached the gate, quickly released his seat belt, and lunged down the aisle . . . unfortunately at the precise moment the pilot braked suddenly to avoid hitting an errant baggage carrier.

The sudden forward acceleration caused his flailing arms and legs to slam into the backs and armrests of four separate seats, triggering a series of startled screams and angered curses in his wake as his head, knees, chest, and elbows bore the brunt of his headfirst slide along the rough carpet . . . until finally, thanks to the effects of abrasive friction and the amazingly sturdy cockpit barrier, he came to a sudden halt.

Stunned and bleeding, Whatley managed to regain his feet and brace himself against the low ceiling, ignore the glares and mutterings of his fellow passengers and the perplexed look of the youthful copilot, who struggled to open the combination door and collapsible stairway, stagger down the stairs of the small plane, snatch his briefcase and suit bag from a baggage handler, and run for the terminal building.

Once inside the terminal, Whatley continued running—elbowing his way though the densely populated Horizon boarding area, charging down the hallway and up the seemingly endless ramp, then sprinting across the main terminal, plunging through another security checkpoint and bolting down another long hallway—to the United gate where, seventeen minutes later, red-faced, wheezing, oozing blood from his knees and el-bows, and barely able to hold his briefcase and suit bag in his cramped and fatigued hands, much less stand upright on his wobbly legs, he learned that the flight to San Francisco would be delayed.

It was probably just as well for all concerned—the airline repre-sentative at the gate, the nearby security guard who was scrutinizing Whatley carefully, and Whatley's fellow passengers, not to mention his as-yet-unblemished rap sheet—that it took the senior congressional staffer another ten minutes to regain his breath, color, and strength . . . which, in turn, gave him a fighting chance to regain what amounted to a very tenuous grip on his composure.

Only then did that sorely abused congressional district office manager finally comprehend that he couldn't check his suit bag in, right here, at the Portland gate—for automatic transfer to the American Airlines red-eye flight—because the anticipated delay would give him, at most, only a very few minutes to make his connecting flight at San Francisco International Airport.

"So we can't check your luggage, sir," the polite airline representative explained in a professionally patient voice. "Because even if you manage to make your connection in San Francisco, any luggage you check here definitely will not."

With understandable amazement, then, at 11:55 that Sunday evening, Simon Whatley—bandaged, exhausted, sweat-soaked, aching, and thoroughly numbed by the six drinks he'd consumed at the Portland Airport and on the United flight—finally stuffed his suit bag, briefcase, and coat into the overhead compartment of the American Airlines 757 red-eye flight to Washington Dulles, and collapsed into his rearmost aisle seat adjacent to two of the plane's three toilets.

Understandably, too, any plans to review the messages from Lt. Colonel John Rustman's rogue hunter-killer recon team prior to his next meeting with Regis J. Smallsreed, Sam Tisbury, and the harrowing presence in the shadows of Smallsreed's congressional office, immediately evaporated when Simon Whatley fell into a deep and exhausted sleep.

At precisely seven minutes after midnight Monday morning—just as the American Airlines 757 jetliner bearing the unconscious body of Simon Whatley arced into the night, and just as Bravo Team leader Larry Paxton taped the next-to-last aluminum cover to the next-to-last giant-tarantula-filled terrarium with hands that definitely trembled with exhaustion and the surrounding cold—special agent/pilot Thomas Woeshack made a relevant discovery.

"Hey, Larry," he called, holding up a box filled with a fifty-fifty mix of long red and purple light tubes, "weren't we supposed to put these IR and UV lights back in those terrarium lids you drilled *before* we taped them shut?"

Chapter Forty-four

The impact of the 757 jetliner's wheels against a solid surface jarred Simon Whatley out of a deep sleep.

Christ, what was that? Did we hit something?

Whatley's eyes snapped wide open just as the spinning rear wheels struck the runway for the second time, whereupon he became aware — once again — of the stench of the nearby chemical toilets, and the noise of the rear cabin, where at least a half dozen small children now yowled from the effects of the sudden change in cabin pressure.

Landing? Can't possibly be there yet. What time is it?

Whatley tried to blink his sleep-blurred eyes into focus enough to see the hands of his very expensive Rolex.

Quarter to five. Can't be Dulles. Way too early. Not supposed to be there until . . . oh, right.

Seven-forty-five.

Three hours difference. Time zones.

God, we are here, he realized, blinking his eyes at what his numbed brain finally recognized as daylight — in the form of dreary clouds and the inevitable rain — through the windows of the now taxiing plane.

He immediately gave immensely grateful thanks that the first leg of this latest in a series of nightmarish trips had finally ended.

Not until the plane came to a final stop, and he stood up on his stiff, aching legs to retrieve his suit bag and briefcase from the overhead compartment did he realize . . .

Oh Jesus, the messages from the drop box. I haven't even looked at the damned things yet.

Simon Whatley felt sorely tempted to sit right back down and go through all of the messages from Lt. Colonel John Rustman's rogue hunter-killer recon team right there. Very tempted indeed, because Smallsreed had given him the specific task of reading, analyzing, and digesting their contents and presenting a summary of the relevant information to the congressman, Tisbury, and the horrifyingly ominous shadow-man who haunted the dark corners of Smallsreed's private office . . . and scared Whatley far more than any one individual he'd ever met.

But Smallsreed's bagman immediately realized that any such effort—

with kids whining, and babies crying, passengers trying to recover their luggage and other carelessly stowed personal items, and the flight attendants hovering with amazing patience, trying to get everyone off the plane so that they could get off, too—courted disaster.

Christ, what if I drop one of them . . . and some kid grabs it . . . and it ends up in the hands of some nosy law-enforcement official?

Or worse, much worse, someone from the Washington Post?

The mere thought sent a chill down Simon Whatley's spine.

In the taxi, he told himself as he slowly shuffled his way out of the plane. *Read them in the taxi on the way to the hotel. Check in, shower, change clothes, whip out a quick summary, and go to Smallsreed's office.*

He glanced down at his watch again.

Plenty of time.

Simon Whatley calculated the relevant time and risk factors associated with his scheduled appearance before Regis J. Smallsreed, Sam Tisbury, and the shadow-man at almost exactly eight o'clock in the morning in Washington, DC. Smallsreed didn't expect him to arrive at the private office at the Longworth House Office Building until eleven. Thus, even taking the heavy rain and the notoriously congested DC metro area commute into account, the senior congressional staffer felt certain that he would be in his hotel room by nine-thirty that morning at the very latest.

It would take him one hour to shower, shave, change clothes, glance through the drop-box messages one last time, write a quick summary, and then take the elevator down to the lobby, where a very solicitous concierge and doorman would personally escort him to a waiting taxi with an open umbrella and a cheerful smile.

Add another ten-minute taxi ride—fifteen at the very most—to reach the front steps of the Longworth House Office Building, followed by a pleasant five-minute walk through the halls of power . . . and Whatley would stand in Smallsreed's office, sipping a cup of coffee and chatting with the senior members of Smallsreed's staff, with a good fifteen minutes to spare.

Plenty of time.

Accordingly, when Simon Whatley removed the three thinnest drop-box message envelopes from his briefcase and carefully placed them in his jacket pocket, he didn't think anything at all about handing his over-coat, suit bag, and briefcase—containing his wallet, keys, airline tickets, Congressional Office Building pass, and the thick envelope with the hunter-killer recon team's surveillance photos of their intended targets—to the taxicab driver, who placed them all in the trunk of the vehicle before shutting Whatley's door.

It was ironic, then, as the cab approached the Dulles Access Road junction with the Washington Beltway in the drizzling rain fifteen minutes later, that just as the finally relaxed congressional district office manager started to reach into his jacket pocket for the messages from Lt. Colonel John Rustman's hunter-killer recon team, a daydreaming commuter suddenly realized where he was, slammed on the brakes, and swerved right in a desperate attempt to make the exit . . . initiating a chain reaction that sent Whatley's cab spinning out of control into the off-ramp divider.

The highly professional and experienced paramedics who responded to the multiple-car accident at the intersection of the Dulles Access Road and the Washington Beltway, wasted no precious time worrying about the individual identities of the bodies lying or hanging in the twisted wreckage that comprised three distinctly separate cars and a cab.

They quickly and methodically extracted all of the survivors from their vehicles before any of the spilled gasoline ignited; provided immediate first-aid treatment for airway obstruction, bleeding and shock; transported the victims to the nearest hospital as quickly as possible; and then got back on the air to take the next priority call.

On rainy days, that last task ranked almost as highly as the other three. At last count, and according to the harried dispatchers who repeatedly put calls out for any available emergency-response team, nine accident calls awaited response, four of which involved serious injuries.

All in all, a typical rainy day in metropolitan Washington, DC.

Accordingly—and very much unlike the Jasper County, Oregon, paramedics who actually took time to try to identify Wilbur Boggs—the team that transported Simon Whatley and the cab driver to nearby Fairfax County Hospital in northern Virginia simply rolled the two unconscious victims out of the back of the ambulance and into the waiting hands of the emergency-room medical team; tossed a pair of plastic bags—one of which contained Whatley's shoes, coat, jacket, tie, and the three dropbox messages—on the curb; secured two freshly made-up gurneys in the back of the ambulance; signed a clipboard-mounted form; then vanished into the dreary, rainy morning with lights flashing and sirens wailing.

Simon Whatley's briefcase, containing, among many other things, his wallet, keys, airline tickets, Congressional Office Building pass, and an envelope bearing the surveillance photos taken by First Sergeant Aran Wintersole's hunter-killer team, remained in the trunk of the demolished cab which, at that very moment, was being towed to a local storage yard several miles from the crash site.

Like Wilbur Boggs before him, Simon Whatley quickly disappeared into the bowels of an overwhelmed emergency-medical-treatment system.

Chapter Forty-five

At precisely 0600 hours on a fairly typically cold and drizzly Monday morning in southern Oregon, Special Agent Henry Lightstone (AKA Henry Randolph Lee) stepped out from under the protective overhang of the Dogsfire Inn, quickly levered his motorcycle into the back of a dark green–painted pickup truck, secured the tailgate, and got into the passenger side of the vehicle driven by a decidedly determined-looking young man wearing a cast on his wrist.

The two men greeted each other in a carefully neutral manner, each fully aware that they must set aside any lingering personal matters for another day.

Moments later, the truck backed out of the driveway and disappeared into the surrounding mist-enshrouded trees.

As it did, an equally determined-looking young woman whose gold-flecked green eyes clearly mirrored the conflicting emotions running through her mind, slowly closed the blinds and retreated into the dimly lighted bedroom with the ever-faithful panther close at her side.

Two hours later, at 0800 hours Pacific standard time, in an open-sided barn with leaky gutters that served as a training facility for the Chosen Brigade of the Seventh Seal, First Sergeant Aran Wintersole stepped onto an array of surplus wrestling mats and introduced martial-arts instructor Henry Randolph Lee to his first four students.

At that precise moment, three time zones and twenty-six hundred miles away, on an equally cold and drizzly Monday morning in Washington, DC, Regis J. Smallsreed impatiently buzzed his chief of staff and demanded to know why the hell Simon Whatley wasn't in his office, where he was supposed to be.

Approximately two dozen increasingly frantic phone calls later, the staff chief informed Smallsreed via the intercom (with some degree of apprehension, because every member of Smallsreed's staff knew to stay the hell out of the congressman's luxuriously appointed private office between the hours of ten and noon unless the president and Congress had declared war on some country actually capable of putting up a decent fight), and cautiously advised his mercurial boss that Whatley had apparently vanished.

Yes sir, the staff chief confirmed, according to Whatley's people, Whatley got on the plane in Medford last night; but no sir, according to the hotel manager, he had not checked into his reserved room yet. Perhaps, sir, given the tight scheduling of the flights, Whatley got held over in either Portland or San Francisco; but no sir, he hadn't called or left a message to that effect, as far as anyone knew.

Already in a foul humor because a lucrative piece of legislation seemed almost certain to lose by a single goddamned vote he couldn't scare up anywhere in this new, godforsaken Congress, Smallsreed was in no mood to hear such a report from anyone, let alone his obsequious chief of staff, whom he often compared, unfavorably, to a drooling bird dog who couldn't find his way back to the blind if harbor buoys marked the path.

Accordingly, the now thoroughly irritated congressman repeated his order.

"Find Whatley—wherever he is, and whatever he's doing—and get him here, *now.*"

At precisely 12:01 that Monday afternoon, Smallsreed's understandably nervous chief of staff asked the man catering the luncheon to hand Smallsreed a sealed note which basically said, in standard bureaucratic weasel words: We have no idea where Whatley is, but we're working on it.

At 12:55, Smallsreed's extremely apprehensive chief of staff bribed the same man (who came to pick up the remains of the luncheon) to deliver a second sealed note which basically said, in that same tail-covering verbiage: Nobody has any idea where Whatley is, but everyone in the entire office is working on it.

Regis J. Smallsreed waited impatiently until the white-uniformed attendant cleaned up the catered lunch and departed, closing the door to the private office behind him.

"The son of a bitch crapped out on us," he announced to his two companions.

"What is that supposed to mean?" Aldridge Hammond, the powerful chairman of the ICER committee, and the only man in the world that Congressman Regis J. Smallsreed truly feared, demanded from his shadowy corner of the room.

Apart from the psychological impact of having a deep and cultured but ever-so-threatening voice coming out of the darkness, there was a more practical reason for the ICER chairman's partiality for darkened corners. He was one of those genetic human rarities: a black albino whose melanin appeared in small and irregular light-to-dark brown patches over his entire skin surface . . . which made him extremely susceptible to the damaging effects of any source of UV light. That, in addition to his incredibly pale brown eyes and yellowish brown hair, and the gracefully fluid movements that belied his sixty-four years, gave Aldridge Hammond the chilling appearance and demeanor of a very dangerous feline creature. It was an image that more closely approached the truth than a far-less-powerful man like Congressman Regis J. Smallsreed cared to think about.

Smallsreed's power lay in his ability to compromise and reach consensus with the 434 other Democratic and Republican members of the House of Representatives, whereas Aldridge Hammond was singularly capable of destroying the efforts of a small country to form a democracy with an almost effortless signature at the bottom of a page. The slightest nod of Hammond's head could—by means that he need never know about—easily result in the death of a man for the simple sin of getting in the ICER chairman's way.

In effect, Aldridge Hammond wielded an incredible amount of power in a manner that was almost gentle in its subtlety. Working with him in a cooperative manner required careful and constant attention to the most imperceptible of cues.

But at the moment, Congressman Regis J. Smallsreed was being anything but careful.

"For his sake, I hope it means he's shacked up with some four-star Hollywood harlot, or shit-faced drunk, or asleep in some godforsaken airport lounge." Smallsreed's porcine eyes gleamed dangerously. "Because if it means anything else, at all, he's a walking dead man."

"You think he went to the FBI?" Sam Tisbury's words conveyed all of the controlled rage of a man who had lost a father, a son, and a daughter to—in his opinion—the malicious and inexcusable actions of federal law-enforcement agents. He had absolutely no intention of losing anything to such people again.

Smallsreed shook his head.

"I don't think so. Whatley may not be the smartest fellow on the block, but he's pretty damned loyal, 'cause he's been doing my dirty work for so long, nobody else can stand having him around." The old man chuckled. "And he sure as hell knows what would happen to him if he ever *did* go sideways on us." The congressman snapped a number two pencil between his fingers for emphasis.

"A frightened man who feels threatened and trapped can make some incredibly stupid decisions," Aldridge Hammond reminded the politician.

"Lord knows that's the God's truth, too," Smallsreed agreed. "But I've got a lot of IOUs out there. If Whatley went to the FBI, I'm sure I would have heard about it by now."

"And if you're wrong?"

"Haven't been wrong yet all these years, have I?" The Oregon congressman gave his guest a hard-edged smile.

"So where does that leave us?" Sam Tisbury interjected impatiently.

"Same place as before." Smallsreed shrugged. "Getting ready to make a little statement, exact a little vengeance, blow any evidence all to hell, and then maybe, if we're real lucky, take the credit for saving the day. Only difference," the crafty veteran politician added, "is that maybe we ought to change our plans a little bit."

"How?" Hammond inquired in his deep, cavernous voice.

"Instead of killing them outright, I think we ought to capture all of those wildlife agents alive."

"What?" Sam Tisbury's head came up sharply.

"Hear me out now, Sam." Smallsreed raised a placating hand. "Once we do that, we have the Chosen Brigade—dear misguided souls that they are—issue a news release saying they've taken several federal wildlife agents captive, and intend to put them on trial to prove to the world that all those black helicopter conspiracy theories are, by God, true as can be, and that they'll kill them—one at a time, right in front of the TV cameras—if the FBI or anyone else tries to interfere."

"But you really don't want that to happen, do you?" the powerful shadow-man suggested. "The trial, that is."

"Hell no. 'Course not!" Smallsreed exclaimed. "So we have Rustman's team rig the entire trial site with every pound of explosives they can lay their hands on. Now I'll grant you, when news media show up, our militant friends might seriously hurt one or two of those agents to keep the FBI backed off. But at the proper time, just before—or"—Smallsreed smiled thoughtfully—"maybe just after the Chosen Brigade lets a select number of the media in to monitor the trial, we make it look like the FBI jumped the gun. Then, before you can say squat, that trial site goes up in a hundred million pieces, all the agents—FBI, Fish and Wildlife, this Lightstone fellow in particular—and all the media types die in the explosion. Rustman's team fades away in the confusion, and guess who gets blamed?"

The veteran congressman chuckled over what he considered his brilliant plan.

"I want him to see it," Sam Tisbury insisted flatly.

"Say what?" Smallsreed blinked his beady eyes.

"I want agent Lightstone to see it happen," the wealthy industrialist clarified. "I want him to know, beyond any shadow of a doubt, that he's responsible for all those deaths."

"Oh hell, that's easy." Smallsreed dismissed the industrialist's primary concern with a wave. "All Rustman's people need to do is keep him separate from the main explosion. Then, at the proper moment, they can point out the realities of life to the young fellow, let him know that his pals probably wouldn't thank him for his dedication . . . and then maybe blow him up all by his lonesome, a little diversion to make sure our people get out of there okay." Smallsreed rubbed his meaty paws together as he fleshed out his plan. "Come to think of it, we ought to add a nice little wildfire, too, just to make sure we don't leave any of that trace evidence behind."

"Considering what he did to my daughter, that sounds like a very appropriate finale." Sam Tisbury nodded his head in apparent satisfaction. "One final thing though. I still want it videotaped."

"You want what videotaped?" So many different aspects of his glorious plan filled Smallsreed's mind, he couldn't imagine what Tisbury meant. "The fire?"

Sam Tisbury shook his head irritably.

"No, I want to see Lightstone's expression on tape when he finally comprehends the magnitude of his loss. Same conditions. I guarantee I'll destroy it once I see it."

"Far as I know, that's already part of the game plan. But I'll verify it when I talk with Rustman," the politician assured his old friend genially.

"Then I'm satisfied. Make it happen, and you'll never need to worry about campaign funds again," the wealthy industrialist promised.

Smallsreed turned toward the figure sitting in the shadows, the fearsome chairman of the ICER committee, who simply nodded his head.

"All right then." Regis J. Smallsreed opened his hands in a benevolent gesture. "You've got yourselves a deal."

"But how will you get word to Rustman's team about the changes if you can't find Whatley?" the shadow-man's voice echoed hollowly in the large room.

"Don't worry about that." The veteran congressman smiled broadly. "An old poker player like me's always got an extra ace or two up his sleeve. You just never know when you might need to fix a temporary run of bad luck."

Chapter Forty-six

A beep from the pager on Lt. Colonel John Rustman's belt interrupted him as he methodically cleaned one of his favorite over-and-under shotguns, using a fine-wired brass brush meticulously to loosen the seared gunpowder residues that had collected under the twin extractors.

Frowning, he set the small implement aside, extracted the pager from his belt with his free hand, briefly examined the digital message, and blinked in surprise.

Approximately forty-five minutes later, at precisely twelve noon Pacific standard time, the retired military officer stepped into a phone booth at a gas station located just across the Jasper–Jackson County border, punched in a long-distance number, waited, fed the requested number of quarters into the slot from the open roll in his jacket pocket, and waited again.

"Hello?"

"I got your message," Rustman replied in a neutral voice. "What's up?"

"We have a change in plans," Regis J. Smallsreed announced casually.

Smallsreed surveyed the area surrounding the public phone booth located in the basement of the Longworth House Office Building one more time, making sure no one paid him any special attention. Then he outlined the new scheme that he, Sam Tisbury, and the chairman of ICER—the notoriously misnamed International Commission for Environmental Restoration—had agreed upon earlier.

After going through the new plan in some detail, Smallsreed paused for a moment, then asked, "What do you think?"

"No problem at our end," Rustman replied cautiously. "But what happened to our mutual friend?"

Translation: "Why isn't Simon Whatley making this contact, in person, the way we agreed, instead of you—which is a risky idea under the best of circumstances?"

"We don't know where he is."

"What?"

As a highly competent and experienced combat officer long

accustomed to recognizing—and reacting to—potentially hazardous situations at a moment's notice, Lt. Colonel John Rustman immediately realized that Simon Whatley's disappearance posed a significant threat to his operation . . . and to his men.

"I have no reason to think it's serious . . . yet," Smallsreed cautioned the other man. "There were scheduling problems with his flight to DC this morning, and he might have missed one of the connections."

"But he hasn't called in."

It wasn't so much a question as an accusation.

"No, he hasn't," Smallsreed admitted.

Rustman slowly inhaled, then released a deep breath.

"We need to find him, immediately," he insisted after a moment's reflection on the impact Whatley's defection could have on the remaining years of his life. It had already occurred to him that Smallsreed probably didn't know about the summary execution of Lou Eliot; otherwise, he wouldn't be nearly so calm about his underling's disappearance.

"Yes, we do need to find him . . . and we will," the powerful congressman hastened to reassure Rustman while he continually scanned the public access area around the isolated phone booth. "But in the meantime, we need to put the new plan into motion right away."

Rustman hesitated.

"Are you sure that's wise right now?" he finally asked.

"Yes, I am . . . financially and otherwise."

Smallsreed's insistence certainly arose from his awareness of Sam Tisbury's promise of political funding, not to mention the deadly consequences that would befall him if he failed to meet his promises to Aldridge Hammond, the shadow-dwelling chairman of the ICER committee.

However, Lt. Colonel John Rustman considered quite different consequences—such as the financial impact of the loss of Smallsreed's operational payout on his future retirement plans. While significant, however, it paled beside the thought of spending the rest of his life on the run from federal or state prosecution for the murder of Lou Eliot.

Even though they approached it from two quite different standpoints, both men realized that, in the context of the financial issues and otherwise, Simon Whatley had become a very expendable resource.

Resolving the expendable part was easy.

But they had to find him first.

"How do you intend to handle it?" Rustman finally asked.

"What?"

"The search."

Meaning don't sic a private investigative agency, much less a federal government law-enforcement agency, on Whatley, because even if he didn't talk, someone was bound to make the connection.

"We'll handle it in-house," Smallsreed replied evenly.

"What does that mean?"

The congressman sighed heavily.

"It means"—an audible edge crept into his gravelly voice—"that if the members of my Washington Office staff would like to remain attached to the public tit, then they'd better find the son of a bitch before I do."

It took Rustman another three hours to arrange a face-to-face meeting with Wintersole.

They sat sheltered in a small grove of evergreen trees and undergrowth on a low hill overlooking the Chosen Brigade's hidden training compound. The Army Ranger first sergeant listened carefully as Rustman detailed the change in plans.

"We can handle our end just fine," he assured Rustman when the latter concluded his recitation. "Fact is, the new plan makes everything a lot easier all the way around. Only problem is, we're still waiting for those agent profiles."

That final remark brought Rustman's head up in surprise.

"Did you remind Whatley?"

"I sent him two separate messages through the drop box," Wintersole reported. "One last Thursday, then a reminder with the surveillance photos over the weekend. Haven't gotten a thing back."

Rustman cursed, and then considered this latest revelation carefully.

"Do you really need the profiles?" he finally asked.

Wintersole shrugged. "We do if we want to be sure about Lightstone. Based on that 'male white, medium height, medium weight' description, we can narrow it down to one out of two, but we've got a lot of bonus money riding on that videotape," the hunter-killer team leader reminded him. "It'd be nice to have a photo confirmation before we set something into motion we can't stop or correct."

"I'll see what I can do," Rustman promised.

Wintersole nodded agreeably, then stared at the narrow valley for a long moment before turning back to his trusted commander.

"What are we going to do about Whatley?"

Wintersole asked the question knowing he and Rustman would be the first ones hunted down if Whatley had lost his nerve and run to the FBI. And neither man maintained any illusions of their limited ability simply to disappear into the countryside. If Whatley talked, both of them—along with the rest of their rogue team—would immediately become the targets of nearly a million federal, state, and local law-enforcement officers, not to mention the more focused and very personal targets of the US Army Ranger MP teams, who would not take kindly to the assault on their own hard-earned reputations.

If Whatley had talked, or intended to, they needed to get out of the country . . . fast.

But to do that, they needed the money—which meant they needed Whatley and his access to the payoff and bonus accounts.

"Smallsreed says not to worry about it," Rustman replied. "He intends to find the son of a bitch himself."

"You think he can?"

"I think a man like Regis J. Smallsreed can do damned near anything he wants to do, especially to save his own ass."

"But does he know his ass is on the line?" Wintersole asked pointedly.

"Oh, I think the congressman understands that very clearly." Rustman nodded his head solemnly, a deadly look narrowing his eyes. "Very clearly, indeed."

Wintersole waited until Rustman disappeared. Then he took the long, narrow, and winding path down to the training compound where, one by one, he contacted the members of his team and relayed the change in plans and related instructions.

Set the bait tonight, at 2100 hours.

Spring the trap tonight, at 2300 hours.

Note the important change in plans: unless absolutely unavoidable, do not kill the agents.

Withdraw all escape-route sets of explosives except one for use in the planned obliteration of the Chosen Brigade's compound.

And under no circumstances harm the female agent or either of the two medium height, medium weight, male Caucasian agents tentatively identified as Henry Lightstone. They needed them to earn the bonus.

One by one, the members of the hunter-killer recon team at the training compound withdrew to their new assignments, until finally only Wintersole and the man he knew as Henry Randolph Lee remained with his nearly exhausted—but still visibly enthusiastic—students.

Wintersole waited until the almost-too-painful-to-watch session finally ended with some futile attempts by the trainees to apply some of their new skills against each other. Then he walked into the open-sided barn as the members of the Chosen Brigade of the Seventh Seal began staggering down the hill toward their waiting trucks.

"Well, how did it go?" Wintersole asked as he helped his new martial-arts instructor roll the mats into the center of the open barn.

"Pretty much the way you thought it would," Lightstone admitted with a wry smile. "The only ones with decent potential are the two kids. They need more discipline, but that will come with the training. The rest of them will be lucky if they make it all the way through the course without making a couple trips to the emergency room."

"They are a pretty sad lot," the hunter-killer recon team leader conceded thoughtfully.

"You know, I really don't get it," Lightstone ventured as he covered the mats with a waterproof tarp.

"What?"

"You said these guys plan to confront the feds someday. That's a joke, right?"

"You don't think they can pull it off?" A slight smile appeared on Wintersole lips.

"Pull it off? Are you kidding?" Lightstone scoffed. "They might be able to hold their own against a bunch of paper-pushing federal bureaucrats . . . if you could limit the fight to paper targets and theoretical bullshit. But if you're talking about them facing down a bunch of federal agents — or even regular police officers, for that matter — it wouldn't even be funny. More like suicide, if you ask me."

"Then maybe what we really need to do is open their eyes a bit, in terms of the real world," the hunter-killer recon team leader suggested.

Henry Lightstone eyed his new employer.

"I take it you have something in mind?"

"As it turns out, I've got an interesting field exercise planned for this evening," Wintersole explained. "Something my associates and I dreamed up the other night to give these people a little better grasp of reality. It's a little complicated, and we could use some help with the logistics if you're free tonight."

"Well . . ."

"And if you do have other plans for this evening," — the hunter-killer team leader smiled knowingly — "you might be interested to know that our employer authorized a thousand-dollar bonus for each participating instructor."

"A thousand dollars?" Lightstone blinked. "What would you expect me to do? Shoot a couple of those jokers?"

Wintersole chuckled. "Actually, something a little less violent, but equally instructive."

"No actual wounds. Just scare the hell out of them?"

"Something like that."

"But a thousand dollars for one night's work?" Lightstone pressed, remembering to stay in character. A thousand dollars was a hell of a lot of money for a man supposedly in between jobs who had just spent a goodly amount of his reserve funds on a used motorcycle.

"Actually, probably only five or six hours, max. I plan to start at 2100, sharp, and finish around 0200 in the morning. Payment in cash, on the spot, assuming everything goes okay," Wintersole added helpfully.

Lightstone smiled.

"Where do I go, and what time should I be there?"

"Be at the entrance to their main compound at, oh, say 2000 hours — 8:00 P.M. I think that would work out just about right. Plan on doing a lot of moving around in the dark, minimal noise, maximum concealment, then all of a sudden popping up out of nowhere to mess with their minds, that sort of thing. We'd be looking for you to take a couple of them out of the picture silently with some quick take-downs and choke-outs if you can get into the right position. Basic psy-ops stuff. Make them sweat a little when their teammates start disappearing, and they don't know why. You ever use any night-vision gear?"

Lightstone shook his head. "Nope. Matter of fact, I don't think I've ever even seen any night-vision gear."

"No sweat. The new-generation stuff is real easy to use. We'll run you through the drill, get you qualified in fifteen minutes. Just make sure you bring a good pair of boots — high-tops if you've got 'em, lot of rocks and holes in the area where we set this up — wool socks, gloves, long johns, and a warm jacket. We'll supply everything else."

"Why do I get the strange feeling I'm being recruited?"

Wintersole smiled. "By the Brigade, or by us?"

"All things considered, I'll be a hell of a lot safer working with you. Especially if these Chosen Brigade characters are really serious about taking on the feds."

"Oh, I think they're serious. No question about that." A shadow flitted across Wintersole's cold gray eyes. "The question is, can they pull it off — or even make a reasonable showing — if they try. That's what we're going to find out tonight."

"You don't sound too optimistic."

Wintersole shrugged. "Just like the old army game, Henry. You do the best you can with whatever resources you're given. Sometimes the best you can do is play for pride."

"Well, whatever the game is, I'm certainly looking forward to it. Especially the money part." Lightstone smiled cheerfully. "Twenty hundred hours, front entrance, main compound." He waved his hand as he began walking toward the distant road.

"Glad you feel that way, Henry," First Sergeant Aran Wintersole whispered to himself as he watched his lanky new recruit disappear into the surrounding woods. "I'm looking forward to it, too."

Chapter Forty-seven

It had grown completely dark that Monday evening by the time Henry Lightstone worked his way through the tall stand of old-growth trees, across a shallow stream, and up a long incline to the edge of an open field, pausing every hundred yards or so to check his compass bearing.

Then, after pausing one last time at the edge of the open field to catch his breath, he knelt and leaned against the rough bark of a concealing thirty-foot evergreen, cupped his hand over his wrist, and checked the luminous hands on his watch.

Seven oh five. Shit.

It had taken longer than he expected—and much longer than he had hoped—because he'd doubled back on his tracks on two separate occasions . . . once as a routine precaution, and then a second time when a branch snapped somewhere behind him.

He'd spotted the deer on his second loop back, which left him with a vague sense of uneasiness when the animal finally noticed him and bounded off into the surrounding brush. While an incautious deer might snap a twig, the agile young men employed by the pale gray–eyed man they referred to as sergeant could easily move through a dense old-growth forest without their boots coming anywhere near a dry branch.

Trouble is, Lightstone thought, *they could be all around me right now, and I probably wouldn't even know it.*

He felt tempted to turn around, right there, and hike back to his motorcycle. Very tempted, in fact, because he also had a very uneasy sense that these six extremely fit and confident young men, along with their ominously cold-eyed leader, wouldn't hesitate to take out anything or anyone which happened to get in their way.

Including a couple of federal agent Special Ops teams, he thought uneasily.

Earlier in the afternoon, during a break from the hands-on instruction, Lightstone had located the shooting ranges and watched two of Wintersole's men work the pop-up targets with a pair of M-16 assault rifles. From Lightstone's limited view, it appeared they did so with tightly choreographed precision and deadly accuracy that spoke of many long hours in the military version of the FBI's Hogan's Alley. One moved, the other covered, one reloaded, the other covered, back and forth . . . a random, forward, leapfrogging that sent short deadly bursts from at least one — and often both — of the assault rifles into every pop-up target that sprang into view.

Christ, we don't stand a chance if they're all like that . . . and there's absolutely no reason at all to think that they aren't, Lightstone reminded himself.

And that memory, plus the nagging awareness that something — or someone — had placed some event, some action into motion drove Henry Lightstone now. He had to get word of his suspicions to his team as soon as possible.

Accordingly — and after one last futile pause to listen for any sound of movement amid the chirping of what sounded like hundreds of cheerful crickets — he glided forward in the darkness, crouched against the wall of the building, and rapped his knuckles in three quick double-strikes against a cold metal door.

The chorus of crickets came to an immediate halt.

An instant later, the tiny sliver of light seeping from under the now-much-more-securely sealed side door went out.

Moments later, the door swung open cautiously.

"It's me," he whispered, then slipped quickly inside and waited against the inside wall until he heard the door close. Anticipating the blinding effects, he shielded his eyes as the lights came on.

It took Lightstone's eyes a few moments to adjust. Then he simply stood and blinked in amazement.

"What in the hell have you guys been doing?" he asked as he surveyed the mass of wadded clumps of duct tape that almost completely covered the warehouse floor.

"Don't ask," Larry Paxton warned as he reholstered his pistol.

"Yeah, don't," Dwight Stoner agreed as he leaned the pump shotgun against the side of the team's rental car. "He's in a real shitty mood tonight."

"Okay, then, what the hell did you guys do to those terrariums?" Lightstone's eyes swept across the rows of glass containers now festooned with hundreds of irregular wads, shreds, and strips of duct tape. "And," he added, "what's the deal with all the ice?"

From Henry Lightstone's viewpoint, all of the plastic swimming pools now filled with mostly melted blocks of ice, and the dozens of empty plastic bags — not to mention large puddles of water — scattered around the warehouse floor strongly suggested the previous presence of dozens of additional ice blocks.

"That's part of what you're not supposed to ask," Stoner cautioned his fellow agent.

"Ah."

Lightstone then heard the resident chorus of chirping crickets start up again, then gradually increase in volume to highly irritating levels.

"The next time we run an operation like this, if we ever run another operation like this, which we won't," Paxton announced ominously, "I get the sexy witch, the panther, and the whole gang of militant idiots all to myself. The rest of you get all the snakes and spiders and crocodiles . . . and the goddamned crickets. Ain't talking about it anymore. That's just the way it's gonna be."

"He's a little upset 'cause we had to take all the terrarium lids off to put the lightbulbs back in after we'd taped them all shut," Thomas Woeshack explained cheerfully. "We tried to freeze them again real quick so nothing would get out, but I guess the cold didn't bother the crickets all that much, 'cause most of them got out anyway. Then a couple of snakes almost got out, and one of them almost bit Larry, 'cause he was trying to hurry . . . and then one of the spiders ran up his arm real fast, and three of the crocs got loose when he fell backwards into their pool . . . and then we ran out of duct tape, and there isn't any more in the whole town, so . . ."

A warning wave from Stoner caused the eager special agent/pilot to terminate his briefing.

Lightstone examined Larry Paxton's expression carefully, while attempting to ignore the ever-increasing volume of cricket chirps.

"Are you okay, Larry?" he asked carefully. "No problems with stress, lack of sleep, bunch of crickets running loose, anything like that?"

"Oh hell yes. Just fine and dandy. Don't hardly hear the damned things anymore."

Lightstone decided to dismiss the slightly glassy look in his supervisor's eyes . . . at least for now.

"Yeah, Larry's fine, Henry. No different than he always is. So what've you got for us?" Stoner prompted the team's wild-card agent.

Another triple-series knock on the door interrupted Henry Lightstone just as he was in the process of describing his new job. He moved forward quickly and turned off the light in the suddenly silent warehouse, then cautiously opened the door as the other three agents stood with firearms ready.

Moments later, a flabbergasted Bobby LaGrange and Mike Takahara stood in the warehouse surveying the disaster around them.

"What the hell . . ." Bobby LaGrange started to ask when Lightstone interrupted.

"Don't even ask," he warned. "First things first. How's Susan?"

"She's fine." The ex–homicide investigator smiled as the happy cricket chorus started up again. "Got her tucked away with a couple retired cops we know out by the Rogue River. She's got her .357, her fishing rod, and a couple of first-class bodyguards. Said to come get her when we were finished playing, but not to hurry." LaGrange allowed his eyes slowly to sweep the warehouse. "So all the crickets got loose, huh?"

"It's not a subject we talk about in Larry's presence," Lightstone suggested gently. "So what are you doing here?"

The ex–homicide investigator shrugged. "Susan doesn't need me around to bait her hook, and I figured you boys might need some help sorting out the good guys from the bad guys." A glint of something decidedly cold and malicious flickered across Bobby LaGrange's still-smiling eyes. "I was heading this way when I ran across Stoner and offered to take over his surveillance of Charlie Team. In retrospect, I guess I should've come here and helped Larry instead." He scanned the warehouse once more, but no trace of amusement remained in his smile.

Henry Lightstone knew that look all too well. Bobby LaGrange would not tolerate even the idea of someone making a threatening move toward his treasured wife.

"So what's Charlie Team doing now?" Lightstone asked as they all sat down in the folding chairs that Dwight Stoner set up in a tight circle.

"From what little I saw, not much," LaGrange reported. "At a little after six, everybody went into what Dwight told me was the team leader's room at the motel. I waited around for something to happen, but nothing did. So at seven, I linked up with Mike and we headed over here. If anybody else was surveilling them, I sure didn't see it."

"Me neither," Mike Takahara added, "but I did pick up something with one of my scanners that might explain . . . ."

"Wait a minute, Mike," Larry Paxton interrupted, the familiar no-nonsense supervisory tone back in his voice. "Before we get into that, I want you all to hear about Henry's new job."

Relieved to see Paxton assuming control again, Lightstone told them about his activities in and around the Dogsfire Inn and the Chosen Brigade compound during the past three days.

"Where exactly is this training compound?" LaGrange asked when Lightstone finished.

"Direct line, a little less than a mile northwest of here." Lightstone described the route he'd taken to get to the warehouse. "There's a rough trail of sorts, but it branches off in several places along the way. Pretty easy to get lost if you don't have a compass and a map. It's about fifteen minutes away if you take the long way around by road."

"You going to be able to find your way back to your bike?" Mike Takahara asked dubiously.

"Yeah, sure, it'll just take a while." Lightstone glanced down at his watch. "In fact, I've got to get going pretty soon. I'm supposed to be back at the compound by eight to help with some kind of night training exercise."

"Don't worry about it," LaGrange assured his former partner. "I'll drop you off at the gate."

Lightstone started to argue that he shouldn't reestablish the link to the LaGrange ranch, but Bobby LaGrange remained adamant.

"Don't worry about it," he repeated. "They've probably already seen us together anyway. This way, maybe one of them'll decide to follow me around for a while." The ex–homicide investigator's expression made it readily apparent that the idea appealed to him very much.

"I don't think so," Lightstone countered. "At least not tonight anyway."

"Oh, yeah? Why not?"

Lightstone described what little he knew about the night exercise, and then relayed his growing concern that something very big—and presumably very dangerous—involving the Chosen Brigade and Charlie Team had been set into motion.

"A thousand-dollar bonus for one night of playing tag in the woods with a bunch of self-righteous, antigovernment loonies? I don't think so," Larry Paxton muttered. "You're right, Henry, these assholes are up to something, no doubt about it. The question is, what?"

"Actually, I think I might know the answer to that." Mike Takahara's remark caused all eyes to turn instantly in his direction.

I think they plan to draw Charlie Team in, using Boggs as bait."

"What?" all five voices echoed in unison.

"What makes you think that?" Larry Paxton demanded.

"I tapped into one of Charlie Team's cell phone calls earlier this evening."

"Hey, wait a minute," Bobby LaGrange said, "I thought you said you guys were all using encrypted cell phones now."

"Yeah, we are." Mike Takahara shrugged.

"So then how . . ."

"We, uh, managed to acquire Charlie Team's encryption code when we were all at Glynco a couple weeks ago," the tech agent explained.

"That was how we knew all about their plan to hide Donato and Green up in the loft, and have Marashenko hide her gun under a rock by the dirt path," Thomas Woeshack added cheerfully.

"But which, naturally, never showed up in our exercise reports," Dwight Stoner further elaborated for Bobby LaGrange's benefit.

"A minor discrepancy. Nothing worth bothering Halahan or Moore about," Larry Paxton said dismissively as he zeroed in on Mike Takahara's comment. "So what's the deal with Boggs?" he asked the tech agent.

"We know Charlie Team's been trying to work out an illegally guided hunt at the Windgate National Wildlife Refuge with one of the Chosen Brigade members, right?"

All five heads nodded.

"Well, according to the conversation I picked up between Donato and Riley, one of their local contacts apparently called Donato at his motel room, told him the hunt was on for tonight, and not to worry about any problems with the local game warden because they knew exactly where Special Agent Boggs would be all evening."

"And just where is that?" A perceptible edge replaced the exhaustion in Larry Paxton's voice.

Mike Takahara shrugged. "I couldn't tell for sure from the conversation, but I got the impression that Charlie Team thinks the Chosen Brigade managed to capture Boggs—apparently sometime after he walked out of Providence Hospital—and that they're hiding him until they can put him on trial."

"For what?"

"Who knows." The tech agent shrugged. "Being a law-enforcement agent. Representing the federal government. Intruding on the God-given rights of local deer poachers. Something like that."

"What the hell kind of sense does that make?" Paxton demanded.

"Hey, I only tap the conversations. I don't psychoanalyze them."

"So what's Charlie Team going to do? Notify Halahan and have him send us in as backup?" Dwight Stoner asked hopefully.

"I don't think so." Mike Takahara shook his head. "In fact, not only do they seem to have no idea that we're here, I got the distinct impression they're planning to play hero."

"Oh no . . ." Lightstone whispered.

"You mean they intend to send Donato and LiBrandi in on the illicit hunt, tag everybody, and then try to take everybody down and rescue Boggs . . . all by themselves?" Larry Paxton's face turned a distinctly paler shade of brown.

"That's the way it sounded to me." The tech agent nodded solemnly.

"Oh, shit." The Bravo Team leader said what every one of them was thinking.

"We need to call them. Right now," Henry Lightstone declared emphatically. "I don't give a damn what Halahan said. They may think they're taking on a bunch of incompetent losers, but from what I've seen and heard, they're walking right into a nest of ex–Army Rangers."

"Assuming these ex-Rangers are part of the plan," Larry Paxton reminded his wild-card agent.

"Hey, if they're not, fine. We end up looking like a bunch of idiots. Who cares?" Lightstone shrugged indifferently. "But if I'm right, and this night-exercise deal is nothing more than a setup to trap Charlie Team, then everything's going to go to shit real fast. And if it does," the covert agent went on, "we're going to lose a bunch of agents."

"And if it is a setup, Henry, where does that leave you?" Bobby LaGrange reminded his former partner.

"I'll worry about that later." Henry Lightstone gave Paxton a pleading look. "We've got to call them, Larry. Right now."

Larry Paxton hesitated for a brief moment, then nodded at Mike Takahara, who immediately reached for his cell phone and punched in a memorized number.

For a good thirty seconds everyone stared at the tech agent—who finally folded up the phone and shook his head.

"No answer. They probably left the cell phones at the hotel."

"Which means they're already gone." Henry Lightstone looked stricken.

"Doing it just like we taught them," Dwight Stoner growled. "Get out to the meet site early, monitor the area, see what happens."

"Shit!" Larry Paxton exploded angrily.

"Did Riley or Donato give any indication of what they planned to do?" Lightstone asked hopefully.

Mike Takahara shook his head silently.

"Nothing about the Chosen Brigade compound at all?"

The tech agent shook his head again and held his hands out in a helpless gesture.

"They could meet their contacts for an illegal hunt anywhere on the outskirts of the refuge, Henry," Bobby LaGrange pointed out. "And that includes literally hundreds of miles. Plus, don't forget, this whole night-exercise business could be a ruse, just to distract *you*, too."

"I think we need to call Halahan, brief him on the situation, tell him to get us some help out here," Dwight Stoner suggested. "FBI, DEA, somebody with some serious firepower."

"Yeah, but what about right now?" Lightstone looked down at his watch. "It's almost quarter to eight now, and I'm due back at the compound in fifteen minutes. By the time he manages to get anybody out here, whatever's going to happen will be all over."

For a while, only the sounds of the crickets filled the warehouse.

Everyone in the warehouse was silent for a long moment.

"One thing's for certain"—Larry Paxton finally spoke slowly and deliberately—"we can't let them walk into a trap completely blind. Regardless of anything else, we have to at least try to back them up."

Everyone nodded in agreement.

"Trouble is, though, Henry's right." Bobby LaGrange noted as he slowly pulled an old .45 semiautomatic pistol out of his waistband, dropped the magazine into his hand, and stared forlornly at the exposed round-nosed bullet. "If we try to face down a team of hotshot Army Rangers armed with M-16's on our own, we could get ourselves seriously killed."

Henry Lightstone stared gloomily down at the warehouse floor, only vaguely aware of the scattered clumps of tangled duct tape and discarded plastic bags.

Suddenly, a smile appeared on his face.

"But then again," he whispered softly, "who says we have to fight fair."

Chapter Forty-eight

Remembering his new employer's comment that it would take no more than fifteen minutes to learn how to use the night-vision gear, Henry Lightstone made a show of paying careful attention while his wrist-cast-hampered fellow instructor demonstrated how to secure the binocular night-sight goggles over his head, and adjust the spacing, aperture, and focus of the eyepieces to give him nearly perfect stereoscopic vision.

Unbelievable, he thought to himself, amazed at the degree of improvement in the latest generation of night-vision equipment. Unlike with the second-and third-generation light-magnifying tubes Lightstone was familiar with, the flow of light green images in these new goggles appeared multicontrasted and almost razor-sharp.

Pretending to master the technology, Lightstone rotated his body in a 180-degree arc. In doing so, he observed two other members of Sergeant Aran Wintersole's training team standing in the trees about twenty yards away from the main group.

A chill went up his spine when he realized that both of these men carried night-vision-scoped bolt-action rifles—very much in contrast to the five trainers grouped around him who all wore standard military-issue Beretta 9mm semiautomatic pistols. In addition, all of the men wore military camouflaged flak jackets with a bullet-deflecting breastplate insert. A half dozen canister grenades dangled from rings on each side of the breastplate on Wintersole's and two of the other soldiers' jackets, and all three carried what looked like a roll of duct tape attached to a loop at waist level opposite their pistol holsters. The other two instructors carried a roll of tape, but no grenades.

Two plus five equals seven, Lightstone told himself. The same number of soldiers he'd seen conducting the surveillance of Charlie Team, all present and accounted for. In spite of the chilling sight of the two night-vision-equipped snipers partially concealed in the nearby woods, Light-stone felt relieved. That meant that if Charlie Team wasn't the focused target of this supposed night training exercise, they wouldn't be wandering around the perimeter of the nearby Windgate National Wildlife Refuge in the dark and under active surveillance by a bunch of lethally trained combat troops . . . unless, of course, Lightstone reminded himself, the re-tired Army Ranger first sergeant had held some of his resources in reserve.

But in any case, Charlie Team wouldn't be out there alone. Whether they liked it or not, Lightstone smiled, the more experienced, manipu-lative, and treacherous members of Bravo Team would cover them on the perimeter, once again ready to do whatever it took to win.

Not that we'll be much help if things don't go our way, the covert agent's smile faded as he returned his attention to his injured companion.

"Feel comfortable?" the young soldier inquired.

"Just fine," Lightstone acknowledged.

"How do you like them?"

"Pretty amazing." Lightstone put just the right amount of wonder in his voice. "I feel like I'm walking around in some kind of green daylight."

"That's exactly the idea." The young soldier laughed. "The earphones are separate from the goggles, so if you ever have to take the goggles off, you'll stay linked to the rest of us. Your collar mike's an autosensor, so just talk and listen. Try not to interrupt someone else, unless it's an emer-gency. Everything clear?"

Henry nodded.

"Good." The young soldier removed something from the box behind him. "Here, let me help you put this on."

"What is it?"

"Flak jacket. Basically an armored vest."

"What the hell do I need an armored vest for?" Lightstone asked as the young soldier secured the wide Velcro straps tightly around his shoul-ders, chest, and waist.

"Didn't the sergeant tell you?"

"Tell me what?" Lightstone wheeled to face the team leader who, to Lightstone's amazement, actually appeared less menacing with the bin-ocular night-sights over his cold pale gray eyes.

"Just to make it a little more interesting for our side, our opponents are going to be firing live rounds tonight."

"What?"

"Don't worry about it." First Sergeant Aran Wintersole noted, then casually dismissed Lightstone's reaction. "They have pop-up reflector tar-gets—which they can hardly hit in the daylight when they're twenty feet away—to aim at. And they'll be stumbling in the woods, about 90 percent blind, even before the first flash-bang goes off. Just stay low, maintain your cool, keep your goggles on, and you'll be fine. Probably'll have a better chance of getting taken out by a falling meteor."

"Yeah, right." Henry Lightstone shook his head in amazement. "What the hell's a flash-bang?"

"These little gems here." Wintersole reached forward with both hands and tapped the underside of the two grenades that hung from Lightstone's flak jacket like a pair of small firm breasts. "They're basically stun grenades, but they generate an extremely bright flash in addition to the concussion. You ever throw a hand grenade?"

"I've seen it done in the movies," Lightstone responded dryly.

Wintersole chuckled. "Same process. But if you do your job right—move in close, take them down one at a time, disarm them, and then tape them up tight—you won't need any grenades. But, in case you get caught out in the open, just slip the grenade off your vest, hold the lever with two fingers of your throwing hand like this"—he demonstrated with a grenade from his own vest—"pull the pin with your other hand, and throw."

"Wonderful," Lightstone muttered.

"Just remember," Wintersole warned him, "you've only got about two and a half seconds after the lever kicks out before it goes off, so try to aim for something thirty feet away—or at the very least, get behind a big tree after you throw it. Otherwise, you end up on your ass with your clock rung. And don't look directly at the flash. These fourth-generation tubes aren't supposed to flare out if they get too much light, but there's no sense in taking a chance."

Wintersole looked around at his team.

"One more thing. I was just advised that the Brigade leaders authorized one of their women to take part in the exercise tonight. I don't want her hurt, so I figure we'll leave her to our martial-arts expert."

"Watch out for your balls, man," one of the soldiers chuckled, and immediately froze when Wintersole glared at him sharply.

"Any more questions?" the eerie team leader inquired.

"Yeah, several," Lightstone replied evenly.

"Then come with me," Wintersole ordered as the rest of the team dispersed into the woods. "I'll see if I can properly educate you before your students show up."

Forty-five minutes later, settled into a concealed position on the outer perimeter of the designated contact zone, Henry Lightstone saw the first sign of movement.

Fifteen minutes later, feeling both relieved *and* increasingly uneasy, he had all of them spotted but one.

Riley and Green in place on the far side. Wu on the near side. Which means it's going to be Donato and LiBrandi on the hunt. He moved his head slowly in a 270-degree sweep, searching the entire outer perimeter of the contact zone one more time. No more bodies. And no movement.

So where's the wildcat?

He began another slow sweep knowing full well that Riley wouldn't let his most volatile and unpredictable agent get too far out of his sight, but then two bright red flashes at the edge of his vision suddenly brought his head back to the designated contact point.

He immediately spotted Special Agents Gus Donato and Mark Li-Brandi standing in the clearing, each of them holding a bolt-action hunting rifle and a flashlight.

Moments later, a second pair of red flashes emerged from the light in Donato's hand, and an identical pair of flashes immediately answered from the far edge of the clearing.

As Lightstone watched, two figures wearing military flak jackets—sans grenades—entered the clearing carrying flashlights that now emitted steady, bobbing bright red beams within the light green world of the night-vision goggles. The four men stood together talking for perhaps thirty seconds when the familiar voice of First Sergeant Aran Wintersole whispered in Lightstone's earphones:

"Okay, take them down, now!"

Lightstone had only a brief moment to see the four distant figures suddenly become two paired sets of grappling combatants when three intensely bright green explosions erupted within the perimeter zone, sending three bodies tumbling. He had just started to come up to his knees, and out of his concealed position, when the first gunshot streaked over his head.

Special Agent Natasha Marashenko was still moving forward, holding the old second-generation night-vision spotting scope to her left eye with one hand and firing her Smith & Wesson 10mm semiautomatic pistol with the other when Lightstone came up, knocked the pistol out of her hand, and then drove his shoulder into her stomach in a lunging tackle that sent the two of them tumbling to the rock-and-brush-covered ground.

Only the fact that he'd knocked most of the air out of her lungs with his shoulder tackle saved Henry Lightstone from serious injury in those first few seconds when—unable to give her any kind of reassuring warning because of the microphone attached to his collar—he tried to get into position for the chokehold while Natasha Marashenko kicked, bit, gouged, scratched, and otherwise fought for her life.

Even so, by the time he finally managed to get the inner portion of his right elbow pulled tight under her chin, grabbed his left biceps with his right hand, looped his left arm around the back of her thrashing head, and then tucked his head in tight against the side of her head as her carotid arteries became tightly compressed against the biceps and forearm muscles of his right arm, Lightstone felt convinced the female agent's jackhammering elbow had broken every one of his ribs.

Several very long moments later, Lightstone felt her go limp in his arms . . . just as Wintersole and one of his soldiers came running up.

"Get . . . her . . . off . . . me," Lightstone gasped.

"Hey, man, I warned you," the soldier whispered as he knelt down and pulled the limp body of Marashenko aside.

"She . . . okay?" Lightstone had a hard time getting the words out. Among many other things, his solar plexus seemed unwilling to cooperate.

First Sergeant Aran Wintersole quickly knelt and pressed two fingers against the side of the young woman's throat.

"Good strong pulse. She's fine," he announced, then motioned for the soldier to tape her up quickly.

Then he moved to Lightstone.

"You okay?" the hunter-killer recon team leader asked with what Lightstone considered a very mild degree of interest or curiosity.

"That was one of the Brigade women?" he whispered in what he hoped sounded like a sufficiently raspy and disbelieving voice.

"That's right."

"Then I take back every smart-ass thing I ever said about these people confronting the federal government," Lightstone apologized as Wintersole easily pulled him to his unsteady feet and helped him readjust the night-vision goggles. "Tell those Brigade characters to stay home and send their women out to fight. The damn government won't stand a chance."

At a little after midnight that Tuesday morning, while Wintersole's soldiers secured the stunned, bound, and gagged agents from Charlie Team into their new underground jail quarters, the hunter-killer team's medic tended the wounds of their severely beaten new martial-arts instructor, and the Chosen Brigade stared in awe at their new captives while animatedly chattering about their long-awaited trial, First Sergeant Aran Wintersole hiked up the narrow pathway to the rocky outcrop overlooking the blackened expanse of the Brigade's training grounds, where Lt. Colonel John Rustman stood waiting.

"How did it go?" the retired military officer asked.

"Real smooth. By the way, that little female agent was everything you said—and more." Wintersole chuckled coldly. "Damn near beat our new hand-to-hand instructor half to death before he managed to choke her out. But other than that, everybody looks like they're in pretty good shape."

"No other injuries?"

"Just a few cuts and bruises. Nothing serious."

"Excellent." Rustman nodded approvingly. "Now all we need to do is identify and isolate Lightstone, set up a reasonably secure area for the trial—they're going to use that old barn, right?"

Wintersole nodded.

"Good. Then rig the explosives, and call the media," Rustman finished with a look of satisfaction on his tanned face.

"Well, there is one more problem, sir.

"What's that?"

"Agent Lightstone. We still don't know what he looks like."

"Right." Lt. Colonel John Rustman mused silently for a long moment. "Tell me, Sergeant," he finally spoke, "you still have Special Agent Boggs in custody, do you not?"

"Yes sir, we do."

"And wouldn't you expect agent Boggs to recognize Special Agent Lightstone?"

Wintersole shrugged. "Yes sir, I guess I would."

"Well, then, why don't you ask him?"

Chapter Forty-nine

Consciousness returned to Simon Whatley in the form of pain.

Deep, throbbing, and—evidently thanks to whatever mixture dripped into his IV tube—essentially controlled pain; so controlled he felt tempted simply to lie there on the firm but yielding mattress and allow the soothing drugs to work their wonders on the frazzled synapses of his severely battered nervous system.

But something drifting around in the back of Simon Whatley's sedated mind kept demanding his attention.

Something about a plane ride.

And a meeting.

And some letters that had something to do with his being—what?— early?

No, not early.

Late.

Simon Whatley's eyes flew open . . .

Oh my God. Where am I?

. . . and then immediately slammed shut in response to the agonizing burst of pain the light caused to shoot through the back of his eyeballs and then ricochet repeatedly in the center of his brain.

His deep and heartfelt moan caught the attention of one of the floor nurses.

"Hi there, sport, how are we doing this morning?" she whispered in a professionally gentle and concerned voice as she automatically felt for his pulse.

Morning? Thank God. Maybe I'm not too late.

He tried to whisper a question, but his lips and tongue simply refused to cooperate.

"What's that, hon?" The nurse put her head down next to Simon Whatley's bandaged face.

He tried again, this time forcing the air through his vocal cords with an effort that sent another streak of pain ripping through his muddled brain.

"Time is it?"

The nurse glanced down at her watch.

"Five-thirty, almost exactly on the nose."

Five-thirty. Five-thirty. What time do I have to be there? Eleven in the morning? Whatley sagged down into the mattress in relief. *Thank God. Plenty of time to call Smallsreed, tell him . . . wait a minute. Five-thirty? How can that be? It was seven forty-five when . . .*

"Nurse?" he rasped again.

"Yes, hon?"

"Are you . . . sure . . . it's five-thirty?" It hurt his mouth very badly to articulate the words, but he had to know.

The nurse glanced down at her watch again.

"Five-thirty-two, to be precise, on what is supposed to be a beautiful Tuesday morning. But before you start . . ."

Tuesday?

No, can't be. It's Monday morning. Has to be Monday morning.

Simon Whatley felt his chest constrict in fear and pain.

What happened? Got off the plane in Dulles at seven-forty-five. I remember that. Terrible ride. Goddamned kids. Filthy smelly toilets. Too tired to read the drop-box messages. Got into the cab. Driving to the hotel . . . was going to read the messages . . . reaching into my jacket pocket when the cab swerved . . . everything went crazy . . . upside down . . .

Accident.

Oh God, no.

"Nurse, get me a phone!"

He thought he yelled the words at the top of his lungs, but in fact, what barely sputtered through his painfully swollen lips and missing teeth sounded like little more than incomprehensible muttering.

The nurse laid a soothing hand across Simon Whatley's forehead. "Take it easy, hon. Don't try to talk."

"Need a phone!"

Another burst of sputtering, but this time she heard the word "phone" clearly.

"Listen," the nurse stroked his feverish brow, "you just rest. I really don't think you're up to talking with anybody yet."

"Please!" He implored the caregiver with his reddened eyes, putting every bit of energy he could muster into an effort to speak clearly through his damaged mouth. "I need a phone. Right now! Please!"

Three time zones to the west, another seriously injured man experienced equal difficulties communicating with the people trying to provide him with basic medical care. But in this case, however, the breakdown in communications didn't occur because of a lack of understanding.

Special Agent Wilbur Boggs knew exactly what the young man in the military fatigues wanted to know.

And the young Army Ranger—recon team designation one-six—sitting in the chair in front of him knew exactly what the severely injured federal wildlife agent thought about his persistent questioning. Boggs had been very explicit in his commentary, which was why he was now wearing a wide strip of duct tape across his mouth.

In fact, only the numerous loops of duct tape that held the middle-aged agent's muscular arms and legs securely to the chair kept the absolutely furious Boggs from demonstrating in much more explicit—not to mention extremely violent—detail, exactly how much the young man's questioning displeased him.

But the restraining loops of tape didn't prevent the enraged and nearly exhausted wildlife officer from driving his forehead into his first inquisitor's face, smashing the young Army Ranger's nose in a virtual explosion of blood, and causing him to retaliate with a savage backhand to the face that sent Boggs rocking backwards in his chair just as First Sergeant Aran Wintersole entered the small shed.

Unimpressed by his soldier's carelessness, as well as his lack of control, Wintersole had immediately ordered the chagrined and bleeding soldier outside, and replaced him with one-four—his other injured instructor—along with orders to get the information out of Boggs in whatever manner proved necessary.

That had occurred almost two hours ago and, as Boggs appeared no closer to talking now than before, the frustrated young soldier abandoned his threats and pressure points, braced his plaster-covered hand against Boggs's cast . . . and ripped the nail off the federal agent's right little finger with a pair of pliers. That, to the young soldier's absolute amazement, only fueled the severely injured agent's stubborn resistance.

It was a mistake to bring the female in, the young soldier thought, looking over at the bound and gagged young woman who, if anything, was making more of an effort than Boggs to get loose and tear into her captors. *She's as bad as he is, if not worse. And having the two unidentified agents in here, too, isn't helping things either. They're just egging him on.* But he wasn't about to voice that opinion. Not with Sergeant Aran Wintersole in the room.

Sighing to himself, one-four prepared for the next phase, which would almost certainly mean carrying out his threat to do precisely the same thing to the young woman's right little finger if he—Boggs—didn't get with the program. Suddenly, another figure entered the shed.

"Does anybody here know where I can find Sergeant . . . hey, what's going on here?" Henry Lightstone demanded from the doorway.

"What are you doing here?" the youthful inquisitor responded. "You're supposed to be with the Brigade."

The young soldier started up out of his chair, immediately suspicious and on the alert because Wintersole had made it very clear that their newly hired replacement was to be given run of the Chosen Brigade's training facility, but he was not to be trusted with any sensitive aspect of their mission.

But before one-four could do or say anything else, First Sergeant Aran Wintersole intervened.

"It's all right, David," Wintersole said as he came up beside Lightstone. "Come on in." He reached around and pulled the shed door shut. "So how are the Brigade members getting along with their night field problems?" the hunter-killer team leader asked calmly.

Henry Lightstone spent a few moments staring at the four figures who were bound to the chairs—noting that the glassy-eyed and bandaged older male strapped into the chair farthest away from the door and the young soldier whose wrist he had broken in the Dogsfire Inn both had fresh blood all over their plaster casts—before he finally answered.

"They're stumbling around a lot, mostly running into trees and getting in each other's way, but nobody's broken a leg or shot anybody yet—which is pretty amazing all by itself."

"How's their spirit holding up?"

Lightstone shrugged. "Probably a lot better than their physical conditioning, but that's not saying much. By the way, I may have insulted Colonel Rice when he offered me a major's rank to join up with the Chosen Brigade. I told him a single stripe would be fine, because every military brigade ought to have at least one private, but I don't think he noticed. Fact is, I get the impression this business of taking prisoners really threw the entire group off their stride," Lightstone added pointedly. "Which brings me to a relevant question. Am I interrupting some critical part of the exercise here?"

He nodded his head in the direction of the two chair-bound figures. Wintersole shrugged. "No, not really."

The fearsome pale gray–eyed soldier seemed to hesitate for a brief moment, as if not quite certain how he wanted to play the situation. But then he went on in what Lightstone thought was an amazingly calm and controlled voice.

"We have an interesting problem here, Henry. It seems a competing paramilitary group in the neighborhood doesn't think much of the Chosen Brigade's brand of politics or religion. So instead of simply agreeing to disagree, this other group decided to send three of their members to infiltrate the Brigade and monitor their activities."

"I thought you said she was one of the Chosen Brigade women." Lightstone rubbed his aching ribs gingerly as he watched Special Agent Natasha Marashenko's eyes widen in recognition over her duct-tape gag as she reacted to the name "Henry" by turning and staring.

"She was supposed to be." Wintersole appeared to contemplate the fiercely glaring figure who had finally stopped struggling against her bonds. "But it was dark, and we didn't pick up on the switch until we found the woman who was supposed to be part of the exercise out cold in the bushes."

"She doesn't look like much of a spy to me." Lightstone's comment earned him a furious glare from the captive Charlie Team agent.

"None of them look much like federal wildlife agents, either, as far as I'm concerned," Wintersole commented.

Lightstone blinked. "Federal wildlife agents?"

"That's their story, although all four of them apparently forgot to bring along their Special Agent badges or whatever it is they carry for ID. Oh, and by the way, they'd like us all to know that we're under arrest."

"For what, holding a training exercise?"

"Apparently we carried out our roles a little too realistically for their tastes." The hunter-killer recon team leader smiled.

"I don't understand." Henry Lightstone donned a thoroughly confused look. "These people from a competing militant group tried to infiltrate the Chosen Brigade posing as federal wildlife agents? What the hell kind of sense does that make? I mean, how did they . . . hey, wait a minute, didn't you say three?"

Wintersole nodded his head solemnly.

"According to our sources, the old fart in the far chair was supposed to infiltrate another couple into the Chosen Brigade during our exercise this evening. The woman next to him—the one you captured—and presumably one of these other two supposed federal wildlife agents"—Wintersole smiled again—"who happens to be named Lightstone."

Henry Lightstone felt a cold chill run down his spine, but he forced himself to remain calm and unresponsive.

"For what I assume are obvious reasons, the Brigade leadership would like to identify this third infiltrator," Wintersole went on. "We have a rough ID—male, white, six foot, one-eighty—which both of these guys more or less fit, but nobody here wants to cooperate. And then, as luck would have it, who pops in at just the right moment but you."

"Me?" Lightstone cocked his head curiously, already judging the relative positions of Wintersole and his already-injured young martial-arts instructor, whose right hand had been converted into what was now, unfortunately, a fairly handy club.

Wintersole nodded. "Whoever comes up with a positive identification of Lightstone gets a five-thousand-dollar bonus. We've been interrogating these two for the last couple of hours on a fairly casual basis and getting nowhere. We were getting ready to try a more serious form of persuasion when you showed up."

A decidedly cold look passed through Wintersole's eyes. "However," he went on, staring directly at Lightstone now as if trying to gage his reaction, "before we do, and taking into consideration the amount of damage you took to your ribs from this little hellion a couple of hours ago, I thought you might like a shot at that bonus money first."

"Five grand, just to find out which one of those other yahoos out there is named Lightstone?" A contemplative look appeared on Henry Lightstone's face as he continued to stare down at the four captive agents—all of whom, for very different reasons, continued to glare right back at him.

"That's right."

Henry Lightstone shrugged. "Tell you the truth, I'm kind of tired of listening to this one screaming in my ear." He nodded his head toward Natasha Marashenko. "And those other two don't look like the cooperative types, but if I can have this old fart to myself for an hour or so," he added as he walked over and removed the gag from Wilbur Boggs's mouth, "I think I can make him talk."

A fierce bloody smile formed on the federal wildlife agent's lips as he looked up at Lightstone and said in a nearly exhausted but clearly unimpressed voice:

"I don't think so, asshole."

Chapter Fifty

At precisely 5:44 East Coast time that Tuesday morning, Simon Whatley's call was finally routed through to Regis J. Smallsreed's Georgetown apartment.

Less than an hour and a half later, Whatley found himself transported upward in an elevator and wheeled into a large, dimly illuminated private room in a very secure and restricted area of Fairfax County Hospital reserved for persons of wealth and influence recovering from their socially acceptable or unacceptable ailments in a manner more befitting their station in life.

From Whatley's prone position, he could see the concerned faces of Congressman Smallsreed and Sam Tisbury.

"Hello, Simon, how do you feel?" Tisbury asked solicitously.

Whatley tried to mumble something through his swollen lips while Smallsreed spoke to the white-coated orderly.

"Those are Mr. Whatley's personal effects," the young orderly explained, handing the congressman a large plastic bag.

"Thank you. We'll take care of everything." Smallsreed ushered the hospital employee toward the door as he spoke.

"And please, don't let anyone disturb us for the next hour," the congressman ordered as he began to shut the door.

"But . . ."

"We'll call if Simon needs anything," Smallsreed smiled reassuringly, then firmly shut and bolted the door in the orderly's face. He then drew all the curtains and turned off all the lights, leaving only the overhead night lights as a dim source of illumination in the serenely wallpapered room, while Sam Tisbury spread the contents of the bag on the foot of Whatley's bed.

Moments later, the door to the adjoining bathroom opened and a tall, gracefully moving figure emerged.

"Does he have the drop-box messages?"

Whatley immediately recognized the voice as that of the ominous shadow-dwelling presence in Smallsreed's office, and sucked in his breath.

"Right here." Tisbury held up the three envelopes.

"I tried . . ." Simon Whatley mumbled, but the three men in the room ignored him.

"What do they say?"

"Just a second." Tisbury tore open the first envelope, unfolded the piece of paper and read out loud: " 'What's the game? Blindman's bluff?' "

"Blindman's bluff? What kind of message is that?" Aldridge Hammond demanded irritably.

"Must be some kind of code," Smallsreed suggested.

"If it is, nobody gave us the key. And there's no signature either," Tisbury added as he ripped open the second envelope. "This one's from Wintersole." He quickly scanned the contents, then read out loud, " 'Please send us the agent profiles ASAP. We need them to positively identify Lightstone.' "

Smallsreed looked down at Simon Whatley as though seeing him for the first time that morning.

"I thought you said you delivered those profiles to the drop box last Wednesday," he accused the injured man.

"I did . . . I mean, we did . . . I had one of my aides . . ." Simon Whatley mumbled frantically, but the congressman turned back to Tisbury.

"What's the date on that second letter?" he asked.

The revenge-seeking industrial executive examined the letter again.

"Last Thursday. Five days ago."

"What about the first one?"

Tisbury examined the first envelope and letter again. "No date, no postmark," he reported.

"How the hell does that happen?" Confusion dimmed Regis J. Smallsreed's ruddy features. "If it went through the post office, it has to have a postmark, doesn't it?"

"Maybe they didn't pick up their mail that next morning for some reason. I mean, I know we . . ." Simon Whatley continued protesting his innocence from his prone position on the hospital bed, but Smallsreed silenced him with a fierce glare while Tisbury opened the third envelope.

"What the hell . . ." the wealthy industrialist whispered as his eyes quickly scanned the letter.

"What does it say? Read it out loud," the ICER chairman ordered from the back of the room.

"It says 'Better yet, would the congressman and the bagman like to play, too?' "

"WHAT?" Regis J. Smallsreed almost screamed in outrage as he ripped the letter out of Sam Tisbury's hand.

"No date on it either," Tisbury informed the other two in an amazingly calm voice as he examined the outside of the third envelope, "but it's postmarked last Saturday . . . and while I'm no expert, I'd say the handwriting looks identical to that on the first one."

But Smallsreed didn't hear him. Instead, he grabbed the front of Simon Whatley's hospital gown and was in the process of wrenching his severely injured district office manager into an upright position while roaring "congressman and bagman, my *ass*! What the hell is that all about, Simon, you stupid bastard?" when the bolted door to the room clicked open and a brilliant white light suddenly filled the darkened room.

From his upright position, Simon Whatley had a brief but terrifying view of Aldridge Hammond's very pale brown eyes, yellowish brown hair and mottled complexion before the almost ghostly figure turned away, shielding his eyes and cursing.

Sam Tisbury lunged for the door, shut off the lights again, and intercepted the startled youth about to extract his master key from the door lock and enter the room.

"We told you not to interrupt us," Tisbury snarled at the young orderly.

"Uh, yes sir, I know, I'm sorry, sir," the orderly nodded frantically, his eyes still wide-open in shock from Tisbury's sudden confrontation, the memory of the incomprehensible words he felt sure he heard Congressman Smallsreed yelling, and his brief glimpse of his patient being hurled backwards onto the bed in the dimly lighted room before he switched on the lights. "But this briefcase just arrived from the tow yard, along with a suit bag and an overcoat. I know you didn't want to be disturbed, but according to the ID tag, the briefcase belongs to Mr. Whatley, and I thought you might want to . . ."

"Thank you, we'll see that Mr. Whatley gets it." Sam Tisbury took the briefcase and, after using his upper body to force the young orderly back out into the corridor, immediately shut and bolted the door.

"Keep that damned door closed!" a furious Aldridge Hammond ordered. "Barricade it if you have to."

"No problem." Sam Tisbury slammed the briefcase onto Whatley's bed, causing the terrified congressional district office manager to flinch and barely stifle a scream of pain. "Check that out, Regis," the wealthy industrialist ordered Smallsreed as he took up a protective stance with his arms folded and his back against the door.

Regis J. Smallsreed snapped open the briefcase and immediately saw the fat manila envelope.

"What's this?" he demanded, glaring at Whatley as he held up the envelope. "Something else you didn't tell us about?"

Simon Whatley tried to stammer an explanation of how he fell asleep on the plane, and didn't have time to read the materials and prepare a summary before getting into the accident, but . . .

Totally disregarding his underling's babbling, Smallsreed tore open the envelope.

"There's a message and a bunch of photographs," he announced as he began to read the handwritten note. His face turned beet red with rage as the words sank home.

"It's a message from Wintersole," Smallsreed snarled as he glared viciously at Whatley. "He says he's still waiting for the agent profiles, but he's enclosed some surveillance photos they took of the agents in the hope that somebody out here can make the ID. The goddamned letter is dated," the congressman went on, his eyes narrowing dangerously, "last Saturday — three fucking days after you said you sent him those profiles, you worthless piece of shit!" Smallsreed screamed as he wadded up the letter and threw it into the face of a stunned and now completely mortified Simon Whatley.

"But . . . but . . ." Whatley stammered desperately, but Smallsreed turned his back on him and flipped through the photographs, examining the labels on the back of each one, and separating them into two piles.

"Okay, Simon" — Smallsreed finally waved the larger of the two piles in front of Simon Whatley's bandaged face — "here's the way it goes. You will get these photos to someone in the Department of the Interior who can positively identify Special Agent Henry Lightstone. I don't care who you go to or how you do it, but if you want a job tomorrow morning, you will get Lightstone positively identified, and you will do it now."

Sam Tisbury suddenly came to life.

"Wait a minute," he exclaimed. "What the hell . . . give me those things! Christ, what am I thinking? I know what that bastard looks like!"

Tisbury took the stack of photos out of Smallsreed's hand, rummaged through them quickly, then looked up in frustration.

"He's not here."

"But he must be. Wintersole *said* . . ." Smallsreed started to protest, but Tisbury shook him off.

"I'm telling you, the bastard's not here! Christ, Regis, you think I don't know what he looks like? I still see the son of a bitch in my . . . Wait a minute!" Tisbury suddenly pointed toward the smaller stack of photos on Simon Whatley's bed. There he is! That's Henry Lightstone!"

Confusion constricted Regis J. Smallsreed's porcine features as he picked up the top photo and examined the label on the back again.

"No, it's not." He shook his white-haired head confidently. "According to the label, this is some local guy — the boyfriend of the woman running the post office."

"You *idiot*!" Tisbury screamed, his eyes bulging with rage as he snatched the photo out of Smallsreed's hand and flapped it in the congressman's face. "Listen to me, goddamn it! I'm telling you, *this* is Henry Lightstone!"

"But what in the world would *he* be doing..." Smallsreed started to protest, but then the light suddenly dawned.

"Goddamn it all to hell," he whispered.

As it happened, the man who caused Congressman Regis J. Smallsreed to take the Lord's name in vain was very much aware of the dawning light, too.

Only in Henry Lightstone's case, he couldn't do much about it because his light came from the soon-to-be-rising sun and resulted from bad timing.

By the time he helped Wintersole get the bound and gagged Donato, LiBrandi, and Marashenko—who, as far as Lightstone was concerned, outdid themselves struggling, kicking, and otherwise fighting their captors—transferred to the hand-dug, belowground, Vietnam-era "tiger" cages where Brigade members now proudly guarded their new prisoners... and then checked the night-exercise area, where the last of the students made valiant efforts to attain their assigned objective... the east horizon had begun to lighten perceptibly.

Which would be a problem, Lightstone realized, as he and Wintersole walked back to the shed housing the crusty old bastard Lightstone thought was Wilbur Boggs, because darkness played a crucial role in his plan, plus he had no desire to beat up a fellow agent.

He tried to disregard the idea that Wintersole might test him with a ringer... or worse, just make him torture someone out of a warped sense of amusement.

"How's he doing?" Lightstone asked as he entered the shed ahead of the hunter-killer recon team leader, hoping at least to eliminate the first possibility.

"He passed out," the obviously exhausted young Ranger replied. "It's your turn now."

Henry Lightstone walked over to the figure slumped in the chair, lifted up the bruised head, casually peeled back the badly swollen and bleeding upper lip, then smiled when he discovered the two missing upper front teeth.

Wilbur Boggs opened one eye, gave Lightstone a wide, bloody, and gap-toothed smile, then drifted away again.

Okay, Boggs, I seriously doubt any of the Chosen Brigade volunteered to sacrifice their front teeth just to play a role for some maniac Army Ranger first sergeant, so you're probably the man Charlie Team's been looking for... which means one more problem resolved, Henry Lightstone thought. Now all I have to do is figure out how to identify myself to you and keep the rest of Charlie Team from saying anything while I'm wearing this damned microphone.

He sensed Wintersole and the young Army Ranger coming up beside him.

"What time is it?" Lightstone asked, contemplating the slumped form of Wilbur Boggs.

Wintersole glanced at his wristwatch.

"Oh-four-forty hours."

"You in a real big hurry to get that information?"

"The sooner the better," the hunter-killer recon team leader replied. "Why?"

"I don't think this guy can stay conscious any longer, much less talk, no matter what we do to him, and I'm about half-asleep myself. So what do you say we tuck him away for a few hours while we all get some rest and regroup?"

Wintersole hesitated, and appeared ready to order Lightstone to begin his interrogation anyway, when the younger Army Ranger spoke up.

"We're all getting a little ragged, First Sergeant. And we still need to get all of that, uh, hardware rigged and tested by this evening."

Wintersole nodded his head slowly.

"And besides," Lightstone added, "I think I know how to get this guy to tell us anything we want to know."

"Lots of luck on that," the young Ranger commented.

"What do you have in mind?" Wintersole's pale gray eyes expressed far more interest than usual.

"You familiar with the expression 'psychological warfare'?"

Wintersole nodded.

Yeah, I'll just bet you are. Lightstone allowed himself a few moments to watch Wilbur Boggs's ragged breathing settle into a steady rhythm before he turned his attention to the man who—for whatever reason—clearly represented the greatest threat to Charlie and Bravo Teams.

"Good. Then I'll let you guess what I plan to do once I find myself a nice, big, poisonous snake."

Chapter Fifty-one

According to the paperwork filed with the FAA, the brand-new Falcon 900-EX that took off from Washington Dulles International Airport at 3:00 Eastern Standard time that Tuesday afternoon was one of three such aircraft owned by an international conglomerate of oil executives who leased the luxuriously appointed jets to clients on a trip-by-trip basis . . . and usually on very short notice.

Which explained the availability of planes, pilots, maintenance and ground crews on a twenty-four-hour call-out basis.

In point of fact, however, Samuel Tisbury, the Chairman and CEO of Cyanosphere VIII, as well as the number two man in the industrial conspiracy known as ICER, owned, operated, and piloted the very expensive three-engine jet. And, in a testimony to Tisbury's incredible wealth and infamous lack of patience, the ground and maintenance crews managed to completely reconfigure the plane internally, fuel and flight-check it a good half hour before Tisbury and his companions arrived at the private hangar.

The Falcon was still climbing—rising high over the Appalachian Mountains, on a basically straight-line course for the Rogue Valley International Airport in Medford, Oregon, with Tisbury and a copilot at the controls, an extremely attractive flight attendant solicitously attending Regis J. Smallsreed and the backup pilot in the forward cabin, and an extremely professional paramedic monitoring a deeply sedated Simon Whatley in the rear cabin—when Larry Paxton notified Special Ops Chief David Halahan that they hadn't heard from Special Agent Henry Lightstone or any of the agents of Charlie Team in the last fifteen hours.

The plane had leveled off at its cruising altitude of twenty-seven thousand feet, and was passing over Columbus, Ohio, when Lightstone decided that he'd slept enough for one morning—*make that afternoon*, he corrected himself, as he glanced down at his watch and discovered that it was already 1:15—and then proceeded to stand up, slowly and carefully, so as not to wake any of the loudly snoring members of the Chosen Brigade, most of whom sprawled belly up in their military-issue sleeping bags strewn over the dirt floor of the low-ceilinged cave.

The reserve pilot had just taken over the controls above Kansas City,

Missouri, so Sam Tisbury could join Regis J. Smallsreed for an exquisitely prepared dinner in the forward cabin, when Lightstone—moving carefully through the rocky outcropping above the Chosen Brigade's training facility theoretically in search of a particular variety of snake supposedly prone to sunning itself on rocky outcroppings at this time of year—spotted Wintersole and three of his men carefully setting the last of their high-explosive packets in and around an old and decrepit horse barn mostly filled with sacks of homegrown chicken manure that the Brigade men never quite found the time to spread in the fields as they promised the women they would. However, in spite of its odorous contents, the Brigade leadership felt the building would make a perfect trial site for Federal Wildlife Agent Wilbur Boggs and his fellow Special Agents from Charlie Team, to say nothing of the entire federal government as a whole in absentia.

The plane was approaching the Rocky Mountains, and climbing again to escape some mild turbulence—to the delight of Congressman Regis J. Smallsreed, who helpfully placed a steadying hand directly across the flight attendant's ample chest as she leaned forward to refill his and Tisbury's wineglasses—as Henry Lightstone watched the first sergeant carefully lock a small transmitter in the SAFE position, then hand it to the young Army Ranger with the cast on his hand.

As the plane passed directly over Salt Lake City, Utah, and began its initial descent, Lightstone retrieved his new cellular phone from one of his cache sites and called Mike Takahara to tell the tech agent what he wanted . . . which, in turn, enabled Bravo Team leader Larry Paxton finally to contact Halahan and advise the increasingly anxious and frustrated Special Ops chief as to the current status of Special Agents Henry Lightstone, Wilbur Boggs, and all of the members of Charlie Team.

And as the Falcon 900-XE crossed over the high desert of eastern Oregon at precisely 5:42 P.M. local time—with Congressman Regis J. Smallsreed enjoying a delightfully sensuous neck and shoulder massage from the multiskilled flight attendant, while Sam Tisbury nodded sleepily under the equally soothing influence of a half bottle of expensive Chardonnay—Henry Lightstone finally met Tech Agent Mike Takahara in the woods about a half-mile west of the Chosen Brigade's training compound . . .

And obtained his snake. . . .

And then went on to describe, in great detail, the final necessary elements of his plan.

At exactly 5:45 that same Tuesday evening, an exhausted Al Grynard, who was determined to maintain as much contact as possible with the agents assigned to his special investigations team, finally returned to the FBI's resident agent office in Medford, Oregon.

"Looks like you had a long day," Senior Resident FBI Agent George Kawana commented as Grynard collapsed into the chair behind his borrowed desk.

Sighing heavily, Al Grynard closed his eyes and leaned as far back as he could in the amazingly uncomfortable government executive chair.

"So help me God," he vowed, half to himself, "if I ever agree to take on another assignment like this, somebody please have the decency to collect my gun and credentials, and file my retirement papers."

George Kawana nodded sympathetically. "I think everybody in the agency agrees that you definitely set a new standard with this investigation."

"A new low, you mean."

"Well, yes, as a matter of fact, that *is* what I meant," the senior resident agent conceded. "But I was trying to look at it from a positive point of view."

"There is no positive point of view on this case, George," Al Grynard announced tiredly, keeping his eyes firmly closed as he tried to find a comfortable position in a chair obviously designed for someone with no lower back. "The whole thing sucks, no matter how you look at it."

"I suppose that means you don't want to see the latest set of, uh, surveillance photos?"

Al Grynard's left eye slowly opened.

"What do you mean by 'uh'?" he inquired suspiciously.

"Oh nothing, really." The senior resident agent shrugged indifferently. "I mean if it was my case, I'd certainly want to see those photos. But I can see where someone in your position might not necessarily want to know what . . ."

Al Grynard came straight up in his chair with both eyes open.

"Where are they?"

"Manila envelope, right in front of you."

Grynard reached for the envelope and hurriedly unwound the string tie.

"And then, too," Kawana went on as he watched his longtime friend and fellow agent pull a dozen eight-by-ten glossy color photos out of the envelope, "if this was *my case*, and I knew I'd be held completely responsible for anything that went wrong, I'd probably be a little curious as to what . . ."

Al Grynard emitted an explosive curse that almost caused the senior resident FBI agent of the Medford office to choke in surprise.

"You know, Al," Kawana pointed out after he regained his composure and observed the stunned expression on Grynard's decidedly pale face, "all these years we've known each other, I don't believe I've ever heard you utter that word inside an FBI office."

"That's . . . that's Lightstone. Goddamned Henry fucking *Lightstone*,"

Grynard sputtered angrily as he hurled the photo onto the desk like a hot coal that burned his hand.

Senior Resident Agent George Kawana slowly got up from his chair and walked to Grynard's desk to reexamine the photo he and his colleagues had already examined with great interest a few hours earlier.

"So *that's* Henry Lightstone, huh? Your old wildlife agent buddy? We kinda wondered who he might be. Not to mention what he was doing lying around naked and bleeding with that . . ." Kawana continued, but Grynard no longer listened.

As Senior Resident Agent George Kawana watched in amazement, Al Grynard lunged out of his chair, ripped open a nearby weapons locker, pulled out a pump shotgun, a vest, and a box of four-ought buck, and ran for the door.

At precisely 6:04 that Tuesday evening, at the very moment the Falcon 900-EX private jet bearing Congressman Regis J. Smallsreed, Sam Tisbury, and Simon Whatley touched down on the main runway of the Rogue Valley International Airport in Medford, Oregon—coming in almost directly over the rapidly accelerating sedan driven one-handed by supervisory FBI Agent Al Grynard, who shouted into the cell phone held in the other—the woman known as Karla carried a shovel, broom, mop and scrub bucket into the interior enclosure of the Dogsfire Inn where her awesome pet spent her unsupervised hours of the day.

The panther greeted her mistress with a complaining yowl.

"I don't want to hear about it," Karla muttered as she scooped and swept, then began mopping the concrete floor with an antiseptic solution, very much aware that the panther no longer used the fenced-in area outside her enclosure and adjacent to the Dogsfire Inn to relieve herself.

If anything, the panther's response sounded even more plaintive.

"Look, he's not here. He's out doing his own thing. That's what males do, so you might as well get used to it."

Evidently unwilling to accept the well-intentioned advice, the huge cat emitted an irritated snarl and lunged into her overhead loft. Moments later, the sound of ripping paper filled the air.

Jesus, Karla thought to herself, *next the two of us will start discussing our dating problems like a couple of sexually frustrated teenagers!*

She had just resumed her mopping when shredded pieces of paper began to rain down upon her.

"Hey, what are you doing up there?" Karla demanded, but the shower of paper continued unabated, punctuated by occasional frustrated yowls.

Muttering to herself, the resident cage-cleaner knelt and was starting to pick up the pieces of paper sticking to the wet concrete floor when a very familiar image suddenly floated by.

What the . . . ?

As she leaned forward to catch the partially shredded, folded sheet, the identity of the image crystallized in her mind.

Henry?

What the hell?

Having no idea at all why a torn picture of Henry Randolph Lee should flutter down from the loft inhabited by her pet panther, Karla carefully unfolded the wet paper . . . then blinked in shock when her eyes saw the name beneath his photograph.

Henry Lightstone?

Special Agent Henry Lightstone?

Oh my God.

Stunned and disoriented, it took her several moments to collect her thoughts. Then forgetting all about Sasha, she stumbled to her feet and ran to the phone in her bedroom.

She punched in the number from memory and let the phone ring eight times. Fighting off a growing sense of panic, she tried a second number, and got an answering machine.

"Goddamn it, where are you?" she screamed in frustration as she slammed the handset down.

Realizing that she had to warn them, right now, before it was too late, she reached under her bed, pulled out a sawed-off 12-gauge pump shotgun and a bandoleer of shotgun rounds, and ran for the door.

She was in her truck and fumbling with the key in the ignition when she felt something heavy hit the bed of the vehicle.

What?

She had already reached for the door handle with her left hand and started to come around with the shotgun clenched in her right, when a flash of black in the rearview mirror caught her eye.

A pair of bright yellow eyes with coal black pupils stared back at her calmly.

Sasha? How . . . ?

The image of the open enclosure door filled her mind.

Oh shit!

She hesitated, torn between conflicting emotions.

Goddamn you, Henry Who-ever-you-are!

Unwilling to lose the time necessary to return the agitated panther to her enclosure, Karla shook her head in frustration, invited the panther into the cab, and quickly fitted the crucial control collar over the complaining animal's thick neck.

After assuring herself that all three of the small, flexible antennas for the tracking, syringe-activating and drug-injecting systems were extended and clear, and that she now had complete control over the dangerous cat, she started the truck and accelerated out of the inn parking lot with a steely look of determination in her gold-flecked green eyes.

*   *   *

The Sage was puttering down the road on his underpowered motorbike toward the Dogsfire Inn when the familiar truck went roaring by, the panther in the cab yowling through the partially opened window in either recognition or distress—the Sage couldn't tell which—as the swirling currents of the truck's wake covered him with dust, dirt, and other assorted debris.

Shaking his head in dismay, he pulled over to the side of the road to clear his eyes and mouth, then got back on the road at a much-accelerated pace.

When he got to the inn, he found the restaurant wide-open but abandoned.

Puzzled and increasingly apprehensive, the old man progressively worked his way into the back living quarters, where he discovered Sasha's open enclosure, the abandoned scrub bucket and cleaning tools, and the concrete floor littered with wet shreds of paper.

Only when he worked his way into Karla's bedroom did he discover the partially torn, still-wet picture of a very familiar individual lying next to the phone on her bed stand.

Five minutes later, cursing to himself in a manner suggesting a far more interesting background than one might expect of the average, supposedly blind soothsayer, the Sage kicked his aging motorbike into life and roared back down the road in pursuit of Karla and the ever-protective Sasha.

And while all of that transpired, Henry Lightstone and Mike Takahara slowly and carefully worked their way under the truck that Lightstone had abandoned on the outskirts of Loggerhead City.

"Can you see it?" Lightstone whispered.

"Oh, yeah, I can see it all right," the Bravo Team tech agent muttered.

"Well?"

Takahara ran the powerful beam of his tiny flashlight one more time around the dual-antenna device someone had attached to the transmission of Lightstone's truck with a thick adhesive patch.

"How badly do you want it?" the tech agent finally asked.

"Will it blow up if you pull it off?"

"No, I don't think so."

"Then I want it," Lightstone replied grimly.

"Okay, you're the boss." The tech agent sighed, then reached up with a heavy screwdriver, popped the device loose with one quick motion, and tossed it to the ground next to Lightstone.

"What in the hell did you do that for?" Lightstone demanded, still somewhat shaken from Takahara's unexpected action.

"You said you wanted it," the tech agent reminded him calmly. "No big deal. It turned out to be what I thought it was."

"You mean an MTEAR-42. Just a simple little flash-bang and red smoke? You're sure about that?" Lightstone pressed as he studied the device warily. "No C-4?"

"I don't know if I'd call it a simple little flash-bang. Those puppies can give an Abrams Main Battle Tank a decent jolt, and that takes one hell of a pressure wave. I definitely wouldn't want somebody to set it off while we're under here. But to answer your question, yeah, I'm as sure as I can be without actually taking it apart. If you look in there"—Takahara directed the small flashlight beam at one of the vent holes in the side of the device—"you can see where the smoke and flash-bang charges are mounted. Plus there's not much room in there for anything else . . . unless you really worked at it," he added thoughtfully.

"Okay, I'll take your word for it." Lightstone grabbed the device and began working himself out from under the truck.

"That mean we're done?"

Henry Lightstone smiled as he pulled the tech agent out from under the truck and up to his feet, then reached down for the wriggling canvas bag next to his feet.

"Oh, no. That was the easy part. It's the next phase when you really start earning your pay."

Chapter Fifty-two

Henry Lightstone and Mike Takahara waited in the darkness on the outskirts of the Chosen Brigade's training compound until the Army Ranger known as Azaria began to set up her video-recording equipment.

They then took advantage of the commotion that followed—the Brigade members preening and posturing at the entryway of the compound with the bound and gagged Natasha Marashenko and Gus Donato, while Wintersole's hunter-killer team members observed the entire scene carefully from the surrounding woods—to work their way into the back of the ancient barn, almost two hundred yards from the compound entrance, where Lightstone had observed Wintersole and his team working earlier that day.

Initially, the smell of rancid and decomposing chicken manure practically overwhelmed the two agents. But they quickly forgot about that when the reddish beam of Mike Takahara's red-filtered flashlight located the first of the explosive packets.

"Jesus Christ," the tech agent whispered as he traced the wires . . . and quickly found eight more packets.

"What's the matter?" Lightstone called softly from his sentry position inside the barn's open doorway.

"There's gotta be at least five or six hundred pounds of C-4 in this place. Maybe more, because it looks like some of it's buried."

"Five or six *hundred* pounds?" Lightstone turned to stare at the crouching Bravo Team member in the very dim light. "Are you serious? To blow up a barn that'll fall down the first time somebody sneezes too hard?"

"Don't ask me. I'm just the guy with the wire cutters who would like to be somewhere else right about now."

For the first time, Lightstone noticed the tables and chairs arranged to form a crude—but very distinctive—courtroom setting.

Oh man, just what we need, he thought, feeling mildly nauseous at the thought of five hundred pounds of C-4 going off in the relatively small and enclosed space. They'd be lucky to find enough pieces to ID all of the victims. He turned back to Takahara.

"How's it rigged?"

"Everything's wired to a central receiver for remote detonation, just like you thought. It looks like the receiving antenna's mounted on the roof."

"What kind of range are we talking about?"

"No way to tell, but probably quite a ways."

"Can you deal with it?"

"Yeah, sure, if I've got enough time."

"Well, get to it. I'll keep an eye out here as long as I . . . Oh, shit!"

"What?" the tech agent demanded.

"Wintersole. He's headed this way!"

"What are we . . ." Mike Takahara started to ask, but Lightstone interrupted him.

"Keep working. I'll try to keep him and everybody else away from here as long as I can."

Lightstone was heading out the back door of the structure when Mike Takahara whispered to him frantically, "Wait a minute, I need to hook that microphone back up!"

Twenty seconds later, Henry Lightstone hurried around the far side of the barn, heading toward the shed housing Boggs a hundred yards away, and almost ran into Wintersole, who now wore night-vision goggles on his forehead over a black knit cap. Streaks of camouflage grease covered his face, and he carried an M-16 assault rifle in a manner suggesting that he'd gladly use it on the first person who got in his way.

"Where the hell have you been?" the Army Ranger first sergeant demanded angrily.

"Trying to scare up a poisonous snake, like I told you I would last night. They're hard to find in cold weather." Lightstone held up the wriggling cloth bag that very clearly contained a large and active snake. "I really had to dig."

Wintersole instinctively stepped back.

"What's going on over there?" Lightstone asked, nodding in the direction of the female Ranger who was in the process of videotaping the Chosen Brigade members and their captives at the compound entrance.

"Never mind." Wintersole shook his head impatiently. "We need to identify Lightstone, and we're running out of time."

"Then let's get to it," Henry Lightstone replied, moving quickly away from the barn and toward the shed.

When Henry entered, he found Boggs glaring fiercely at his interrogator, blood streaming from the agent's rebroken nose and split lips. Startled, the young Ranger brought his uninjured hand down to his holstered pistol, then stopped when he saw Wintersole behind Lightstone.

"I was beginning to think you'd run out on us." The young soldier glared at Lightstone accusingly.

"If I had any brains worth talking about, I would have. I don't like reporters and TV cameras," Lightstone commented, noting that, like Wintersole, the young Ranger wore his night-vision gear ready to go on his forehead, which reminded him that he'd left his own gear somewhere in the cave. He walked to the bound agent and examined his face critically, very much aware as he did that the eyes of all three men focused on the writhing bag in his hand.

"This guy ever tell you anything?"

"Nothing useful or polite," the young Ranger replied, looking down uneasily at the wiggling bag dangling less than two feet from his leg.

"So what do you think, Mr. Special Agent Boggs?" Lightstone asked in a soft, almost whispery voice. "You going to cooperate with us now? Or are you going to force me to make the rest of your life very short *and* very miserable?"

"Depends." Wilbur Boggs spoke through bloodied lips in what Lightstone considered an amazingly calm voice considering the circumstances. "What's in the bag?"

"Nothing you'll like very much." Squatting down, Lightstone slightly twisted the top of the bag, untied the securing cord, and then held the top loosely in one hand to create a half-inch-diameter opening.

He waited until the snake just poked out of the hole . . . then in one quick motion, grabbed it just behind the head with his thumb pressing into the base of the reptile's skull, and yanked it out of the bag.

The sight of the black-and-red snake—the common blacksnake brought by Mike Takahara from the warehouse—frantically wrapping its thick three-foot body around Henry Lightstone's right hand and arm caused both Rangers to step back even farther. Although tightly strapped to the chair, and unable to move, Wilbur Boggs simply studied the snake critically.

"Where in the hell did you get that thing?" he demanded suspiciously.

Much too late, it occurred to Lightstone that an experienced wildlife agent like Boggs would certainly know that common blacksnakes were anything but common in the Pacific Northwest. In fact, as far as he knew, other than the ones that Bravo Team now possessed, and perhaps a very few more in a couple zoos, they were simply nonexistent . . . which should have made it extremely difficult, at best, for Lightstone to find one anywhere near the Chosen Brigade's training compound.

But before he could think of something to say to distract Boggs, Wintersole interrupted.

"Never mind where he found it. Worry about what he's going to do with—"

The sound of animated voices and running footsteps distracted the Army Ranger first sergeant, and he opened the shed door just as one of the other young Rangers came running up.

"First Sergeant, we've got FBI agents at the compound gate."

"How many?"

The young soldier hesitated. "Uh, just two or three, I think. They're in a stand-off position at the entrance. When I left my post, they were arguing with Colonel Rice, and he ordered all of the prisoners taken to the barn to begin the trial."

"What's our status?"

"We're all standing back . . . completely out of it so far."

"Excellent." Wintersole smiled as he turned back to Lightstone and the young soldier. "You two get that information on Lightstone out of him, *right now!*" he ordered. "And keep your mikes live. I want to hear what's going on."

And before Lightstone could say or do anything else, he disappeared.

The young Ranger interrupted Henry Lightstone's thoughts as he stared at the door of the shed, ignored the frantically thrashing poisonous snake in his hand, and tried to make sense of this latest development.

"You heard the sergeant, we're running out of time," he reminded Lightstone. "Let's get going."

"Yeah, I guess you're right," Lightstone agreed, and then casually tossed the writhing blacksnake into the other man's hands.

The soldier instinctively caught the snake, but then an expression of horror replaced the surprised look on his face, and he emitted a high-pitched scream as the snake whipped around and buried its fangs into the fleshy base of the young man's thumb.

Lightstone swiftly grabbed the snake by the tail and—in one quick motion—ripped it loose from the young Ranger's hand, swung it and lightly slammed its head against the back leg of Boggs's chair ... and quickly popped the stunned reptile back into the bag.

"Don't panic, I milked it before I brought it here. Not enough poison left to kill you," Lightstone softly assured the hunter-killer staring down at his bitten thumb. Then before the young martial-arts-trained soldier could react, Lightstone hammered him to his knees with a pair of punishing body strikes to the solar plexus, then finished him off with a sharp elbow strike to the base of the neck that dropped him to the floor, unconscious.

Wilbur Boggs observed Lightstone in wide-eyed silence as the covert agent brought his left index finger up to his lips while working the collar mike and belt pack loose with his right hand. After setting the mike unit on the floor next to Boggs's feet, he leaned down and whispered into the battered agent's ear:

"It's okay. I'm Henry Lightstone, Special Ops, Bravo Team. What I need you to do, *right now*," he instructed, pointing to the communications unit on the floor, "is groan as loud as you can, and then say something appropriate."

To Boggs's credit, his eyes blinked and lower jaw dropped for only a brief instant before he recovered ... and emitted a loud and very realistic agonized groan, followed by a muttered curse.

"Okay, good." Lightstone grinned. "Keep it up."

As Wilbur Boggs continued to groan, and curse and thrash around in the chair, Henry quickly cut away the duct tape binding the resident agent's wrists, arms, and legs. Once he freed Boggs, he quickly knelt, collected the young soldier's pistol belt, night-vision goggles, and communication equipment, then searched the pockets of his flak jacket for the transmitter.

"Here, take this," Lightstone whispered, handing Boggs the heavy pistol belt.

"Thanks," Boggs whispered back between groans and curses, "but you take it. I can't even stand up."

Lightstone ignored the offered handgun.

"You going to be okay if I shut off the light and leave you in here with this kid?"

"Oh, hell, yes," Boggs replied in a tired whisper.

"Then just keep groaning and cussing—but like you're starting to come around," Lightstone softly instructed the battered agent, "and keep your head down. Things could get crazy around here any minute now."

Then before Boggs could say anything else, the covert wildlife agent turned off the light and disappeared into the darkness.

Crouching behind the shed to avoid the powerful flashlight beams now flickering back and forth around the distant trial site, Lightstone put on the communications mike and earphones and adjusted the night-vision goggles he'd taken from the Ranger.

When everything he viewed appeared in bright, contrasted shades of green, and he could clearly monitor the occasional terse commands and acknowledgments Wintersole and his troops exchanged as they hid in the forest surrounding the compound, he began moving toward the milling crowd.

Lightstone specifically looked for Takahara and Wintersole, but as he got closer, he could see at least twenty people moving in and around the barn now: the members of the Chosen Brigade, and Charlie Team . . . and a much smaller group, consisting of three clean-cut-looking men wearing blue jeans, boots, and down jackets who apparently argued with Brigade Colonel Rice, and three other Brigade members armed with M-16s standing about twenty-five yards away from the barn entrance. Plus he saw another Brigade member guarding Special Agent Natasha Marashenko, with her hands tied behind her back and a pistol at the back of her head.

Come on, Mike, where are you?

It took Henry Lightstone a few moments to realize that one of the men in the jeans, boots and down jackets—the one in the center arguing with the self-appointed colonel—looked vaguely familiar.

When the man turned to say something to one of his companions, Lightstone smiled in sudden recognition.

Grynard?

Well I'll be damned. What are you doing here?

But before Lightstone could factor the unexpected presence of his old nemesis into the picture, a cold and demanding voice crackled over his earphones.

"One-one to one-four, what's your status? I need an answer, now!"

Shit! Lightstone thought, surveying the area even more intently now, knowing Wintersole wouldn't wait long if he didn't get a response.

Come on Mike, where are you?

"One-four, report. What is your—" Wintersole demanded again over the hunter-killer team's scrambled communications net. Only this time, a deeply furious voice interrupted him.

"You want to talk to this kid, Sergeant, then you get your ass back over here, and we'll discuss the matter," Wilbur Boggs rasped harshly. "And by the way, you and your little toy soldiers are all under arrest." The sound of a 9mm round being jacked into the chamber of a military-issue 9mm Beretta semiautomatic pistol clearly echoed over the earphones.

Boggs, you idiot!

Almost immediately, Lightstone saw the easily recognizable figure of First Sergeant Aran Wintersole moving deliberately toward the shed.

Henry Lightstone, too, turned toward the shed, knowing all too well that Wilbur Boggs had just committed a brave, but foolhardy and very likely fatal, mistake. But then a loud voice thundered out of the darkness to his right.

"HENRY, LOOK OUT, BEHIND YOU!"

Lightstone only had a brief moment to recognize Mike Takahara's voice before he heard the figure coming, ducked under the downward sweeping butt-stroke, and spun on his hands to kick the legs out from under his swiftly moving assailant. He heard the black plastic stock of the M-16 assault rifle clatter against a rock, but then lost his night-vision goggles when the muscular young Ranger slammed a forearm against the side of his head, then nearly connected with an open-handed killing stroke aimed at his throat, which Lightstone barely deflected in time with the palm of his hand.

Working instinctively in the darkness, Lightstone parried another strike, and a third . . . then lashed out sharply with his elbow at a point where he judged the young soldier's face should be, heard a confirming grunt of pain when soft tissue gave way under the impact, then extended the muscular Ranger's arm out and twisted it sharply, wrenching it out of the shoulder socket.

The soldier was still screaming and thrashing around in the darkness, and Henry Lightstone was feeling on the ground for his goggles and the transmitter, when the beams of two flashlights converged on his face.

"LIGHTSTONE? WHAT THE HELL ARE YOU *DOING* OVER THERE?!" a familiar voice yelled out as he tried to shield eyes.

Oh yeah, definitely Grynard.

"HENRY, YOU IDIOT!"

What?

Karla?

What the . . . ?

In that brief instant during which those two remarks aimed at Henry Lightstone filled the air, the wild-card agent sensed Wintersole coming to a dead stop, and turning in his direction with the M-16 raised . . . and he dived for the transmitter suddenly visible in the shifting beams of the two flashlights, thumbed the A and B switches as a pair of 5.56mm rounds kicked up dirt and rocks mere inches from his head, then rolled away as the nearby barn erupted in a bright flash followed by a violent explosion that sent hundreds of pounds of rotten board fragments, dirt, and rancid, decomposing chicken manure flying in all directions.

Henry Lightstone had a brief glimpse of First Sergeant Aran Wintersole being flung to the ground by the force of the manure-bag-contained MTEAR detonation (and at least a few pounds of C-4 that Mike Takahara evidently missed, because Lightstone couldn't imagine any kind of a training device, military or otherwise, creating an explosion like that), and then . . . once he managed to get his night-vision goggles back on . . . the amazing sight of the Chosen Brigade, Natasha Marashenko and the other members of Charlie Team, FBI Agent Al Grynard, and his colleagues all staggering to their feet dripping with clumps of decomposing chicken manure.

Lightstone was continuing his desperate search, this time for the M-16 assault rifle that his attacker had lost, when someone—a feminine voice? He couldn't tell—began screaming "CANVASBACK! CANVASBACK!"

The furious voice of First Sergeant Aran Wintersole snarled in Lightstone's earphones.

"One-one to Fire Team One, target one-sixty-degrees relative is Special Agent Henry Lightstone . . . and he's got one-four's transmitter. Get that bastard, *now!*"

Realizing that the remaining members of Wintersole's hunter-killer team effectively surrounded him, and were very close to trapping him, Henry Lightstone abandoned all thoughts of finding the lost M-16.

Instead, he ran.

Chapter Fifty-three

The first fifty yards were the worst because Henry Lightstone knew he remained well within the hundred-percent kill range of a trained Army Ranger armed with an M-16 automatic assault rifle. He scrambled on his hands and knees at several points, then threw himself sideways on two separate occasions, to escape the seemingly endless, short bursts of 5.56mm rounds coming at him from all directions, shearing off fragments of bark, branches, and rock that flew into his face and tore at his clothing as the projectiles whipped past his head.

Somewhere in the background, he thought he heard the sound of 12-gauge shotgun and high-velocity pistol rounds, but he was much too busy trying to stay ahead of the shadowy figures working very hard both to keep up and to circle around in an effort to cut him off to worry about such things.

But as he got deeper into the woods and the thick pine and fir trees became more plentiful, the short bursts of 5.56mm rounds came further apart, and nowhere near as close, which gave him hope . . . and he continued to run, now driven by the sounds of boots scattering small rocks and crunching lightly on the thick carpet of dried pine needles, forcing himself to ignore his aching legs and burning lungs.

At one point, he heard a feminine voice start to ask something—but Wintersole immediately cut her off with an order to maintain radio silence.

Halfway to his goal, Lightstone paused to rest, taking in deep breaths to fill his lungs and replenish the oxygen debt in his rapidly fatiguing muscles. As he did so, he could hear the muted sounds of other heavy breathing in his earphones.

That's why he didn't want them talking with each other, Lightstone realized. *I can hear them . . . which means they can hear me, too.* Shaking his head in frustration, he quickly flipped off the microphone switch.

But as he did so, the first of the oncoming figures appeared in his night-vision goggles and immediately sent him off running again.

As he ran, Lightstone stayed on the winding path because he'd only traveled the route once before and figured this offered the least chance of spraining an ankle on a loose rock or unseen branch. He briefly considered circling back and trying to catch one of the trailing soldiers by surprise to acquire one of the M-16s, but immediately abandoned the idea, knowing that if he stopped—or did anything at all instead of run— he wouldn't stand the slightest chance against the team of professional soldiers who trained together, leapfrogging, surrounding, and killing multiple armed targets with Swiss-watchlike precision.

Instead, he continued to run, stopping only briefly every few minutes to check his compass and gather his remaining reserves . . . until, finally, he emerged from the tall stand of old-growth trees, crossed a shallow stream, and sprinted up a long incline to the edge of an open field.

He paused briefly at the top of the slope, looked back, saw two of the dark green figures materialize at the edge of the forest, and then, with the last remnants of his strength, staggered toward the darkened warehouse.

※   ※   ※

First Sergeant Aran Wintersole lay prone at the top of incline with the barrel of his M-16 assault rifle extended, waiting until the two members of his fire team signaled that they were in their proper flanking positions. Then he directed the figure lying next to him to set the crosshairs of her target scope on the slightly open side door of the warehouse nearest their location.

She did, and shook her head.

"I'm getting a diffuse heat source, but no movement," she whispered while continuing to scan the front of the warehouse with her IR-heat-sensing target locator.

"Wait a minute," she corrected herself. "I've got heat and movement. Looks like it's coming from the gap between the siding and the floor."

"How many?" Wintersole demanded.

"Two . . . no three, at least three targets. Definitely three."

"Where?"

"Far front corner of the warehouse, opposite side from the open door, in close to the main roll-up door," the communications specialist reported confidently.

Using hand signals, Wintersole quickly informed one-two, his heavy-weapons specialist, of the location of the three targets inside the warehouse, and ordered the corporal and his team to take the near door and go in hot while he and his team stayed outside to pick off the expected runners.

Once the Ranger first sergeant verified that everyone was in place, he signaled "Go!" with his raised right hand.

As Wintersole watched with professional calm, the Rangers took the door without hesitation. The roar of automatic weapons fire filled the night air as the lunging and rolling soldiers sent overlapping streams of 5.56mm rounds into the front and side corrugated metal walls of the building.

Then came the distinctive sound of full magazines replacing empty ones.

And then dead silence, broken only by a softly whispered, "Oh shit."

Another distinctly feminine and near-panicked voice whispered, "Help, I'm stuck."

"One-two, give me a sit-rep!" Wintersole immediately ordered.

Another period of silence.

"We've got a . . . a situation . . . in here, First Sergeant," the team's heavy-weapons specialist whispered in a shaken voice.

"Get us out of here, First Sergeant," the feminine voice pleaded.

"One-two to one-one, request permission to withdraw," the heavy-weapons specialist whispered.

"Negative, one-two. Hold your position," Wintersole ordered. "Do you have Lightstone?"

Another long pause, then a soft, "I don't know, First Sergeant."

First Sergeant Aran Wintersole blinked in disbelief.

"Then go look and see, Corporal," the hunter-killer team leader ordered in a slow, very clear, and definitely threatening manner.

A much longer pause followed this time.

"We can't, First Sergeant."

The unimaginable words from arguably the toughest member of his Ranger hunter-killer recon team brought the combat-hardened first sergeant immediately to his feet. He charged toward the partially closed side door of the warehouse, reflexively thumbing the selector switch of his M-16 to full auto as he did so.

Once at the side door, Wintersole paused, M-16 at the ready position, and motioned to one-seven on the other side of the door opposite him. Without hesitation, the young soldier dived in through the doorway, sending a stream of 5.56mm rounds streaking over the heads of the other hunter-killer team members and punching through the far side wall of the warehouse . . . then rolled to the floor, automatically ejecting the empty magazine as he reached back for a full one with his left hand.

The instant he heard one-seven hit the floor, Wintersole slammed the door aside with his shoulder and lunged through the doorway, finger tightening on the trigger of his M-16, ready to kill the first thing that moved . . . and then stood, stunned and uncomprehending, as he stared at the incredible scene before him.

"Oh my God . . ." one-seven whispered, but Wintersole ignored him, feeling a very unfamiliar fear-induced chill run through him when he saw the hundreds of slowly moving eyes and legs glowing in varying combinations of bright red and iridescent blue in the bright green viewfinder of his night-vision goggles . . . and then the six, much larger bright eyes glowing in the far corner of the warehouse by the roll-up door.

But as the hunter-killer team leader moved toward the hundreds of slowly moving, bright red and iridescent blue creatures, he began to put it all together.

Snakes and spiders?

Then he stepped on something sticky.

What the hell . . . ?

At that moment, a deep voice with a distinct, South Carolina accent called out from outside the front roll-up door of the warehouse.

"THIS IS SPECIAL AGENT LARRY PAXTON OF THE U.S. FISH AND WILDLIFE SERVICE. WE HAVE THE WAREHOUSE SURROUNDED. THROW YOUR WEAPONS OUTSIDE THE DOOR, AND COME OUT WITH YOUR HANDS OVER YOUR HEADS!"

"BULLSHIT!" Wintersole roared as he spun and emptied the thirty-round magazine waist high across the front wall of the warehouse.

Ordering his troops to maintain their positions, Wintersole calmly knelt on the concrete floor, reloaded his weapon, and waited.

"What do you think?" Larry Paxton asked. With a Smith & Wesson 10mm semiautomatic pistol clenched tight in both hands, he was crouched next to the largest tree he could find among the meager collection surrounding the warehouse parking lot.

"Definitely sounded like a 'no' from here," Bobby LaGrange replied from his prone position next to the adjoining tree. The retired San Diego Police homicide detective aimed the 12-gauge pump shotgun held tight against his shoulder at the main roll-up door of the warehouse.

"Yeah, that's what I thought, too."

Sighing to himself, the Bravo Team leader slowly stood up, positioned himself in a barricade position next to what now—thanks to the barrage of bark-shredding 5.56mm rounds that had come flying in their general direction—seemed like a very small tree, yelled out, "OKAY, IF THAT'S THE WAY YOU FEEL ABOUT IT," and then carefully and deliberately fired two 10mm rounds into the metal wall of the warehouse.

The crash of breaking glass immediately followed the sound of punctured sheet metal . . . and then, some moments later, a high-pitched scream.

"GIVE UP YET?" Paxton called out.

Dead silence.

"I SAID, DO YOU GIVE UP YET?" Larry Paxton repeated.

More silence.

"IN CASE YOU'RE WONDERING, THOSE YELLOW-EYED THINGS ON THE FLOOR ARE CROCODILES, THE TARANTULAS HAVE FANGS LIKE YOU WOULDN'T BELIEVE, AND EVERY ONE OF THOSE DAMNED SNAKES IS POISONOUS . . . ESPECIALLY THE TIGER SNAKES AND THE DEATH ADDERS. AND NO, I AIN'T GOT NO IDEA AT ALL WHAT I'M AIMING AT," Paxton tried hopefully.

No response.

"Give them another shot," Bobby LaGrange suggested sensibly.

Muttering a heartfelt curse, Paxton raised his 10mm semiautomatic again.

Two more rounds punched through the corrugated metal, followed by more breaking glass, another high-pitched scream, and some extremely heated profanity.

Moments later, four M-16 assault rifles sailed through the side door and clattered on the ground.

Wait a minute. How many were there? Five or six? Henry Lightstone stood at his barricade position behind a nearby tree, trying to remember exactly how many figures he'd seen following him in the woods and then entering the warehouse. *They started out with seven at the training compound. Boggs had one-four under control, and I took out another one—broke his nose and dislocated his shoulder—which leaves five. Right.*

"That's only four, Wintersole," Henry Lightstone spoke into his reactivated collar mike. "I want them all, or I'm tossing in a flash-bang."

Following a brief pause, a familiar voice echoed in his earphones. "Lightstone?"

"Special Agent Henry Lightstone of the United States Fish and Wildlife Service to you, First Sergeant," Lightstone replied tersely as he cautiously moved toward the side of the warehouse. "Boggs already told you you're under arrest, and Larry wasn't kidding about those snakes being poisonous, so toss out all your weapons and get your people out here, now!"

After another brief delay, the fifth rifle came flying out the side door, followed by four camouflaged figures with their hands over their heads.

Henry Lightstone took up a barricade position by the side door, holding Woeshack's 10mm Smith & Wesson at the ready, with Bobby LaGrange standing guard with the shotgun, while Stoner, Takahara, Woeshack, and Paxton moved in, collected the M-16s, and took the four young Rangers into custody, quickly handcuffing their wrists behind their back, and laying them facedown in the middle of the parking lot.

Then Lightstone backed away from the building, and into the middle of the parking lot to give himself a better view of the front roll-up and side doors with his night-vision goggles while Takahara and Woeshack assumed blocking positions on the back sides of the warehouse.

"Come on, Wintersole, get your ass out here," Lightstone finally spoke softly into his collar mike.

"Why don't you come in and get me, Henry?"

"What's he saying?" Larry Paxton demanded in a hushed voice as he came up beside Lightstone.

Lightstone reached down and shut off the collar mike.

"He wants me to go in there and get him."

"Forget that crap." Dwight Stoner held up one of the flash-bang grenades he'd taken off one of the Rangers. "Let's toss this in and we'll see how fast he comes out."

"Shit, don't do that!" Larry Paxton whispered urgently. "You'll blow out every piece of glass in the damned warehouse, and every snake and spider in there'll get loose!"

"How about we turn the lights on so we can at least see him," Lightstone suggested.

"Can't." Paxton shrugged apologetically. "I had Mike shut off the main and then cut the feed lines coming out of the panel to make sure these guys couldn't turn on any lights and figure out real quick that we weren't in there."

"What about flashlights?"

"We've got six of them," Stoner replied sheepishly. "But they're all in the warehouse."

"Wonderful," Lightstone muttered, then grew silent when he heard Wintersole chuckling in his earphone.

"Come on, Henry. Just you and me. We'll have some fun, see what kind of Ranger you would have made."

"What's he saying now?" Paxton demanded.

"Son of a bitch is getting impatient." Lightstone looked down at the four Rangers sprawled facedown and quiet in the almost pitch-black parking lot. "Hey," he whispered, "what happened to their night-vision goggles?"

"They weren't wearing any," Dwight Stoner replied.

Lightstone quickly knelt and rapidly searched all four of their captives before pulling Paxton and Stoner about twenty feet away.

"The bastard had them take the goggles off before they came out," he informed his teammates in a hushed voice. "Same with the communications gear and the red-lensed flashlights they were carrying. Military thinking. Don't give up any resources that the enemy can use against you. I've got this one set of goggles, but what about our stuff? Don't we have any night-vision gear?"

"Nope, just Mike's spotting scope." Larry Paxton was starting to look thoroughly frustrated now. "Look, how about Dwight and I take the far door and go for the flashlights, while you guys keep him pinned down?"

"No deal." Lightstone shook his head. "This guy's a Ranger first sergeant. You go in there blind, and he'll tear your throats out before you even see him."

"Come on, Henry." Wintersole's voice reverberated in Lightstone's headset again. "Just you and me. If you try to get tricky and bring your friends in too, you know I'll kill them . . . and you'll have to live with the fact that it was your fault for the rest of your life."

"That's it," Lightstone muttered as he ripped the earphones off his head and threw them on the ground.

"Hey, what do you think you're doing?" Larry Paxton demanded.

"I'm going in there and arrest that son of a bitch."

And before the Bravo Team leader could say or do anything else, Henry Lightstone ran toward the warehouse . . . picked up speed as he approached the almost completely closed side door . . . then slammed it open with his shoulder, dived into a forward judo roll as the door swung shut behind him . . . and came up in a semisitting position with the Smith & Wesson extended in front of him in a double-handed grip.

The incoming roll threw his night-vision goggles off kilter, and Lightstone quickly readjusted them so he could see clearly.

What he saw made his flesh crawl.

With no starlight to enhance his view in the almost-total darkness of the warehouse, the sensors of the new-generation light-vision goggles picked up only IR and UV fluorescence.

As a result, and thanks to the reflected light from the dozens of terrariums aligned on the shelves along the rear wall of the warehouse, Lightstone could easily see the bright red legs and eyes of the sixty-to-seventy giant red-kneed tarantulas and the iridescent blue eyes of the two snakes which had escaped when Larry Paxton's randomly aimed 10mm bullets shattered their containers.

Between them and the hundreds of slowly moving bright red and iridescent blue legs and eyes in the background, Lightstone might never have seen Wintersole at all . . . had not fifteen or twenty glowing tarantulas effectively outlined his seated form as they slowly walked up, over, and around his body.

Keeping an eye on the two sets of free-roaming iridescent blue snake eyes, one set of which had crossed in front of Wintersole, Lightstone moved slowly forward with the 10mm aimed at the center of the Ranger first sergeant's forehead.

"You're under arrest, Wintersole," he announced softly. "You have the right . . ."

"To remain silent," the Ranger first sergeant finished as he slowly rose to his feet so smoothly that the inquisitive bright red–glowing legs barely hesitated before continuing on their wandering path.

"If you move again without my telling you to do so, I'll drop you . . . right here, right now," Lightstone warned.

Watch the snake, the covert agent reminded himself, well aware that Wintersole was perfectly capable of slinging the reptile at him with his foot, trusting the leather of his combat boot to defeat any bite and knowing that Lightstone, at best, could deflect it with his pistol . . . or more likely, his arm. A dangerous tactic, especially if Paxton's random shots had freed one of the tiger snakes or death adders.

"I don't intend to move, Henry," the Ranger first sergeant spoke softly, apparently indifferent to the tarantula slowly inching its way from the collar of his fatigue jacket to his ear, or the other one under his chin, whose iridescence illuminated Wintersole's face. Even in the hot reddish glow of the slowly moving eyes and legs, the soldier's expression appeared cold.

"She'll do my moving for me."

At that moment, Lightstone became aware of the movement to his left.

But before he could move, or swing around with the Smith & Wesson, or do *anything* at all, a very familiar voice whispered . . .

"Hello, Henry."

The click of a releasing safety catch told him all he needed to know.

There really had been six, after all.

"Hello, Natasha," he greeted her softly, keeping his eyes and gun on Wintersole. "You moonlighting now?"

"Always have been, Henry. That's what I like best about the American free-enterprise system. So many wonderful opportunities for a young woman who wishes to move up in this world."

"Especially a treacherous one."

"Oh yes; that, too. It would have been much easier if Halahan had transferred me to Bravo Team, but . . . there are always ways."

"*What* would have been easier, Natasha?" Lightstone asked in a quiet voice.

"Oh, that's right." The female Special Agent giggled. "You don't know, do you?"

"No, he doesn't," Wintersole reiterated the point as he brought his boot down quickly over the slowly approaching pair of iridescent blue eyes, picked up the snake carefully behind its head, and then walked slowly toward Lightstone, holding the pair of blue eyes out in front of him . . . all the while ignoring the 10mm Smith & Wesson still aimed at his forehead.

"It's a very poor exchange, Henry," Wintersole explained the basics as he stopped directly in front of the gun muzzle. "You kill me, she kills you . . . and then she kills them. And she will, too. I understand she's very well trained, and very good with that pistol; not that it will make much difference since she'll have every possible advantage," the hunter-killer team leader added with a cold smile. "My guess is that your friends won't stand a chance. Imagine all of them dead because of you. That's your biggest fear, isn't it, Henry?"

"I won't bargain for my life against theirs, Wintersole, and I won't put this gun down." Lightstone kept his index finger firmly on the trigger of the Smith & Wesson, and the front sight centered just above the Ranger first sergeant's nose to emphasize his point. "If she pulls that trigger, reflex action will set this one off . . . and you'll die. To tell you the truth, way I feel right now, I'd just as soon take you with me."

"I'm sure you would, Henry." Wintersole smiled faintly. "But that won't be necessary. If you come with us, your friends get to live, and you get to see what this is all about. It's either that, or like you said . . ." Wintersole adjusted his grip on the snake's head, closing its mouth tightly between his forefinger and thumb, and then slowly and carefully brushed the scaled head lightly against the exposed knuckles of Lightstone's tightly clenched hands, ". . . we both die. Right here. Right now.

"And, since you brought it up, I wouldn't mind taking you with me, either," he added with a sardonic smile.

Henry Lightstone felt the cool head of the snake against his fingers, then saw the outline of the head in the combined light of the bright red and blue iridescence.

Tiger snake.

The worst one of the whole batch.

Absolutely deadly.

Of course, Lightstone thought with an odd sense of detachment. *What else would it be?*

Then he blinked in surprise when Wintersole crushed the snake's head with his fingers and let it drop to the floor.

"It's nothing personal, Henry. I'm just doing what I'm getting paid to do."

Wintersole continued to smile, a menacing but ultimately indifferent smile.

"So which will it be, Henry? You're the one who has to choose. And you have to choose right now."

Two minutes later, Henry Lightstone walked slowly out of the warehouse with his hands over his head.

"LARRY, BACK EVERYBODY OFF!" he called out. "WAY BACK. I'M GOING TO GO . . ."

Then he stopped dead still.

"LARRY?"

"BOBBY?"

No answer.

"If your friends are playing games . . ." Wintersole hissed in Lightstone's ear.

"If they are, it's a new game to me," Lightstone informed his captor calmly, scanning the area with the night-vision goggles. As far as he could see, the entire parking lot, the adjacent warehouses, and all the surrounding sparse woodlands appeared empty.

No handcuffed Rangers.

No Bravo Team.

No Bobby LaGrange.

Nobody.

"This isn't . . ." Natasha Marashenko never completed that statement because Wintersole cut her off.

"Get going, now!" he ordered her urgently.

They had just reached the edge of the clearing where the land sloped down to the increasingly dense stands of evergreens, when a bright searchlight suddenly illuminated the area from the side of the adjacent warehouse and a voice bellowed out over a bullhorn.

"FBI! DROP YOUR WEAPONS AND PUT YOUR HANDS UP!"

Cursing, First Sergeant Aran Wintersole spun, sent four 10mm hollow-tipped bullets streaking in the direction of the searchlight—which immediately exploded in a glaring flash, then flared out, plunging the entire area into pitch-darkness again. Turning back, the hunter-killer recon team leader threw a surprised Lightstone aside and rolled down the incline, then came back up into a zigzagging sprint toward the trees as gunfire erupted from all sides.

Natasha Marashenko had already started to run before Wintersole destroyed the searchlight and was halfway down the incline when she tripped on an exposed root. She tumbled to the ground, screaming in surprise and anger, and was scrambling back up when the bullets began whipping over her head . . . which slowed her down enough that she was still a good six feet away from the first big tree when Lightstone caught her from behind in a running tackle.

The impact sent the Smith & Wesson flying; but instead of trying to twist loose and scramble for it, Natasha Marashenko swung her elbow back and caught Henry Lightstone square in the face, destroying his night-vision goggles and causing blood to pour from his nose.

Stunned, blinded, and enraged, Lightstone lunged and grabbed Marashenko by the waist of her tight jeans, spun her around, drove a crippling elbow into her thigh, tried for an arm bar, lost it, and had to cover to protect when the female agent jackhammered a series of potentially lethal elbow and hand strikes at his face and neck.

Then, before he realized what had happened, she was off him and hobbling toward the forest.

Ignoring the bullets smacking into trees above his head, Henry Lightstone dived forward, twisted behind a large tree for shelter, came back up to his feet, and was taking off after her again when he suddenly found himself flying through the air and landing hard on his back.

"Let her go, you idiot!" a familiar voice snarled in his ear.

But the adrenaline still surging through Henry Lightstone's bloodstream caused him to fling her aside and try to get back up again.

This time, when he landed hard on his back—knocking a goodly amount of air out of his lungs in the process—and tried to get back up again, she pinned his left arm behind his back and wrapped her right arm around his throat in the first move of a carotid chokehold.

"What the hell . . . !" he gasped, and reached up with his right hand to deflect the choke . . . then almost screamed when the huge cat came tearing through the brush and lunged at him, the impact sending both him and his assailant tumbling backwards into the dirt.

Henry Lightstone had a brief instant to realize that he lay on top of the sensuous body of a very strong woman who still had one of his arms pinned and *her* arm pulled tight around his throat . . . with a panther firmly planted on his chest, digging her painfully sharp claws into his heaving chest muscles while nuzzling his face with her thick-whiskered nose, and rumbling in apparent amusement or contentment . . . before another familiar voice yelled out above him.

"FBI, YOU'RE UNDER ARREST!"

A subliminal sense of awareness totally unrelated to the shouted order suddenly caused Henry Lightstone to jerk his head upward and stare past the head of the panther who also stared into the dark sky at . . . what?

He blinked, tried to focus, gave up, and looked helplessly over his shoulder at the grinning dirty face now visible in the flashlight beams.

"Under arrest?" he echoed. "Me?"

"Uh-huh," the woman known as Karla acknowledged, while Sasha rumbled in agreement and several blue-jeaned figures wearing FBI raid jackets and carrying sound-suppressed, night-scoped M-16 rifles moved slowly and cautiously past him into the woods, and a number of other blue-jeaned figures gathered around them at a safe distance.

"You're an FBI agent." Lightstone said it more out of wonder than anything else.

"Brilliant deduction, Sherlock," Karla chuckled in his ear. "We'll make a federal agent out of you yet."

"And so am I, sonny. Been retired for a lotta years, but they brought me back special just for this case . . . so there," the skinny, bearded, and supposedly blind old soothsayer otherwise known as the Sage announced with a wide grin as he proudly displayed his FBI raid jacket and badge.

"Dear God," whispered Lightstone as he looked around at the other familiar faces—Larry Paxton, Mike Takahara, Dwight Stoner, Thomas Woeshack, Bobby LaGrange, and Danny-the-Cook in an FBI raid jacket—who all wisely kept their distance from the glaring, but seemingly contented panther.

"And just in case you wondered, sport," Karla spoke softly in his ear, "Danny's one of our tech agents, in addition to being a half-decent cook."

"You swear in this damned cat, too?" Lightstone inquired, glaring into the adoring bright yellow eyes, and wincing when her claws dug deeper into his chest.

"I'd be happy to, but I don't think she'd take the demotion."

"Ah."

"Okay, Karla, I think you and Sasha can let him go now." FBI Supervisory Agent Al Grynard let out an exaggerated sigh as he joined the group, looking down at the female members of his unconventional FBI covert agent team disapprovingly as he reholstered his sidearm.

"Umm, no, I can't," Karla announced after a moment.

"Why not?"

"Because you just arrested him."

"But that was just for show . . . to keep them running," the FBI supervisory agent—who now radiated the aura of a man sorely put upon—reminded her less than patiently.

"I know, but who cares? I got him, and we won." The dirty-faced female grinned, much to her supervisor's visible dismay.

"You know, Grynard, you FBI folks run one hell of an undercover investigation when you put your minds to it," Larry Paxton commented as he gingerly brushed off some of the fetid debris adhering to Grynard's dark blue FBI raid jacket. "Supposedly blind old-fart soothsayers who ride around on motorbikes, witches who run government post offices, Cajun cooks, real live panthers, exploding sacks of chicken shit. Don't think I've ever seen anything quite like it."

"I was *not* responsible for the chicken shit," the supervisory FBI agent muttered darkly.

"Right, which was why I was thinking maybe we could just transfer Henry directly over to you guys, seeing as how . . ." Larry Paxton smiled hopefully.

"Actually, I kinda liked the way two female agents in a row stomped the shit out of Henry," Dwight Stoner interrupted before the incredulous FBI supervisor could respond in some manner that he might later regret.

"Yeah, speaking of which," Lightstone remarked, looking up from his sprawled and—digging panther claws aside—relatively comfortable position, "how come you guys held back so long, and then just let them . . . oh."

"The light dawns." Karla smiled.

"It's about time," Mike Takahara commented.

"From the FBI's standpoint," Al Grynard explained, trying his best to maintain his dignity and composure in spite of his splattered and odorous jacket, "the Chosen Brigade of the Seventh Seal was a classic example of a basically inept and disorganized militant group ripe for manipulation by a more serious antigovernment organization. Jim—the Sage—Karla and Danny were keeping a loose eye on them as well as a couple of other groups in southern Oregon, when Wintersole and his team showed up and started nosing around . . . which put us on alert."

"And then a bunch of *our* Special Ops agents wandered into the picture, followed by Bobby LaGrange and me, and things started to get confusing?" Lightstone easily completed the sequence.

"Yeah, to put it mildly," Grynard replied sarcastically. "Only nobody knew who you were because it took so long to get any decent surveillance photos," he added, glaring down at Karla.

"Hey, you try to run a post office and a restaurant *and* take covert pictures of every federal undercover agent who wanders through the door." The female FBI agent shrugged. "And besides," she added with a mischievous grin on her dirt-smeared face, "he wouldn't go to sleep so I could take his picture. Sasha kept waking him up."

The huge panther purred agreeably at the mention of her name.

"I don't want to hear about it," Al Grynard repeated.

"Yeah, me neither," the Sage agreed.

"As I was saying, seeing as how this is supposed to be a real, honest-to-God FBI investigation, the plan was—and still is—to track Wintersole back to what we assume are the main players in this little put-the-federal-government-on-trial scenario," the FBI agent supervisor made no attempt to control his sarcasm.

"But then, Mr. White Knight"—Grynard pointed at Lightstone—"you almost screw everything up when you decide to come to the rescue of a covert FBI agent perfectly capable of protecting herself . . ."

"Yeah, so I noticed," Lightstone grumbled, rubbing his neck.

". . . not to mention also being protected by her two cover agents *and* a goddamned panther, and break the arm of one of Wintersole's men, which distracts Wintersole who, for some unaccountable reason, decides to drag you into their game. And then, of course, after everything goes to shit at the compound and it looks like Wintersole and this Marashenko—whoever the hell she is, in addition to being one of your agents—just might try to link up with somebody higher up in the organization to tell them what went wrong, you,"—Grynard glared down at Lightstone—"manage to end up in the way . . . *again.*"

"He's not real smart," Karla conceded as she rubbed the carotid-choke-inducing edge of her wrist against Henry Lightstone's exposed throat, "but he is kind of cute."

"Wait a minute," Lightstone protested. "It was you guys . . . and these two in particular," he added, referring to Karla and Sasha, "who deliberately let Wintersole and Marashenko get away, in the middle of the woods, and in the middle of the night, I might add. So just how in the hell do you intend to follow them anywhere?"

"Actually, Henry," Mike Takahara glanced down at his still confused partner, "I think Danny's planning to track your Army Ranger pal electronically."

"What?"

"Come on, Henry, use that cat brain for a minute or two," Karla smiled pleasantly as she adjusted herself more comfortably under her captive, and then lightly fingered the center medallion of the cougar-claw necklace around his neck. "How do you think we kept track of you?"

Chapter Fifty-four

The next day dawned cold, wet and dismal, an absolutely perfect day for hunting ducks.

Or at least that's what Regis J. Smallsreed told Simon Whatley, who sat mute and huddled in the far corner of the main VIP blind, numbed by the only partially effective painkillers, shivering from the cold in spite of his down pants and jacket, and, in every other way imaginable, feeling more miserable than he had ever felt in his entire life.

"They're calling it an 'unexplained explosion' at the training compound of the Chosen Brigade of the Seventh Seal," Lt. Colonel John Rustman read from the second page of the *Loggerhead City Gazette* now that he had enough light to see the fine print. "An unidentified source reported seeing what looked like numerous body bags being loaded into a refrigerated truck. The FBI sealed off the scene and refuses to answer any questions at this time."

"What the hell does all that mean?" Sam Tisbury cradled one of Smallsreed's expensive auto-loading shotguns and watched the horizon, to all outward appearances a man at peace with himself and the world.

"Probably means there was a bunch of federal wildlife agents in those bags, and they're not happy about it," Rustman explained, "but we'll find out soon enough. Wintersole reported in last night. Said he'd meet us here sometime this morning to brief us in person."

"What took him so damn long to check in?" Smallsreed demanded impatiently when the sky remained free of birds. The entire episode made the bloodlust flow through his veins, and he could hardly wait to kill something too.

"SOP." Rustman continued reading the paper that one of his employees had surreptitiously delivered to the blind earlier that morning. "You make the hit, go to ground, and pop back up in a remote location, twenty-four to forty-eight hours later, after the follow-up hunt dies down. Standard hunter-killer recon procedure."

"That's assuming there actually *is* someone out there looking for them," Tisbury commented. "We don't know that yet."

"There's *always* a follow-up hunt," Rustman replied without taking his eyes off the text. "You hit somebody as bad as Wintersole and his people did, you'd damn well better count on it. And don't forget, we went after federal agents," he reminded them.

"Federal agents aren't any different," Regis J. Smallsreed dismissed Rustman's comment indifferently. "They get in the way, they either get moved . . . or removed like everyone else. Simple as that."

"Did Wintersole say anything about the tape?" Tisbury voiced his primary concern.

"No, just sent a coded message. Standard phrases. But I don't think you have to worry about First Sergeant Wintersole." Rustman looked up from the paper calmly. "He's a professional soldier who knows exactly what he's doing. That's why we put him in charge of the field aspects of this operation."

"Yep, that's exactly it," Regis J. Smallsreed agreed, bobbing his massive head vigorously. "You want something done right, you go out and hire yourself a professional . . . 'cause when you do, everything always works out just fine . . . including that out there." The congressman's eyes glittered greedily as he pointed toward the far horizon.

"What've we got?" Tisbury asked, readying his shotgun.

"Looks like a bunch of cans, if my old eyes are any judge." Smallsreed glanced over at his host hopefully for confirmation.

"Wouldn't be a bit surprised." Rustman smiled briefly as he glanced toward the horizon, then reluctantly put his paper away. "This is a good spot for them."

Silently, the three men crouched in the blind and watched as the formation of migratory birds announced their low-to-the-water approach with intermittent quacks, long necks extended forward as their powerful wings sliced through the chilled morning air in precise, synchronized strokes.

"Yes, by God, cans!" Smallsreed whispered as much to himself as the others in the blind.

Caught up in the pure sensory pleasure of the moment, Congressman Regis J. Smallsreed uncharacteristically allowed his hunting companion to take the first shot.

Moments later, the concussive roar of Sam Tisbury's shotgun shattered the moment into illusionary fragments as the lead canvasback tumbled in an explosion of feathers, tissue, and blood.

The shock wave had barely registered on the gun-wary instincts of the remaining birds when nine more blasts erupted from the blind, sending nine more tight patterns of lead pellets streaking upward in intersecting paths with the left and right sides of the rapidly separating formation. Nine more bloody explosions sent nine more lifeless canvasbacks plummeting into the water.

Which left one canvasback—severely wounded by the stray pellets from the pattern that had obliterated his wing mate—veering off in a desperate, zigzagging effort to escape the deadly barrage.

Regis J. Smallsreed stood with an open mouth and an empty shotgun, and watched in anguished disbelief as the crippled bird somehow remained airborne—desperately quacking and flapping its wings as it tried with every ounce of strength it could muster to reach the weed-choked sanctuary of the far-distant shoreline.

He wore that anguished look because Congressman Regis J. Smallsreed remained as greedy as ever.

As always, he desperately wanted to kill them all.

Lt. Colonel John Rustman took one look at the directional vector of the duck's erratic but determined course, cursed silently, and activated the small radio transmitter on his belt.

"Wintersole," he whispered tersely into the mike. "Take it . . ."

But then he remembered. No Wintersole. Not today.

Or at least not yet, anyway.

Sorry, duck, you'll just have to suffer. Rustman shrugged as he automatically glanced at his own empty pump shotgun in the VIP blind's gun rack. *Must not be your day.*

The congressman was still standing there, clutching his empty shotgun and glaring angrily at the out-of-range canvasback—*his* canvasback—a good eighty yards away and slowly gaining distance with each feeble wing stroke, when two dark-hooded figures suddenly stood in the adjoining blind with .223 Mini-14 semiautomatic rifles in their hands.

A moment later, a single sharp, explosive crack echoed across the water.

Ninety yards away, the terminally injured bird suddenly spun in mid-air, its bloody feathers momentarily fluttering protectively over the splash points created when its carcass struck the water.

"Holy shit!"

As Sam Tisbury's astonished exclamation rang out across the water, Lt. Colonel John Rustman and Regis J. Smallsreed wheeled and stared openmouthed at the dark-hooded figures in the adjacent blind.

"Who . . . the hell is that?" Sam Tisbury's face still bore an absolutely astounded look.

"That, I believe, is First Sergeant Aran Wintersole, reporting for duty as ordered," Lt. Colonel John Rustman replied, unable to keep the supervisory pride out of his voice.

However, it did occur to him as he spoke those words, that the figure wearing the purple scarf around—her?—throat had made the shot. Wintersole just stood there with the Mini-14 held comfortably in his arms, watching the female Ranger with what Rustman guessed was an equivalent amount of pride.

He started to say something to that effect, to explain to his companions in the VIP hunting blind how meaningful that demonstration of faith had been. But the appearance of a small plane coming in low over the horizon suddenly caught his attention.

As Rustman, Tisbury, and Smallsreed watched in silence, the erratically flying float plane stalled, recovered, then stalled again as it suddenly veered in their direction.

"My God!" Sam Tisbury gasped. "He's going to crash right into us."

"What?"

Simon Whatley staggered desperately to his feet and stared in horror, with the other three men, at the oncoming plane.

"Oh, shit!" he whispered.

"GODDAMN IT, HE'D BETTER NOT . . . !" Regis J. Smallsreed screamed, but it was too late.

Before the congressman could say or do anything else, the pilot seemed to regain control at the last moment, powering the small aircraft forward in such a manner that the two floats mounted beneath the plane hit the water hard about twenty feet in front of and just to the right of the four helpless duck hunters . . . sending a huge spray of water flying in the air that literally drenched them, and generated a huge swell that surged toward the blind.

Blinded by the spray, Simon Whatley staggered backwards, bumped into Smallsreed, then grabbed onto him for support just as the swell struck and nearly upended the anchored blind . . . effectively sending both desperately flailing men catapulting through the open doorway and into the freezing water.

Just as Smallsreed and Whatley came up for air, the congressman livid with rage and screaming himself nearly hoarse, the pilot of the more-or-less-landed aircraft made a sharp right-angled turn and cut the engine . . . generating another series of waves that choked off Smallsreed in mid-scream as his white-haired head disappeared beneath the surging ice-cold water.

In the brief moment before the plane slammed into the anchored blind, federal wildlife agent Wilbur Boggs and FBI supervisory Agent Al Grynard managed to exit hastily the rear seats of the aircraft and make it out onto the floats. The impact sent Rustman and Tisbury tumbling to the floor, while Boggs and Grynard held on to the wing struts for dear life.

More accustomed to such landings by Fish and Wildlife Service agent/pilots, Wilbur Boggs let go with one hand, waved his replacement Special Agent badge, and jubilantly roared, "Federal agent, you're all under arrest!" Meanwhile Grynard clung to the struts with both hands and glared at the pilot until he remembered *why* they had attempted an insane landing like that. Then he quickly fumbled for his gun.

By this time, Lt. Colonel John Rustman had staggered to his feet at the far corner of the blind, holding a pair of shotgun shells in his left hand and his pump shotgun in his right.

The retired military officer prepared to combat-load the empty shotgun—to pull back on the slide, palm the first shell in through the ejector port, jack the slide forward with his left hand, and then trigger the high-based round into the face of the still-fumbling Al Grynard with his right.

But then he, too, appeared to remember something.

First Rustman—and then Tisbury—turned and stared across the water at the two now-unhooded figures still standing in the adjoining duck blind with their Ruger Mini-14s held up in a ready position.

That's right, Colonel. Real bad idea, Henry Lightstone thought to himself as he and Karla stood side by side in the slowly rocking blind. *If she can hit a moving duck at eighty yards . . .*

He slid his index finger inside the trigger guard of the stainless-steel semiautomatic rifle.

And don't even think about turning that gun this way, in her direction, or you're a dead man.

"Lightstone," Sam Tisbury whispered in disbelief.

Numbed with shock, Lt. Colonel John Rustman allowed the pump shotgun to slide out of his hands.

"You know, I think the older fellow on the left—the one who looks like he's about ready to have a heart attack—recognizes you," Karla suggested, easing her own index finger away from the trigger of her Mini-14 as she watched her noticeably displeased and airsick boss order the two men to put their hands over their heads . . . right now.

"Oh yeah, he knows me, all right," Henry Lightstone whispered as the missing pieces all began to fall into place. "That's Sam Tisbury."

Karla turned her head and stared at Lightstone with a puzzled look on her face.

"Okay, I give up. Who's Sam Tisbury?" she asked reasonably.

Henry Lightstone shrugged. "Just a very wealthy and crooked industrialist who doesn't like me very much."

"You mean *seriously* doesn't like you?"

Lightstone nodded his head.

"So what you're telling me is all of this rogue-Army-Ranger-hunter-killer-team-for-hire business is finally starting to make some sense?"

"Actually, I think it's starting to make a great deal of sense." Henry Lightstone wore a thoughtful look on his face. "Tisbury's an extremely rich and powerful man from an even richer and more influential family. And I'm pretty sure he blames me for the deaths of his father, son, and daughter. But if *that's* what this whole deal is all about, then I think he just screwed up big-time."

"Sounds like it couldn't have happened to a nicer person," she remarked as they watched Wilbur Boggs—from his sitting position on the aircraft float—lean out and grab Simon Whatley's frantically waving left hand, slap one end of a set of handcuffs around the wrist, pull Whatley's arm around the float strut, then close the second cuff around the right wrist of a red-faced and sputtering Regis J. Smallsreed, leaving the congressman and his bagman dangling in the water on either side of the main float strut.

"Him and Rustman both," Lightstone agreed. "In fact—"

"Hold it a second." Karla held up her hand and listened intently to the voice in her earphones for almost two minutes.

"Okay, we copy. Good job, Danny. Thanks." She terminated the exchange and then turned to Lightstone. "The Hostage Rescue Team found Wintersole and Marashenko a few minutes ago, about five miles north of here," she reported in a peculiarly quiet voice.

Lightstone noticed the unusual inflection immediately.

"Found? You mean alive?"

She shook her head. "No, they were both very dead."

It took Lightstone a couple of seconds.

"Not by us, I take it?"

She shook her head again, this time more slowly. "Apparently somebody put a single bullet through each of their foreheads, at point-blank range. Danny could see powder burns on both wounds."

Henry Lightstone blinked in disbelief.

"That's not . . ." he started to say it wasn't possible, but then he hesitated. "Were they tied up?"

"No. According to Danny, their hands were free and both of them were armed with M16s. They found them lying on their backs in the middle of a small clearing barely big enough for our chopper to land."

"So they were executed . . . presumably by the same people sent in to pick them up," Lightstone murmured softly as he stared across the water at Sam Tisbury. "That's interesting."

"If you say so." She shuddered as if suddenly very cold . . . but her mood improved almost immediately when she replaced the Mini-14 in the blind's gun rack. "Oh well, look on the bright side"—she smiled—"at least they didn't show up here."

"We'd have had our hands full if they had, no doubt about it." Lightstone placed his rifle in the rack next to hers, then stared across the water again.

"You sound disappointed."

"What, that we didn't get to take on a vindictive Army Ranger first sergeant, fully armed, in his playground, with the element of surprise on his side?" Lightstone smiled. "Are you crazy?"

"Don't give me that bullshit, Henry Lightstone." She cocked her head and studied him thoughtfully. "When you get right down to it, Wintersole was just another bully, and you couldn't wait to confront him, could you? In fact, I'm really amazed you didn't throw a fit and insist on being part of the search team."

Lightstone couldn't keep from smiling.

"If you must know," he replied as he once again considered the sensuous features of the beautiful young woman in the early light, "Wintersole and I had our confrontation. In the warehouse. I guess from his perspective—and mine, to some degree—he was just a professional trying to do his job. And long as I kept him away from the people I cared about . . ." Lightstone shrugged. "I don't know, I guess I just didn't see him as all that evil. Malicious, and scary, and dangerous as hell, sure, but not evil. So I figured let the FBI Hostage Rescue Team—or whoever," he added thoughtfully, "hunt him down. The more interesting people—the truly evil ones, if you will—are right here. And in my own way, I got to confront them, too."

Lightstone remained quiet for a while, then added, "Larry and Al were right. Once that female Ranger told us virtually everything that happened out here the day Wintersole executed Boggs's informant—and we won't discuss how Sasha just happened to brush by her shoulder when she wouldn't talk and Grynard turned his back for a moment," he added with a brief smile—"somebody had to go after Rustman and Smallsreed. And who better than us? I'm just glad they *found* Wintersole's body, so we won't have to spend the next few months looking over our shoulders and wondering where the hell he is."

"What do you mean 'they'?" she demanded indignantly. "Who do you think put the transmitter on him in the first place?"

"Well, okay, you, Danny, and that crazy-old-fart retired agent Sage, whoever he is."

"You mean Dad?"

Henry Lightstone blinked in shock.

"What?"

Karla shrugged. "Figured I'd better tell you before Grynard did . . . just in case you're concerned about my background," she added with a cheerful smile. "However, I wouldn't worry about it too much. Mom claims that Dad's more of the sleight-of-hand, carny-barker type. All of the serious witchcraft runs in her side of the family, and only gets passed on to the daughters."

"Dear God," Lightstone whispered.

He remained silent for a few moments, still trying to capture that elusive thought, listening to the sounds of the rapidly approaching FBI and Fish and Wildlife Service boats, and watching Grynard and Boggs handcuff and search Rustman and Tisbury before going back to retrieve a grateful Simon Whatley while leaving a furious Regis J. Smallsreed handcuffed to the float strut and dangling in the cold water.

He gave himself over to the thought so completely he didn't realize the beautiful covert FBI agent was studying him carefully until she spoke.

"You don't really believe it, do you?" she finally asked. "You don't think that all of the evil ones are here."

Her certainty caused Lightstone to recall how he had looked up with Sasha into the dark sky and saw nothing . . . but knew that *something* truly evil and threatening was there.

"No," he conceded quietly, "I really don't believe they're all here."

She reached out for his hand and the two of them stood in the bobbing blind, each of them lost in their own thoughts.

"So tell me," he finally said, "setting aside the problems of your crazy-old-fart father and reassuring mother for the moment, what made you so sure that Wintersole would keep wearing that bear-claw-necklace transmitter?"

"Actually, I think we can thank Sasha for that." Karla smiled back at him. "Nothing quite like a little adrenaline surge to make the typical macho male deeply superstitious."

Lightstone glanced down at the cougar-claw necklace he still wore around his own neck.

"That goes for you too, sport," she replied with a mischievous grin. "However, in your case, I think there may have been some rampant hormones involved in the process."

Henry Lightstone nodded sheepishly. "I guess I have to plead no contest on that one."

"Bet your ass," she nodded. "And speaking of pleading, you think Rustman or Whatley will testify against Smallsreed? He's the one Grynard really wants."

"What do you think?"

"Well, unlike our dear departed Sergeant Wintersole and very possibly Lieutenant Colonel Rustman, Mr. Simon Whatley and the Honorable Regis J. Smallsreed don't strike me as guys who would back each other up to the death," she said, rubbing the small of Lightstone's back. "I think it's probably more a question of who gives the other up first with the best supporting evidence. What was that you called them when they went into the water?"

"The congressman and the bagman." Henry Lightstone smiled at the memory of Charlie Team agents Donato and LiBrandi struggling helplessly in the bottom of the Glynco septic tank. "Hell of a pair from day one."

"And we got it on tape, too," Karla tapped the waterproof tape recorder strapped to her waist.

"You got it?"

"Every word. Including, I believe, some interesting comments earlier this morning relating to the death of someone named Lou Eliot . . .

which, as I understand the situation, should please the indomitable agent Boggs as much as that female Ranger's confession."

"It will please Mike, too. He went to a lot of work installing those microphones in that blind."

"He's a nice guy. Too bad he couldn't be here to see it."

"Actually," Lightstone mused thoughtfully, "knowing Mike, I'd be willing to bet a nice bottle of wine and a cozy evening *without* Sasha hanging around that he mounted a video camera somewhere in this blind."

"No bet," she laughed. "I'm wearing one of them."

"Really?" Lightstone looked suspiciously at the ornate clasp that held the purple scarf above his partner's Kevlar and flotation-vest-padded chest. "Where?"

"None of your business. Not yet, anyway."

"Ah."

They both remained silent for a long, more tantalizing than contemplative moment.

"Just one more question before they come for us, Agent Lightstone?"

"Yes?"

"Were you *really* serious . . . about what you said this morning?"

"You mean . . . ?"

"Uh, huh."

Lightstone hesitated.

"Well, now that you mention it . . . maybe it's not such a great idea after all. I mean, you saw it with your very own eyes."

"You trying to take the chicken-shit way out on me again, Special Agent Henry Lightstone?" A soft smile formed on her lips.

Lightstone shook his head. "Nope. I don't think I could ever top my last chicken-shit act. And besides, I wouldn't necessarily call it being chicken shit. It just seems to me that if we really are going to spend some time together in a remote Alaskan wilderness cabin, without Sasha like you promised, then maybe we should find ourselves a better bush pilot to get us there."

"What's the matter with Woeshack? I think he's wonderful. Just because he scared Al half to death with that evasive-maneuver landing . . ."

"No, it's not that," Lightstone sighed as he put his arm around the ever-enticing federal-government postmistress, witch, FBI agent, waitress, and fortune-teller who—it suddenly occurred to him—might or might not really be named Karla, another little detail they'd yet to discuss.

"I just thought you ought to know . . . that's pretty much the way he always flies."

"Oh." Her eyes glittered in anticipation. "Well, you did promise me the trip would be interesting. Something I've never done before. I'm sure that Woeshack's flying will be a memorable part of that experience."

"If we actually get there in one piece, I'm sure it will be, too." An odd look suddenly crossed Lightstone's face. "And speaking of memorable experiences, I just remembered: I'm supposed to tell you that our crime lab people are very interested in that hair you gave me."

"Really? How come?"

"Well, according to their report, the hairs are bearlike *and* primate-like, but they don't match any bears or primates in their collection."

"How odd." Her gold-flecked green eyes suddenly lit up with amusement.

"That's pretty much what they said, too, since as far as they know, they've got hair samples from every species and subspecies of bear- and primatelike creatures in the world. So what they'd like to know is, first of all, what is it? And second, where did you find it?"

A mysterious smile played on her sensuous lips.

"Well, I really don't know *what* she is, but I *do* know she's quite happy living on your friend's ranch—with the others."

Henry Lightstone tried to say something but at first nothing came out.

"You mean . . ." he finally got out, but she quickly put her finger on his lips.

"There's a little one, too, Henry, and she's precious. Let's let them be."

"But . . ."

"Like Dad always says," she whispered in a distinctly sultry voice that instantly made Henry Lightstone forget all about mythical creatures who might be real, "nothing is *ever* as it seems."

Epilogue

Aldridge Hammond, the spotted, reclusive, and deadly chairman of ICER sat alone in the dim light of his private office, allowing the memory of the incredible chain of events that had—once again—claimed a powerful member of his carefully orchestrated conspiracy, to flow through his mind.

He was still sitting there, an hour later, when his executive assistant entered the private office through a side door, placed a state-of-the-art infrared videocassette on his desk, and whispered a question in his ear.

He nodded his mottled head silently.

Some moments later, Hammond watched in fascination as the two camouflage-clad green figures instantaneously recoiled from the door of the helicopter, first in shock . . . then in death.

He had his assistant stop the tape at that point, freezing the almost painfully sharp image at that precise moment of betrayal, the instant First Sergeant Aran Wintersole realized he was to be sacrificed in a failed—and in retrospect, meaningless—attempt to protect Tisbury and Smallsreed.

Then Hammond motioned for the assistant to go back to the beginning, seeking the earlier segment that had caught his attention.

She located it, and this time he watched a different green figure hit the ground hard, start to fight his way out of the encircling chokehold, and get knocked back by the sleek green creature that lunged out of the trees . . . But then the two of them hesitated and looked up—directly into the far distant lens—at what?

The silenced helicopter?

The camera?

Me?

"You see *something*, don't you?" he whispered fiercely, irresistibly drawn to the glaring eyes of the panther and the searching eyes of the man who—thanks to some incomprehensible twist of fate—had become the nemesis of ICER.

And, so it would seem, my most dangerous enemy.

He signaled his assistant again, then watched silently as a thin white rectangle appeared on the screen . . . then enlarged to frame the two dissimilar heads. Moments later, the printer stopped churning, and she placed the resulting digitized photograph on his desk.

He stared at it for a long moment, slowly dissipating his tightly controlled rage with soothing thoughts of his yet-unused resources.

Then, in a deliberate action that spoke volumes about his future intentions, the chairman of ICER slowly placed his mottled fingers over the glaring eyes of the panther and the seeking eyes of Special Agent Henry Lightstone.

And obliterated them from his sight.

About the Author

A former deputy sheriff, criminalist, and police crime lab director, Ken Goddard is currently the director of the National Fish and Wildlife Forensics Laboratory in Ashland, Oregon. His previous novels include *Balefire*, *Prey*, *Wildfire*, *The Alchemist*, and *Cheater*.